Happenstance

TESSA BAILEY

TESSA BAILEY

Dedicated to @blondebookbabe on BookTok
Thanks for getting me into this mess.

CHAPTER

ROOSEVELT ISLAND IS A WEIRD-ASS PLACE.

Being that my *life* is in a weird-ass place at the moment, I seem to be in the right spot.

I shift in my stool near the window of the pizzeria, careful to keep most of my body partially hidden behind the cinderblock pillar in the center of the dining room. I'm the only one in here, even though it's dinnertime, making it pretty difficult to blend in. When I lean back slightly, I can see the group of men across the street, although they're obscured by foliage and a strategically parked van.

Definitely up to no good.

There's a tingle at the center of my spine and I twist in my seat to find the pizzeria owner glaring at the half-eaten slice of pepperoni sitting in front of me.

"Something wrong with the pizza?"

"No, it's great." I take an exaggerated bite to prove I'm telling the truth, even though it's thoroughly mediocre. "I'm just a slow eater."

"Hmm."

He goes back to filling the red pepper flake shakers.

Truth is, I'm on my first stakeout and my stomach isn't what you'd call *settled*. And speaking of stakeouts, picking this sparsely populated island to surveil New York City's deputy mayor was a rookie move. Accessible only by ferry or tram, Roosevelt Island is a random strip of land in the middle of the East River, in between Manhattan's east side and Queens. The main attraction—besides the view of the city skyline —are the ruins of a smallpox hospital, so, you know. There aren't crowds of people *flocking* to see the sights. Not the best place to be inconspicuous.

Why am I here?

Good question.

I certainly wasn't assigned this mission by anyone in a position of authority.

I guess you could say I'm a rogue sandwich girl.

I'm using my illustrious position as deliverer of deli meats to get my foot in the door at the *Gotham Times*, New York City's most respected newspaper. I couldn't just start off with a smaller paper, like the *Village Voice* or the *Brooklyn Eagle*. Not me.

Elise Brandeis aims right for the top—and she never quite makes it.

That doesn't stop me from trying, though. Especially not now when my tank of ambition has dwindled down to a measly few drops.

The bite of pizza gets stuck halfway down my throat and I gulp hard to swallow it. *Stop feeling sorry for yourself and focus on the task at hand.* I'm in the middle of rousing my motivation when the deputy mayor steps into view—and I see them.

I see both of them together for the first time.

Deputy Mayor Alexander and Jameson Crouch, union boss of Local 401.

Two men who really, really don't want to be seen together, especially by me—a wanna-be reporter. Which is obviously why they chose to meet on Roosevelt Island, home to a bunch of empty parks and eerie sculptures. The two men cast wary glances over their shoulders and I duck behind the cinderblock pillar before they spot me watching them. When I venture another peek, they're shaking hands. Holding my breath, I swipe open my phone to snap a picture, but the pizzeria owner blocks my view, slinging a white towel over his shoulder and planting his hands on his hips.

"You don't like the pizza. You want something else?"

"It's honestly *great* pizza. I'm just…" I get my camera app open and raise it above the man's shoulder. "Look at this amazing sunset. I need to get a picture."

Eyebrow raised, the pizzeria owner turns slowly, looking out at the street. "You can't see the sky from here. I have cannoli. You want to try some cannoli?"

Oh boy. Definitely no time for dessert. Alexander and Crouch have apparently concluded their undercover meeting. The whole pack of men seem to break at once, like a business casual football huddle. Are they coming this way? Maybe grabbing a slice before boarding the tram back to the less haunted island across the river? Some of them appear to be, yes.

Meaning, I need to get out of here. Fast.

"Is there a back exit?"

"Through the kitchen," says the owner without missing a beat. He's done this before.

See what I mean? Roosevelt Island. It's a weird-ass place.

I'm off the stool like a shot, jogging through the kitchen and out the wrought-iron storm door. The street is mostly empty, apart from a few regretful tourists hoofing it to the tramway. I shoot a backward glance toward the rear of the pizzeria on the off chance I've been followed, scanning the sidewalk for anyone that might be termed a goon. When I don't spot any suits and ties among the casually dressed pedestrians, I turn the corner at the end of the street and pick up my pace toward the tram entrance. I think I got away with it.

Didn't get the picture, but there's always next time.

A gust of cold November wind blows my long hair into multiple directions, a shiver coursing through my limbs and raising goosebumps on my bare skin. Wait…bare?

Damn. I forgot my jacket.

"Oh, come on."

Pausing mid-stride, I consider returning to the scene of my two-hour stakeout. Not a good idea. I already left my departure to the very last second. If I double back to Carmine's, I'll be spotted for sure. I will also have to deal with another round of questioning about my half-eaten pizza. Unfortunately, it's not exactly unusual for me to leave something unfinished.

I do everything halfway. Leaving a project done somewhere in the middle is my specialty. In the closet of my apartment, one would find a half-knitted sweater, an application for culinary school completed to page five out of ten, and a crate full of arrowroot starch and essential oils leftover from the natural deodorant business I semi-started—and by semi started, I mean I bought the ingredients and thought of a clever name.

Pit-ter Patter.

Okay, it's *sort of* clever.

At least I will make it all the way home tonight where I will face plant in some tequila.

That I can do without stalling out somewhere in the middle.

There's no line for the tram, thankfully and when the attendant waves me forward, I jog closer in my thrifted heels, praying the cable car is heated. I step inside a moment later and sigh, finding it slightly warmer than the outside temperature—

It's also occupied. By three men.

"Oh. Nope." I briefly register that all of them appear to be south of thirty-five, before I turn around with the intention of getting out and waiting for the next empty car, because frankly, I'd rather swim home in a hurricane than have a conversation with strangers. But as soon as I set foot back on the sidewalk, I see Deputy Mayor Alexander turn the corner with his black ball cap pulled down low on his forehead. He's surrounded by suited individuals, one of whom appears to be communicating via an earpiece. If I wait for the next car, there is every chance I'm going to end up on the same one as these dudes.

And that cannot happen.

If the deputy mayor and his security team register my face, there's a good chance they'll recognize me the next time I follow them. In the spirit of anonymity, I reverse into the cable car holding the three men, exhaling in relief when the door closes and the tram begins to move, carrying us upward and toward the East River.

"What changed your mind, love?" one of the men asks, his accent upper crust British. Deep and polished. "Was it my sheer animal magnetism that drew you back in?"

I knock on the window, drawing the attention of the tram attendant. "Too late to swim?" I call to him through the glass. He either doesn't hear me or isn't amused by my joke, because he stares back blandly as we pass. "Note to self: bring an inflatable raft next time," I mutter, taking my phone out of my purse and scrolling through emails, hoping British will take the hint and leave me alone for the duration of this three-minute ride.

It's not so much to ask.

Curious by nature, however, I can't resist a peek at my fellow passengers via the window reflection and…oh.

Okay, wow.

My roommate would refer to these men as contenders.

They're all appealing in different ways, but they *are* indisputably appealing. And stumbling across three attractive men on the Roosevelt Island tram is the dead last item on my list of things I expected to happen this evening, right after Zendaya showing up and informing me she's my fairy godmother. Or a promotion to staff writer at the *Gotham Times*.

Now that would be far-fetched.

But hopefully not for long.

Because I definitely saw Deputy Mayor Alexander meeting with the union boss who is currently in a very publicized feud with the *actual* mayor. By all accounts, they should be enemies. Deputy Mayor Alexander is the mayor's right-hand man. Why is he having clandestine meetings with Crouch, the union boss who smears the mayor every chance he gets?

"You're staring, love," taunts the British man.

He's right. I've been staring at him in the glass reflection. Because there is something familiar about him. Something I can't quite put my finger on. Did he bartend at that hotel where I trained as a concierge three years ago before getting bored and throwing myself into the natural deodorant space? No, that's not it. Where do I know him from?

"Porn," he says from his elegant lean against the interior wall of the tram. "You know me from pornography, darling," he drawls, his mouth spreading into a grin. "The good shit."

I'm turning around before I can stop myself, because holy hell. He's right.

That dark blond hair, the incredible bone structure, that bedroom rasp.

I don't remember his name—I'm not a porn junkie, although I like a visual aid as much as the next twenty-six-year old girl—but I used to have more than a few of his videos bookmarked on my phone. And right now, I'm staring at him with clear recognition, so I snap my gaping mouth shut, turning to gauge the reaction of the other two men.

They're both frowning at British.

"That's enough," says a guy who has the best posture I've ever seen. His back is perfectly straight, his arms crossed over his impressive chest. For a moment, I think I recognize him from somewhere, as well, but no. He just bears a striking resemblance to the Duke from season one of *Bridgerton*. As in, he's a perfect ten, emphasis on perfect. There is not a stitch of his impeccable overcoat and pleated slacks out of place. I could eat the second half of my pizza slice off his shiny wingtips. This man is exacting and apparently in the habit of coming to the defense of women he doesn't know. Very Duke-like, indeed.

"That's enough of what?" inquires British, amusement twinkling in his eyes as he turns his attention to the second man. "Charisma? It cannot be turned off, unfortunately. Women upon women have performed very thorough searches of my person looking for the switch."

I can't help it. I'll probably cringe about this for the rest of my life, but my attention drops to his crotch.

"That's the on switch, love. Not the off one."

Something slightly dangerous flashes in the Duke's eyes, but before he can say anything, the third man clears his throat and stands up. And up. And up. He's so tall, the top of his shaved head almost brushes the ceiling of the cable car. The word Hercules whispers through my head. That moniker wouldn't be misplaced. His muscle-bound presence, however, is softened by a face that, once upon a time, was definitely a baby face. Until he did too much frowning, perhaps.

Hercules paces forward a step, his paint splattered boots scuffing along the floor—and he settles into a cross-armed position between me and British, *No Trespassing* written clearly across his rough features.

"It's not polite to talk about your privates in front of a girl."

I laugh a little in disbelief. What is happening? "Well this is definitely the most interesting ride of my life."

"Ah…" replies British without missing a beat. "If only I had a nickel for every time a woman said those words to me…"

The other two men turn to face him, visibly done with his shit.

That's when the cable car grinds to a halt.

The lights flicker and go out, leaving us in a dim evening haze.

What little heat was being pumped into the tram goes bye-bye.

Long seconds pass in silence while we wait for the conveyance to start moving again.

It doesn't.

"This is not happening, right?" I say, looking down at the river below, unnerved by the sudden absence of the mechanical hum and watching in jealousy as boats move beneath us on the water toward civilization. "I mean, this thing freezes like once every four years. What are the odds?"

"Slim to almost none," sighs the Duke, taking out his phone, thumb zipping across the screen. "Guess we're just lucky."

Hercules is still posted up between me and British, a furrow between his dark brows. He appears to still be coming up to speed on what exactly is happening.

"Wait," says the big guy slowly. "It's frozen?"

We answer him in a chorus of three yeses.

A voice comes over the speaker, but it's really just a burst of static and unintelligible words, reminiscent of the subway. "Very reassuring." I toss my purse down on the plastic bench and rub my arms vigorously. The heat has only been off for thirty seconds and I'm already shivering. "Just this morning, I said to my roommate 'the train has never been more unreliable.' Roosevelt Island tram? Hold my beer."

Hercules watches me trying to warm myself from beneath his gathered brows, fingers twitching in the crook of his elbow. "Do you want my sweatshirt?"

He jerks his bearded chin downward at his navy blue hoodie, which is covered in paint and cement splatters, like the rest of him.

"No," I say immediately. "But thanks."

"How about my overcoat?" asks the Duke, very smoothly. Already taking it off.

Hercules hangs his head a little.

"No, thank you." I have to lean sideways to answer the Duke, because Hercules is taking up my entire line of vision. For some stupid reason, I feel the need to add, "I…wasn't turning down his sweatshirt because it's dirty."

"Why did you turn it down?" British wants to know. "You're shaking. And I—"

"You're an expert on shaking women," I interrupt. "Yeah, we get it, dude."

There's a hint of a smile on Hercules's mouth now and I don't know why I feel relieved about that? Was I worried I hurt this stranger's feelings by turning down his sweatshirt? I really *do* need that tequila faceplant.

"I like boundaries. They're healthy and give me a sense of power in a world where I don't have much," I say, pulling up the internet browser on my phone, hoping to find a contact number for whichever city agency runs this godforsaken tram. "That's why I turned down the sweatshirt and the overcoat. While I'm at it, I'm preemptively turning down whatever you're going to offer me, too, British. I have a feeling it's flesh colored and curves slightly to the right."

He belts out a laugh. "I fucking knew you recognized me."

I have raised the eyebrows of both Hercules and the Duke, but I ignore the slight burning sensation in my cheeks and continue my hunt for the right phone number. "Don't look at me like that. You've probably…been entertained by him, too. Maybe you were just more focused on his acting partner?"

"Ah, love. They never have to act." British sticks out his hand toward the Duke. "Tobias Atwater. Pleased to make your acquaintance."

"We're dangling above the East River in a death trap," says the Duke, very succinctly. "'Pleased' is not the word I would use. Quit the inappropriate bullshit. She's not interested."

They shake, despite the very clear fighting words, although they look like they're trying to rip one another's hands off, jaw muscles snapping formidably. "It's obvious the woman can handle herself and doesn't need you speaking for her," Tobias responds with forced charm. "Although if you were speaking for her, your name would be..."

A sharp nod. "Banks Pearson."

They still appear to be contemplating whether or not to toss each other through the glass window into sewage-infested waters below.

Hercules grunts and takes a step closer to me. Like he wants to guard me against any potential violence. And it's so odd, because I find it very difficult to trust people—but I almost move into the circle of his warmth without thinking. Just like that. He must be an Aquarius and my chaotic Gemini energy is simply vibing with his.

Oh, I took an astrology class last year. Dipped out halfway through it, of course.

When Tobias and Banks finally stop shaking hands and retreat to their corners, I tap the number I found on Google. The line rings four times, then descends into a series of beeps. I call back three more times before someone answers with a harried, "Yes?"

"Yes, hello." I plug my opposite ear out of habit. "Myself and three other passengers are stuck up here. What's going on?"

Quite a lot of noise is happening in the background. Ringing phones, voices, a blaring television. "Mechanical failure. The technician is on his way."

"Any idea how long before we're moving again?"

"Not at this time, no. As soon as possible."

"Is there a way to turn the heat back on?" I whisper. It's a dumb question. The answer is obviously no, but I am trembling now and beginning to pity myself, my brain projecting images of sweatpants and my fluffy white bed comforter. God, I would give anything to be under the covers in some fuzzy socks right now. Experts say to dress for the job you want. I want to be a reporter. A staff writer at the paper. So I'm wearing a pencil skirt and a white, button-down, cap-sleeve blouse. My tombstone is going to read: Here lies Elise Brandeis. Disappointing daughter. Human icicle.

The line has gone dead in my ear, so I blow out a breath and hang it up, searching for a distraction from my imaginary epitaph—too real. And if I'm engaging strangers in conversation, that's when I'm truly desperate. "So." I try to keep my rear teeth from clenching and fail. "What brings you three to b-beautiful Roosevelt Island?"

None of them answer.

They're all distressed in their own way over my condition. I'm no expert, but said condition is probably verging on frostbite. Without a mirror in front of me, I have a feeling my lips are turning blue. They obviously notice—and I think it's why they each take a measured step in my direction.

"Will you please take one of our jackets or…" Banks starts, raking a hand down his face.

"Or allow one of us to keep you warm?" Tobias finishes for him, visibly enjoying the proceedings. "Is that where you were headed with your suggestion, mate?"

"Not in the way you made it sound," Banks clips.

A shiver passes through me, so powerful that my teeth actually chatter.

They take another collective step, all of them annoyed at each other for having the same idea. Or compulsion. Or whatever is happening. I put up my hand to stop the advance of the man closest to me, which happens to be Hercules. The palm of my hand connects with the middle of his chest and the worn cotton of his hoodie. The thick muscle beneath that leaps under my touch.

My breath catches.

For the first time, I notice the white logo on the right pec.

Local 401. That's the same union I came to Roosevelt Island to investigate. At least, 401 union boss Jameson Crouch's connection to Deputy Mayor Alexander. The two men I saw shaking hands from the pizza parlor. But based on the five minutes I've spent in *this* guy's acquaintance, he is probably not involved in any behind-the-scenes corruption. What kind of corruption? I'm still working on that. More than likely, though, Hercules is on the island to work on the housing development that's under construction at the hands of 401.

He could know something useful, though.

This man might be able to give me rare insight into my investigation. Or help me. If I want the managing editor at the *Times* to take me seriously, I have to bring her a story. I've been trying to piece together this bombshell piece for weeks and today, I most likely had my suspicions confirmed. Deputy Mayor is the mole who has been feeding harmful information to Crouch, giving him ammunition for his feud with the mayor. But even after seeing them together today—and on friendly terms—I still only have smoke and mirrors. A theory.

And a sandwich cart with wheels.

A cart that I push through the corridors of the *Times*, serving hoagies to the *real* reporters. I don't want to do it anymore.

I want to be a writer and I don't want to quit halfway this time.

Before I think better of it, I curl my fist in the front of Hercules's sweatshirt and pull him forward, not missing the lump that moves up and down in his throat.

"You haven't told us your name yet," I say quietly, caught off guard by the invisible feather that drags along the lowest regions of my belly.

He takes a deep breath while his eyes trace the part of my hair. "Gabe Gatlin."

"Gabe." My lord, his voice is deep. "I'm Elise." Suddenly, I'm second guessing my intention to finesse information out of this giant, but it's too late to turn back now because my breasts meet his chest. "You'll keep me warm?"

His swallow is loud in my ear, his arms coming up around me, locking me close to his powerful bulk. "Yes, please."

CHAPTER

Two

IT'S VERY silent now that Gabe's arms are around me.

Silent except for the loud rapping of his heartbeat near my ear.

I'm not going to lie, I forget my ulterior motive for several long moments, the ample heat of his big body sinking into mine and ceasing my shivers. He smells like a construction site—sawdust and paint and coffee—and somehow I know that going forward, I will always associate those smells with warmth and comfort. I'm almost cross-eyed at the sudden rush of heat to my bones and before I can stop myself, I melt against him a little, seeking more.

I don't even get annoyed when he sniffs my head.

"She…Elise…asked us what we're doing on the island," Banks says briskly after a full minute. It's impossible not to notice the deeper resonance to his tone. It's either resigned due to my choice of Gabe for warmth…or irritated. Or both. "Would anyone like to share with the class?"

"I came for some routine acupuncture," Tobias says, followed by a brief sniff.

Lie. I'm pretty good at determining when someone isn't telling the truth. It's what led me to the field of reporting. And that subtle hitch in his tone has my eyes flying open. When did I close them? Actually, am

I drooling on this guy's sweatshirt? Not quite, but I'm close. "You came all the way out here for acupuncture? Why couldn't you see an acupuncturist in Manhattan?"

A beat passes. "Mine is more of a specialist."

I'm leaning sideways to look at Tobias now, beside Gabe's shoulder. "You said it was routine."

Suddenly we're in a stare-off across the stalled cable car. Banks shifts to face Tobias, an eyebrow arched in curiosity and there's a speculative rumble in Gabe's chest. My first impression of Tobias was fairly simple. He's a cocky idiot who doesn't know when to shut up. But over the course of a few breaths, that impression begins to change and it has everything to do with the sudden tension bracketing his mouth and drawing up his shoulders. The playful twinkle is gone from his eye—briefly—before he's laying it on thicker than ever.

"You caught me," Tobias drawls, smoothing his collar. "I was conducting an affair."

Banks and I trade a skeptical look. An identical one. One that surprises me. I can count on one hand the people in my life with whom I've shared this kind of intuition and it was developed over the course of years. With Banks, there's a weird sense that we're on the same page. Though...that can't be possible when we've known each other a matter of minutes.

"If you were having an affair, you definitely would have told us immediately. Bragged, even," Banks says, his incredibly rich brown eyes still fastened on mine, like he's reading the words right out of my head. "But since none of us want our ears to bleed when we're unable to call for medical attention, let's move on. Gabe, I assume you were here working on the housing development?"

Gabe grunts in affirmation.

"Who put you in charge of interrogating everyone?" Tobias wants to know. "I have a lot of experience playing a cop and wouldn't mind putting it to use."

"It's not an interrogation," Banks clips. "But if we're going to be here for a while, we might as well know who we're sharing air with."

Tobias laughs. "Don't act like you give two shits about our explanations for being on Roosevelt Island. You're only asking as a formality, so it won't seem odd when you ask Elise about hers. Be a little less obvious, mate." The Brit is sharper than we've given him credit for, even if his charmingly affable expression is back in place. "On second thought, stare at her with a little more psychotic intensity. Maybe you'll kickstart the engine and we can all go home."

"No, thank you," Gabe mutters.

My head tilts back so fast to observe his face that my neck gets a crick. In the last few minutes, the construction worker has become this silent monument of comfort, but with the low utterance of those three words, he becomes the focal point of the tram car. When he realizes he's turned himself into the center of attention, the tips of his ears turn a dark shade of red, starkly obvious on his Irish-looking skin. "Never mind. I'd just...rather not go home."

"Why?" I ask, my attention drawn to the strong column of his neck where a tattoo peeks out from his hoodie, stretching up toward his ear. It looks like a wing of some kind. There's some lettering on the other side, as well. How far down those neck tattoos stretch? There's so much ground to cover. "Why don't you want to go home?"

He hesitates. "My brother lives next door."

"You boys in a tiff or something?" Tobias asks absently while looking out at the skyline.

"Sort of," Gabe replies. "But it's more that he's living with my ex-wife."

I trade a wince with Banks, our expressions once again indistinguishable.

What the heck is up with that?

While I'm continuing to wonder about my oddly immediate kinship with Banks, I'm only half aware of my palm sliding up and over the rock-solid mound of Gabe's right pectoral. My hand is moving of its own volition, as though compelled to give him comfort. And when my fingers trace the outline of the wing tattoo on his neck, I begin to wonder if the air is thinning in this cable car. Or if some kind of delirium-inducing toxin has been released into the scant space, because I don't just go around stroking the pectoral muscles of strangers. *Talking* to strangers is a stretch for me, unless it's strictly work related.

This *is* work related.

Gabe is a portal into the deputy mayor's relationship with Jameson Crouch.

You're going to question Gabe about what he's heard. Seen. Right?

Yes. I am.

As soon as he spills the tea on his brother and ex-wife. "Why are they living together?"

"It's not a very nice story," Gabe says, hesitating for a beat, before stroking a hand down the back of my long, dark hair—and God help me, I'm shivering now for an entirely different reason. Am I attracted to this big bear of a man? "Are you sure you want to hear it?"

"Yeah," I whisper, my attention ticking over to Banks, then Tobias. They're both watching Gabe's giant paw travel down the length of my hair and neither one of them seems to like it. Not one bit. Why? They just met me. They have zero claim on me and I don't have one on them. Or Gabe. Apparently, that toxin in the air is potent and nothing makes sense anymore. "Tell us."

Gabe hums. Adjusts his stance.

"My brother and Candace were both popular in high school. Everyone wanted to be him, be with her. But they were with each other. Only. Until after graduation, I went to trade school. Got this job as a foreman and started making money. At the same time, my brother was unemployed. Drinking too much. They broke up, a few more years passed." A lump slides up and down in his throat. "And suddenly she wanted to be with me. For stability, I guess, since we were pushing thirty. But I guess she never really got over my brother, because, uh…"

"You found them turning each other's cranks," Tobias finishes. "Been there. On the crank turning end of things, of course."

I shoot Tobias a venomous look.

He winks back at me—and he's very lucky the windows on this tram don't come down or I might "accidentally" push him out of one. It occurs to me in that moment that I am having vastly different reactions to these three men. Tobias riles me up, irritates me. Banks is like looking into an emotional mirror, giving me a strange sense of camaraderie. And Gabe? I'm protective over him. A man twice my size.

Like I said, nothing makes sense anymore.

Giving myself a mental shake, I refocus on Gabe's story. "I'm sorry that happened. It can't be easy living next door to them."

"They act like it *didn't* happen. The marriage. And they park on my lawn." His tone is disbelieving and I get the impression he's never said any of this out loud. "Their wheels are only a few inches onto my property but it kills the grass. I like my grass." He splits an annoyed look between all three of us in defense of lawn maintenance. "Anyway. They...expect me to follow their lead and act like the marriage never happened and I don't know how."

"That's because it's impossible, Gabe," I say. "An impossible thing to expect from you."

He nods, studies my face closely. The sun has gone down and it's growing darker in the small car. Suddenly everything is *more*. The intimacy of our position—my hands on his chest, his arms wrapped around my hips. Banks and Tobias observing closely, not breathing. All four of us are sort of suspended in animation, but my pulse is galloping, moving faster when Gabe wets his lips, his hand flexing on the small of my back. Oh my God, I think he's going to kiss me. Right here, in front of these other men. Why doesn't that seem as wild and crazy as it ought to?

I mean, it does. It's bananas. But in the near-dark private world above the river, it's almost like we've momentarily slipped out of reality.

Gabe's breath shallows—and I feel it. His erection spears up between us, almost shockingly hard, and he immediately drops his arms from around me, backing toward the other side of the car and turning around, bracing his hands on the metal frame that surrounds the glass. "I'm sorry. I didn't mean to, uh..."

Skin flushed, I nod once, stammering, "I, yeah. I know."

"Sweet hell, if I apologized for my dick every time it got hard, I would be hoarse twenty-four hours a day," Tobias declares, looking down at the appendage in question. "I'd advise you all to buy stock in throat lozenges, because I'd be going through bags of them like water."

The absence of Gabe's furnace-like heat starts to take effect immediately. It's like walking out of a hot shower into a snowstorm. I'm even colder than before, because I've been to the Promised Land. Gabe must hear my teeth chattering from across the tram car, because he shoots me a miserable look over his shoulder…

But suddenly Banks is stepping into view, blocking Gabe.

Blocking, well, everything.

He wraps his overcoat around me and draws me up against his body. And when I say my mouth begins to water over his scent, it's not an exaggeration. A scent has never intoxicated me. At the mere suggestion that I might one day lose my chill over cologne, I would have laughed—until now. It's smoky and sensual and ever so slightly sweet. And where Gabe is thick and rounded, Banks is ripped and tight. He looks me right in the eye while heating me up in very precise, proficient manner that leads me to believe he's been envisioning how he would do it this whole time.

I've been in denial for the last few minutes. Trying to ignore the fact that I was aroused by Gabe. The packed press of his strength, our size difference, his capable energy. But I can't deny it now when Banks is holding me accountable with eye contact that I can't seem to break. My nipples are puckered inside my bra and there is a teasing tingle between my thighs that is growing harder to ignore. It was there when Gabe held me and it's only growing more potent now that I'm in Banks's arms. So which one of them is doing this to me? It can't be both, right?

Banks presses a thumb into some magical pressure point at the very base of my spine and I make a breathy, whimpering sound before I know what's happening.

All three men seem to expand in the darkness. Like they're grown attuned to me and I've just turned some knob to raise the volume. This has to be a dream. I'm going to wake up any second now and be home in bed, my phone chiming on my bedside table. I'm definitely not hanging suspended over the East River with three men, two of whom my body seems powerless to ignore.

This is insane.

Try and view what's happening as a necessity, rather than a choice.

I need body heat. They are giving it to me. We all do what we have to do to survive in the wild, right? There is no difference between me being pressed up against this gorgeous man's gym-perfected body than stranded campers huddling together for warmth in the wilderness.

Right.

I clear my throat and try to ignore that thumb drawing circles on my lower back. "So, Banks." I pretend I don't notice that my voice has fallen approximately fifty-two octaves. "Are you going to tell us why you're on Roosevelt Island?"

CHAPTER

I'M close enough to Banks that the slightest pop of muscle in his cheek is like an avalanche. But I only see it in my periphery, because he's still holding eye contact. It boggles my mind that I haven't looked away yet. There is something about a person looking at me too closely that is usually unnerving. Why is that not the case here? The longer this continues, the more my raving pulse seems to carry downward to the juncture of my thighs. To…everywhere. I'm an exposed nerve and he's rubbing me more and more raw with that freaking thumb.

And his unwavering stare.

I asked Banks what brought him to Roosevelt Island. Is he going to answer?

No one inside the car seems to be breathing, our collective focus narrowed down to the two of us. The fact that we're touching feels massive. Important.

"I'm here to see my mother," Banks says finally—and that's when his gaze finally flickers away from mine. It's only a split-second loss, but it tells me there is more to the story.

"And it didn't go well?" I only murmur the question, but we're all so close, so in thrall with each other, that my question reaches everyone.

Banks doesn't seem surprised by my astuteness. As if he's already noticed, too, that there is some sort of intuition between us. "No. It never does."

His jaw pops, as if to say, *conversation closed.*

I'm not great at taking orders, silent or not. "Why?"

A second ticks by. Then his thumb drags up my spine—firmly—almost as a reproof for pressing him on the issue of his mother. His trip to the island. For several breaths, I don't think he is going to answer me. I think he is simply going to let my gasp hang in the air. But finally, he says quietly, "She won't take my money."

No one is expecting that. Even Tobias tilts his head curiously.

"Why not?" Tobias is speaking. "You did mention she's a woman, correct?"

"Did I mention you're a shithead?" I fire over Banks's shoulder.

"Lots of people share your opinion, love."

Banks pulls me closer, as if to soothe. I can't believe it works. At least until Tobias's lips pull into a grin. It doesn't reach his eyes, though. No, those are locked on Banks's hand moving beneath the material of the overcoat. Was Tobias purposely trying to get under my skin with that comment because he's...?

No. No way he's jealous.

Not one of the top-grossing adult film actors of all time. He can't possibly have the ability to feel envy in his line of work, right? Especially over a woman he just met—one who he had an antagonistic relationship with from the word go.

I shrug off the notion and go back to Banks. "Does she need money?"

"Yes. She's accustomed to having a lot more of it, but she..." Banks's swallow is loud near my ear. "She fell on hard times after my father passed. I'm making enough to support us both, but she is letting her guilt get in the way of good sense."

"Guilt over what?" Gabe asks.

We all jolt a little, maybe since none of us expected him to speak so soon after the boner incident. "I played rugby growing up," Banks begins after a few beats. "Loved it. Chose it over following in my father's footsteps in finance and they....specifically she...didn't support me. Since I found success as a player and now a coach, she doesn't feel right about accepting the benefits. She'd rather live paycheck to paycheck out of pure stubbornness."

I study the rigid set of Banks's chin. "I bet you're a lot like her, aren't you?"

For the first time since meeting him, the edge of his mouth tips up into an amused smile, and good God, he was handsome before, but now he's dangerous. "You'd be right about that, Elise. Doesn't make it any easier to come here every week and have my assistance rejected." His thumb travels along the waistband of my skirt, slowly. So slowly. Then his fingers splay on my back, his palm riding my spine all the way up to my shoulders, back down with increased pressure, stopping just before my backside and I don't know how he's done it, but I want him to go lower. I want to feel that skilled hand on my bottom, pulling me close. Which, hello, would be entirely inappropriate. We don't know each other and there are two other people in this car. Yet I can't seem to stop myself from leaning in until my nose is almost buried in the notch of his throat and breathing the perfect scent of him into my bones. "And you, Elise? Why are you here?"

His voice has dropped considerably, his head tilted to the right, focus latched on my mouth. Just like before, with Gabe, I get the sense that he's going to kiss me.

Am I going to let him?

Who am I and what happened to the girl who refused to borrow any of their outerwear for warmth? I am all about boundaries. Ask my roommate, Shayna—I strive to keep my relationship formal with her, despite her best efforts. But the lines between me and these men have blurred so much, I have no idea which new territory we've entered.

Banks dips his mouth closer to mine, creating an urgent tug in my belly.

My toes stiffen automatically, lifting me. The energy of the other two men seems to go on high alert—and then a phone rings.

Wait. Huh?

It's Banks's phone, vibrating between us.

The spell doesn't dissipate completely, but when I take a hard gulp of cold air, there's a tic in his cheek and we allow a few inches between our mouths. Inches that should have been there all along, because my goodness, he's a stranger. He studies me, I study him back, and I can see the moment he deems it wise to take the call.

Without breaking eye contact with me, he tugs the phone from the inner pocket of his coat, answering it with a slip of that magical thumb. "Hello?"

"Bad news, coach," comes a voice from the other side. "Trainers are putting Vankman on the injured list for the next two weeks. Goddamn ankle. He won't play on Tuesday."

Banks tips his head back, his breath visible as it curls toward the ceiling. "Fuck me."

"Why don't you take the call?" Tobias suggests, closer now. Right beside us. "I've got her."

"Like hell you do," I counter.

"Take my coat," Banks says, removing the garment with one hand and wrapping it around my shoulders, phone still pressed to his ear. With a warning look in Tobias's direction, he paces a few feet away and continues the call, leaving me with the man on this tram that puts me most on guard. Mentally, I'm stacking bricks in between him and I, slathering on mortar and slapping on a DANGER sign for good measure.

"I've got the coat," I say, pressing a finger to his stomach and pushing him back a step. "I don't want or need your body warmth."

"That's a shame." He drags his full bottom lip through his teeth. "I'd love to give it to you."

I've seen what he wants to give me. Many times. It's very photogenic.

"Not interested."

"Liar." His lips twitch. "Tell me which scene lives in your head rent free. The one where I play a male escort? Fan favorite, that one."

I should slap him upside his head for being so forward, when I've made it abundantly clear that I'd like him to back off. He deserves a good shove at the very least. "Actually, the ones you did with two women were always the best," I say, batting my eyelashes. "Your mouth was too busy to do much talking."

An appreciative grin flashes across his seductive mouth and I have the dumb urge to return that smile, even though I'm beyond irritated. Is the altitude affecting me?

"Do you speak to every woman with this much familiarity?"

There's a twitch somewhere in the neighborhood of his right dimple, but he maintains his smirk. "Sometimes. But I'm not all that interested in their answers," he says, seeming to catch himself off guard. "The way I am with yours."

"Why me?" No answer. His mischievous grin dulls ever so slightly and his blue eyes grab onto mine tightly, holding—and I see something vulnerable there. I get a fleeting glimpse behind his tomcat façade and it...affects me. "You behave like this as a distraction, don't you?"

He chuckles. "A distraction from what?"

I shrug a shoulder. "The real you. Whoever that is."

Amusement fades from his expression. "The real anyone is usually a disappointment."

"What are you more afraid of? Being disappointed? Or doing the disappointing?"

Tobias breaks our stare quickly, shoveling fingers through his thick head of chestnut hair. "Who says it can't be both?"

The thrum in my veins grows thicker. I'm tethered to him by a rope of intimacy that was objective before, but it tightened, became personal, with a brief glimpse at the man underneath. I'm becoming magnetized against my will.

This isn't real. Seriously. I have to be imagining this.

My brain has conjured this entire bizarre scenario.

A *third* man cannot be making my pulse race. Fast. Faster. In a way that confuses me, because it's reminiscent of fight or flight, except the rapid-fire pounding in my veins is a lot thicker. And lower. My erogenous zones are well acquainted with this man—his chiseled face and deep, promissory voice—and they've fired up at his nearness, forcing me to press my knees together in an attempt to quell a spreading ache.

He notices.

His chest rises and falls with a curse.

But I don't expect him to look pained over my embarrassing, telltale move.

Briefly, he closes his eyes. When they open, his gaze travels up the side of my neck, over the crown of my head, as if he's taking my measurements. "The uptight one asked you a question, Elise." His tone once again cajoling. "What business do you have on Roosevelt Island?"

Reality comes back to me in degrees.

Obviously I can't tell him—them—the truth.

Not with Gabe sitting directly behind Tobias. A quick peek at his reflection in the window tells me the construction worker is listening closely, too. I'm not a good liar. I'm much more likely to tell an uncomfortable truth and damn the consequences, but in this case, I'm better off telling an itty bitty white lie. The last thing I need is Gabe tipping off his boss that someone from the *Gotham Times* has connected him to the deputy mayor.

The sandwich girl, but hey. Semantics.

And maybe there is a tiny part of me that is embarrassed to tell them I sling ham on whole wheat all day. Maybe there is even a little annoying part of me that wants to *impress* them, especially since I haven't impressed anyone lately. Especially myself.

"I'm a reporter," I say, just as Banks hangs up his call, his attention immediately zipping back to me. Staying there. All three of them are hanging on my every word. Why? No way am I physically disturbing all three of them the way they are disturbing me. "I was on the island to get some details about the housing project."

"This late on a Thursday?" Tobias asks, arching a dark brow. "Very dedicated."

"Yes. I am."

Gabe's boots scuff the floor as he stands. "I can help you with that. If you want. I've been working on it since the beginning and I know every corner of it."

"I'd like that," I say, guilt making my throat dry. Best to see the deception through before I lose my nerve. "Maybe we can meet over coffee. Are you doing anything Saturday night?"

Those words cause a silent commotion in the tram car.

I'm pinned by three different sets of eyes, that jealous energy I thought I imagined earlier now coming from both Tobias and Banks. It creates a disturbance in the air.

Too bad.

I'm not getting a boyfriend out of this wacky turn of events. I'm getting a point of contact for the exposé I'm writing. The one that is going to land me a staff writer position. I decided to pursue a career in journalism and I have to see my journey through this time. I've done too many things halfway and not only have my parents lost faith in me...

I've completely lost faith in myself.

I need it back. I don't know who I am without my confidence.

"Saturday night? Oh yeah. I've got this fancy party. For work." Gabe looks like he's waiting for the punch line. "Wait...you're not asking me out, are you?"

I'm smiling, but it wavers. He's a nice guy and he's been through a lot. Why couldn't it be Tobias or Banks that had a potential inside track on Jameson Crouch?

I realize I wouldn't like that either and feel a flash of impatience with myself.

Something is very wrong with me.

"Yes, Elise," Tobias clips, smiling once again in that way that doesn't reach his eyes. "Are you asking out the one with the erection?"

Over Tobias's shoulder, Banks tilts his head, expression questioning.

"Maybe I am." I wet my lips. "And that's between me and Gabe."

"Is that to say there's nothing between us?" Tobias asks. And then with a wink and a nod in Banks's direction, he adds, "Or you and him? Let's not pretend something isn't happening here. All of us feel it."

If I thought the air was charged before, nothing compares to the way it crackles with electricity now. With those words, the odd attraction between me and these three men has been acknowledged. I haven't been hiding it, as I assumed I was. Maybe I was too surprised by my reaction to them to play it cool. I don't know. But they're all coming closer to me now, at the same time. They are circling me. Tobias in front, Gabe behind, Banks to my left.

Our breaths are white in the air and the puffs of condensation come quicker, quicker.

I'm getting blasted with heat now from all sides. My pulse is haywire.

They're all taller than me, even in my heels, and I'm shocked to find I'm turned on by being the shortest. By being the object of their attraction. All three of them? How?

"Is Gabe your choice then, love?" Tobias asks, tipping up my chin. Studying my face.

"If you want him to stop touching you, say the word, Elise," Banks says. "If you want any of this to stop, I'll make it happen."

Gratitude floods me and I nod, my hand reaching out before I think twice, my fingers threading through the longer ones of Banks.

"Yes," Tobias says, jaw flexing. His hand sliding feather light from my chin down to my throat, his knuckle stroking downward over the slight lump, his grip circling the entirety of my throat loosely. "Tell us if you want to stop."

"We will listen," Gabe says gruffly, his mouth buried in the back of my hair now.

I'm touching all three of them at once. It's like having a triple-pronged electrical current running through my body. My nipples are in points, my skin is hypersensitive. And then Tobias squeezes my throat, just barely, and I whimper—bringing all three of them forward in a heated rush, their hard bodies converging on me from three different sides.

Oh holy shit. Holy shit.

I start to shake, their muscles flexing against me in response. Almost like a protective move that they can't help. "I don't know what's going on."

"Join the club," Banks says through his teeth.

"Me either." This from Gabe, who unexpectedly wraps his forearm around my waist and draws me back tightly to his chest. "But I'm the one she asked out."

There's a flash of something dangerous in Tobias's expression. "Allow us the opportunity to change her mind. It's only sporting."

Banks brings my hand to his mouth and exhales roughly against the small of my wrist, razing the sensitive region with his teeth. I suck down a greedy inhale, my right knee jerking up in response to the intense pull between my thighs. Tobias catches my knee in his left hand without looking, proving he's an expert at his trade. He yanks my knee up to his hip so suddenly that I gasp, powerless to do anything but reel while he balances it there, his exploratory hand sliding higher on my hip, just beneath the hem of my skirt. Squeezing until I cry out.

At the same time, Gabe fists my hair and brings it to one side, his open mouth on the nape of my neck, Banks taking my hand and placing it inside his buttoned shirt. He pauses with my palm over his heart and it's rioting out of control. Mine is doing the same.

"Are you hot for all three of us, Elise?" Tobias asks, his thumb pressing into my hip abductor in such a knowing and skilled way that a sort of languidness rolls through me. As though he's hit a pressure point to rob me of tension. "There's no shame in it."

Logically, I already know that. But I welcome hearing it out loud. "I know. I've just never been with…" I'm breathless. "I can barely tolerate one man, let alone three."

I've never been the recipient of a more heated look. "If you want this, tell me. I'll guide us." He wets his sensual bottom lip. "Free of charge."

Am I crazy to nod in the face of such arrogance? To say, "Yes"?

Maybe. But I do it anyway. I don't want to break free of their hold. Not yet.

A little more.

"Good girl. Now kiss him," Tobias rasps, framing my jaw in his hand and turning me toward Banks. "Kiss him while my hand is up your fucking skirt."

I've never experienced this painfully wonderful kind of clench before, the one that makes my panties feel like they've melted onto my body like hot wax. I'm wet. I'm wet and trembling and my lust is directed full circle, three times as potent because there are more places for it to go. To land and flourish.

Banks crowds in closer, his lips drawing back from his teeth like he's in pain, brow furrowed. A hot breath later, his mouth moves over mine and we moan into a kiss. A bolt turns in the dead center of my stomach, wild colors and patterns splattering on the insides of my eyelids. I've never kissed or been kissed back with so much urgency.

"Gabe would like to get his dirty hands on your tits, Elise," Tobias murmurs with his forehead nuzzling my temple, his grip still around my throat, somehow keeping me anchored, instead of alarming me whatsoever. Maybe because I believe them when they reassure me that we can stop at any time. "Do you allow that, love?"

Oh my God. Being asked for permission in such explicit terms makes me want to wrap my other leg around Tobias's waist, but I'm too weakened by the kiss to do anything but nod my consent. I'm boneless between three hard bodies. They're holding me up. Tobias by the throat, Gabe supporting most of my weight from behind, Banks keeping me in utter thrall with his mouth—a mouth I gasp into when Gabe flattens my breasts with his hands, his middle fingers stroking roughly around my hard nipples—and I'm shaking almost violently now.

"What about you?" Gabe rumbles into my hair, pinching my nipples between his knuckles, increasing the pressure until I'm panting, breaking the kiss with Banks. Staring back into his glittering eyes in wonder. From both of us. "What are you going to do to her?" Gabe asks again, his lap making contact with my bottom, lifting me onto my toes.

"Me?" Tobias winds the sides of my skirt in his hands, dragging the material up my thighs, landing my now-bare bottom in Gabe's lap. "I'll tend to the pussy, of course."

He starts to kneel—

The lights turn on in the tram car—and it jolts into movement.

A voice crackles over the loudspeaker, the words as impossible to discern as before, but the jarring feedback is enough to send me screeching back into reality. I'm sandwiched in between three men I just met. I'm kissing one of them, another is fondling my breasts and I have no idea what the third man is about to do, but I'm pretty sure I've seen him do it before on the screen of my phone while turning up the speed setting on my vibrator.

We are going to be on the other side of this ride in like, under a minute and I'm flushed, shaken, breathing like I just surfaced after a dive to the bottom of the ocean. In a way, I have. I'm so aroused, I'm almost disoriented while stumbling free of the three-way tug-of-war they're playing with my senses, gulping down air while attempting to straighten my clothing.

"What was that?" I ask to no one specific. Or maybe I'm asking myself. "I don't know what that was," I clarify haltingly. "But I don't just...I don't do things like this."

I cringe over the clichéd statement. It feels like something women are supposed to say to hide the fact that they enjoy sex, when we should be allowed to own it. I *do* own it on occasion. But this—three men I know so little about—commandeering my entire being like this has unnerved me. I'm an impulsive person when it comes to changing professions and trying new things. However, I am the opposite when it comes to personal relationships. My constant job hopping is the perfect guarantee that I don't have time or energy for friendships or romantic entanglements. And this four-person affair, which I'm not entirely sure isn't a shared psychosis, is nothing if not a giant tangle. As such, I'm desperate to break free of this shared bubble and get some fresh air. Get some space to think and breathe.

I make the mistake of glancing back at Banks, Tobias and Gabe. It's a mistake because they all very obviously want me back between them, even if they seem a little thrown by what just happened, too. What prompted the whole thing?

Right. I asked out Gabe.

He's looking at me now from beneath hooded eyebrows, as if he wants to revisit that invitation very badly. Now. But...I find I can't do it. My mouth won't form the words that will establish a second meeting with him. I won't use this guy for my story. It feels wrong.

The door of the tram opens and I propel myself off, ignoring the baritone chorus of voices calling my name behind me, their footsteps hitting the sidewalk several yards behind. I hail the first yellow cab I see, resisting the urge to turn around in my seat as it flies down Second Avenue, secure in the fact that I'll never see these men again.

And surprised when that realization makes me sad. Restless.

But I bite down on my lip to stop myself from asking the cab driver to go back. I'm not going to get distracted from the story. I'm not going to forget my purpose for the sake of something that has no viability.

No chance of lasting. I've done that way too much throughout my life —and the cycle stops now. It has to.

I open my purse to get my credit card out, so I can pay for the cab when it arrives outside my building. After some increasingly frantic rooting around, my pulse skitters like dimes across a hardwood floor.

My *Times* badge is gone.

CHAPTER

Four

Banks

WE ALL STAND beneath the tramway watching Elise go, oblivious to the sudden pandemonium at the tram station. While we've been stuck above the river, news stations have arrived, concerned loved ones have gathered and...apparently I've been dropped into an alternate universe where I become starved for a woman at first fucking glance.

I'm not sure about Tobias and Gabe, but I've certainly never had the impulse to run after a member of the opposite sex before. I've got more discipline than to follow through on the urge. So apparently do the other two men, though it's obvious we're all considering it.

I've made my living in rugby. It's in my nature to adapt fast, to strategize and make the most advantageous choices, but at this very moment, I'm at a loss.

What happened on that tram?

Tobias is the first one to speak. Obviously.

"What in the bloody hell was that?" says the Brit in wonder, ten fingers buried in his hair. An adult film star. I've just shared a woman with an adult film star—granted, we didn't get any further than making out. Still, this was definitely not on my bingo card. I should be on the phone with Vankman's replacement, scheduling extra training sessions to get him ready for the match on Tuesday. I should be on the phone with my mother's landlord, trying to convince them to take a payment from me, despite my mother expressly forbidding it.

Instead, I am obsessing over the way Elise's tongue moved with mine. Like we've kissed before. Or like we'd been dreaming about it and finally got the chance.

Her mountain air scent is on my palms and I can't stop myself from pressing both hands to my face and inhaling, the fly of my slacks still snug even though she's long gone. Growing tighter at the renewed tease of her smell in my nose.

Again, what happened up there?

I feel almost drunk, but my senses are somehow sharper than ever. Awake.

"I can't believe she asked me out," Gabe says, staring after the cab. A forlorn giant. "That beautiful girl asked *me* out."

"That's not a girl, that's a woman," Tobias says, wiping the back of his wrist across his mouth. Trying to hoard the taste of her, like me? The possibility irritates me, even as I understand it. Elise was—is— nothing short of extraordinary. Long limbs, that wild tumble of dark hair, eyes that could snap between vulnerable and skeptical in a matter of seconds. Sharp wit that was on display the moment she stepped onto the tram.

Of course all three of us were attracted to her.

But I can't pretend that's all it was.

"Dammit," Gabe says, shoving his hands into the pocket of his sweatshirt. "I should have just said yes."

Tobias claps a hand down on the construction foreman's shoulder. "Don't beat yourself up over it, erection boy. She still would have chosen me eventually."

"She hated your ass," I say, blithely.

"Yes, but she would have loved my cock." He smiles at both of us, this man who talks about his dick more than a presidential candidate talks about healthcare. "Actually it sounds like she's been loving it for years."

"I don't watch porn," Gabe says, still staring up Second Avenue, as if she might turn around and come back. And God, I wish she would. I'm feeling pretty forlorn myself, truth be told. Maybe I'm still trapped in the alternate tram universe, but my gut insists she…belongs back here with the three of us. I feel that way even though I'm jealous of these men for touching her. She's simply supposed to be here. "I have a stack of magazines I found in my old man's closet when I was thirteen and I've never needed anything else," Gabe continues.

"That's tragic as fuck, mate," Tobias murmurs, a line ticking in his cheek.

Now all three of us are staring at the avenue in heavy silence.

"Do you think there is any way to track her down? Purely out of curiosity, of course." Tobias asks, finally, his tone slightly more unraveled than before. I can relate. There is this sense of unfinished business that is pulling at my nerve endings and it's become more intense the longer she's gone. Is it possible they're feeling it to the same degree?

"A way to track her down apart from searching for women named Elise living in New York City on social media?" Not that I plan to do that. At all. Surely. And definitely not the second I get home. "No. And tracking her down in any way, shape or form would be inappropriate."

"Are you always such a boring old rule follower?" Tobias shifts, lets out a breath. "She did mention she works as a reporter."

I already thought of this, but unlike him, I'm not sharing my strategy for finding her and okay, yeah, apparently I'm willing to be highly unethical when it comes to Elise. Unusual for me, to say the least, but the way she made me feel is unusual, too. The effect of her is still turning over and over in my stomach. "She didn't mention which news outlet."

Tobias tilts his head. "No, but 'reporter' gives me a valuable Google keyword."

"Like I said, computer shit is too complicated. I just went ahead and stole her badge," Gabe says, holding up a lanyard with an ID card dangling on the end. "Her name is Elise Brandeis and she works at the *Gotham Times*."

We both gape at the foreman.

"Just when I thought this night couldn't get any more bizarre," I mutter, dragging a hand down my face. "You stole her property? Did you think that would earn you any brownie points when you see her again?"

"I didn't think that far ahead. I rarely do." At least Gabe has the grace to look slightly sheepish. "Stealing is a product of growing up with a brother and a shit ton of cousins that never left my damn house. You want something, you better take it before it's gone. I didn't get this big by letting someone take the last pork chop."

Tobias is incredulous. In this one instance, we are of the same mind. "Let's find a nice pub and have a stiff drink, shall we?"

Gabe

I face the two men across the table.

Both of them are staring at the lanyard wrapped around my fist, the ID card hidden in my hand. They want to look at Elise's picture, but I want it all to myself. That selfish reaction makes me feel guilty, though, so I finally sigh and open my fist. And we all stare down at the picture of her glaring at the camera. Hell, I miss that glare and it's been less than an hour.

What is going on here?

Under normal circumstances, I never would have spoken to these guys.

They're not my people.

One is polished and permanently agitated, drinking some kind of Belgian wheat beer, instead of Budweiser or Coors Light, like a regular dude. He's built like someone who trains like a motherfucker at the gym, instead of lifting shit and getting dirty, like me. And the other one—the porn actor? Forget about it. He's like some kind of strange, alien species with his accent and expensive sweater. Cashmere, isn't it? He checked his reflection in a spoon when we sat down. He talks about his penis in front of a girl. No, a woman. Bottom line, I've never spent actual time with anyone like him. We have nothing in common.

Except Elise.

She's why us three very different men are sharing a drink together.

We all want her and it's not a mystery as to why. I'm not the sharpest crayon in the box, but I've never been struck dumb by the sight of someone. Never gotten hard so fast in my life.

The way she snuggled into me, her breath on my throat…

A groan tries to leave my mouth, but I drown it with a sip of beer at the last second.

She's gorgeous. Smart. Smells so good. Didn't freak out when the tram stalled. And she seemed to like me. Let me put my arms around her. So I might have overreacted in the genitals department. Technically, I'm still overreacting a little because I haven't had any alone time since it happened. *Deep breath, man.*

Why didn't I just keep my mouth shut about the ID card?

I could be home by now. Could have used the ID card to find her before the others. But no. I had to open my big, dumb yapper. Now I'm in competition with super-fit sports guy and a man who has sex for a living. I couldn't even compete with my lazy brother. Do I stand a chance against these two?

Maybe. She asked me out, didn't she?

Looked at me with softer eyes than the other two, unless I completely imagined that.

It's possible. What could she want from me?

What would *any* women want from me, let alone Elise who is so full of life and secrets and curiosity, it made my throat burn just to look at her?

My failed marriage was all about providing. I was pretty comfortable with my ex, because I'd known her for so long. But I never felt like she was one hundred percent present with me. Not like I did when Elise tipped her chin up and seemed to stare right into my soul.

"I think I'll just take this and go," I say, pushing aside my beer—and attempting to leave with the ID card. "Nice meeting you both."

They stand simultaneously, shoving me back down into the wooden booth.

Sex guy is stronger than I thought.

"Not so fast," Banks says, visibly trying to hold on to his patience. "Let's just finish our drinks and figure this out."

"Figure what out?" I question him, warily.

"What happened up there," Banks explains, taking the orange peel garnish out of his beer and tossing it onto the napkin. First, he looks at Tobias. "This sort of thing might be typical for you, but I've never shared a woman like that."

"Me neither," I say, trying not to think too hard about the curve of her butt in my lap. The way she pushed it up against me and grinded, slowly, wiping my brain clean. "I don't really want to start now, either."

Their eyes snap to mine. I've put them on guard.

That's fine. I don't have a lot of friends. Not like my brother does. I've gotten used to being the odd man out. I just really don't want that to happen with Elise. Something really deep in my stomach tells me she's important. How this situation is handled is important.

"And there's the elephant in the room," Tobias drawls, rapping his knuckles on the table. "We were all...affected by this woman. We all want to sleep with her."

"If you don't think it was more than that, you weren't there," Banks states.

Tobias becomes fascinated by his martini. A martini. Who is this dude? I have no business hanging out with him. But I'm more interested in what Banks said. Until now, I swear I had some kind of instant, cosmic connection with Elise.

What if it wasn't only me, though?

"What do you mean?" I ask, narrowing my eyes at Banks.

The rugby coach lets out an exhale, shakes his head. "I can't find the adequate words to explain it. Except to say...she never felt like a stranger. Not for a single second. I wanted to protect her immediately. I wanted her to..."

"Like you?" Tobias supplies, seeming to shock himself. "Really, genuinely like you. Because she seemed like someone whose opinion matters."

"Yeah," Banks and I say at the same time.

We're all trading wary glances with each other.

Shit. They do get it. I'm not the only one.

Tobias

Fucking hell.

What am I doing here?

As galling as it is to admit, I don't think I've got a chance with Elise. She has definitely rubbed a few orgasms out to my impressive visage, but she thinks I'm a twat. Hell, I *am* a twat. Talking about sex and making filthy insinuations is part of my charm. However, I'm usually capable of turning it off in mixed company. Tonight? I couldn't. It doesn't make any sense. I wanted her to like me and yet, I couldn't seem to stop doing the very thing that pissed her off.

Almost as if I resented the very need to be liked.

My therapist—the real reason I was on Roosevelt Island—would be impressed.

Whatever the reason I behaved like a boor, here I am, trying to be part of her fan boy club when I've all but obliterated my chance to sleep with her. And fuck me, I really, really want to sleep with her. There's also the peculiar matter of wanting my chance at keeping her warm. The way Erection Boy and Banks did. That lost opportunity sits in my stomach now like a paperweight. So I drink my piss-poor martini and stay put, the chance of seeing her again keeping me glued to the booth.

Hopefully when I do see her again, this gnawing need to be somehow important to her goes away. Throughout my adult life, I've only been important to people if I'm making them money. In some cases, that wasn't enough. They wanted more. As much as they could squeeze out of me, even if it came at the cost of a friendship. Because at the end of the day, no one really wants to be my friend, do they? They don't like me, they like what I can do for them.

Sexually.

Financially.

This girl, this Elise, is the first person in a long time whose opinion made me give a shit.

"Right. We have the ID badge. That gives us her last name." I lean back in my chair, oh so casual, though I'm feeling anything but. "Do any of us still use Facebook? We can probably find Elise there, send her a message."

"There are two problems with that," says the coach, immediately.

He's the smart one.

Gabe is the muscle.

I'm the sexual riptide.

"One," Banks continues, "who is going to message her? One of us? Or all three? Because it seems like three messages might overwhelm her and none of us will hear shit back."

"Or she might only message back one of us," Gabe points out.

"That's a pretty sizeable risk," I tell Gabe with a serious expression, completely taking advantage of his naivete, but listen, I am the Least Favorite of this pack and I'll use every tool at my disposal. "You know how indecisive girls can be. Too many choices and they shut down."

That's all bullshit, but again. Least Favorite. I can't risk her choosing before I have another chance to make an impression. Though I have zero guarantee I'll do better next time.

Still…

"Probably for the best if we elect a representative to message her on behalf of all three of us," I say. "Make a plan for all of us to see her again."

Banks clears his throat. "That brings us to the second problem."

"Enlighten the group," I sigh, refusing to let him know I'm interested.

"Do we trust the elected representative?" Banks sips his beer. "I'll be honest, I'm not sure either of you should trust me not to ask her out. Alone."

"Same," Gabe says, his expression saying he holds the winning lottery ticket in his giant mitts. "I'd cook a pot roast for her."

"And if she's vegan?" I ask, popping my green olive into my mouth.

Gabe pales.

"Bottom line…" Banks doesn't look happy about what's he's going to say. "Social media leaves too much up to chance. I think it has to be in person."

I pause mid-chew. "You're saying we should simply show up at the *Gotham Times*?"

"She's going to hate that," Gabe and Banks say in unison.

"Yeah, she will," Banks continues, turning his beer in circles on the table. "But I genuinely think we've seen the last of her otherwise."

"He's right," I find myself saying. For the life of me, I can't see Elise answering a Facebook message and agreeing to meet with us. "So we go to the newspaper and…ask her to choose. Is that your shite plan? Because I fancy keeping my balls."

Banks is silent for long moments. "I don't know. Should we ask her to choose?"

Gabe leans forward, head tilted like he's trying to hear a song playing on the radio at low volume. "What's the other option?"

A muscle jumps in Banks's cheek. "We don't."

"We don't see her again at all?" Gabe sputters.

"My God, man, you're thick," I groan, massaging the bridge of my nose.

"No, Gabe. We don't ask her to choose." Banks is visibly surprised he said it out loud, the bronze of his neck darkening slightly. "Look, I coach a team. We have two players I consider all-stars, but they can't win the game alone. The team behind them—that's what makes them great. When they try to be heroes and score without that supporting cast, that's when they fail, right?" He pauses. "What if…there was something about us as a whole that appealed to Elise? Not only as…individuals."

We're all silent for a moment and I know what they're thinking about. They're replaying how she turned to putty as soon as we were all surrounding her. Touching her. When the four of us connected, a tangible change took place in her. In her energy. In the air. "She enjoyed having triple the attention and fuck, she deserves it," I say without thinking.

Gabe is shaking his head. "I don't know how to do that. One of her, three of us."

"You were doing it," I point out.

The foreman drains his beer.

"This might be a good time to address everyone's sexual preferences," I say. "I've experimented with men, but it's the pussy life for me. What about you two?"

"Straight," Banks says.

Gabe stares over my shoulder, like he's trying put a puzzle together. How does this guy even tie his shoelaces? "A guy on my crew is gay."

I stare. "Yeah, that doesn't count."

"I'm straight."

"Okay, fine," I say, in my element now. "So this is just about Elise. We're all about her pleasure. And getting pleasure from her."

Gabe shifts in his booth, very obviously still dealing with his erection. "Yeah."

"Not from each other."

They both shake their heads.

"Then are we being selfish by only offering her one of us? Bear in mind, I have the ability to provide the same amount of orgasms as three men, possibly four, but...she did seem to have an odd fondness for you both." I polish off my martini and signal for another. "Enjoy that while it lasts, because I'll eventually be her favorite."

Says he, with absolutely no confidence.

Banks snorts. "Whatever, guy." He hesitates. "But the rest of what you said makes sense. I liked...watching her get overwhelmed. By what we were doing. At the same time. One man can't give her that. I can't believe I'm going to say this, but I think our best chance of spending time with her is...together."

"Fuck," I mutter, along with Gabe. "Another round, then?"

CHAPTER

I PUSH my sandwich cart through the sea of cubicles, soaking in the sound of ringing phones and cable news. It's noon on Friday and the only time I become the most important person in the newsroom. Because I'm peddling everything from a classic pastrami on rye to caprese on ciabatta. My cart has a squeaky wheel, which has turned into a Pavlov's dog situation. When the staff writers hear the wobbly whine coming their direction, they turn with hungry expressions and begin extracting money from their wallets and purses.

Someone holds out a ten and I already know this guy wants the turkey wrap, so I hand it to him without stopping, depositing his cash in my apron, tossing two singles onto his desk.

"Enjoy your eight-dollar sandwich," I murmur, my attention directed squarely ahead, as usual. On the managing editor's glass office walls. Karina Grazer sits on a giant turquoise exercise ball behind her desk, shaking her head at whatever is being said on her Zoom meeting. Her shoes have been kicked off, her nylon-covered arches digging into the foot massager beneath her desk. There are two pictures hanging behind her on the wall. One of Karina meeting the president. One of her getting arrested at a reproductive rights rally.

I slow my cart down so much that I'm only eating up an inch every ten seconds. I've become an expert at timing my Karina sandwich delivery, so I can catch her in between the morning editorial meeting and her afternoon call with the big bosses. The tone of our conversation very much depends on the outcome of those Zoom meetings and today, I'm desperately hoping to find her in a good mood, though I've brought along an extra cup of her favorite garlic aioli just in case she's in a shouty state of mind.

A woman waves at me from across the chaos—and I recognize her as a wild card. She always takes several minutes to decide what sandwich she wants. Oftentimes she decides against purchasing a sandwich at all. Then she asks if I have any soups with a bone broth base, which obviously I do not. I have no soup at all and never have. I'm the sandwich peddler.

Normally I would be annoyed by this, but it's going to work to my advantage today, because Karina doesn't look anywhere near ending her call.

"Hey Elise," says my customer, rubbing her palms together, perusing the selection of artisan sandwiches prepared by a deli in Chelsea. "Is there anything new?"

Nope.

Up ahead, I watch Karina end the Zoom and slump forward onto her desk.

With urgency bubbling in my blood, I face my customer again with a smile. "They added honey to the mayo of the chicken club. Really transformed it. Total chef's kiss."

"Ooh okay, I'll take that."

"Fab."

I place the sandwich on her desk, quickly make change and wheel my cart toward Karina's glass office. I lied about the honey in the mayonnaise, but listen, she'll convince herself she tastes it and I needed a swift exit. When it comes to food, the devil is in the details. People will order a meal because of pickled onions or the words *avocado crema*. I learned that when I tried to launch a food truck called The Kitchen Sink. A diner on wheels, serving everything from burgers to biscuits and gravy. I didn't listen when my parents told me I needed food service experience and after a few hectic days at a street festival in

Greenpoint, the Kitchen Sink...well it sank. There was only one silver lining and it was selling the truck I'd spent weeks fixing up and the profit paid my rent for six months while I figured out my next career.

Karina lifts her head and spies me coming, her dark eyes narrowing into slits, probably gauging my mood the same way I gauge hers. There are days when I simply deliver her tuna on whole wheat and leave. Today is not one of those days.

No. After last night, I'm even more determined to make the *Times* job happen. I need to know I'm capable of having aspirations, pursuing them and succeeding. I can't take another failure or halfway accomplishment without my self-worth dwindling down to nothing. I'm dangerously close already. Not to mention my parents, who only gave me a tired smile when I informed them I was going to be a reporter. They've had it with me.

I never thought I would see the day. As long as I worked hard, they never cared if my efforts went into ceramics or coding. Hard work always pays off, they would tell me—and that advice came from experience. My mother emigrated from Mexico as a teenager. After months of teaching herself English by watching talk shows and sitcom reruns, she found work as a bilingual nanny, a position in high demand in southern California. Eventually she tutored children in her community so they could have an easier time finding their own opportunities. Now she operates her own childcare service. She's dedicated. Amazing.

And my father, an Irish-American boxer turned marine, is the most reliable human I've ever met in my life. He's never *not* answered his phone when I call. His handyman skills are unmatched—he can fix anything that's broken. When he makes a promise, he keeps it.

How did these remarkable people end up with a commitment-phobic daughter?

"Ah, there she is. The bringer of nourishment herself." Karina bounces a few times on the exercise ball, stretching her limber brown arms high above her head and letting them drop with a thud onto her desk. "Since you have wheeled your entire cart into my office and closed the door, rather than simply deliver me the mediocre tuna sandwich, I can only assume that you have a story idea you would like to pitch to me. Again." She holds up her hand when I try to speak. "Here is a story I would like covered. Why no celery in the tuna? Why does the deli have against texture?"

"Excellent question," I say brightly, laying a napkin down in front of her and presenting the boxed sandwich with a flourish. "You obviously have a discerning palate."

"I know when you're buttering me up." She pauses in the act of popping open the cardboard tabs of her sandwich box, shrewd eyes zipping to the lanyard dangling around my neck. "Is that a new badge?"

That simple question is all it takes for the tram incident to come roaring back in surround sound audio. I can feel Gabe behind me, thick and sturdy, his breath on the back of my neck, Banks and his hungry mouth slanting over mine, a groan growing louder and louder in his throat. Tobias rucking up my skirt. What would have happened if the electricity hadn't returned when it did? Would I have been intimate with them? *All* of them?

"Um…" It takes some work to bring my voice back to even. "Yes, this is my new ID. The picture was old."

Karina holds the sandwich in front of her mouth, preparing to bite in. "You've only been working here for a month, Elise."

"I know, but I had a mole removed and I wanted the picture to reflect the current me, so…" She's getting ready to debunk that easy-to-verify lie, so I rush to continue. "Anyway, that's neither here nor there."

"Just like the mole," Karina says around her first bite.

My laugh is cringingly loud. "Good one." I park myself in the chair facing her desk, pretending I don't notice her eyeroll. "There is something you should know. I've been following a story for a couple of weeks. Really, it just started as a hunch—"

"Elise, I appreciate your tenacity, but you are not employed here as a writer." She gestures to the gigantic cubicle graveyard behind me. "All of those reporters and staff writers out there have paid their dues. Most of them suffered through J-school and a master's degree to belong in these hallowed halls. This is the goddamn *Gotham Times*, sandwich girl. I like you, but you can't just cut to the front of the line."

My throat tightens like a zip tie has been pulled taut around it. She's right. I know she's right. But I'm not cut out for long hauls. I'd make it through one year of journalism school, tops. Forget about a master's. I don't have that kind of dedication inside of me. I'm not a sticker. I never stick. The consequences of my modus operandi were made very obvious earlier this year when I attempted to join the military, like my parents. To become a marine. I was running out of time to make them proud and this? It was surefire.

Except the marines didn't want me.

"Hear me out, Karina. You know the feud going on between the mayor and that union boss, Jameson Crouch? They keep taking shots at each other in the press and somehow, Crouch seems to have inside information. Damaging information that is hurting the mayor's approval rating, right before an election." I wet my lips. "I started looking into his closest advisors and Deputy Mayor Alexander has some longstanding ties to Crouch. They went to the same high school, moved in the same crowds. So I started following Alexander and—"

"You did what?" Slowly, the managing editor sets down her sandwich. "You followed the deputy mayor?"

"Yes."

"Are you out of your ever-loving mind, sandwich girl? Do you have any idea how politicians behave when their power is threatened? They can be downright dangerous when push comes to shove." She swipes the napkin across her mouth and gears up to deliver what can only be a scathing lecture about safety—which I am prepared to accept—as long as she lets me pursue the story. But something stops her. Karina's eyes fasten to a spot beyond my shoulder and widen considerably. "Who is that? Who are they?"

"Who?"

"They." She gestures impatiently. "Those men."

The bottom is already dropping out of my stomach when I turn around. There is no reason I should assume it's the guys from the tram. We had a memorable encounter, sure, but to show up at my place of work the following day? That's crazy. Right? Yes. Still, based on Karina's reaction and some weird gut intuition...I somehow know who I'm going to see when I twist around in the chair. Maybe because seeing them again—and soon—felt inevitable.

There's Gabe in his paint-splattered sweatshirt and jeans, holding a hard hat to his chest, looking woefully uncomfortable among the gawking staff writers.

Banks has already spotted me, his gaze cutting through the buzzing office and hitting me in the chest like an arrow strikes a bullseye. And obviously Tobias is leaning against the wall, grinning and wearing my missing badge around his neck.

"Oh my God," I whisper, whipping back around, my face burning.

"You know them," Karina says—a statement, not a question. There's a reason she's a managing editor. Her teeth were cut in the field of journalism as a White House correspondent. She can sniff out a lie from a hundred yards away. "How do you know them and what are they doing here? I already let you get away with the mole removal bullshit, so it better be the truth."

"I...you're my boss. I can't tell you that truth."

Karina throws up her hands. "Good God. I am not your boss. You report to the deli."

I don't receive that statement. "Do I, though?"

"Yes."

"Technically, I work at the *Gotham Times*, though. See? I have a badge."

"To get through security—" She cuts herself off, audibly grinding her teeth. "I already go to therapy twice a week. Don't make me go a third time. Who are those men?"

My heart is palpitating at an alarming rate. "You know how the Roosevelt Island tram got stuck last night?"

"Yes, the story is on page three."

I nod. "I was on one of those stalled cars with them. It was close quarters." At a loss for how to explain, I shrug my shoulders all the way to my ears. "I lost my mind."

For the first time in the month I've worked here, Karina is momentarily stunned into silence. "You played hide the eggplant—excuse me, eggplants, plural—with those three slabs of beef right there?"

"It didn't get that far. No eggplants were hidden." I bury my face in my hands. "Oh God, you're never going to take me seriously as a reporter."

"I didn't take you seriously as a reporter before, Elise."

"I was wearing you down," I say weakly.

She ignores that statement. "Hold on. A couple of witnesses claim Deputy Mayor Alexander was on the tram, but he hasn't confirmed or denied. You were on Roosevelt Island following him, weren't you?"

I hum in affirmation.

"Then you deserved to get stuck. That was reckless and stupid and it will not happen again. Do you understand me?" She jabs the air with a finger. "Drop the story or I'll fire you."

"Technically, you can't fire me, I work for the deli."

She snatches up her phone and begins punching the screen with both thumbs.

"What are you doing?"

"Scheduling a third therapy session."

"Oh." I wince, warmth spreading across my shoulder blades. A tingle that tells me I'm being watched—and not just by Banks. "They're still standing by the entrance, aren't they?"

"Oh yeah." She whistles under her breath. "Forget the tuna. Bring me one of them on your sandwich cart on Monday. Any of them will do. I'm not picky." Suddenly she grabs up her glasses from their resting spot on her desk and puts them on. "Is that...?"

"Tobias Atwater, the adult film star with over one hundred and eighty films in his catalogue at the age of thirty-three. Yes. That's him." I might have browsed his Wikipedia page on the train this morning. Just out of curiosity. Gabe's name turned up nothing, no social media presence whatsoever. When I slapped "Banks Pearson, rugby, coach" into the Google search bar, I gave a cursory scan of his biography which was located on the team website. Very cursory. Hardly remember any of it.

Liar.

Banks, also known as the Duke, is quite a big deal in his own right. With collegiate national titles under his belt as a team captain at Penn State, he's now the first Black coach in the United States Rugby Union, not to mention the youngest. He rules the sideline for the New York Flare—and he's undefeated this season.

Not that I memorized any of those details.

"I better go get rid of them," I mutter, pushing to my feet. There is no way I'm going to make any headway today with Karina, especially with these three clowns posted up by the elevators. How dare they show up to my place of work? What could they possibly want?

Before I can leave Karina's office, she shoots up from her exercise ball, sending the inflatable zigzagging toward the window. "Wait. Wait a second."

Hope leaps in my chest. "You're rethinking the whole 'deputy mayor is a mole for the union boss' story? I can show you my notes—"

"Nope. I've made my position very clear on that front, Elise. Do not try me." She keeps our gazes locked until I nod, very discreetly crossing my fingers behind my back. "I'm about to give you a big opportunity that you do not deserve in any form or fashion. I'm offering you a chance to write something for the lifestyle section. A week in the life of a woman in a polyamorous relationship."

All I can do is stare. "I'm not in a polyamorous relationship. I'm not in any relationship, but if this were one, I...don't *think* it would be referred to as polyamorous, since they...I mean, I could be wrong, but they didn't seem at all interested in each other..."

"Fine, so a quad?"

I let out a low whistle. "You definitely know more about this than I do."

"I've led an interesting life." She pauses, leans forward. "Elise, in no way am I pressuring you to pursue a relationship, but if you made that decision independently, that is a story I would be interested in from you."

"No. No way. I'm...no. First of all, they could just be here to return my old badge. I might have dropped it. Second, on the off chance they are here to ask me out or something equally insane, I don't even like having one boyfriend, let alone three. Men are a pain in the ass." My mind is conjuring nightmare scenarios, one right after the other. "There would be no way out of a group text situation if I had three boyfriends. It would be never-ending. That is three sets of crusty friends I'd have to meet and impress. Three sets of parents. I'm dying a rapid death inside just thinking about it."

"Say no more." Karina collects her ball and sits back down in front of her sandwich, her lips twitching with a smile. "I totally understand. Maybe you could just tell them to get lost and write about the tram experience itself. Whatever you decide is fine with me, but under no circumstances do you continue with this harebrained stakeout of Deputy Mayor Alexander. Okay?"

I swallow. Nod. Start to leave again and stop with my hand on the door.

"Why are you hesitating?"

"Just enjoying the last few seconds before they realize I'm a sand-wich delivery girl."

"The best sandwich delivery girl." Karina sinks her teeth into her tuna sandwich and waves me toward the door. "Even if you're reckless and annoying."

"Such flattery."

She snorts. "Drop the story, Elise."

I turn away from her so she can't see my eyes are crossed. "It's dropped."

Briefly, I consider running for the emergency exit located on the opposite side of the floor, but my mother didn't raise a coward. So with no choice, I lift my chin, wrap my fingers around the metal bar of the sandwich cart and push it toward the trio of men who are absolutely joking if they think I want anything to do with them.

My internet search history notwithstanding.

CHAPTER

Six

ON MY WAY across the cubicle graveyard, I build up a hot head of
steam. Every eyeball in the place is turned toward the tram trio and
these Ivy League-educated reporters are quickly putting together the
pieces, probably since I am plowing my cart toward Tobias, Banks and
Gabe like a one-sided game of chicken. Not only are they likely stirring
up speculation about me, but they've put me in a weird position with
Karina who will henceforth refer to me as Hide The Eggplant Girl.

The fact that Tobias pushes off the wall and casually drawls,
"Utterly heartwarming. The Tram Fam is back together," does nothing
to even out my mood.

By the time I reach the men, I'm so irritated that I send the cart
sailing straight into Tobias, hoping to knock the wind out of his sails—
or perhaps maim him in some such way—but he catches the cart with
one hand, his grin only stretching wider.

"Ah now," he says with a sniff. "I can tell she missed me."

I peer over my shoulder to find everyone and their sister draped
over the tops of their five-by-five patch of real estate, their recently
purchased sandwiches forgotten in their hands. "What are you doing
here?" I scream-whisper at them through my teeth. "This is my place
of work." I reach over and snatch the badge from around Tobias's

neck. "Did you steal my badge so you'd have some way to track me down?"

"I did not steal it," Tobias responds, hesitating for a drawn-out dramatic pause before pointing at one of the men to my right. "Gabe did. He swiped himself in through security and let us in the back entrance."

"Gabe stole it? You really expect me to believe that?" There's no way. Not soft-spoken, wounded-by-betrayal Gabe. But when I glance over, he's avoiding eye contact with me and the tips of his ears are the color of a fire engine. "Gabe. You didn't."

"Sorry, Elise," he rumbles, scrubbing at the back of his neck. "You asked me out and I didn't get the chance to...you know."

"Close the deal on the date," Banks supplies, his eyes unwavering on me, as always.

"Yeah," Gabe says, taking a step in my direction. "You left so suddenly. Before I could get my shit together. I saw the strap of your ID hanging out of your bag and I thought...this is how I'll get to see her again."

"Wait. I'm confused. Which one is the sandwich girl dating?" someone says behind me, followed by a storm of whispered guesswork. Afraid of what I'll find, I nonetheless glance back over my shoulder and people appear to have joined from other floors to witness this.

"That's more or less what we're here to find out," Tobias informs them, cheerfully.

At this point, I'm surprised steam doesn't blow my head through the ceiling. "Can I speak to you three somewhere private?" I say through my teeth.

"Of course," Banks answers immediately. "Lead the way."

The only room I have access to is the kitchen, so I breeze past the three men and the elevators. "Tram Fam on the move," Tobias announces to the office.

"I'm going to kill you," I whisper at him over my shoulder.

He beams back at me.

We continue down the short hallway to the other side of the elevator bank and hook a left. Surrounded by three men who each have several inches of height on me, I unearth the key from my apron and slide it into the lock, ordering my fingers to firm up and stop trembling. There's no reason to be nervous. None at all. I'm going to explain to these men that I have no interest in dating any of them and shortly, they will disperse toward their respective corners of Manhattan, leaving me to figure out my next move with Karina. If there is one.

How did I get stuck in another unachievable pipe dream?

That's the question echoing in my head as I step inside, flip on the light—and far too late recognize that the kitchen is only half the size of the tram car.

They've already piled in, arms crossed, looking at me expectantly.

We're standing very close to one another, their big chests offering me warmth. The showered cleanliness of them so inviting, I mentally sob. No single man has ever been so touchable to me, but somehow *these* three beg for welcoming strokes from my palms. Valiantly, I try to ignore the effect their nearness has on my pulse. Or…is it one of them? All of them? I'm so confused. "What?" I ask semi-unsteadily, closing the door. "You have the nerve to show up here—at my job—and look at me like I owe you money?"

They all react differently to my gripe.

Tobias rocks back on his heels, Britishly amused.

Gabe hangs his head slightly.

Banks clears his throat, seeming to realize at once how intense the trio of them are coming across. "Allow me to explain, Elise. After you left last night, the three of us went out for a drink."

"None of us ordered Michelob Ultra or something equally ghastly," Tobias interjects. "So rest assured we all have a pair of balls."

"Wasn't really concerned about it, since I never plan on seeing them," I shoot back.

Banks sends Tobias a look. "Maybe it's best if you say nothing for a while."

"Shut up and perform, Tobias. Not the first time I've heard that."

"Great," Banks says dryly, before returning his attention to me. "As I was saying, we went out for a beer and…" He pauses to adjust the collar of his dress shirt, which I already know smells incredible. Smoky and sweet. "I think it's safe to say we were all dumbstruck by what happened on the tram. I don't know how else to describe it. But none of us has experience with—"

"Objection." This from Tobias. Obviously. "I've been in a foursome."

"Not without getting paid, I'm guessing?" Banks says.

Tobias gives a very sage nod. "You are correct about that. Maybe it's you lot that owes me money."

"I am leaving in thirty seconds," I inform them with a bright smile.

This pronouncement makes Gabe very unhappy. He shifts right to left in his boots and seemingly forces himself into speaking. "After what happened with my brother and ex, I haven't dated anyone. Didn't have any interest. It's definitely a shock to me that the first time I do have some interest—a lot of interest, Elise—I'm sharing her with two other dudes. It doesn't really make any sense after what I've been dealing with personally." He swallows, visibly confused by the next thing he says. "But it didn't exactly feel...wrong, either."

It's a challenge to keep my expression neutral when the memories of last night are crowding in from all sides, making me ache in places I shouldn't be aching while on the clock. But I can feel Gabe's calloused hands taking ownership of my breasts, his slow tug of my nipples through my shirt and bra. I remember Banks's breath on my mouth, panting, hungry. And Tobias...I truly hate him for making me obsess over what he'd been planning to do before the lights came back on and the spell was broken.

I'll tend to the pussy, of course.

The word "tend" makes me think of farming.

Like driving a tractor. Or plowing.

Had he planned to plow me? Am I overthinking this?

"When I said we had a drink, I lied. Slightly." Banks glances briefly at the men beside him. "It was more like three. By the time we got to the third one, we admitted that, uh..."

"We loved the idea of you getting the maximum amount of pleasure," Tobias finishes, heat replacing the amusement in his blue eyes. "Maybe it's the fact that we all met you at the same time, but the sharing felt good, because it benefited you. Don't get me wrong, there is some definite jealousy among the ranks. If two of us turned our backs, the third would rob you like an art thief with a chance at stealing the Mona Lisa."

"I prefer to be compared to the Birth of Venus, but okay." It's getting very difficult to pretend that my knees aren't shaking. "Point taken."

That dimple makes a brief appearance on Tobias's cheek. "I think I speak for all of us when I say, we want you individually, all to ourselves, but this situation…"

"It calls for something more evolved," Banks finishes. "You do. You will get more satisfaction out of the three of us. None of us can find fault with offering you *more*. In fact, it seems like a crime to do otherwise."

"We'd like another chance to worship you. Do you happen to have an opening in your schedule?" Tobias's gaze runs down the front of my apron and snags on my thighs. "Today would be great. Within the next hour would be preferable. Happy to host at my place."

There is an intense flutter between my legs that I've never really experienced before. It's like a second heartbeat. It's instinct. My body is quite aware that they would give me something that it would never forget, but my brain is very adamant that pursuing this…arrangement is a bad idea. This, these men, is something I wouldn't be allowed to do halfway. My intuition is telling me they would require all of me. Every little bit.

I don't even know what *all of me* looks like.

I haven't given my all to anything in a really long time.

"Just a brief rundown. You've come here to ask for a foursome." I look each of them in the eye. "In broad daylight. Stone cold sober."

They trade glances and nod.

"Why me? Is it just because I'm…I seemed willing—"

"Why you?" Gabe growls, his brows pinching together. "Why you?"

Tobias nudges Banks with his elbow. "She's asking, why her."

There's a tic in Banks's right eye. "First of all, you are fucking beautiful, Elise, just in case you haven't been told so a thousand times in your life. Second…" He stops to shake his head, his wingtips carrying him a step in my direction, making me very aware that I'm against the door. "The second reason is not very easy to put into words. Except to say, as soon as you stepped onto the tram, you had all of us by the throat. And overnight that hold only got stronger."

"It's like it was supposed to happen," Gabe adds, almost to himself. "The four of us being on the same car. The electrical shortage." His eyes lift to mine, then travel down over the curve of my neck, his chest beginning to rise and fall at a quickened pace. "All of it."

"We realize that sounds quite insane," Tobias says, serious for once. "I half expected them not to show up today. I thought perhaps my imagination was making everything that happened sharper. Stronger. But now that you're standing back in front of me, I know I was wrong. I didn't imagine any of it. *We* didn't."

I'm still waiting for the punch line.

Or my alarm clock to go off.

Beneath my apron, I pinch my thigh just to be sure I'm truly awake. Even though I already know the answer. I'm bright eyed and bushy tailed—and I could never dream these three men up in such specific detail. Could never imagine three presences so…tremendous.

There is no way I'm considering this. Obviously. Because it's straight up kooky. Just like everyone and everything in my life, they will expect more from me than I know how to give.

"Do you guys need me to walk you out? Or can you find the exit yourselves?"

A lip twitch from Banks.

Gabe seems powerless to do anything but gravitate closer to me.

"You're not even going to consider it?" Tobias asks, with his signature smile that doesn't show in his eyes. "That's all?"

"That's all," I confirm. "Honestly, men are nothing but irritating. Once or twice, I thought I found a decent one and officially started dating him. Sure, it starts out great. Then suddenly I'm required to check in all the time. Let him know where I'm going, when I'll be home. I have to be available for daily phone calls. About *nothing*. Why do women subject themselves to this?" I gesture at the row of incredibly good-looking men, wondering in the back of my mind if I have a screw loose to turn down their offer to worship me. "Showing up at my office like this doesn't really give me casual vibes. It feels like a trap. I'm not getting sucked in by the promise of orgasms. Then suddenly I'm picking up three pairs of dirty socks on my floor. Uh-uh. Nope."

"Elise, I'll eat your pussy like it's the last slice of chocolate fucking cake," Tobias deadpans. "You know how I do it, love."

"I should punch you in the face for talking to me like that," I manage, using all of my control to hide the fact that my legs have turned into gelatin molds. *Chocolate. Cake?*

"Why don't you?" Tobias winks at me. "Is it because I'm too pretty?"

"Once again, I am asking that you please shut up," Banks bites off.

Tobias holds up his hands in surrender.

"If you said yes..." Gabe begins, slowly unzipping his hoodie, taking it off and laying it on the kitchen counter that runs along the wall to his left. Beneath it, he's wearing a white T-shirt that is so thin and ancient, I can see right through it. To the maze of tattoos on his beefy chest. The colorful patterns of ink run all the way up the right side of his neck. They take up every inch of space on his thick arms. I start to question why he's taking off his hoodie when he is moments from leaving the building, but...it becomes very obvious why.

Everything south of my belly button is melting like hot wax.

I can't help but envision that powerful body on top of me. Behind me.

Gabe's hoodie removal is *effective.* Even more so when he comes closer, hitting me with soulful eye contact and the smell of sawdust. "If you say yes, I promise not to expect phone calls from you," he says gruffly, working man's fingers flexing at his sides. "But I can't promise I won't be happy when I get one."

"Same," Banks says, his voice an octave lower.

"Make that three," Tobias sighs.

"We're not..." I sputter, pressing my back tighter to the door. "This is not a negotiation of terms. I'm saying no. Hell no, actually." My rapidly dampening underwear is calling me a liar, but I ignore the barb. "Are none of you going to address that I lied to you about being a reporter? No one is going to point out that, in reality, I'm a sandwich delivery person?"

That question brings them up short.

It brings me up short, too. I wasn't planning on saying that.

"And I used to come on camera for a living," Tobias says, narrowed eyes riveted on my face. "No one is passing any sort of judgment here. Your profession is irrelevant."

"Maybe to you," I rasp, suddenly feeling winded. "When you three walked in—"

"You mean the Tram Fam," Tobias interrupts.

Banks smacks him in the shoulder.

Gabe whips a growl in the Brit's direction.

"I will never say those words out loud," I inform the room.

"Please continue, Elise," Banks says, refocusing on me. "When we walked in…?"

I have to take a deep breath before I continue, because they are so close and their scents combine to create some kind of intoxicating super scent, which must be the reason I have goosebumps all down my arms and legs. "When you walked in, I was telling the managing editor, Karina, about my trip to Roosevelt Island. I didn't lie about being there as a reporter. Problem is, I am not *employed* as a reporter, as you can tell by this incredibly unflattering apron." I look at Gabe, resisting the urge to walk into his arms when I remember very distinctly how warm and secure I feel inside of them. "I was there to follow a different story. One involving your union boss, Gabe. Jameson Crouch. I asked you out so I could…I thought maybe you could give me closer access to him, because I think he might be in cahoots with the deputy mayor. I think they might be sabotaging the mayor. But… using you for information didn't feel right. I *couldn't* use you like that. So I left without making firm plans. Okay?"

No one moves for long moments as that confession settles over the room.

Banks reaches out and tips my chin up. "Why didn't using him feel right?"

I look at Gabe and find him watching me steadily. Maybe a tad warily—and I can't blame him, but the wariness hurts. More than it should.

"Did it feel like you were betraying him?" Tobias asks.

I'm distracted by the intensity in Gabe's expression, which is why this next part slips out. "Yes. And it felt like I was betraying the group." Which is something I had no idea was true until the words are hanging in the air between the four of us, leaving me shaken down to my toes.

"It's the Tram Fam effect," Tobias murmurs.

We all roll our eyes at him.

"Elise," Banks says, an underlying sense of urgency in his tone. That finger is still tipping up my chin, making me feel very vulnerable. And God help me, extremely turned on. I'm standing before three very interested men who appear to be poised to pounce if given a single word of encouragement. "I understand why you're hesitant. This whole thing is...unexpected. The kind of thing other people do." He presses his thumb into the center of my chin and drags my mouth open, allowing a soft whimper to escape past my defenses. "Let's try it on for size, anyway. You can back out at any time."

I'm exposed. My head is spinning. I would be lying if I said I wasn't...attaching myself to these three men in this moment. It's happening whether I like it or not. Or maybe it happened last night over the East River. Whatever the reason, I find myself confiding in them. Opening myself in ways I've rarely done with anyone. "I do everything halfway. I'm afraid to do the work and have it mean nothing, so I look for shortcuts. I'm...this...you are going to require too much of me."

Tobias props a forearm on the door above my head, his mouth dropping to the space just above the curve of my neck. "Say yes, anyway," he implores me hoarsely. "If any of us leave socks on your floor, you get a free dick punch."

I laugh. It's a breathless, tinkling sound I don't recognize, almost a little hysterical. And why wouldn't I be hysterical when Gabe is staring at my breasts while wetting his lips, Banks's fingers leave my chin and slide into my hair, tugging the strands at the roots and releasing a delicious rush of endorphins that twist my nipples into hard spikes. Then there is Tobias mouthing the words *chocolate cake* at me.

God, I hate him.

Don't I?

"I can't do this here," I whisper, voice trembling.

Three sets of eyes zip to my face. "But you *can* do it?" Gabe asks, low, urgently.

The universe seems to hold its breath. I'm poised on the edge of the unknown.

What am I thinking?

"One time," I breathe. "One time, yes."

The word "yes" is like a gun firing at the start of a race.

Banks uses his grip on my hair to turn my head to the right, just in time for Gabe's mouth to swoop down and claim mine. It's like unspoken choreography. Poetic. I don't get a breath in before it's happening, before Gabe is wrapping me in some kind of euphoric spell, hard, desperate lips working mine over like he hasn't experienced anything pleasure-related in a long time. Maybe he hasn't. Isn't that what he implied earlier?

I'm caught up in the give and take, the stroke for stroke rhythm of his tongue in my mouth, the bristle of his beard on my chin and cheeks, when Banks begins unfastening my apron, tugging down the top half so he can palm my breasts. As soon as Gabe releases me to come up for air, Banks arrows toward my neck, razing me with his teeth from shoulder to the patch behind my ear. It's so raw and sensitizing that I cry out, reaching out, desperate for purchase. One of them. All of them. I don't know. All I know is I get my fists wrapped in Banks's shirt and Tobias's hair and they love it. They groan over being touched by me.

Tobias moves in to claim the other side of my neck, licking me in a bold claim, before his lips press in tight to my ear. "Been dreaming of getting my fingers up that skirt since last night. Are you going to set me loose on it, love?"

I think we all know the *it* he's referring to. It knows. It clenches in response.

The next words out of my mouth need to be *no. Later. Stop.*

But while I was perusing—okay, devouring—his Wikipedia page earlier, I returned to the moment on the tram a hundred times. The moment when he said he was going to tend to me.

So perhaps quite unwisely, I eek out the word, "Yes."

Tobias smiles against my ear.

All three men suspend in animation, watching Tobias's fingertips trail slowly up my knee, my inner thigh, disappearing beneath my skirt. I'm not a lip biter, but there is no choice but to bite down hard or scream at him to go faster. He knows that's what I want, because he's chuckling against my ear. At least until his fingers reach the cotton of my panties and he releases a slow hiss, two very knowledgeable fingers pressing lengthways into my slit through the thin material, gently sawing back and forth, seizing the air in my lungs.

"What does she feel like?" Gabe asks in a hoarse voice, stroking a hand down the front of his jeans. "I need to know."

"Tell us," Banks demands, still using his lips and teeth on my neck, his fingers unfastening the buttons of my shirt one by one.

"Firm and wet." His breath is hot against my ear. "Fucking perfect."

That description—which, I'll admit, has a nice ring to it—visibly brings Gabe to the edge, his weathered face contorting in pain. He steps around Banks who is groaning into my neck, his mouth moving feverishly, arousing me more with every targeted lick and nip of my sensitive skin. And suddenly Gabe's lips are moving over mine, his big, heaving chest the final thing I see before my eyes slip closed and I'm nothing but a receptor for sensation. My mouth belongs to Gabe, my aching flesh to Tobias and for some reason, Banks is bliss and reassurance all at once. His face close to mine makes me feel secure, like I can tackle this extreme event that is happening—and his hands. They are inside my shirt now, strumming my nipples through my basic cotton bra and I'm carried away, I'm boneless and cared for and exultant.

There is a full minute of the worship they spoke about before it all spins out of control.

Tobias goes down on his knees in front of me, leans down and sinks his teeth into the inside of my knee, a sound of pure hunger kindling in his throat. Banks drags a hand down the small of my back, lower, where he kneads one side of my bottom, groaning roughly, before beginning to gather the back of my skirt in his hand.

"Do you want him to use his tongue on it, Elise?" Banks exhales shakily, his lower body crowding toward me slightly, letting me feel his substantial erection against my hip. "Your call. Whatever you want to do, I've got you." He whispers the next part into my hair. "You can decide on me. I'll take you home right now. Just us. Wet you down again and make you fucking scream."

Wait. Is he asking me to ditch the other two?

I'm still examining those urgent words when Gabe drops into a kneeling position beside Tobias, surging forward to press his panting open mouth to my belly, his huge hands beginning to participate in the act of drawing up my skirt, too. "I want her first," Gabe rasps.

"Life is full of disappointment, mate. She's mine." This from Tobias, who has finally shoved my skirt high enough to reveal my white cotton underwear, of which the crotch is embarrassingly soaked—and they both stare with open appreciation for several beats, before converging on me at once. Gabe's mouth arrows toward the cotton triangle, but Tobias wraps a forearm around my hips, ripping me to the right at the last second, his mouth fastening to my drenched mound of cotton and suctioning me through my panties.

I'm trapped between protest and…utter lust. How is he…how. How is he inflicting so much pleasure on me with a barrier between us? He has stiffened his bottom lip and he's rubbing side to side over the top of my clit and I'm already panting. My left leg is lifting to wrap around his head, because if he stops, the bliss comes to an end and it can't end. It can't.

There is a scuffle below and suddenly it's Gabe's mouth providing the friction, the unabashed, urgent licking through my wet underwear —and it's so good, different than Tobias's mouth, but somehow exactly what I need, too—and it comes to a stop when Tobias elbows his way back in, jerking me toward him with that arm wrapped around my hips. A tug of war is ensuing between Tobias and Gabe, which is bad enough, but then Banks enters the mix, enfolding me in his arms and dragging me away from the scene. At first I think it's to disengage me from the battle happening between Gabe and Tobias, but when our laps press together, he curses under his breath and backs me toward the kitchen counter. Pins me.

"Do me a favor and wrap those legs around me nice and tight, angel," he urges, reaching down for my knees as if to jerk them up— and I'm shocked to find that I want to. My core tightens expectantly, excited by the imagery of his demand. He wants to take me here, against the counter, roughly if his harsh breathing is any indication. But over Banks's shoulder, I see the other two approaching with twin expressions of possessiveness and I know we've taken a wrong turn. They're literally fighting over who gets me first. Consider my mind blown.

"Stop," I mutter, still trapped in the need they've woven around me.

They stop.

On a dime.

They're not happy about it, but apart from their chests heaving up and down, their movements cease immediately—and I've never felt more powerful. Seen. Heard. Sure, my skirt is around my waist and I'm wedged in between a seriously aroused man while two more seethe behind him, visibly restraining themselves from stealing me, but I'm in control of this situation. And control feels incredible. I have to triple lock my apartment door to keep danger out and can't go places alone at night, so the way these men respect my wishes is…well, it's how it *should* be, but it's also fucking glorious.

They've just fed me something I've never eaten before.

It's also a very good thing they know how to listen to the voice of reason, because these three have lost their damn minds.

"No. I'm not the rope in a tug of war." I push Banks back a step and work my skirt back into place, my diaphragm expanding and contracting with staccato breaths. "What happened to all that 'sharing you felt right, because it benefitted you' talk? Were you lying?"

"No." Banks answers first, dragging an unsteady hand down his face. "No, I don't know what came over me. I just couldn't stand not being the one to—"

"Take you first," Gabe grits out, obviously still working on getting himself under control, his nostrils flaring, sweat dotting his upper lip. "Make you happy first."

"It's tough being the only enlightened one," Tobias sighs, but his casual tone is forced. Does he think I can't see the strain around his jaw? The white knuckles of his fists.

"This isn't going to work," I murmur. It's a statement of the obvious, right? "I don't think any of us are cut out for this. A four-person..."

"Relationship. You can say it, And you were loving every second," Tobias argues. "We are the ones who fucked it up." He shoves five long fingers through his hair. "I'm not acquainted with jealousy. I didn't know how to handle it, I guess."

"He took the words out of my mouth," Banks says, brown eyes steady on me. Regretful.

Gabe takes longer to speak. So long that we all look at him expectantly until he finally speaks in that deep rumble. "I guess I've gotten tired of letting other people take what I want."

That sentiment catches me in the dead center of my chest. It doesn't align with my personal issues, but I understand what it's like...when it seems like everyone around us has life figured out and we're still in beginner mode. There's a thread of that frustration in what Gabe is saying and it pulls at me like a gravitational force.

I start to respond when Gabe's head lifts and he tacks on, "And I don't understand it, but I've never wanted anything or anyone like I want you." His eyelids fall and he visibly struggles with the next part. "It's the same for them."

Banks nods, grips the edge of the counter beside me, his scent teasing my nose. "Give us another chance to do it right, Elise."

Everyone looks at Tobias. He snorts. "I'm not apologizing. I called dibs."

"Why are you the way that you are?" I ask, tilting my head.

Something guarded travels through his eyes. "Now, love. Don't open Pandora's box."

That ominous statement settles over the room and I can't help it. I'm beyond curious about what makes these men tick. I want to know what turned Tobias into a giant tool. Want to know more about Banks and the situation with his mother. Gabe? I just want to defend with a sword, even though he's not the simple golden retriever I initially pegged him to be. Apparently he's also a hot, tattooed thief.

"I suppose..." Gabe goes on. "Remember that fancy party I told you about tomorrow night? It's being held to support the mayor's reelection. After all the feuding between my boss and the mayor in the press, the gala is basically the mayor offering an olive branch to Crouch and the rest of 401. My brother and Candace are going to be there. It's sort of an introduction of them as a couple. I guess having it hanging over my head set me off. I'm sorry, Elise."

Why can't I just accept his apology and walk out of here? These three are going to be a ton of work and I've established that work usually leads to me bailing halfway.

I...don't want to do that to them.

Except maybe Tobias.

"Gabe..." I take a long breath. "You stole my ID badge and tried to physically fight Tobias for...dibs." I can't believe I just said that with a straight face. "You're able to admit when you're wrong and talk about uncomfortable things at the cost of your own pride. You're obviously capable of a lot more than you think."

His chest lifts and falls, eyes guarded but hopeful. "You think so?"

"Yes. I do."

Gabe is silent for a moment. "Then I want to invite you to the gala. As my date." He chews the inside of his cheek, visibly working through something. "But since you think I'm capable of more, then, uh...yeah. I want to make up for today. So I guess I'm inviting all three of you to the gala."

Everyone performs a double take.

A clap from Tobias breaks the silence. "I am a devil at parties."

"You're the devil, period," I fire back.

His grin is infuriatingly sexy. "If you want to experience my forked tongue, love, just ask."

"Enough," Banks grinds out. "You want to ruin this for all of us, British? Keep talking."

Tobias doesn't quite lose his smirk, but he drops sideways against the wall with his arms crossed and goes silent, the feigned boredom not reaching any higher than his curved mouth.

Gabe's proposed invitation to the gala is still hanging very noticeably in the air. Prior to my meeting with Karina this morning, I would have jumped at the chance to get this kind of access to Alexander and Crouch. Now? I'm hesitant. If Karina tells me I'll be fired for chasing down this story, she means it. No, *if* I attend this party, it needs to be about Gabe and the personal obstacles he needs help overcoming. And it would be.

If I decide later to keep hunting down the truth, it needs to be on my own time.

For now, my biggest hesitation in accepting the invitation is, well, the obvious.

"I appreciate you making an effort, Gabe, but I'm not sure about going on a public date with three men. I don't even know what that would look like. That seems like a lot, really fast."

Banks's energy is sizzling. "It doesn't have to be a date with all three of us. You go to the party with Gabe as his date. Me and this prick are just...there, too."

"Why?" I genuinely want to know.

"To be near you, Elise."

They're all looking at me in the exact same way. As if that's it. That's the truth of everything. They want to be near me.

"I'm not sure." I shake my head, scrutinizing each of them closely. "But the answer is definitely no if you're going to turn this into a competition. I'm not interested in being the prize. Or the bone you three fight over. You'll need to get on the same page."

Tobias, Banks and Gabe trade long looks, going from questioning to resigned to determined in the space of a few seconds. "We'll keep our egos at home tomorrow night," Banks says. "This is about you. Not our male pride."

"My ego doesn't detach," Tobias says, rolling a single shoulder. "That being said, it bothers me that we have upset you and I don't anticipate doing it again. At least not by trying to pull you apart like a wishbone. I can't help what comes out of my mouth."

"We noticed," I say, trading a smirk with this man I used to fantasize about daily.

The way he holds my gaze, subtly licking the corner of his lips definitely doesn't raise the temperature of my skin to sizzling. Definitely not.

Lies.

"I'll need to find a way to get you added to the guest list," Gabe says, splitting a glance between Banks and Tobias. "I don't have that kind of pull on my own."

Wheels turn swiftly behind Banks's eyes. It's like looking in a mirror. "I'm the head coach of the New York Flare. We're always looking for a good cause. Reelecting the mayor who has been a vocal supporter of the team is as good a cause as any."

We simultaneously look at Tobias. "I'm the ultimate novelty. I'll get in." He huffs a laugh. "Coincidentally, I'm a novelty *because* I always get in."

I don't give him the satisfaction of reacting to that. "I don't know. It's still…a lot."

"We won't make it obvious." Banks tips his head to one side, a corner of his lips quirking up, his manner sort of cajoling. He's been so intense since we met, the charm hasn't quite made an appearance, but here it is. He's barely turned it on and my stomach has flipped over. "One more chance, Elise?"

"If I say yes, will you leave?"

"Yes," they reply in unison.

I circle the three men, poking each of them in the shoulder. Their very hard, very muscular shoulders. Goodness. "I am not, under any circumstances, going to end up in a long-term relationship with you three. This is…I don't know. An experiment that probably won't go beyond tomorrow night. A diversion. I don't have time for group chats and your knucklehead friends. Okay?"

"I don't have any friends," Tobias brags. "Does that give me an advantage?"

"Goodbye," I call on my way toward the door, phone in hand. Is it my imagination or do they all seem to sniff me as I pass? "Gabe, which number is yours? I'll air drop you mine."

He lists the last four digits of his phone number and I shoot him my contact information.

"Ah, I see how it works," says Tobias. "Steal from the lady. Start a fight during the orgy and still be the one to win her number. I've been going about this all wrong."

"Apparently we both have," Banks tacks on, dryly.

"See you all tomorrow," I toss over my shoulder, not quite able to stop the smile that blooms on my face. But it fades in degrees when I find Karina watching me from the opposite end of the hall. She doesn't look angry. No. Although she does raise an eyebrow at my askew clothing, not to mention the bickering male voices coming from the kitchen behind me. And while she doesn't say it out loud, I can hear her reminding me about the article she suggested I write, instead of the deputy mayor/union boss exposé.

A week in the life of a woman in a quad.

After emerging from the kitchen looking like I bumped into a tornado, it's going to be very hard to deny that I am in some kind of entanglement with them.

But a relationship?

No way. Nah. Never.

CHAPTER
Seven

Banks

I'M NOT one hundred percent focused on practice. Closer to forty.

That much is obvious when I find my players breakdancing in the middle of the pitch when they're supposed to be running a long passing drill. I fumble my whistle slightly on the way to putting it in my mouth, my clumsiness unusual. I issue the two, shrill staccato blows that my team is well acquainted with. It means I'm not happy.

"If you've got so much energy," I shout across the freshly mani-cured grass. "You'll have no problem running stadiums. Last man back runs it a third time."

Another blow of the whistle cuts through their groans, but they waste no time sprinting off toward the stands, running up and down each row of stairs in a haphazard line. Truthfully, it's not their fault I can't concentrate enough to run a decent practice session today.

It's her fault. Elise's. Theirs, too.

Might as well get used to Gabe and Tobias. They are clearly as invested as I am.

And Jesus, I am very invested. It's Saturday. Tonight is the mayor's reelection gala. I'm attending as a designated fifth wheel. I should be exasperated or humiliated by my willingness to attend a date Elise is having with someone else, yet I find myself checking the time on my phone every eight minutes, approximately. Anxiously waiting to see her again.

My players hit their second round of stadiums, drawing my eye to the stands. Normally, the steep collection of royal blue seats is something I avoid. When I emerge from the locker room at the beginning of a match, I peruse the family section to determine who is there. After that, I refuse to glance at the crowd, whether they are cheering, sitting in silence or jeering the referee. There is no one there for me. I don't need to be reminded of that when I'm trying to focus on winning the match.

"You got something on your mind today, coach?" says my assistant, approaching from midfield to where I stand on the sidelines. "You worried about playing without Vankman on Tuesday?"

"Yes and no," I say curtly, embarrassed to have been caught staring into space. "I think Parnell will fill in nicely, but we still need to work on his attack. He's offloading the ball too soon. I'd rather him take contact then pass into a crowd."

"I'll stay after practice and work with him for a while."

"Good. Thank you."

He's quiet for a moment, observing me. "Normally, you would offer to stay as well. You have somewhere else to be?"

Yes. Watching the woman I can't stop obsessing about go on a date with someone else.

I clear my throat hard. "Just meeting a friend."

"Sure."

I stare balefully into his bright smile.

Chuckling, he begins to walk away, but stops and comes back almost immediately. "Sorry, I forgot. There's something I need to ask you." He hesitates, my odd mood clearly throwing him off balance. Usually there is an easy camaraderie between me and Pete, but it's difficult to be in an affable mood when I have Elise on my mind...and no idea if there's a way to keep her. It figures that I've found someone who engages me mentally, physically, emotionally and she's anti-relationship, whether it's with one man or fucking three. In a way, it serves me right for living the first thirty-two years of my life as a sworn bachelor.

"I'm sorry for being distracted," I say to Pete, watching as the players return to the field and collapse into the grass to recover. "What's up?"

He hesitates, before jerking a thumb over his shoulder. "Our ticket rep called. He wants to know if you still want to leave that ticket at the box office? Same way you do every game?"

A hole forms in my stomach, but I don't let the sudden blow to my midsection show on my face. Do I want to keep setting myself up for rejection? "I'm not sure. I'll let you know tomorrow."

"Sounds like a plan," Pete says easily. But I can interpret his expression. It's pity.

How much longer will I continue to leave a match day ticket for my mother, before I realize she's never going to show up? At this point, it's beginning to become pathetic. How many voicemails have I left, asking her to come sit in the designated family box? How many times have I looked into the stands, hoping that just once, there will be someone here for me?

Too many.

I don't know how much longer I can allow myself to care before I shut down that muscle, numb it, and pretend I don't give a shit. But I don't think it'll be very long.

As a younger man, there might have been resentment toward my parents for scoffing at my dreams of playing rugby, instead of falling into line in the financial sector, like the men in my family who came before. They made their protests clear by refusing to attend matches or pay for the travel teams. So I practiced my ass off and became good enough for scholarships. Onto the elite squads where I was visible enough to be recruited by Penn State.

During my junior year, my parents divorced. Bitterly. Money had become an issue after my father made some bad business decisions, eventually being asked to step down at his firm. He is remarried now and making ends meet, but my mother...she won't allow me to give her the help she needs. I have the means for her to live more comfortably and she won't take it, because I make my living in rugby. The profession she always laughed off.

I'm over the past. But she isn't.

And so we live life in a constant stalemate.

Me wanting my mother's support while she laments the time she spent not giving it.

My eye is drawn back to the stands and this time, I picture Elise. Warmth pushes down my arms into my fingertips, the digits of my right hand flexing around the whistle.

Damn. I'd love to see her there. For me.

She would get all of this. She would understand the importance I place on winning.

Somehow I know she would. Without question.

I raise the whistle to my mouth and shout my players into a scrimmage to round out the end of practice. I check my phone and only seven minutes has passed since the last time I looked. Seven minutes closer until tonight.

But I can't seem to make myself wait to speak with Elise. It took some cajoling, but I was able to get her phone number off of Gabe. At the risk of pissing her off, I pull up her contact information and tap out a text.

Me: *Hey. It's Banks.*
Elise: *Gabe strikes again, huh?*
Me: *He handed over your number for a meatball sub.*
E: *That's fair. I'd hand over state secrets for a meatball sub.*
Me: *Good to know.*

Some of my players are looking at me curiously and I realize there's a mile-wide smile stretched across my face. I replace it with a frown, signaling them to pay attention to the match. Apparently I'm resigned to being a shit coach today.

• • •

E: Take a picture of what's in front of you, Banks. No cheating.

Me: Nope. I have half a brain, so there isn't a chance in hell I'm sending you a picture of two dozen sweaty rugby players.

E: I had no idea you were so selfish.

Me: With you I am.

E: I noticed.

I'm bombarded by the memory of her trapped between me and the counter in that tiny room at the *Times*. Her legs were just beginning to creep up around my hips when sanity returned, but Christ, I really think I'd have banged her into oblivion then and there, if given the green light. When I'm touching her, my surroundings have no meaning. There is only connecting with her. Feeling as much of her as possible as quickly and greedily as I can. Still…

Me: The plan is to try and not be so selfish. To learn to share. I realize that.

E: I think we're making up the plan as we go.

Me: Maybe. But you're part of it, so I'm in.

A minute passes. And then a picture comes through.

It's a selfie of Elise.

She's rolling her eyes, her index finger pointing into her mouth.

E: Gross.

My laugh stops everyone mid-scrimmage and I shock them all by ending practice early.

Gabe

I drop down onto a bench, take off my hard hat and swipe a sweaty forearm across my forehead. It's fall and the weather is cool, but I've been hauling my ass all over this building site since eight o'clock this morning, hence the perspiration soaking the front of my Local 401 T-shirt. I open the brown bag in front of me and take out half of a meatball sub, leftover from yesterday, plus a can of Coke, cracking it open.

Both lunch items have vanished within two minutes and I'm still left with fifty-eight minutes of my break. Normally I would catch a nap in the back of my truck or something, but I can't relax.

Tonight is my date with Elise.

I'm definitely going to fuck it up somehow. I don't know how yet, but I will.

I'm good at construction. I build. I frame, insulate, do masonry, interpret plans from the architect with ease. Building is my one and only skill. What I know about women is slim to none and I was *married* to one. Actually, I think I know *less* about women now that I've been married—a fact that has never been more troubling as it is right now. When I've got this beautiful, badass chick meeting me tonight. She wouldn't like me calling her a chick and that only makes me smile more. There is just something about a woman who snuggles with a man one second and tells someone to fuck off in her next breath.

Am I already in love?

Damn. I might be.

With a gusty sigh, I lean back against the concrete pillar behind me, phone in hand. As I've done several times today, I pull up the picture of Elise's ID card and zoom in on her picture. I did embarrassing things while staring at this photo last night—and it's only from the neck up. I'd barely gotten myself warmed up before I finished all over my stomach, the Mets game playing on the screen of my bedroom television. Didn't even have time to grab a tissue.

I've never had trouble lasting in bed. In fact, with my one and only partner, I had a hard time staying focused at all, my mind consistently drifting to other things. Like food. Or building permits. Eventually I would find the rhythm I needed to finish, but I'm fairly positive it used to take me at least twenty minutes. Masturbating to the thought of Elise? Twenty seconds.

It won't be like that when and if we have sex. In real life.

It won't. Right?

Shaking off the concern, I add the photo to her contact and the temptation to text her becomes too much. I haven't sent a personal text to anyone in weeks. Only work ones. The last time I texted anything personal was to my brother, reminding him not to park with his tires on my lawn. He responded with a picture of his middle finger and continued to do it anyway. Maybe it's just something I have to learn to live with. How many times in my life have I resigned myself to being inconvenienced or overlooked?

What difference does one more time make?

I rub at the uncomfortable notch in my throat and pull up an empty text screen with Elise. I already feel better just seeing her name. Even better when I start typing.

Me: You're so beautiful.
Elise: Hi Gabe.
Me: I hope you're not texting me to back out of our date.
E: You texted me.

I'm such a bozo.

E: I heard you gave my number up for meatballs.
Me: Sort of. I gave Tobias a fake number.
E: You're my favorite, Gabe. Despite your thievery.

My dick starts to turn stiff over that. Being her favorite. Is she just saying that? Shit, I don't want to know. I'm just going to pretend like she does.

. . .

Me: What are you doing right now?

　E: Getting dressed for a yoga class.

　Me: Oh. Jesus.

　E: ??

　Me: I have a little thing for yoga pants. By that I mean I have a thing for wanting to see them on you. Don't send me a picture.

　E: Why not?

　Me: You remember my issue on the tram? It'll become an issue again. Real fast.

A picture comes through of her and I shake my head, "Nope," starting to put my phone back in my pocket. Yeah, right. I don't make it five seconds before I'm tapping download on the image and then heat is running rampant through my body, with an emphasis on a certain appendage. She has sent me a shot of her in a white sports bra and navy blue nylon pants. They're so tight, I can make out the shape of her pussy clearly. And the low-rise band of said pants gives me a view of those little peach fuzz hairs under her navel. The shape of her hips. Her breasts, nipples clear as day. This woman is artwork in human form.

E: See you tonight, Gabe.

　Me: I'll be seeing you pretty much all day, every time I blink.

　E: #Favorite.

When I recover from that single word, I take a gulp and overdo it. Can't help myself.

Me: I needed this. To talk to you.

. . .

A chunk of seconds passes before she answers.

E: I told you. You're capable of more than you think, Gabe. Remember that.

When I return to work at the end of my lunch hour, there is a little more steel in my shoulders, energy in my step, and her words echoing in my head.

Tobias

I knew the muppet would only change one number—and the last one at that.

Within five tries, I've reached Elise.

I'm sitting in the waiting room at my therapist's office when she texts me back.

Elise: Gabe only changed one number, didn't he?

My laughter startles the receptionist. After catching her breath, she gives me a sly, questioning smile. Understandable. Normally I'm leaning across the desk by now, flirting with her until my appointment time arrives—what else is there to do? But Elise must have completely ruined me, because the only thing that turns me on at the moment are venomous insults. Furthermore, the idea of flirting with another woman turns my stomach sour.

Alarming, to say the least.

Especially considering Elise still can't stand the sight of me.

I wiggle my fingers in anticipation of texting Elise back. Maybe a carefully selected nude? God knows I have plenty of those. It would be a shame not to immortalize my physique now and again in my iPhone camera roll. Something tells me that will get my number blocked, however, so I settle on something that will encourage her to reply.

Because I want to talk to her. I want to know her.

What the fuck is this change taking place inside of me?

Before I can ask about her day—blech, how common—my therapist arrives in the doorway, summoning me inside. I come very close to canceling the entire session, just so I can text back my brown-eyed beauty, but I've come all the way out to Roosevelt Island and these appointments don't run cheap, so I sigh and follow her into the familiar room full of house plants and colorful furniture.

The first time I walked into this office, I didn't think Dr. Bunton and I would be a good fit. Her taste in décor is unrefined and she wears rainbow Crocs, for the love of God, but she got me talking. Acknowledging my shit out loud. That's more than I can say for the last three shrinks who tried to figure me out.

"It's nice to see you again, Tobias. How have you been since the last time?"

I have to chuckle. "Life has been interesting, to say the least."

She settles into a giant mustard yellow armchair. "How so?"

After removing my overcoat and laying it across the back of a leather couch, I take a seat across from Dr. Bunton. "I met a woman. She loathes me. It's fabulous."

Her mouth opens and closes. "You like the fact that she loathes you?"

"No. I hate it. But for now…I think it's fabulous that she feels something for me. Anything. If you met her, you might understand." Finding the right words to explain here is almost impossible. How can I describe the seismic shift that happens in my bones when Elise flicks me a mere glance? "Having her acknowledge me feels like winning no matter her opinion, even if I would like to change that opinion. Drastically."

Dr. Bunton is silent for a few beats. "Your words are carrying a lot of weight today."

"Are they?" I throw my ankle up onto my knee. Casual as you please. "Hmm."

The ticking clock in the room suddenly seems louder.

"You came to New York from London five years ago and you've yet to let anyone close. All of your acquaintances are surface level and almost always sparked by your persona. Most of your time is spent in your apartment."

"It's a lovely apartment," I interject, somewhat dully, a throb happening in my chest.

"Yes, I'm sure. And it's very understandable that you'd choose to hide away after what happened with your manager." She pauses, tilts her head. "Are you beginning to feel more inclined to be social? Perhaps less fear when it comes to allowing people to get close?"

"God, no. I just think…" I shrug. "Maybe a little fear is worth…her in return."

It's plainly obvious she's trying not to smile. "She must be something."

An image of her stepping onto the tram assails me, her long, dark hair blowing out behind her, sharp, intelligent eyes cataloguing everything in a one-second sweep. "Yes."

"Have you told her about what happened in London?"

I scoff. "Why would I tell her that? It makes me look like a fool."

"No. It makes the person who took *advantage* of you look foolish. Not the other way around. You have to forgive yourself, Tobias."

I'm shaking my head like a baby who doesn't want to eat his broccoli, so I stop.

"When you met this woman, did you play your part of the smarmy adult film star—"

"Fucking hell. Smarmy?"

"Or were you this man sitting before me? An honest, loveable person who might have a concerning naughty streak, but also has weaknesses and faults, like everyone else."

Several seconds tick by while I consider this. "I was smarmy, of course."

"Why?"

I throw up a hand and let it drop. "People enjoy the smarmy porn star."

"The surface level people do." She lets that sink in. "They're entertained by it for a night, maybe two. Someone that might consider a deeper relationship with you might not take you as seriously, however."

This is cutting a little too close to the bone. I'm not ready to admit how scared I am to let down my guard. To take off my mask. The last time I did that with someone, they betrayed me. Pulled the rug straight out from under my feet and the world hasn't looked the same since. I'm going to work on this part of myself, but for now I'm more comfortable changing the subject.

Luckily, I have the ultimate card to play.

"Did I mention, she and I are part of a foursome?"

Dr. Bunton chokes on her sip of coffee.

Forty minutes later, I'm walking to the tram, my thumb smoothing over the screen that still holds Elise's text message.

Elise: Gabe only changed one number, didn't he?

Me: Afraid so. But I'm willing to let him think he outsmarted me if it makes you detest me a little less.

E: Hmm. Not worth it.

My bark of laughter carries down the street. This woman. I've got it fucking bad for her.

Me: I can think of something that would make you hate me a lot less, love, but it can't be accomplished through the phone.

The message is done and sent before I can stop myself. I'm very aware that I'm falling back on my faithful routine of acting like a cad. It's a defense mechanism. I'm not going to stop utilizing it overnight. Hell, maybe ever. What do I know?

E: Please. You've accomplished it many times through the phone, as you well know.

 Me: It doesn't come close to real life.

 E: We need to change the subject.

 Me: That tells me two things. I'm making you horny. And you want to keep talking to me. Consider me pleased as punch.

 E: Consider me pleased to punch you.

 Me: Ah, Elise. You little treasure.

 E: Shut up.

 E: Send me a picture of what's in front of you right now.

I find the request oddly...fun? And I don't hesitate to snap a picture of the tram, firing it off within seconds.

E: YOU'RE JOKING. Why??

I hesitate. Then I hear Dr. Bunton's voice calling me loveable, of all the ghastly adjectives available in the English language. Why did I enjoy hearing that about myself? Is it...true?

Me: I'm here for therapy. Attempting to believe I'm someone worth knowing.

Sending that message makes me feel winded and shaky. I feel exposed as I step onto the tram, locking and unlocking my phone, willing her to send me some manner of response, just to put me out of my misery. Her messages come through just as I'm reaching the other side of the river.

. . .

E: Ughhh. You're worthy of knowing.
    E: And obviously dick punches. Bye.

I think today might be the best day of my life.

CHAPTER

WHAT DOES one wear on a date with three men? Red seems like the obvious choice. Too obvious? Perhaps leather? Oddly enough, I'm not feeling a lot of pressure about my wardrobe considering they almost fought each other over me while I was wearing an apron.

Realizing I'm smiling kind of stupidly into space, I jam a hand into the crowded dress section of my closet, vowing to wear the first garment I pull out. Sputtering out a drum roll, I open my eyes to find I'm holding a pink dress. An A-line fit and flare with a heavy skirt and a low neckline, purchased years ago at Marshall's and never worn in public. It's flirty. Sweet. No one will suspect that I'm the main attraction of a three-ring—er, man—circus.

Maybe I'll come to my senses after one drink.

Said no one ever.

I still can't believe this is happening. That I'm doing this.

That I...want to.

Temporarily.

Holding the dress against my chest, I sit down on the edge of the bed and replay yesterday afternoon in the kitchen of the *Times*, especially the part where they closed in on me, claiming they wanted to give me the "maximum amount of pleasure" even if it meant sharing, which none of them obviously prefer. What would it be like if they all actually got on the same page about that and followed through? What if the three of them could really operate as one entity of...giving?

Pleasure from men is not something I actively seek out. I can do it myself, thank you very much. It's specifically *these* three men. The combination of their energy, their unique effects on me, that has my fingers curling into the satin material of the dress, a flush creeping up the sides of my face. Maybe I should release a little tension before I meet them tonight so my brain is capable of making objective decisions?

I'm already breathing fast and setting aside the dress on my bed... when my apartment buzzer goes off. "Huh?"

When I walk out of my bedroom, my roommate, Shayna, is standing in flannel pants and a Tinkerbell T-shirt, eyeballing the speaker warily. We haven't spent a lot of time together, at least not in a social sense, but she once left her laptop open to her dating profile and I couldn't help but take a small peek. *Activism and Disney* is her subheading. Many times I've wanted to ask about her job as a non-profit spokesperson. Reminders of the past always hold me back. "Did you order food?" she asks now, pointing a single finger at the door.

"No," I say. "Should we ignore it?"

It buzzes again.

We trade a shrug.

I approach the box on the wall and press the speaker button. "Yes?"

"Flowers."

It's possible I heard that wrong. This speaker was installed during Prohibition. Approximately. "Um...what?"

"Flower delivery."

Okay. Heard him right. But unless my parents are sending me flowers, no one has this address. "You have the wrong apartment."

"How do you know they're not for me?" Shayna wants to know.

Wincing inwardly, I tap the speaker again. "Who are they for?"

A long-suffering groan fills the apartment. "Elise Brandeis."

"Oh." I rear back slightly, baffled. Then I shake myself and hold down the button to allow the delivery person into the building. Keeping the chain lock engaged, I pull open the apartment door slightly and watch the man approach with...not one, but *two* bouquets. My jacket is hanging on the peg beside the door, so I root around in my pocket for the change I received this morning for my bagel—it's a few singles—and when he sets down the flowers in their vases on the hallway floor, I hand him the dollar bills through the slit in the door. "Thanks."

"Yup," he sighs, already heading back in the opposite direction.

Shayna laid down safety rules when I rented the room and they include never opening the door for strangers, and never buzzing anyone into the building without knowing who it is. When I order takeout, I give her a heads-up that someone will be coming to the door and she returns the favor. Apart from the odd, casual conversation, that's really the extent of our relationship.

When I moved in last year, she asked me a few times if I wanted to join her and some colleagues on a night out, but I declined. I'm not great at maintaining friendships, even if she seems like someone I would have liked a lot in a past life.

I wait until the deliveryman is out of view before sliding open the chain lock and bringing the bouquets into the apartment one by one. I set them down on the small coffee table in our common area and consider the cards peeking out among the blooms.

One is roses. Red. All cut the exact same length.

One is a mixture of sunflowers and daisies and big, orange lilies.

Somehow I know they're from my men.

I'm referring to them as my men now? *Ugh.*

The question is, how did they get my address?

My head moves on a swivel, zeroing in on my purse where I left it, hanging on top of my jacket. I'm on my feet, zipping across the apartment under the suspicious eye of Shayna, taking out my wallet to find my identification is missing. I haven't needed it since yesterday, so I wouldn't have noticed it was gone. They must have taken it when they ambushed me at the *Times*. Or *one* of them took it, rather. But they're all accomplices, as far as I'm concerned.

"Gabe," I say through my teeth. "I can't believe I sent him a yoga pants selfie today. I am going to—"

The buzzer sounds off again.

Slowly, I turn to look at Shayna and I'm greeted by an arched eyebrow. "Maybe he forgot you needed to sign something?"

"Yeah, probably." I hit the talk button. "Yes?"

"Delivery."

"That's not the same voice," Shayna points out.

"I know." I lean in toward the speaker again. "Delivery from where? For who?"

"Jesus, I don't know. Uh...the slip says 'Tobias' something?" he says. "Is that you?"

With a headache starting to pound behind my eyes, I let the delivery man into the building. "I hope they are enjoying their last moments on earth right now, because tonight I'm going to kill them."

Shayna clears her throat. "What was that?"

"Nothing," I croak. Sliding the chain lock back into its groove, I open the door a couple of inches. I find a man holding a gigantic eggplant wrapped in a yellow bow. "Great. That's just lovely," I grumble, desperately searching my jacket pockets for more tip money, surprised when Shayna's arm appears over my shoulder, two singles folded between her middle and forefingers. "Thanks," I say a minute later when I've closed the door.

And now I'm standing here with an eggplant.

Shayna gestures to the purple vegetable, also known as the universal symbol for dick, and the bouquets on the coffee table. "What's all this?"

"This? Nothing." Quickly, I toss the eggplant into my bedroom where it bounces twice on the bed, before coming to a rest on my pillow, no doubt leaving the world's biggest dick print. Tobias would be delighted. "Sorry about the interruption," I say, collaring a vase under each arm and waddling them toward my bedroom. "Plans for tonight?" I call.

Shayna is silent for a few beats. "Yeah, meeting up with some school friends in the West Village." She pauses. "You're welcome to join."

I pause inside my room where she can't see me and pinch my eyes closed. Dang, I thought we'd reached the point where she'd given up on inviting me places. It's not that I don't want to go, but...the effort it would take to maintain a friendship with my roommate? All that work and then one day, she'll just move out. Or I will. We'll move on. We'll lose touch and I will have nothing but memories to show for it. Memories that make me sad.

A series of faces flip through my mind. Rebecca from Florida. Josephine from Nevada. Evander from San Diego. Friends I made growing up as a military brat. Friends to whom I would sit in the dark and spill out my heart, only to wave goodbye a week or a month later, on to the next destination where I would have to start all over again. Again. Again. There were no shortcuts when it came to making friends, so eventually I just stopped trying.

I quit trying to do anything the full way.

"I have plans, actually. But thanks for the invite," I call back to Shayna, backing up briefly into the doorway so she can see my smile. "Have fun."

It takes her a moment to nod. She wants to poke around about the flowers. And the eggplant. But in the end, she backs toward her room and closes herself inside.

Ignoring the useless flare of guilt in my middle, I do the same. I set the flower arrangements on my nightstand and pluck out the cards, already dead certain which man sent each bouquet—and I'm right. The sunflower mix is from Gabe. His card reads, *You're saving me tonight, I won't forget it.* The card that came with Banks's roses says, *I'll take everything you've got, even the thorns.*

Wow. Nicely done, men.

Almost nice enough to forget one of them is in possession of my state ID.

I should file a police report and cancel the date tonight. But I can't bring myself to leave Gabe hanging at this gala where his brother and ex-wife are set to make a big splash.

Feeling slightly lost, I pick up my phone where it's charging on my dresser and pull up the contact information for my parents. First my mom, then my dad. Maybe I just need some visual proof that I do have the phone numbers for two people who love me. Or maybe it has been too long since I spoke to them and I'm flying by the seat of my pants here, in desperate need of their grounding presence. Whatever the reason, I find myself tapping the FaceTime option for my dad and sinking down onto the floor, turning around so I can lean back against the wobbly piece of furniture.

My father answers on the fourth ring, squinting an inch away from the screen. "Honey?"

Homesickness billows inside of me like a sandstorm.

Permanent homes were never a thing. But through all of the moves, my parents *were* home. And I've repaid them with disappointment. Not that they would ever say it out loud.

"Hey Dad."

He finds somewhere to prop the phone and leans back, the shamrock tattoo on his right shoulder looking a little more faded than the last time I saw it. "Hey, kid. What's good?"

"Not much. I'm getting ready to go to a party tonight." I tilt my head back briefly to look at the flowers looming above my head. "With some friends."

My father's eyes widen. "Wow. That's amazing. I love hearing you're making friends again."

"Yeah." Why are my palms sweating? I had no idea my father was so aware of my lack of friendships. Why wouldn't he be, though? I stopped trying to form bonds with my peers in middle school while I was still living at home. "How's Mom? Is she there?"

"Anita!" he shouts, pointing at the screen when footsteps approach in the background. "Your daughter is on the phone."

"My daughter? I have a daughter? Who knew?" she teases in accented English, plopping down onto my father's lap. My heart squeezes at the picture they make, their unbreakable union obvious. I could recite the story about how they met at a beach bonfire verbatim. Their features are as familiar as my own, probably since I share so many of them. My mother's brown eyes, her high cheekbones. My father's pug nose. "Baby girl," chides my mother. "You look tired."

"Thanks Mom," I respond dryly. "How's everyone on base?"

"Good! Good." She trades a look with my father that turns a bolt in my stomach. "Actually, we spoke to someone at the recruitment center. They're willing to let you reapply for service, if that's something you were still interested in—"

"Oh! No. No, that's okay." I strive for casual, but there's a winded quality to my tone. "No, I have this great job here at the *Times*," I half-lie, hoisting my pinched together fingers into view. "I'm this close to having my byline printed. It's...good here. I'm good."

I can tell they want to look at each other again. That they'll be weighing every word I say in a lengthy discussion as soon as we end the FaceTime. I love my parents more than life itself. They love me the same way. Despite my untethered upbringing, they've always done everything in their power to make me happy.

But things have changed between us.

They used to get so excited when I told them about a new idea, a new venture. They applauded my ingenuity with the food truck. They cheered me on when I started real estate courses. Through all my hare-brained ideas, they backed me up. But when I was rejected by their beloved marines for service, on the grounds that my work history showed a glaring lack of commitment, they started to lose faith. As did I.

Now, even when I reassure them, they only look worried.

Doubtful.

"Oh my gosh, I just realized I'm running late. Can I give you a call tomorrow?"

My mom's smile is forced. Dad isn't bothering to fake one at all.

With a fist-sized lump in my throat, I hang up before they can say anything else.

Then I stand up and hurry through putting on the pink dress.

If nothing else, tonight is the biggest distraction I could ask for.

CHAPTER

MY UBER PULLS UP in front of the Conrad, a downtown hotel, but I make no move to get out. Instead, I watch through the fogged back window as people climb out of black town cars and limousines, the women in sleek, black dresses, the men in tuxedos. I might be wearing a bright pink selection from the last chance rack at Marshall's, but these people don't intimidate me. Not at all. They wish they could pull off this shade of bubble gum.

No, I'm intimidated by the flutter of protectiveness in my ribcage that happens when I see Gabe standing outside, waiting for me, hands tucked into the pockets of his triple XL tux. He nods at guests who walk past him through the glass doors, almost bashful. A shy giant who steals personal possessions and is ready to throw down for the chance to taste me first. He's more than meets the eye. A lot more.

If only I could stick around long enough to find out.

I'm thanking the Uber driver and climbing out to meet Gabe before I'm aware of my actions, the cold air kissing every inch of my bare skin. He sees me coming and his lips part slightly, a white puff of breath momentarily obscuring his face. Not so much that I can't see his relief, though.

"Elise. You look…unreal." He approaches me like a football player waiting on-field for the kickoff, focused and already taking off his jacket. "I wasn't sure you would come."

"Why?" I raise my chin with way too much attitude to counteract the unfamiliar sensations he's stirring inside of me. "Because you stole my ID? Again? Except you took it out of my wallet this time?"

His ears darken. "I wanted to send you flowers so bad," he says gruffly, draping the warm material around my shoulders. "Why do you never have a goddamn coat?"

My lips tingle when he scolds me in that worried tone of voice. "I didn't have one that matched this dress," I manage.

"That dress..." His chest rises and shudders back down. "I hate dancing, but someone's got to dance with you looking like that."

"You will." I allow him to take my right hand. Hold my breath as he brings it to his mouth and kisses the pulse at the small of my wrist. "That's why I'm here, right?"

He makes a scrape of a sound. "Right."

We intertwine our fingers like we've done it hundreds of times before and there's an answering clench in my stomach. It's different than the comforting tingles I get for Banks. Or the agitating hunger Tobias inspires in me. My reaction to Gabe is protectiveness wrapped in lust, but I can tell he also wants to guard me. I'm his defender when I hold his hand, while also very well aware he would do the same in a heartbeat. That certainty is etched deep, even after such a short period of time.

"Are your brother and Candace already inside?" I ask quietly.

He swallows, something like dread playing in his gaze. "Everyone I know is inside."

I push up on my toes and kiss the underside of his bearded jaw. "Good."

Without stopping to address the question in his eyes, I nod at the doorman and pull Gabe through the entrance. We're guided by tall, flickering candle pillars to an elevator and brought up, past a dozen floors of hotel rooms and conference centers, to the very top of the Conrad. Music starts to pound in the rhythm of a heartbeat before the doors even open—but when they do, I'm struck by a rare, uncharacteristic fear that I'm out of my league.

It's like something out of a movie. It's how the other half parties.

The ballroom glows like the inside of a dark amethyst.

Floor-to-ceiling windows look out over the downtown Manhattan skyline.

Two women hang suspended from the ceiling, twirling slowly in long, white silk, graceful and breathtaking and no one even pays them any attention—and they're just one component of the opulent background. Guests mingle in their finery, sparkling crystal champagne flutes pass by on trays. The air is the perfect temperature, sensually scented. The room is lit just enough to see the faces of the people around us, but dark enough to give a sense of…permission.

"I had no idea the union rolled like this," I murmur to Gabe.

"They do during election years," he replies, gesturing to a man mingling on the other side of the room. After the crowd parts slightly, I see it's the actual mayor of New York City. "My father was a 401 member, too, back in the day. He used to say the unions elect the mayor, not the people. This is how they court us."

"Or in this case, make amends." I tip my head toward Jameson Crouch who is clear on the opposite side of the room as the mayor. "Doesn't look like it's going too well."

"The night is young," Gabe says, following my line of sight. "It's going to take more than one drink to get those two on better terms."

My fingers itch to take out my phone and tap out a few notes for my story, but I don't. That's not why I'm here. Tonight is about Gabe.

Primarily, at least.

There's a warm buzz on the side of my neck and I follow Gabe's attention toward the bar where, sure enough, Tobias and Banks are standing. At opposite ends. I watch long enough to witness a woman approach Tobias and I'm surprised when he gives her a curt shake of his head without looking, sending her away. For Banks's part, he sets his drink down slowly when he sees me and tugs roughly on the collar of his starched white shirt.

Good lord. I only stepped off the elevator a minute ago and already I'm having to focus on my breathing, commanding my pulse to remain steady.

What are these men doing to me?

Gabe's fingers jolt within mine, drawing my attention.

He's no longer looking at the bar. Instead his eyes are locked on a couple across the room. There's no doubt the man is his brother, though there are obvious differences. Both of them are tall and husky, but Gabe is firmer. Packed tight in the muscle area. But after a moment of observation, it's easy to see Gabe's brother has a certain devil-may-care charisma that attracts people like flies to honey. Men slap him on the back as they pass by and he snaps out a greeting that makes them laugh every time. He's loud and attention grabbing where Gabe is more of a strong, silent type.

The woman his brother is dancing with—presumably Gabe's ex, Candace—enjoys the attention he draws. Basks in it even when she's not directly addressed. There's nothing wrong with liking attention. I like it, too, depending on the situation. But bottom line, if this woman was the one who hurt Gabe, we aren't going to be friendly.

I didn't wake up this morning and decide to act as a bodyguard for a man twice my size, but here we are.

Murmurs on all sides of us draw my notice. Eyes shift from one brother to the other, whispers are passed between sips of drinks. There are two very distinct groups in attendance. Men and women who look at ease in their finery. And construction types who seem very uncomfortable in their tuxedos. Half of them already have their bow ties dangling from their pockets. It's that latter group splitting their attention between Gabe and his brother, watching to see what will happen. How he'll react to his ex-wife and brother cozied up in public.

"Are you still in love with her?" I ask Gabe, surprised to find my stomach knotted.

"No." He shakes his head. "No, I'm not sure I ever was. I think I…"

"What?" I prompt him after a few moments of silence.

"I got my growth spurt a lot earlier than my brother." He ducks his head slightly and shakes his head, as if he can't believe he's telling me this. "Growing up, I was only called outside to play if the football got stuck in a tree. I had this broom handle I kept by the door, so I could dislodge the ball from between the branches. Then we got older and I started sneaking everyone into movies, claiming to be eighteen when I was only fourteen. The lady at the ticket counter knew we were full of shit, but she let us in anyway." He tips his chin at the dancefloor. "And then one day, he was as tall as me. I wasn't needed for anything and I didn't...I wasn't as quick with the comebacks and jokes. I just stayed out of the way, so I wouldn't have to feel like I was...out of place, I guess." Very briefly, his gaze flickers to the woman on the dancefloor, before finding my gaze. "It just felt good to be chosen. By someone. Maybe even *anyone*. Is that terrible?"

"No." There's a catch in my throat, so I clear it. "No, it's not terrible. It's human nature."

He seems relieved by that assessment. "The mistake was mine, you know? I should have seen what was happening. Should have recognized my own weakness." He pauses. "I need to take my broom handle and go inside. Let them be happy."

"As long as you make yourself happy, too," I say, tugging him toward the center of the ballroom. "Come on. Let's dance."

"Ah, Elise." His fingers stiffen within mine. "I don't know. I don't really dance."

I grin back at him. "You do tonight."

He's momentarily befuddled by my smile, opening his mouth and closing it. "Jesus, you're so fucking pretty."

"Thank you." Oh dear. That tug in my chest is very ominous. "You're very handsome. We sound like two people who ought to be dancing and enjoying themselves, don't we?"

We pass through a group of men holding pilsner glasses of beer—construction types who watch us speculatively, not bothering to hide their smirks.

"Better keep your date away from your brother," one of them snickers.

A chorus of laughs follows.

Gabe immediately tries to pull his hand out of mine, his jaw turning brittle. He's obviously preparing to confront whoever made the comment, but I hold on tight to his hand, refusing to stop until we reach our destination.

"Look. I'm really not a dancer. All right? It's enough just to have you here with me," Gabe says, pulling roughly on his collar. "I don't need to...to beat them."

I draw him to a stop near the edge of the floor, somewhat in the shadows, noticing the way his Adam's apple appears to be lodged beneath his chin. Being in the center of the room has caused a fine sweat to begin forming on his brow. "You're right. We don't have to beat them, but we're not running, either." I wind my arms up behind his neck, pressing my body in tight to his strength. "Take up space, Gabe."

A groove appears between his brows. "What do you mean?"

"Take up your space and don't apologize for it," I say, teasing the ends of his hair with my fingertips. "Like you said, you don't have to beat anyone. I respect that. It's a healthy way of looking at a really hurtful situation. But maybe...if a person stays quiet and makes everyone else comfortable all the time, at the cost of their own voice, they're beating themselves."

He blinks, considering that. "That's what I've been doing. Trying to make them comfortable when it should be the other way around."

I nod. "So stop."

"Take up my space."

"Yeah," I say, beaming up at him. "That's right."

That's my only warning before I'm walked backward into the purple light, his hands dropping to my hips and gripping them securely. So tightly that a whimper shudders out of me before I can stop it, drawing the attention of a couple dancing to our left. Gabe hauls me upon to my toes in a bear hug that crushes the fronts of our bodies together, his seemingly ever-constant erection spearing me in the belly.

"God. I'm sorry—" he breathes in my ear.

"No. Take up your space." There are very few individuals I wouldn't slap for squeezing me against their boner in public. Or maybe there is only one and I'm dancing with him. I'm different around Gabe. I'm different around all three of them. More aware of my body. My mind. My thoughts are less muddled, almost like energy generated by the four of us together is so loud that it drowns out the outside noise.

Gabe's heat causes my neck to loosen slightly, but I manage to keep my head upright, locking eyes with Banks over his shoulder. Then

Tobias. Neither one of them is moving. Only their eyes, tracking mine and Gabe's movements on the dancefloor.

"I want to know your story now, Elise."

That pronouncement from Gabe brings me up short, my steps faltering, but he only holds me tighter and continues to move in a slow, swaying circle. "What do you mean?"

His thumb finds a home in one of the dimples at the small of my back, presses deep, deeper, until my ankles turn to vapor. "I mean...we all want to know you. Everything about you." He puffs a laugh that sounds more frustrated than anything. "Elise, I'm not going to lie..." His swallow is loud in my ear. "Not knowing every goddamn thing about you is driving us all a little insane. You barely agreed to see us again, so I'm...we're trying not to push."

My pulse is starting to race. "I don't understand."

"You sell sandwiches? Fine. It's a respectable job. Except you pretended to be a reporter. You're chasing this story and you're not supposed to be. Please don't get pissed at me for saying this, but you don't seem like the type to do anything backwards."

"I have to use the ladies room," I blurt, disengaging myself from Gabe on the dancefloor. A lot of guests are watching us with avid interest, so I pull him down for a kiss. One. Two of them. "I'll be right back."

"Elise..." Gabe curses under his breath. "I pushed too soon."

"I'll be back," I say again, throat dry. And then I'm weaving through a sea of tuxedos with a smile tacked onto my face. Tobias and Banks frown at my departure, pushing off the bar as if to follow me, but I shake my head at them, mouthing the word "bathroom." Still, they don't settle, but there is nothing I can do to allay their worries right now.

I'm too busy having an identity crisis.

Men outnumber women ten to one at this party, so the upstairs ladies room is relatively empty. Two older women end their discussion when I walk inside and leave through the still-swinging door. I prop my hands on the sink and meet my own eyes in the mirror, Gabe's voice echoing in my head. *You don't seem like the type to do anything backwards.*

Funny, that's exactly who I am. These days, anyway. Not always.

I wasn't always like this.

Two voices reach me through the bathroom door and my chin snaps up, sending my troubling thoughts scattering like picnic goers in a rainstorm. I know those voices. Recognize them well. One of them belongs to Deputy Mayor Alexander. The other is Jameson Crouch. Gabe's boss, to be specific. Of course, they're both at this party, but meeting alone on a separate floor at the end of a dark hallway? To say people would find it suspicious is an understatement.

I'm here tonight for Gabe. Despite the reminder, though, I can't deny the urge to follow those voices. It's not technically safe. Karina wouldn't like it, to say nothing of the men downstairs who already seem so protective of me. But I don't owe anyone a single explanation about who I am or what motivates me, right? Not to Gabe, not Banks and certainly not Tobias. With that reassurance ringing in my head, I creep out of the bathroom and follow the voices.

"What are you doing?" I whisper to myself. "Something bad. This is bad."

I swore to Karina I would drop this story. But *not* following these men would be neglectful. They've practically fallen into my lap, right? I was just minding my own business, then bam. Potential headline news walks by. Creeping on the balls of my feet to the end of the deserted corridor, I stop just before the turn and listen.

"Let's make this quick before we're missed," Deputy Mayor Alexander clips. "Being caught gossiping like schoolgirls near the bathrooms would raise some eyebrows."

"Jesus Christ," drawls the union boss. "You're in a fucking mood."

"What did you not understand about 'make this quick'?"

"Hey." The union boss takes on a much sharper tone. "I'm suffering through this phony truce between me and the mayor to make sure he doesn't suspect anything. I'm your ticket to becoming the mayor of this godforsaken city, in case you forgot."

"I didn't. That's why I'm here," growls Alexander. "You really want to do this? So far, you've been accepting the information I give you to take potshots at the mayor. But leaking documents and private correspondence to the press is a whole other animal."

"We have no choice but to take this to the next level—they poked fun at the feud on frickin' *Saturday Night Live* last week. No one is taking the debate seriously anymore. Now the mayor invites my union to this gala as some kind of peace offering? I'll let him think I accept, but he's dead wrong if he thinks I'm going to forget the way he's shuffled aside the union too many times. You're going to get in that office and change how things are done. In *our* favor."

"All right. I hear you." There's a sound of metal slapping down on a palm and I hold my breath, listening. "These are emails the mayor sent me prior to the governor's visit last month. He calls the governor a scheming reptile, among other select names. Not to mention what he says about his wife—those are going to be the nail in the coffin. The first family of New York is popular as hell in this town. Floating these emails out for public consumption isn't going to help the mayor come election time. Once the writing is on the wall, that's when I'll reluctantly announce my intention to run."

"A scheming reptile, huh?" mutters the union boss. "Takes one to know one, I guess."

"We're all scheming in our own ways. Some of us are just better at not getting caught."

A few women step off the elevator behind me, their voices carrying down the corridor. Thinking on my feet, I press my phone to my ear, nodding at a pretend caller on the other side, dropping the device as soon as the women disappear into the bathroom. But it gives me an idea. A bad one. Another bad one. But the information being handed to me on a silver platter is too valuable to pass up. Before I can talk myself out of it, I open my camera app and make sure the flash is off. Listening to make sure the union boss and deputy mayor are still engaged in their hushed conversation, I sneak the very edge of my phone past the edge of the wall and snap a photograph, my heart slamming loudly against my eardrums.

No break in their conversation. I got away with it.

Just as fast, I turn on a heel and speed walk for the elevator, exhaling a sigh of relief when the metal door slides open immediately. I get inside, staring at my reflection is disbelief. "That was a stupid risk," I whisper. "That was so utterly stupid and pointless, because you can't show it to Karina. You're going to get fired."

I'm unsettled. Angry at myself for being so impulsive. Normally I would retreat into myself. Handle these feelings on my own. But when the elevator doors open to the party once more, I find myself eager to be around Gabe, Tobias and Banks. I find myself craving their company. Craving the distraction and maybe even the comfort they'll provide.

And when I step off the elevator into the cool, dark purple atmosphere of the party and I'm pinned by three sets of eyes, it's obvious they're more than willing to provide those things.

CHAPTER

Ten

TOBIAS AND BANKS are still in their positions at the bar, visibly relaxing once I'm back. Gabe has joined a conversation with a few men who are definitely part of the construction crew. They've already removed their tuxedo jackets and rolled up their sleeves. The conversation appears easy-going, none of the ridicule Gabe expected. *Thank God.*

I don't want to interrupt when the evening is going unexpectedly well, so I give in to the magnetic force dragging me toward the bar. I'm off-kilter after my eavesdropping session upstairs. My blood is still pumping at an intense pace and Banks's presence will even me out again. Tobias? He'll be there, too. There's no way *he'll* even me out, but maybe he'll piss me off and distract me from what I've just done and heard.

Distract me from wanting to do something about it.

I head in the direction of the bar and fold my hands on the hammered brass surface, enough of a distance between me and Banks —and me and Tobias—that no one will wonder if Gabe's date has gone astray. There is a cocktail menu sitting on the bar and I pick it up, perusing the list of signature cocktails while prickly warmth spreads down both sides of my neck, disturbing my concentration. It's Tobias. It's Banks.

Without exchanging a word with me, I know what they're thinking. Needing.

I glance sideways at Tobias and find him grinding ice in his cheek, his gaze pinned to my neck, and I cross my ankles tightly, a long, winding ribbon of lust unfurling down to my toes. It's almost impossible to keep my expression schooled as I transfer my attention to Banks, watching him circle the tip of his middle finger on the bar in a mini pool of condensation, his throat moving in a rough swallow. My heartbeat reaches my ears and thickens, nipples swelling against the front of my pink dress.

By the time the bartender approaches and asks me what I'd like to drink, I've pretty much forgotten my name, but manage to order something called a French Kiss. I would blame the sudden pulsing weight between my thighs on the sexy atmosphere, but they also did this to me in my sandwich preparation station at work, so sorry, girl, that isn't going to track.

On my left, Banks chances a step closer to me, resting his forearms on top of the bar.

Tobias follows suit from the right. Actually, he takes two cocky, sauntering steps in my direction, a martini raised to his lips. Banks's ego must give him no choice but to rise to the challenge, because he closes in another two feet or so.

"Stop," I whisper, pinning each of them with a look. "I'm here with Gabe."

"Then why are you over here in between us when you're supposed to be playing his supportive new love interest?" Tobias asks.

"Tobias," I return smoothly. "Please tell me more about how a love interest is supposed to behave, so I can do the exact opposite."

He huffs a laugh. "You don't think I have any experience with relationships, cheeky girl?"

A snort from Banks. "With your mirror, maybe."

Banks and I fist bump without looking at each other. It's just…automatic.

So much that we shoot each other a startled glance.

That simple, odd connection I share with Banks visibly annoys Tobias. It appears to push him into what he says next. "I attempted to have romantic relationships at the start of my career." He picks up his drink and salutes us. "I'm sure you can imagine what the arguments were about."

I'm so busy trying to picture Tobias as a boyfriend that I forget to thank the bartender when he sets down my drink and walks away to fill the next order.

"They were smart women to walk away," Tobias continues. "I could have learned a thing or two from them about the stupidity of blind trust. The kind I had for my manager."

"What happened with your manager?" I ask, sliding my purple martini toward me, using the tip of my index finger to spin clockwise the flower sitting on the surface.

Tobias shakes his head. "I hate talking about it, mainly because it's such a fucking cliché. The lack of creativity is completely beneath me."

"We've been warned," Banks says, exhaling. "Still want the story."

"Me too," I'm not sure why I reach over and run a knuckle down the back of Tobias's hand, but he closes his eyes on contact, as if to savor the feeling. "Very well." His voice is slightly uneven and he takes a moment to rein it in. "I trusted my manager completely. So much so that I didn't read the fine print of the paperwork he had me sign. Essentially, I signed over the rights to dozens of hours of recorded… work to him. No compensation for me. Just giving up these really vulnerable moments for free." He chuckles, but the merriment doesn't reach his eyes. "Ripped off by a business manager. See? A tale as old as time."

That bomb drops, explodes and all we can do is let the cloud of smoke billow up.

"Sorry, how is that cliché?" Banks asks, turning fully to face us.

"Yeah, that's my question, too. Were you…friends?"

"Best friends," Tobias clips. "Or I thought we were. He never took me seriously for a minute." Seconds tick by. "I wasn't able to perform on camera after that. Filming scenes had never felt dirty before, but it did after that. I was used. Played." He shrugs. "I bought a one-way ticket to a place I could disappear and I've been in New York ever since."

I've never been short of breath while standing still.

I'm...angry, I realize. On Tobias's behalf—which is so shocking, I should look out the window and see if pigs are flying. I'm also pretty peeved at myself for goading Tobias into telling me such a painful story. For being so dismissive of him when there are clearly undiscovered worlds behind the gorgeous façade. "I'm sorry that happened to you, Tobias," I whisper, leaning over and kissing him on the cheek. "You get the night off from dick punches."

"Kind of you," he releases on a pent-up breath. For a moment, we can't seem to stop looking at each other, but he's obviously still raw from telling his story, because for once, he diverts attention from himself. "What about you, Banks?" He presses a hand to his cheek briefly, where I kissed him, and all I can do is stare. "Any tales of betrayal and woe stuffed in your closet?"

"No one reaches this age without experiencing a little betrayal." Banks clears his throat, straightens. "None of them were quite as dramatic, though."

Back to his irreverent self, Tobias drums his fingers on the bar. "Were they rugby betrayals, perhaps? He didn't pass me the ball enough or he stole my clothes from the locker room and left me naked. That sort of thing?" Tobias shivers. "Scintillating."

Loud voices reach me from the area surrounding the dance floor. Gabe. The ruckus is coming from the group in conversation with Gabe. The men he was laughing with only moments ago now appear to be having a laugh at his expense and it's easy to see why. Gabe's brother and his fiancé are right behind him on the dancefloor. So close he could reach out and touch them. They appear to be oblivious to how close they are to Gabe—but Gabe's co-workers are not. They are cracking up, shoving him in the shoulder, pretending to spank an invisible ass, because men never fully mature, I guess.

"That's my cue," I mutter, stepping away from the bar—and stopping. Splitting a look between Tobias and Banks. "Are you two going to help him or not?"

I can see it. That glimmer of competitiveness that was on display in the *Times* food service room. Maybe they're still hoping to edge each other out in the relationship race with me? If there was a hope in hell of a real relationship, I mean. What is wrong with them? I don't know, but for several seconds, Tobias and Banks stare at each other, waiting to see what the other will do. And then, they simultaneously sigh and push away from the bar.

"I'll create a diversion." Tobias sighs. "It's pretty much what I've been doing the entire evening just by looking like this."

Banks groans. "How has nobody kicked this guy's ass yet?"

He winks. "Too busy *getting* ass for them to catch me."

I stare at him blankly.

"I hate him." This, a simple statement from Banks. Then to me, "I'll hang close to you and step in where necessary."

Tobias holds out his right hand in front of him, picking up my left one and placing it on top, nodding for Banks to do the same. "Tram Fam on three."

Banks and I drop our hands and walk away in disgust. As soon as I get within earshot of Gabe and the others, I'm cringing over what's coming out of their mouths.

"You were just keeping her warm for big bro, right?"

A round of raunchy laughter. My skin crawls.

"Can you hear them going at it through the walls? Good thing you know how to insulate."

"Maybe he doesn't want to. Maybe he's a cuckold."

Two of them are doubled over at this point, holding their sides, tears of mirth rolling down their cheeks. And honestly, one would have to be drunk to think any of these one-liners are killing. I'm going to shut them up for the sake of comedy alone.

I arrive at Gabe's side, pretending to be oblivious about what's happening and I intertwine my fingers with his. The jokesters freeze in the act of sipping their drinks, a couple of pairs of eyebrows nearly hitting the ceiling. Satisfied that I have their attention, I lift up onto my toes and kiss Gabe's ear, asking loud enough to be heard, "Can you take me upstairs now?" I open my mouth against the side of his throat and breathe heavily, eyes closed. It starts out as an act, but his sawdust and coffee and soap scent hits me in the pit of my stomach and claws lower until it's me. It's me wanting to inhale him. "I need you."

Remembering myself and my mission, I pass a shy look around the circle of men.

"So sorry to steal him, gentlemen." I stroke my finger along the curve of Gabe's chin. "But I'm sure you all have dates to keep you company, right?"

At first, they just appear stunned by my arrival—and more than a little impressed, thank you very much—but my question soon sinks in and they begin to shift in their wingtips, like three trees blowing in different directions. "We're stag tonight," one of them says, finally.

I push out my lower lip. "Awww. Can't imagine why."

Some uncomfortable laughter fills the silence.

They're trying to tell if I'm joking, but I don't give anything away.

"How the hell did Gabe pull this girl?" asks one of the drunker ones.

Irritation zaps in my fingertips, throat. "Actually, I asked *him* out. Best decision I've made in a long time." I snuggle suggestively into Gabe's side, taking his big hand and sliding it slowly along my hip. "And I'm getting impatient to have him all to myself. Good night, gentlemen. We're going to find a much more enjoyable way to spend the evening."

They watch us leave as if trying to figure out whether or not I've insulted them. They figure it out when we're about ten feet away. "Hey," shouts the same guy who wondered out loud how Gabe pulled me. "You know who you're on a date with?" He sways a little, coming toward us. "The laughingstock of—"

I see and hear it all happening in slow-motion.

Tobias holds up his martini in the middle of the dancefloor. "Gather around, everyone. I'll tell you about the time a royal—who shall remain unnamed for legal purposes—snuck me into Windsor for a game of truth or dare involving ski masks and rubber duckies..."

While that tale is being spun, Banks oh-so-casually spills his drink on the floor. The leader of the punk posse steps directly into the puddle, his foot eliciting a wet squeak. He pinwheels for a few seconds, before landing smack on his butt in front of everyone. I want to revel in the wonder of it all. I really do. But I don't need a crystal ball to know this situation is going to escalate. Fast.

"Come on." I tug a stunned Gabe toward the elevators. "We're making a run for it."

"Oh." He sounds dazed. "Okay."

Thankfully an elevator is opening and letting off more people as we arrive and I pull Gabe in behind me. Once inside, I hold my index finger down on the door open button. "Come on, come on, come—"

Banks slips through the entrance of the elevator, buttoning his tuxedo jacket as if he didn't just deliver a smackdown of justice. Right on his heels is Tobias, who is grinning ear to ear, martini still in his hand. "Now that is entertainment."

I laugh breathlessly, Tobias and Banks immediately joining me. They even trade a high five with one another, so hell itself must have frozen over in the last three minutes. The sight of them bonding causes a happy jump in my stomach, catching me off guard, but I shake off the surprise and give in to the celebratory laughter. I don't stop until my eyes are full of tears and it's only when I blink them away do I notice that Gabe is still silent.

"Gabe?" I ask, worried, wiping the moisture from my cheeks. "Are you okay?"

He looks down at his hands. "Yeah." There's a glimmer of a smile, but it drops as quickly as it appeared. "I appreciate you three doing that. I do. It's just…I'm not sure it'll change what everyone thinks of me." He stares forward for a beat. "But hell if I won't be replaying that for the next decade."

The four of us are laughing now, even if Gabe's chuckle is slightly reluctant.

It's an important moment.

A change is taking place right in front of my eyes. Even if things are different tomorrow, right now we're a team. We looked out for one of our own—that's how it feels. It scares me how close I feel to these men right now. It's so scary because I know what it's like to grow and change with someone and then have to say goodbye. It's scary because my attention span is shorter than a gnat's and the thought of hurting any of them—even Tobias—makes my belly churn.

Maybe for tonight, I can tear free of the hold my psyche has on me…and just live and breathe what's happening here. And what's happening is…I am brutally attracted to all three of these men for different reasons. My protectiveness of Gabe is what's pulling the hardest at me right now. He still has shadows in his eyes and I want them gone. Now.

Before I can dissect and analyze my impulse to death, I grab Gabe by the collar and pull his mouth down for a kiss.

CHAPTER

Gabe

I'VE ONLY BEEN with one woman in my life.

As soon as Elise's mouth is on mine, I wish I could erase the other experience and have only this. Only Elise. I want to blanket myself in this fucking feeling she brings me. She accepts me and encourages me, the way a best friend might.

Except the way I feel about her can't be defined as friendly, whatsoever. Not when she makes me start sweating on sight. Not when I am so hungry for the taste of her, I've spent the last couple of days almost delirious. In a fog where only Elise exists, her voice a constant whisper in my ear, the smooth taste of her making me feel wild and out of sorts. Jumpy, like I have somewhere else to be. Something waiting for me that I don't know how to reach, because two other sets of hands are there, too.

I want her for myself.

I want to bring her home.

Yet I know how sick I would feel if she chose Banks and Tobias...

and I don't want that for them. Furthermore, I don't want to deprive Elise of added pleasure in her life. Christ, who could deprive her of anything? The jealousy hasn't totally faded, maybe it never will, but I...like the other two men. I'm grateful to them for defending me downstairs in their own unique ways. And God help me, the idea of sharing Elise with them, giving her maximum satisfaction, is growing less and less unthinkable to me.

No, I'm starting to *need* this. Not only be a part of, but watching her be worshipped.

Faster and faster, it's becoming...inevitable.

Her body molded to mine is right.

Her mouth defies description. The kiss is vulnerable and searching. She's exploring me like she gives a shit, wants to learn me and celebrate me. Know who I am. Mere minutes ago, I was more lost than I've ever felt in my life, but she is saving me, redirecting me, giving me a new name. Hers. That kind of salvation makes me want to get down on my knees, shove up her pretty dress and use my tongue on her pussy. Repay her with bliss.

I'm about to do just that when the elevator dings. I continue kissing Elise's mouth because it tastes like everything good about the world. But I can taste her confusion about the elevator dinging and doors rolling open onto a quiet floor, so I release her lips and appease myself by sliding my fingers into her dark hair and inhaling handfuls of it.

"Why are we here? I was..." She sounds dazed, short of breath. "I was only kidding about having a room..."

"Darling, I always get a room," Tobias rasps.

Banks is closer than I realized, his hand propped to my left on the stainless-steel wall, watching our kiss close up, expression unreadable. "For once, I like the way you think, Tobias." His fingers join mine and Elise's hair, his teeth razing up and down the side of her neck. "Before we step off this elevator, tell us what you want, Elise. No pressure. No confusion."

To my surprise, Elise looks up at me, almost adoringly? Am I imagining that? I don't want to be imagining it. I want to soak it in and believe it. Believe in her and this magic she makes in my chest.

And then she trails her palm down the front of my body and

cradles my erection in her hand, massaging the stiffness until I choke. "I don't know. I just know I'm…" She shakes her head and I can see the thoughts are new, startling. The situation is foreign to her, but she's trying to put her needs into words. Good. The better for me…no, us… to fulfill them. "I just know it has to be Gabe right now. After that, I don't know."

The sound that comes out of me is one I've never heard before. It's a grinding shout let loose from the pit of my stomach. I'm not supposed to be chosen first. In a lot of cases throughout my life, I wasn't chosen at all. How am I the priority for this incredible girl? What does she see in me that no one else ever has?

"This can't be about pity, Elise," I say, sounding strangled. "Please."

"It's not." She shakes her head. "I don't understand it, but there's something…there's something inside of me I'm supposed to give you. There's something inside of you that you're supposed to give me. Don't you feel that?"

If I felt it any more, I'd pass out. "You have no idea."

She nods, relief making her look more vulnerable, more open, while she flicks open the button of my tuxedo pants and delves her hand inside, jerking me off through my boxers, ripping a shuddering groan from my throat. Simultaneously, Banks exhales a gravelly sound against the side of her neck, his own hand busy adjusting the bulge behind his zipper.

"What are you giving him permission for?" Banks grinds out.

"Everything," she whispers, her head falling back on her shoulders for a beat, as if she's reveling in that single word. That single word is hedonism and freedom and it delivers yet another one-two punch of gratitude to my system. It wrecks me.

When she lifts her head again, her pupils are dilated, her teeth creating dents in her bottom lip. "Everything," I huff, dropping my forehead to hers. Her gaze is zeroed in on my mouth and she's breathing fast, like I'm having the same effect on her that she's had on me since the night she stepped onto the tram. Both of the other men have moved to observe her from either side of us, visibly turned on by her arousal. They see she wants me and it's a blast of confidence unlike any other. Confidence and gratitude and hunger.

Christ, I'm so fucking hungry for her.

"And us?" Banks prompts again, his voice an octave lower than before.

"Everything. As long as he's…"

"First," Tobias finishes for her. "We hear you."

I can't take my eyes off her, but I'm aware of Tobias's hand sliding down her back. Slowly. Then he steps behind her completely, taking both sides of her ass in his hands. Lifting her up. "Up we go, Elise," he says, hoarsely—and out of nowhere, her legs are wrapped around my hips, her mouth on level with mine, eyelids heavy.

I'm suspended in disbelief. Mine? Actually mine? That's all my brain can muster before Banks uses his grip in her hair to guide her forward, her lips meeting mine and melting me, just fucking melting me completely. So much that my knees temporarily forget to work and I fall back against the wall of the elevator, her tongue working into my mouth and stroking along the left edge of my tongue, withdrawing, giving the same treatment to the right side. And my dick was already hard, but now it's so stiff, my eyes are beginning to water.

"Do you like this?" she says, tightening her thighs around me and rolling her hips, her pussy flush with my erection and I moan like I'm dying. I'm dying. I'm dying.

"I love it so much. Just…" *Calm down. Focus.* "Give me a minute before you do it again."

"Dear God, he's not going to last five minutes," Tobias mutters.

"Shut up," Elise gasps against my mouth, going back in for more and I give it to her, as much as she wants. I kiss her like I'll drop dead if we stop. Although…

"He's right," I manage, panting, my balls drawn up so tight, they feel like a chin strap. "It's been too long. I'm halfway there just looking at you."

Elise searches my eyes and nods. "It's okay." She rotates her lower body again and I hold my breath, ordering my balls to play it cool, but how am I supposed to do that when the most beautiful girl I've ever met is grinding on me, choosing me, bringing me back to life after being numb for so long? "Bring me to the room." Her teeth graze the underside of my jaw, hips rolling and snapping, flooding me with more lust than I've ever experienced in my life. "So I can take care of this."

"You heard the woman," Tobias says, his mouth in her hair now, too, his index finger slowly brushing side to side over the hard point of her nipple, through the barrier of her dress. "Let's go. Every second she goes without pleasure is a travesty."

Banks's mouth rides across the smooth ridge of her shoulder. "It scares me that I'm beginning to agree with him more and more."

The elevator doors whoosh open and that's when it occurs to me that I actually have to walk while this aroused. Holy shit. I'm barely able to stand. "Just get me there," Elise murmurs against my mouth and I am flung into motion, simply because she asked me. She made the command, and my entire life seems to be about her needs now. Elise needs it and I deliver.

No questions asked.

The three of us are walking down the hotel corridor, Tobias leading the pack, key in hand. I carry Elise in my arms, glancing right and left for threats, as if a monster is going to jump out of the shadows and snatch her away. It's a ridiculous fear, but logic doesn't apply to how I feel about this woman. Banks is behind me and without seeing them, I know they are having some kind of communication through eye contact, the way they frequently do. For some reason, that doesn't make me as jealous as before. He looks out for her. He checks in with her. Elise should have as many people protecting her as possible, shouldn't she?

Tobias taps the key card against its sensor, holds the door open as I carry Elise inside. My heartbeat is rapping loudly in my ears. I'm salivating, my hands moving of their own accord, sliding up beneath her dress to cradle her naked ass cheeks, no way to stop myself from thrusting my hips upward, making her whimper. And we attack each other's mouths, the privacy of the room peeling away that last iota of hesitancy.

A hand on my back guides me through a parlor, a living area and finally we're in the bedroom. I sit down on the edge of a bed without seeing it, Elise a full on cock tease in my lap, riding up and back while pushing the tuxedo jacket over my shoulders and down. Off. Her fingers working the buttons on the front of my dress shirt. She forgets to untie the bowtie, so I must look like a Chippendales dancer. Ask me if I care when she's struggling to breathe against my mouth, her fingernails scraping across my scalp, looking into my eyes and making sense of all the pain and turmoil and confusion I've felt over the last few months. Maybe longer. Maybe my whole life. She's here now and it's fine.

A lamp is turned on with a click, filling the room with a golden glow.

Banks lifts Elise off my lap and I growl, trying to haul her back down. Until he quickly lays a hand on my shoulder. "Relax. I'm undressing her for you." He stares at me hard, but there's no aggression there. Something tells me he's just trying to reach me through the Elise-fog that's surrounding me. "Put on protection for her."

I exhale and try to gather my thoughts, but it's no use. She's consumed me.

And when Banks unzips her dress, grinds his jaw and shoves the garment down to the floor, revealing that her golden tan runs to every lithe inch of her, she sends me a dazed smile. In that moment, I know with total certainty that I'm going to be obsessed with Elise Brandeis as long as I live.

CHAPTER

THE ROOM IS SPINNING.

Hands and mouths caress my skin. My thighs, bare stomach and throat. The snap of my bra is like a firework going off in the cool, quiet room and then my nipples are tightening into a painful pucker, spurred by the air conditioning, the men on either side of me removing my clothes, arousing me for a third man who watches me like a bear who is on the hunt for his first pot of honey after a long hibernation.

Tobias steps in front of me, temporarily blocking my view of Gabe. He looks me straight in the eye and tucks his pinkie finger into the front waistband of my panties, dropping to his knees and slowly, slowly peeling the garment down to my ankles. He is nearly eye level with my sex, but still has to lean down slightly, heat spreading in his eyes, tilting his head as he studies me there. His chest starts to move faster, his hands clenching tightly around my panties.

"She's almost ready." His warm breath on my flesh makes me gasp, my left hand reaching for Banks and he takes it quickly. Tobias watches the movement, his upper lip stiffening. "Almost," he repeats. "Gabe is going to need her right on the edge if he's going to get her to the finish line."

"Stop talking about me like a race car."

"My apologies." He lays a hot kiss on my sex and against my will, I start to tremble. Damn this deeply ingrained attraction to him. I hold my breath and watch as he sits down and lays the back of his head on the edge of the bed. "If you were a race car, you'd be a Ferrari, by the way. That sort of makes us your pit crew." He crooks his finger at me, swallowing hard enough that I can see the lump lift and plummet in his throat. So much bravado. "What say you come closer for a little tune-up, love?"

I want to punch him in the face and feel him on top of me at the same time.

How is that possible?

As if sensing my confusion, Banks kisses my shoulder, his knuckle trailing up and down in the split of my backside. "Do you want that?" He reaches between my thighs from behind, dragging his middle finger through my flesh and spreading the wetness all the way back. Like, *the back,* shooting my eyes a little wider. For a moment, with these three hungry males surrounding me, touching me in places I haven't been touched before, I wonder if I'm out of my depth, but I discard the worry just as quickly. I'm in control here. They've put me in control. "Do you want to kneel over his face, Elise?" Banks asks urgently against my ear. "While I kneel behind you?"

Yes.

Yes, I want to experience everything with these men tonight. They make me feel safe and lusted after and the way I'm attuned to all three of them in different ways is overwhelming. With everything in my life so undecided, they'll make me forget for the night. They'll occupy me mentally and physically until there's only them. Only pleasure.

"Yes," I whisper.

Tobias closes his eyes for a moment, as if relieved. When they open again, I swear I see the flicker of a flame in their depths. "You're going to put your left knee on the bed and lean forward, palms flat on the mattress." His color is deepening, chest heaving rapidly. "Tell me when I find the right rhythm, love. I already know the spot."

With that statement hanging in the air, he takes hold of my bottom in a firm grip and pulls me forward, opening his mouth against my slit and inhaling roughly. "Must be exhausting walking around all day with something so priceless tucked away between your legs." His tongue parts me, moving like a winding river over my clit, then retreating with added pressure, no joke, making me squeal and fall forward in the exact position he asked of me, eyes temporarily blind. "Smart girl. You know you can trust me with it."

He smacks my ass once, twice, the cracking sound crystal clear and sharp, then palms my right cheek and spreads me wide. For Banks, I realize. He's holding me open for Banks. Vaguely, I hear another thud behind me on the floor and acknowledge through the mounting hunger that Banks is kneeling now, too. His breath is on my bottom, between it and because of the way I'm positioned, hips tilted, his breath also ghosts over the underside of my core, where Tobias is asserting himself with slick drags of his tongue, his harsh moans adding infinite enjoyment to the action. Vibrations.

"Never had anything so delicious in my fucking life," Tobias grates, his fingertips skimming up my inner thigh, rubbing a thumb over my entrance before pressing, starting an uncontrollable tremble in my legs. "How does the rest of her taste?"

"I'll tell you in a minute." Banks flattens his tongue against that untouched place and grunts, stiffens the appendage and rides it in swift motions, up, back, up, back then revels in me by rolling his head side to side, his fingers digging glorious bruises into my buttocks. My vision doubles along with the pleasure, my core winding up like a clock, breasts heavy, teeth chattering, hands fisted in the comforter. "She's a little nervous. And a lot excited."

"That's what I'm getting, too," Tobias says, smacking my sex lightly. "That's what makes a good girl tight and wet at the same time, isn't it?"

I'm being set loose into the atmosphere like a stray balloon, and I want to remain here, with my men, so I search out Gabe's eyes and find him watching me with rapt concentration, his fingers busy applying a condom to…a very king-sized erection.

"Oh…God," I cry out at the sight of it, because it's almost too much when my body is already on the verge of a life-altering orgasm. The idea of sinking down onto something so large would normally have me saying *hell no*. But I've never been this prepared. This needy. This wet. At some point, my fingers have snagged and twisted Tobias's hair and I've tipped my hips higher for the unfamiliar sensations Banks is spinning through me. Pleasure converges on me from two sources and a third lies before me, tempting me, my hips beginning to buck in anticipation of sitting on Gabe's lap. "Please, please, please, please..."

"No begging necessary, love. That's our job." Tobias's voice sounds like it's coming from a vast distance when he says, "How close are you?"

"Close," I choke out. And the pure sex in his voice shunts me even closer.

Right to the edge. I could let myself catch fire right now, but I bite down on my tongue and try to ignore the fact that I'm shaking—shaking—and prevent myself from letting go. I want it to be for Gabe. He needs me the most tonight and...I don't know when I started interpreting their needs and fulfilling them, don't know when I started caring about each of them as individuals—and a whole—but here we are. I'm almost desperate to show him how strong he is. How desirable. To feel exultant in the process. Powerful. Alive.

There is a whisper in the back of my head saying *mine*. Unfortunately or fortunately—no idea which—I hear the same claiming whisper for Banks and Tobias.

I'm yanked clean out of my frenzied thoughts when Tobias presses two slow fingers inside of me and grinds out a sound that has me mentally chanting *chocolate cake* and at the very same time, Banks applies unyielding pressure to that untouched place. A secret place inside of me that has never been reached swells, the pressure in my lower body turning my blood to molten metal and my muscles into taut ropes.

"I'm going to h-have—" A tremor rocks through me and I bear down, my forehead on the mattress now. I'm positioned so I can watch what's happening behind me, below me, and the vision of Tobias using his fingers between my thighs, his movements skilled and knowing, will never leave me. Never. It's a fantasy come to life and when he slaps my clit with his tongue and pushes those digits deeper, I know I'm at the end of my line. "I'm there," I scrape out. "Please, I'm—"

Tobias moves swiftly while cursing under his breath, sliding free of the opening between my legs. Banks snatches my hips in a grip, unwilling to let me go, eyes appearing black in the dull light, but Tobias wrestles me loose and drags me up the bed toward Gabe.

"*Fuck!*" shouts Banks. A dazed glance over my shoulder shows him pacing at the foot of the bed, both hands on his head.

Meanwhile Tobias is out of breath, sweat soaking the front of his dress shirt. He seems thrown. Caught off guard. "I should have stopped sooner, but the more I licked it, the better it tasted. And love, it tasted like fucking paradise to begin with." His eyes drift shut and he glides his tongue along the seam of his upper lip, remembering, savoring. "Already imagining next time, Elise."

I can't swallow. The need for release is making me dizzy.

Gabe is reaching for me and I want to go, but a deep, inner urge has me curling a hand around the back of Tobias's neck and bringing him down for a kiss. It's closed-mouthed and sweet, but it's also breathless and there's an unexpected jolt in the center of my chest. Tobias is startled by the kiss, a sound breaking off in his throat, but by the time he starts to take the kiss deeper, I'm pulling away, straddling Gabe while still holding Tobias's hand, fingers clenched tightly together. He's my comfort now? I couldn't stand him twenty minutes ago—

Gabe surges up and captures my mouth in a hard kiss and there is nothing sweet about it. I'm bent backward over his thighs, our tongues tangling, his calloused palms scraping up my back, then downward to take rough hold of my bottom.

"I need to fuck you," he says urgently against my mouth. "Please let me in, woman."

It's the *please* for me. It's so Gabe. It endears him to me even as I'm reaching back, enfolding him in my grip and pressing him to my center. Sliding him up and back until he falls back onto the pillow, his ample muscle flexed and stark.

When I finally take him inside me, four moans fill the room.

Relieved, jealous, tortured, anxious, horny.

Those sentiments are all buried there, converging on me from all sides.

"Christ, I've been beating my cock until it's sore thinking of you and I still won't be able to hold it in," Gabe hisses through his teeth.

"Just can't believe I've actually got my cock inside you. You're warm and wet for me, too. Fuck. Fuck. Fuck."

Gabe's hips are already surging up between my spread thighs, entering me with hard thrusts and it's utter euphoria. Apparently, I've never been properly prepared for sex in my life, because being filled has never, ever felt this mind-blowing. He's big, but I'm so slick, it doesn't feel uncomfortable. No. It's the opposite. It's like having my sense of taste returned after a decade without it. I'm burying my nails in his shoulders, dropping down on top of him and rocking my hips into his pumps, alternating between whimpering and sinking my teeth into his meaty shoulders.

He's expanding inside of me and we're back to that place where he can't take any more, like he was in the elevator. And there is a certain kind of gratification that comes with watching his eyes roll into the back of his head, his breathing pattern turns scattered, his fingers gripping my buns so tight, it would hurt if anything on this earth were capable of penetrating this lust. But nothing is. It's the ultimate armor and a burden at the same time because I'm working, working, working my hips to get rid of it, Tobias's fingers growing tighter around mine, Banks's mouth tracing up my spine and the lust starts to tear at me, the orgasm that approaches so wicked and wild that I'm almost terrified of it.

"My God," Tobias says on an exhale, his hair in disarray. "I've seen it all, but I've never seen anything like you."

Sitting up, I reach out with my free hand and grab the headboard, riding up to the thick tip of Gabe's hardness and scooping my hips back down—*snap*—as I allow him to enter me again, his sex even stiffer than before, his expansive chest heaving. Glowing in the lamplight.

"Elise," Gabe growls. "I can't go much longer."

"I know."

I squeeze him inside the cradle of my body and he rifles me faster on his lap. Up and back, up and back. "I don't want to stop, but…" he pants, looking at the other men in welcome disbelief. "Her *pussy*."

Banks clips off an epithet and I hear his belt buckle coming undone and the clanking sound of metal curls my toes in anticipation of the unknown, makes me buck with more intention. There is so much plea-sure to give, so much to receive. And I feel safe to explore it all. I feel their protectiveness, their wholehearted focus on my whims, my needs.

More than anything, though, I can feel Gabe straining, trying to hold back his finish—and I don't want that. I want to watch him lose it, all because of me. I want him to feel the extreme of pleasure after the pain he's experienced. I want him focused on me and his release and nothing else. *Mine.*

I fall forward, dragging my breasts side to side through his sweaty chest hair, levering myself up enough to lock our mouths together. But I don't kiss him yet. No, I grind down and rotate my hips, covering his lips with mine.

"Fill it up for me," I whisper, biting his bottom lip hard. "Now."

On a strangled bellow, Gabe's back arches up involuntarily and warmth spreads deep inside of my body. *Yes.* Still I grind and snap, our mouths panting together, my front row view of his straining throat muscles better than any sunset.

They're so beautiful, I lick them collarbone to chin.

"Jesus Christ," Banks bursts out, sounded winded.

"You've just seen a man get ruined in real time," says Tobias, his tone reverent.

"Me next," Banks breathes, matching Tobias's tone.

Beneath me, Gabe's hips surge upward, face contorted in pain, the last of his climax thundering through him, finally settling loose the primal roar I sensed he'd been holding in. Part of me has the deepest need to lay down on top of his powerful body and stroke my fingers down his cheek, comb them through his chest hair, praise him, but I'm still on the verge of my own release and I'm immediately refocused on that, because it has gone beyond urgent now.

The last few minutes were about Gabe, but now the necessity has shifted to me. I'm nearing the point of physical pain, not only because I'm hot and aching, but because what I've given to Gabe has satisfied something poignant in me…and I know I'm going to be taken care of now. I have this heavy faith in my chest that I've never had toward anything. Only these men.

I whimper.

That's all it takes and all three men kick back into motion. Gabe jackknifes upward from the pillows to kiss me, immense gratitude in every swipe of his tongue against mine. Tobias is once again manhandling me off Gabe's lap, laying me down on the mattress face up and parting my legs. Groaning into the first taste of me, his hips punching against the edge of the bed. Banks kneels beside me and tips my chin up, searching my eyes.

"Are you okay, Elise?"

"Yes and no," I gasp when Tobias throws my legs over his shoulders, then begins long journeys of his tongue from my back entrance to my clit, teasing that incredibly sensitive bud side to side until I'm fisting the comforter. "Please. I can't stand it much longer."

Tobias reluctantly lifts his head and I see for the first time, his hand is inside of his pants, moving vigorously. His expression is the intersection of starvation and conflict. I think he's going to cover me with his body and fill me. I want that. I want it from Banks, too. I want to be taken while the other two watch and imagine themselves in the same position, happy as long as I'm being fulfilled.

But I'm caught off guard when Tobias stands suddenly, zipping his pants over a thick ridge of flesh. "Fuck me," he grates through his teeth. "I can't be inside of her. It needs to be you now, Banks, you lucky bastard."

Even as Banks maneuvers me around to face him, his shaft already in hand, he shoots Tobias a confused glance. "Why exactly can't it be you? You're as obsessed with her as we are."

His gaze burns into mine. "That's the problem. I think…" He drags a hand down his face. "Good God. I think I actually need her to like me first."

Something like affection infiltrates me before I can stop it, but I don't have time to examine his words or my response closely, because Banks captures my attention. Wholly and completely. As soon as he's looming above me and we lock eyes, that connection between us transforms from comforting to a live wire. My heartbeat becomes something I feel.

Every beat.

"I feel it, too," he whispers against my mouth, his hand coming up to frame my jaw, his teeth grazing my neck. Licking the sting away. "Still yes, Elise?" He drops his hips into the juncture of my thighs and slowly presses his thickness to my slit, the very top where I'm sensitive, and without warning, he bears down, making me gasp. "Still yes to this?"

"Yes," I manage in between harsh pants.

"Are you sure?"

"Yes. *Yes.*"

He reaches down to make an adjustment. And looking me square in the eye, as he's wont to do, he pounds into me. I scream, my fingers flying to his back, nails drawing blood. Because oh my goodness, oh my goodness, *oh God.* Having Gabe inside of me was glorious, but there is something about Banks being on top, that added gravity and weight, that has my sex already seizing up. I once overheard the phrase "boyfriend dick" from my roommate and now I understand. He feels perfect. Way down deep. Not massive like Gabe. Not girthy and broad like I know Tobias to be. Just right.

Now you're the Goldilocks of penises? Get your life together.

But when Banks pulls out of me and sinks back in with a long, shuddering groan, I feel like I do have my life together. How much better can it get?

"I'm going to enjoy the fuck out of making you come on my dick while they watch," Banks says, lips flush to my mouth, beginning a slow ride of my body that quickly turns faster. "Didn't expect to. Didn't expect you, either, though, did I?"

He's got my jaw held tightly in his hand and he's making love to me while our eye contact speaks to me—no, both of us, I'm certain—on an emotional level, too. He doesn't break that connection as he starts to move faster, faster, eventually letting go of my jaw to sling his arms beneath my knees and angle himself forward, bending me in half, his lap smacking off my butt with every thrust. It's exactly what I need. Hard. Crude. In this moment, I want to be held down and used. Made to pay for arousing him in the extreme—and I think he interprets that in my eyes—because he rides me so rough and so fast, Gabe has to stand at the edge of the bed and hold my shoulders, so I don't go flying onto the floor, his thumbs brushing up and down my neck, jaw. Whispering praise.

"I love that," I manage, feverishly watching him occupy me. "Don't stop."

"Jesus, Elise." He pushes deep and holds, muscles jumping, and I can tell he's taking a break to prevent himself from finishing too early. "I was going to take this slow, but you've got a deep little clench that I like too fucking much. It's killing me." He uses the sleeve of his shirt to swipe sweat from his forehead. "And you want this. Look at you. You need it mean, huh?"

"Yes," I say, my throat raw from holding in my screams. "I don't...I don't normally. It's just that I feel safe with you. All of you."

"Good," Banks and Gabe say at the same time.

I become aware of Tobias on my left. He's lounging on his side on the bed, less than a foot away from Banks and I, head propped on his left fist. His posture might be casual, but his eyes are intensely bright and focused on my face. Goosebumps rise on my skin, intimate muscles flexing involuntarily—and I wind even tighter when Tobias leans in and whispers against my lips. "You might be safe with me, but you're not safe *from* me, Elise. Enjoy the reprieve."

"Gabe," Banks grunts, visibly unable to stop himself from bucking into me, releasing a shaky exhale. "Hold her arms down. Above her head."

"Good call, mate. I was going to suggest the same," Tobias says unevenly, stroking the hair back from my face. "Give our goddess what she wants."

Gabe draws my wrists up over my head, stretching me out like a sacrifice, and they all take a minute to peruse me, whispering curses and prayers under their breath. My nipples pucker under their scrutiny, throbbing with every word of praise. I can barely keep my eyes open, the rush of bliss is so heavy and lush.

"What are you going to do for her?" Banks demands to know, beginning to rock into me once again, clearly agitated with the need to climax, but trying to control his response to me.

Tobias smirks at Banks while trailing his fingertips down the valley between my breasts, crossing my stomach and parting the top of my flesh with those smooth digits, finding and massaging my clit with such exacting pressure, I cry out, my thighs jolting violently.

"That's what she needs, isn't it?" Tobias's mouth hovers over mine, his quick, shallow breaths creating condensation on my lips, but he doesn't kiss me. And I want that kiss. Badly. But the denial in his eyes speaks volumes. *I think I actually need her to like me first.*

I show him my displeasure and his smile vanishes, a growl sounding in his throat.

"Don't you dare pout at me when I can't do anything about it," he rasps.

"You can," I gasp.

"Not yet, dammit." The pace of his fingers increases and all I can do is arch up and let the sensations rocket through me.

Tobias stroking the source of my pleasure.

Banks driving into me with thorough, savoring rolls of his hips.

Gabe above me, his thumbs digging into my wrists, a telltale bulge stretching the front of his briefs, his tattooed body, honed from manual labor, covered in sweat, his eyes rapt on the place where Banks enters me.

Hard.

Harder.

"She likes it rough," Gabe pants.

"Then that's what she gets," Tobias says hoarsely. "We'll wear our good girl out every fucking time, won't we?"

"Yes," growl the three of them. An erotic trio of baritones.

Oh my God. We've all found a rhythm now and our movements become base, animalistic. Tobias never stops his perfect torture, luxuriating in every stroke of my sensitive nub. Banks stretches further, filling me deep enough to caress a secret spot that gets my knees shaking. Still imprisoning my wrists, Gabe gets down on his knees and moans into my hair that I'm beautiful, that he needs to watch me come.

"Fuck," Banks says, the word almost unintelligible because he's breathing so hard. "She's even sexier covered in sweat." He rams into me, making me scream. "Those tits, especially. But God help me, it's the way that she looks at me. So trusting. That's what's making me come. I can't stop myself."

"Just a minute longer, Banks," Tobias murmurs, watching my face carefully. "She's holding back, but she's so bloody close."

"We've got you, Elise," Gabe says, kissing my temple. "You're safe."

Banks nods at me, communicating the same with his eyes.

Am I...holding back? I examine the thoughts racing through the back of my head and realize, yeah, underneath the wonder, there's a subtext of worry. That I'll get too close to these men and won't be able to follow through. That I'll abandon whatever is happening here halfway through and be the reason for another disappointment.

Banks leans down and kisses me hard, trapping Tobias's hand and creating an abundance of pressure to my clit. Then he says, "You're ours. No matter what you do, you're ours." And then he presses Tobias's fingers down tighter and I implode. A scream emerges from my mouth that hurts my own eardrums, electric gratification plunging to the deepest parts of me and lighting me up from the inside. My clit throbs while I'm hit again and again by waves of toe-curling decadence. The act of being restrained and worshipped while having an orgasm is unlike anything else. I shake and writhe and babble about the intensity refusing to ebb, my body in beautiful turmoil, three pairs of eyes watching my every move and loving them.

Finally, Banks stiffens and falls down on top of me, bellowing into my neck, his lower body jerking with every ribbon of release, the other two men groaning, as if imagining what Banks is feeling. How it feels to release while inside of me, our bodies slip-sliding together.

"Elise," Banks says between shallow breaths. "What you did to me...I can't even put it into fucking words."

"We'll fight anyone who comes for it," Gabe vows in a resonant tone. "*Ours.*"

"Ours," Tobias rasps, visibly trying to hide his awe.

We plunge into what I can only describe as a catatonic state. Banks drops down, face up on one side of me, Tobias sandwiches me in from the opposite side, still appearing very deep in thought. And Gabe joins us, throwing himself down onto the mattress beside Tobias.

"Try to cuddle with me, Gabe, and you'll regret it," Tobias snaps off, reaching down to hold my hand. But when I squeeze it, he sighs and says, "Not that you don't seem like a good cuddler. I'm just not the warm and fuzzy type, yeah?"

I'm shocked when Tobias reluctantly looks at me for approval.

I give him a dazed smile and he stares, his Adam's apple visibly caught beneath his chin.

At least until Gabe bear hugs him from behind.

Tobias hastily disengages. "What in the hell did I just—"

"Gotcha," Gabe yawns, rolling over to face the pillows.

Banks bursts out laughing and after a moment, we all join him.

Despite the encroaching panic that I was able to temporarily shed while we...made love? Is that what happened here? It feels like much more than sex, as much as I'm scared to admit it.

I take a long, silent breath.

Regardless of the panic I'm experiencing, I force the drowsy smile back onto my face, determined to enjoy the boneless peace and sense of safety they give me—for now. Come the morning, I'll decide what the heck I'm going to do about these three men. Men who I suspect will make it harder than I thought to walk away.

CHAPTER

Thirteen

MY UBER LETS me out on the sidewalk in front of my building and I give the driver a tired thank you while climbing out. I have every intention of going straight into my apartment and taking a long, hot shower—not to mention, a damn good look in the mirror—but a newspaper sitting outside of the bodega next door halts me in my tracks.

The headline of the Post reads: *Leaked Mayor Email Bombshell.*

My stomach plummets as I approach and scan the subheading.

No comment from Albany regarding the scathing insults toward the governor, but sources say the NYC mayor can kiss his endorsement goodbye...

This is what I overheard Alexander and Crouch discussing last night at the Conrad. The information I saw them exchanging on that thumb drive—*God*, they worked fast.

And I know how the story got leaked.

I know definitively that Alexander is the mole.

Furthermore, I have the closest thing to proof.

Instead of going straight to my apartment, I turn on a heel and jog across the street to the twenty-four-hour CVS. One of the great things about New York is walking into a drugstore in a pink party dress and raccoon eyes on a Sunday morning and everyone just minds their own business. The single employee behind the register doesn't even glance up from his phone while I email myself the photograph I snapped last night and print it out in eight- by-ten glossy form on one of their instant photo development machines. I purchase a manila envelope from the stationery aisle and tuck it inside, holding the picture close to my chest.

What now?

Part of me wants to tear up the snapshot and pretend it never existed.

The more stubborn and destructive part of me wants to give it to Karina.

For now, I'm going to do nothing. It's Sunday. I have time to think —and my lord, I have a lot on my mind. Three men, to be exact.

Quietly as possible, I slip into my apartment and remove my high heels, dangling them from a fingertip. The sun is barely up, so I should be able to escape an interrogation from Shayna. If I can just make it to my room without encountering my roommate, I will be four for four in terms of avoiding people, considering I crept out of the room at the Conrad an hour ago without waking a single member of my fan club.

I have to admit, the three of them looked insanely sexy in repose, disheveled and unshaven in their wrinkled tuxedos. There was definitely a few moments of hesitation where I considered waking up Gabe by licking his exposed muscles and giving him another chance to prove his stamina. There is something about helping him build back endurance after a long dry spell that makes me feel ticklish in places that shall remain unnamed.

And Tobias...

Without his cocky smirk, he resembles more of an angel than a devil. Facial muscles slack, two hands tucked under his head. Facing me, as if maybe he fell asleep watching me. Might as well admit it, I'm starting to soften toward him, especially after he tried to moderate his cutting remark to Gabe last night, not to mention the revelations about his former manager. Maybe I'm not softening *completely*, but I am growing more anxious to know about him. And the attraction. Unfortunately, it builds.

Then there's Banks. I got the feeling he wasn't actually sleeping when I left the hotel room. No, some intuition tells me he knew the second I woke up. I have a foggy memory of us both waking up in the middle of the night and him kissing and stroking me back to sleep. Like it was natural and we'd done it for years. I'm painfully attracted to Banks, but also comfortable with him, as I am with Gabe, while Tobias makes me feel uncomfortable. Itchy.

Sweaty.

I'm almost to my room when there's a creak across the kitchen and Shayna steps out of her room, crossing her arms over her chest. "No." She waves a hand at the couch. "You need to sit down and tell me what's going on."

My excuse is locked and loaded. "I stayed the night at a friend's house."

She snorts. "You don't have friends."

I wince. Should have thought that one through a little better. "Wow, you're really going to call me out like that?"

For a beat, she pretends to think about it. "Yes. I am."

Rolling my eyes, I cross to the couch and flop down, tucking the manila envelope under my thigh. She takes her time meandering over to me, propping her butt on the table that serves as a television stand. "Yesterday, you got three gifts in the mail. Sauteed that eggplant last night with some garlic, by the way. Very tasty."

My mouth drops open. "What happened to the separate food rule?"

"You weren't going to eat it," she claps back, as if she had that rebuttal locked and loaded. "You only eat things that require a bowl. Soup, cereal, noodles…"

"Fine. I guess that tracks."

"Also, you didn't leave the address where you were going on the freezer. We both broke a rule, so we're even."

"I never follow that rule."

"You don't go out, that's why. No matter how often I invite you."

"Is this going to get emotional, because I'm…" I scrub my eyes with the heels of my hands, not caring what it does to my already tragic makeup. "I'm drained."

"Why?"

My hands fall into my lap. "Why do you care?"

"Because I like you. You're funny. You're driven. You remind me of me before I started going to therapy." She shrugs a shoulder. "I want to be your friend. Deal with it."

"This conversation makes me want to jump out the window."

"Me too."

"Ooh. Even after therapy?"

"Therapy is an ongoing project. It doesn't fix you."

I exhale toward the ceiling and leave my head there. For some reason, my neck is sore from last night and not having to hold my head up feels amazing. Also, when I'm not looking directly at Shayna, the act of opening up is slightly less repugnant. "Look, it's not you. It's me."

"I know."

I give her a dry look, then go back to staring at the ceiling.

Shayna chuckles. "Tell me where you were last night and I'll leave you alone."

"I don't want to tell you. It's like…" I shake my head, vision from the hotel room vivid, playing out in the front of my mind, stealing a considerable amount of my breath. "Something no one would understand unless they were in this exact situation."

Shayna sits down beside me on the couch. "I'm going to riot unless you give me more."

"Figured that." I study her for a moment, wondering what it would be like to come home and tell her about my day. Listen to a funny story about hers. Have plans to hang out. It would be great, wouldn't it? I'd have that axe-drop feeling the whole time. Still, maybe I could test the waters? After all, I didn't spend last night alone and company didn't kill me. Yet. "Tell me something about yourself first."

She squints an eye. "My dream is to visit the tulip fields in Amsterdam."

"Okay." My pulse beats wonkily. "And you work for a non-profit downtown…"

"Uh-huh. We provide counseling services to young mothers." I notice that her eyes stray to something across the room. It's the newspaper I saw downstairs. On top of a fresh stack at the bodega. "Although if the current mayor doesn't get reelected, I'm not sure we'll keep our funding. He's been a big supporter, but..." She shrugs, looking half dejected, half resigned. "Obviously someone powerful wants him out."

"Yeah," I eke out, trying not to show how fast my blood is pumping.

This is the first time the deputy mayor's mole status becomes more than a story.

His actions are going to affect people. Shayna. The people she helps.

My roommate is clearly starting to find my sudden silence odd, so I reach for a distraction. "What about something more personal?"

It takes her several moments to think. "I lost my virginity on the Staten Island ferry."

"Oh wow." I do a double take. "That's a good one."

She laughs, appearing somewhat distant for a handful of seconds. "It might be, if that dude wasn't the very reason I'm in therapy."

"Woof." I reach out to squeeze her hand, but get nervous and draw it back before making contact. "I'm sorry, Shayna."

"Thanks." She nudges my knee. "Your turn. Who caused this walk of fame?"

That gets a smile out of me. "Instead of walk of shame?"

"Uh-huh."

I worry the hem of my dress. "If that's your attitude toward one-night stands, maybe you won't be too judgmental about the fact that I...I was with three men." Her jaw drops and I rush to continue. "It's a whole bizarre story. I got trapped on the Roosevelt Island tram with them and it's hard to describe, but there's this connection. None of us have ever done anything like this, except Tobias. He's an adult film star—"

"Tobias Atwater?" she breathes.

"Oh my God." I slap my hands over my face. "You know of him."

"Know of him? I've done unspeakable things to myself while watching his films." She stares down at the carpet, as if reminiscing about those things, before her gaze shoots back to mine. "You're *sleeping* with that man?"

"Well..." I hedge. "Not yet. Probably not ever. He's complicated.

They're all complicated. This whole thing is…thorny. That's why I'm going to put the brakes on. I mean, I like them all. For different reasons. Where could this kind of situation possibly lead?"

"Nowhere but a mess."

"Exactly," I say, strangely feeling a little disloyal.

"It would be fun getting there, though," Shayna sighs.

"The road to hell is paved with gold."

We both sit there quietly for a minute, staring into space. Shayna breaks the silence when she says, "Yup. I'd turn straight down that road."

Both of us break into laughter. It's surprisingly nice to laugh with someone else. Come to think of it, this is the second time in twenty-four hours I've laughed with other people. But instead of spreading joy inside of me, I have to tamp down on the need to excuse myself and hide inside my room.

Thankfully, the doorbell ringing saves me from having to make a decision.

Shayna raises an eyebrow at the door. "No one delivers flowers this early."

"No…and definitely not on a Sunday." I stand and cross the apartment warily, hitting the speak button. "Hello?"

A crackle of static. "It's Banks. And the other two."

My stomach slingshots up into my throat, tingles spreading down to my fingertips.

"Is that them?" Shayna squeaks, standing directly behind me now.

"Yes," I reply, trying to sound normal and failing. "That was Banks speaking." I press a hand to my stomach to still the butterflies. "He… he coaches rugby—"

"Hold on. Hold on." Shayna doesn't appear to be breathing. "Which team?"

"Uh…" I search my brain and come up blank. "The Flame or something?"

Shayna storms to the other side of the apartment, hands on top of her head. "The *Flare*, you mean? No. You are lying. I got dragged to a game last year by one of my friends. He is a contender, Elise. All ruthless and sexy, prowling the sidelines. Did you at least sleep with him?"

"Oh yeah," I say on an exhale. "Affirmative."

"Yeah, I bet he was firm."

The buzzer drowns out my snort. I hit talk again. "Keep your pants on."

Tobias's voice fills the apartment. "First time I've heard that."

Shayna gives a dazed laugh. "What do you think they want?"

"More time together, probably," I bite off in disgust that is directed mostly at myself because the pulse of anticipation is growing more and more steady.

"Yeah, sounds terrible." Shayna is thoughtful for a moment. "Who is the third member of this dream team fuck posse, by the way?"

"Gabe." I can't help but sound a little dreamy when I say his name. "He's a sweet construction foreman who might also be a secret kleptomaniac."

"Hot." Shayna stops in front of me. "So. A porn star, a locally famous rugby coach and a construction worker. I don't feel bad about eating your eggplant anymore."

"Fair enough. I've got all the eggplant I can handle." I press down the intercom button. "I'll be down in fifteen minutes."

CHAPTER

AFTER TAKING a quick shower and brushing my teeth, I go downstairs. Banks, Gabe and Tobias look so ticked off and disheveled, I slap a hand over my mouth to trap a laugh. Wrinkled tuxedo shirts and five o'clock shadows galore. "Wow," I say, biting hard on my bottom lip. "I would ask if you boys all woke up on the wrong side of the bed, but someone had to be in the middle."

"That's very cute, Elise," Tobias sniffs, slapping wrinkles out of his sleeves. "Does it look like the Tram Fam is in the mood for comedy?"

My expression is a mockery of seriousness. "No, it doesn't."

"Good." He crosses his arms. "Because we're not."

"You left," Gabe points out, his voice a little rusted. "You didn't say goodbye. Or let us bring you home safely."

Banks says nothing, just glowers.

Tobias elbows him. "It's your turn to express your dissatisfaction, mate."

"I have a better idea," Banks returns evenly. "Let's take a walk, Elise."

He suggests the walk in a low, sort of promissory tone that makes my skin tingle. Like he's not suggesting a walk at all, but a continuation of last night. "I'm fine right here, thank you. But you're more than welcome to take a stroll."

The three of them bristle.

Tobias even throws up his hands and starts to pace.

"Are you three really this angry because I didn't say goodbye?"

"That's part of it," Banks says. "Mainly, you're treating this like it was a one-night thing. We don't know where we stand with you. We know next to nothing about you, either, Elise." He pauses. "But don't you think that what's happening between us deserves more than a six am sneak out?"

"You didn't even leave a note," Gabe points out, visibly scandalized.

My stomach twists. "I'm sorry, Gabe."

"I'm sorry, Gabe?" Tobias echoes, incredulous. "Just a sorry for Gabe, is it?"

"Tobias, I'm not going to talk to you when you're being hysterical."

His bristly jaw nearly hits the sidewalk.

Someone clears their throat behind me in the building entrance. I glance over my shoulder to see that Shayna is watching the proceedings with nothing short of astonishment. I start to introduce her, but the words get stuck in my throat. That feels like a huge step. Introducing Tobias, Gabe and Banks to my roommate. That's a relationship move. I've already attempted to be more forthcoming with Shayna this morning. My evolution is officially taking place too quickly.

All four of them watch me struggle with various forms of curiosity and exasperation, before Shayna finally steps around me, holding out her hand. "Hi, I'm Shayna. Elise's roommate."

Tobias transforms in a split-second from scorned lover to charming devil. "Hello, Shayna." He captures her hand and brings it to his mouth, kissing her knuckles. "My reputation precedes me, I see."

Shayna chokes.

He smiles broadly. "You're staring at my zipper, dear."

My roommate snatches her hand back, laughing nervously. "Oh God. Sorry."

"Don't be," he responds smoothly, giving me a pointed look. "At least *someone* is interested in this award-winning co—"

"Now is not the time, Tobias," Banks interrupts, sharply. Quickly, he shakes Shayna's hand. Gabe does the same, grunting. "Elise, we'd like ten minutes of your time."

"That seems reasonable," Shayna whispers, sounding as if she's in a trance, her eyes skipping around from man to man. To man. "Isn't that reasonable, Elise?"

It's on the tip of my tongue to say no. The reason I left before they woke up this morning was to avoid this conversation. The one where we put labels on whatever this is. The serious talk where we make this an ongoing thing. I knew it was coming. They weren't happy with just one night. I'm not, either, but I'm terrified of what happens after six nights. Or ten. When I've let them see me at my most vulnerable and we've traded secrets, then suddenly, it ends. I've never had a relationship, friendly or romantic, with anyone that didn't come to an abrupt stop and I've managed to avoid that pain successfully for a long time.

Is it so much to ask that they let me continue to do that?

Still, Banks is right when he says our "relationship" deserves more than a sneaky exit.

I can do ten minutes.

I'll take that time to explain to them that I'm done.

It was a very nice experiment, but I'd like to quit while I'm ahead.

"Ten minutes."

"Thank you," Banks says, gesturing for me to precede him on the sidewalk. The other two men mimic his gesture, so I've got three men in wrinkled tuxedos gesturing at me like they're a restaurant maître d' about to guide me to my table. I'm really starting to think my whole life has been one big hallucination since stepping onto that damn tram.

Shayna slowly turns to me, bewildered. "I don't know if I should call the police or a documentarian."

"Welcome to my world," I mutter, stomping through the sea of tuxedos. "Come on, jerks."

We walk for a few moments in silence, the three of them huddled around me like bodyguards. Tobias holds up a flat palm to stop a cab before it can cut in front of us, Gabe keeps a hand on the small of my back and Banks looks busy strategizing, the muscle in his cheek doing gymnastics. We've only traveled the length of a crosstown city block when Banks holds up his phone. "It's going to start drizzling any second now. We should do this in a coffee shop."

"Capital plan," Tobias says briskly. "There's one just ahead."

"There's a better one two doors past it." Again, Banks gestures with his phone. "According to Yelp."

There is something off here, but I can't quite put a finger on it. Maybe the fact that it's a clear blue sky. Not a cloud in sight. It's more than that, though. Banks won't make eye contact with me, which is unusual to say the least and oddly...makes me feel a tad off balance. "It's not going to rain," I say, hoping he'll look at me. He doesn't. "Banks—"

Before I can complete that sentence, I'm hustled through an open door. Into a very small establishment with one non-descript desk and beige, centuries-old carpet. The words *Can You Break Out?* are stenciled onto the wall in red ink, along with a peeling magnifying glass sticker. In smaller print are the words: *New York's Only 24-Hour Escape Room.*

Okay. This is not a coffee shop. Five seconds is all the time Banks needs to gesture to the exhausted woman behind the desk and get a wave in return.

"I called about the prison theme," he says curtly.

"This is who you were talking to on the phone in the cab?" Tobias asks. "I just assumed you were into some weird kink."

I'm guided down a long hallway in too much of a stupor to react. And then I'm locked in an escape room with Banks, Tobias and Gabe.

A red timer appears above the door. Sixty minutes begins to count down.

My gasp can be heard clear to Texas.

No, they didn't. This isn't happening.

"This is kidnapping," I say through my teeth.

"For the record, I didn't know about this," Tobias says, turning in a circle with a chuffed expression. "But I fully support it."

Gabe is still visibly piecing together what is going on. "I didn't know, either..."

"One of you would have given it away." Banks takes a deep breath and grasps my shoulders, turning me to face the room more fully. It's decorated like a prison cell, complete with a metal bunk bed, sink, a stack of books, scrawled words on the wall and a nasty-looking toilet that I'm guessing was there prior to them picking the theme. "When you left this morning without a word, we knew what it meant. You're cutting us off." He tries to cradle the side of my face, but I pull it away, even though his touch feels incredible. Too incredible. "Tell us why."

"I told you already." My heart is starting to hammer. All three of them have closed in on me, studying me with identical frowns in the darkness. I'm not scared—and I probably should be considering they just trapped me in an escape room against my will. But the only thing I'm scared of is revealing myself. All the shit I keep locked down deep with my defenses piled on top. "I told you that day in the kitchen at the *Times*. I don't want to be accountable to three guys. Relationships are messy and annoying and time-consuming. You're asking me to do this to the power of *three*. I'd have to be a masochist."

"Is that really all it is?" Tobias raises an eyebrow. "You think we'd be annoying?"

"You just locked me in an escape room!"

"If I hadn't done this, tell me you wouldn't have already broken this off and gone home." Banks tilts his head, waiting. "I know that's what you had planned."

"I think Banks is the smart one," Gabe muses.

"Glad you're all caught up," Tobias says, patting Gabe on the shoulder.

I want to kick both men in the shins, but I'm too focused in on Banks being so perceptive when it comes to me. "I never said this was going to be long term."

"Why?" Banks asks, patiently.

"I just told you. Boyfriends are a full-time job."

"It's more than that, Elise."

Heat blooms against the backs of my eyes, so I raise my chin defiantly. But I can't say anything without saying *everything*. I press my lips together tighter, shaking my head. Vaguely, I realize Banks is a genius, because there is something about being in this stupid room, locked away in the dark with an hour on the clock, that makes my defenses thin to nothing. This moment is so far from any reality that I'm used to, what does it matter if I say something too personal that I'll regret?

Gabe takes one of my hands. Tobias threads his fingers through the other.

They both squeeze. And at the same time, Banks presses his forehead to mine.

My insides just...erode. Air escapes my lungs, words tumbling along with it.

"Fine. We moved around a lot when I was growing up. I'm a military brat. And, um..." I close my eyes and take a deep breath. "I had so many best friends. I would find someone special and give them all my trust. Take all of theirs in return. Sleepovers whispering in the dark and building forts. When I got a little older, it was confiding crushes and going through puberty together. Then it was time to go. It was always time to go. It was like having my heart ripped out every time. I'd try to keep in touch, but they would find someone else, or the bond wouldn't be the same as being face to face. The good just faded. So I stopped trying. It's so much easier this way. Please just let me make this easy."

There's a long silence.

Then Tobias, "We're in a fake prison cell in day-old tuxedos. I think the easy ship has sailed, love."

Banks and Gabe whack him in the shoulders.

He sighs, looking regretful. "I'm sorry you had to lose people so often, Elise."

"So am I," Banks says, his voice sincere.

Gabe squeezes my hand hard and we simply remain like that for a few minutes.

"What if we agree to a certain length of time, like a trial period?" Gabe surprises everyone by suggesting. "At the end of it, you can decide if you want to continue."

"That's not going to work. I'm going to get too..."

"Attached," Banks finishes for me.

I press my trembling lips into a straight line.

"That was my ulterior motive," Gabe says quietly. "Getting you as attached as we are."

"Gabe, you're secretly kind of diabolical."

"Thank you." He nods for a moment. "What's diabolical?"

Tobias sighs. "I understand your fears, Elise. I lost my best friend, albeit for different reasons. You make an emotional investment and then suddenly, it means nothing. Maybe it meant nothing all along. Investing that energy again seems pointless." He shakes his head a moment, mouth poised to speak. "But this isn't. It's not pointless."

"Give us time to convince you of that," Banks says, kissing my forehead. "We are three men who have nothing in common. We didn't even like each other. In some ways, we still don't."

"Amen to that," Gabe sighs, looking at Tobias.

Tobias rolls his eyes.

"But we feel very strongly about you, Elise. So much that we've learned an entirely new nature. How to be unselfish. How to give instead of take." Those words carry reminders of last night and my thighs flex in response. "This isn't temporary."

That sentiment is echoed in the eyes of the other two men, their intensity snaking around my limbs and pulling me under. Back to the place of willing surrender I was in last night.

Fight it, whispers my last iota of self-preservation.

"You don't understand what you're getting into. My fear of committing has bled out into every other part of my life. Professionally, I take shortcuts, because I'm afraid to do the hard work and fail. It's why I'm a sandwich girl trying to be a reporter." The hard part, the worst part, climbs my throat. Am I really going to reveal my worst shame out loud to these men?

Yes. I am.

I can't believe it, but I am.

"And...I was ready to change. I was. I took a trip home to San Diego and told my parents I was done messing around. Wasting time and money with my harebrained ideas, like food trucks and all-natural deodorant. I enlisted with the marines. I was going to be in the military like my dad and finally make them proud of me, but they rejected my application. They looked at my work history and could see I had no capacity for commitment." I try to pull my hands free of Tobias and Gabe's grip, try to leave the warmth of Banks's body, but they all step closer. They press in on me tightly as I gulp in a huge breath of air. "I went right back to my old habits, because I don't know what else to do. You guys really don't want any part of this."

"Try us," Gabe says gruffly against my temple.

"The truth is, we all have our shit, Elise. We're all carrying baggage around." Banks is speaking. "Maybe I'm crazy, but the shit doesn't feel as heavy when we're together."

"I actually forgot I was carrying mine last night." A frown line appears between Tobias's brows. "To say that's unusual would be an understatement."

I'm caving. I can feel it.

I'm letting a toe edge over my line in the sand.

Because what they're saying is true. For so long, I've been power-less, like I didn't have control of my life or anything in it. Where I moved. What school I attended. As an adult, I can't seem to find success no matter how much I want it. But when the four of us are together, I'm given this wealth of control. Sure, I'm currently locked in an escape room, but I'm usually the one deciding how we proceed. Who I touch. What I want. Yes or no.

They make me wonder what else I'm capable of. Beyond them.

"Do you guys have an actual plan or are you just going to keep showing up and accosting me in public?" I whisper in a big rush.

Their chests start to move faster. Deep exhales of relief. Inhales of anticipation.

"I always have a plan," Banks says, pulling me closer, followed by the other two converging on me. I'm lifted into a four-way bear hug, my feet elevating off the ground.

"I always have the hotel room," Tobias says, his tone a little bumpy. "That's an invaluable contribution and I won't hear any different."

Gabe clears his throat. "I steal things."

"We date. That's the plan, Elise. We date you exclusively. You date us exclusively. We don't have to put a label on this." Banks chuckles softly. "I'm not sure there is one for us."

My groan is muffled by Banks's shoulder. "The group texts trying to schedule dates around four different agendas are going to unalive me."

"Do all four of us have to go on every date?" Gabe asks. "No offense, but I doubt Tobias wants to go to a Mets game."

The Brit rears back slightly from the four-way hug. "What's that supposed to mean?"

Gabe shrugs. "It means they don't serve martinis at Citi Field."

"How do they feel about uncontrollable erections?"

"Break it up, guys," I say.

Both of their mouths snap shut. I could get used to this.

Maybe it's that glimmer of optimism that nudges me into making a suggestion. They can't be the only ones concerting an effort. If I'm agreeing to become a member of a quad, I'm going to be an active participant. "How about...we commit to one date per week with all four of us. The rest of the time, we can do one-on-one dates. But the other two must be made aware. All four of us have to agree to everything. I want..."

"You want...?" Tobias prompts me.

"I want you all to feel like you're in the loop. I want you all to feel...valued."

"Even me?" Tobias again.

I cast my gaze toward the ceiling. "I guess."

He elbows Gabe without breaking the hug. "She's warming up to me."

Banks has been silent for almost a full minute. "I can agree to solo dates. And group dates once a week."

Gabe chews the inside of his cheek for a beat. "Me too."

"I'm in no position to make demands," Tobias sighs, before winking at me. "Yet."

"Do the solo dates include sex?" Gabe asks, his swallow audible.

The air grows thicker in the dark room, their bodies seeming to swell, tighten around me. They settle my feet back onto the ground, stepping back. The four of us eye each other, as if trying to gauge how we feel about that not-so-tiny detail.

"I think I speak for the Tram Fam when I say..." Tobias rakes me head to toe with a look, his middle finger trailing side to side along his waistband. "...there is no way I'd be capable of going on a date with Elise and not try to get her into bed."

"You read my mind," Banks admits.

"God no." Gabe's voice is pure gravel. "Me either."

It would be easy right now to surrender to the darkness of this room and the touch of these three men. *My* men, apparently. My sex is already turning damp and pliant, simply from the way they're looking at me. I'd love to close my eyes and let them feed me pleasure, feel their hands raking over every inch of my skin, their mouths sampling me like it's going to be the last time. It would be so easy to receive their pleasure.

I crook my finger at all three of them, gesturing for them to come closer. In seconds, they are breathing hard, shedding their tuxedo jackets onto the concrete floor. They embody head-spinning lust to the power of three and I'm their target.

Unfortunately, if we're actually doing this, if they have seriously convinced me to give up my bachelorettehood, then this needs to be a teachable moment.

"We have forty minutes left," I murmur, scrubbing my palm up Banks's chest, my opposite hand tugging lightly on Gabe's beard and making him moan. "I can't think of any way to spend it, can you?"

"I can think of a few," Gabe says on a gust of breath, his gaze zeroed in on my breasts.

Tobias appears to be doing mental math. "I can think of one hundred and six. Give or take."

"Just tell us what you want," Banks rasps against my ear.

"Oh, I will."

I allow myself to accept a kiss from each of them, though it's risky in the extreme. Afterward, I only want more. Still...

Garnering my will—and my indignation—I elbow Banks in the stomach, yank hard on Gabe's beard and ram my knee into Tobias's thigh, giving him a dead leg. "Did you think you were going to get away with locking me in an escape room? Against my will? To discuss my *feelings*? Uh-uh. No." I turn and begin to pound on the door while the three of them attempt to recover behind me. "Don't you ever do something like this again. Next time, I aim for the crotch."

"She did something to my leg," Tobias says, panicked. "I can't move it. I think I'm paralyzed."

"You got off lightly," I inform him.

"At least she said there would be a next time," Gabe mutters, rubbing his chin.

Finally, the receptionist opens the door, her attention traveling between the three of us. "You need a clue?" she asks with a yawn.

"Nope. *They* do," I say, skirting past her.

Don't ask me why I'm smiling as I storm out onto the sidewalk. It makes absolutely no sense at all. Maybe it's because I stood up for myself. Maybe it's because I feel lighter after unburdening myself to Tobias, Gabe and Banks. It could be that they just...make me happy, even when they're behaving without any semblance of ethics. And I'm excited to see them again. I'm...relieved. Even a little hopeful. It's been a while since I felt either of those things.

"Elise, wait up," calls Banks from behind me.

I keep walking. "I don't think so, evil mastermind."

"I deserve your punishment. And believe me, there is no worse punishment than having you walk away like this, even if it's not permanent." He catches my elbow and slows me to a stop, slowly wrapping his arms around me. "Then again, I saw you smiling," he growls into my hair.

My mouth continues to betray me, the corners edging higher. "State your business."

He kisses the side of my neck and reluctantly steps back, his mood visibly shifting. Turning more serious. Briefly, he checks over his shoulder to make sure we're separated from the group. "Look, I didn't want to say anything in front of the others, but..." He watches me closely, a vein ticking in his temple. "Elise. That day we showed up at the *Times*, you told us you'd followed the deputy mayor out to Roosevelt Island. That's why you were there that night. We've all seen the story that broke this morning about the mayor's leaked comments about the governor and...that's reaching pretty damn high. I don't know if that information came from the deputy mayor or what, but I know it's unsafe for you to be involved. You've dropped the story, right?"

Remembering the meeting I witnessed last night and the subsequent, very damning picture I printed out this morning, it's hard to keep my features schooled. I'm not sure I completely pull it off. "I can take care of myself, Banks. I know what I'm doing."

"In other words, you haven't dropped it," he says, frown deepening. "Being at a party with your subjects last night proved a little too tempting?"

"I have dropped the story." I hold up a frustrated hand. "I was there for Gabe last night—that's all. If I'm involved at all at this point, it's just getting the information safely into the managing editor's hands."

He nods for a full ten seconds. "Please, we need you safe, Elise."

Instead of lecturing him on my free will, I find myself saying, "I know. I'm being safe."

Because I don't want these men to worry about me. It's not about control. They genuinely care. They opened up to me the night we met. And again last night. I've just exposed myself completely in the escape room. We're not just bed partners, we're…friends. We're confidantes. I don't want to abuse the bond with them that is quickly beginning to feel like a privilege.

No one knows I'm in possession of the picture. I'm going to hold on to it until an opportune moment, then hand it safely over to Karina. I'm not risking my neck for a job I haven't officially been given. For a story that I've been forbidden to cover at that. I'm going to find another way to land a reporter job, whether I actually take up Karina's offer to write that human interest piece or…I actually bite the bullet and enroll in journalism school. I just haven't decided which direction to take yet.

"Listen…" Banks clears his throat hard, going from serious to…a little apprehensive? This is the first time I've seen him anything but confident. "I've got a match on Tuesday. Late afternoon. I would love it if you came. I don't…" He quickly adjusts his stance. "It's rare for someone to attend one of my matches for me. My father lives too far away and has a whole new life. My mother…she can't see through the past to the present."

"She won't support you now because she didn't support you then?" I whisper, pressure weighing down on my sternum.

"Yeah." He inclines his head stiffly. "I think I might finally be done leaving her a ticket at the box office. I've been doing it for years, but... yeah, I think that's it."

I'm not sure why I say, "Leave the ticket for one more match. I have a good feeling."

Maybe I don't like seeing him let go of his hope. Or maybe I *do* actually have a good feeling. Whatever the reason, he gives me a single nod. "All right. If you say so. It can't hurt."

He clears his throat. "Boring baggage aside, I would love *you* to come. To get to know me." He reaches into his jacket pocket and produces a ticket, holding it out. "It kills me to say this, but I'd like to send Tobias with you. It's just an exhibition game but the stands get rowdy, occasionally. I want to know you're safe."

"Sounds like a job for Gabe. Not Tobias," I muse, taking the ticket. "A scuffle might mess up Tobias's hair."

"Gabe has to bring his mother to a doctor's appointment on Tuesday."

My heart turns over. "Awww."

Banks tilts his head. "You've got a soft spot for Gabe, don't you?"

"Yes," I answer, though I'm tempted to make a joke and blow off the question. "I feel differently about each of you, I guess."

He zeroes in on those words, even though I can tell he's striving for casual. "That's the first time you've admitted to having feelings for us, one way or the other."

"Don't go planning the wedding."

"Legally, I don't think we could."

"Thank God."

Banks chuckles, but his expression is anticipatory. "Feelings. Say more."

I roll my eyes, casting a glance over his shoulder to find Gabe and Tobias out of earshot, but watching us curiously. My body is still heavily under the influence of their presence, my nipples pebbled, back of my neck hot. I refuse to regret my hasty departure, though.

Not even a little bit.

Sure.

I let out a breath. "Gabe makes me wish for lazy Sunday mornings in bed with coffee and the smell of cinnamon in the kitchen. Sweet. Tobias is Saturday night. Strobe lights and moaning and…that tipsy feeling, like if you have one more drink, you'll be sorry."

"And me?"

"You are…" I swallow. Being open and honest to someone about how I feel on the inside is harder than I remember. I've been out of practice so long. "You're real life. The place where I'm in my pattern and feel safe. You're not a detour, you're a path forward."

It takes him a while to digest that, staring ahead at me on the windy, wrapper strewn street, sun dipping behind clouds and back out again.

Finally, he takes a slow stride forward. Another one. "I don't mind being real life, Elise." He reaches me, taking two fists of my coat, tugging me close and finally, finally, raking his hard mouth over mine. "But I need to know I make you escape, too." He reaches into my coat and palms my breast, slowly twisting the material of my shirt for friction against my nipple. "I need to know you'll come to me when you want your panties pulled down and those thighs spread open."

My legs decide not to hold me up anymore and I sway against him.

"I would, I do," I whimper, reminded just how easily he can blur my thoughts and have me speaking gibberish. "I will."

"Will. I like that. Good." His treatment of my mouth is tender, but hints at darker promises. "Come to the game, Elise." His voice hitches slightly. "It's important to me."

The kiss winds on for so long, I don't have the chance to answer until a minute later—and quite alarmingly, my heart does it for me. "Then I'll be there."

He strokes his thumb down the curve of my cheek, his smile fading gradually, before finally turning to leave. He looks back at me over his shoulder three times before getting into a parked town car that I didn't notice before and driving away. Gabe waves at me while trudging toward the subway entrance across the street, watching me with a sheepish smile the whole way. And Tobias just kind of stands there, arms crossed, looking thoughtful as I enter my building.

As soon as I'm no longer with them, the last thirty minutes feels like a dream.

But it wasn't—and I'm now in an active, real-life relationship with three men. Three. I must be suffering from temporary insanity. Hopefully it will pass soon.

The haphazard clunking in my ribcage tells me it won't.

The fact that I miss them already does, as well.

My skin feels paper thin without them touching it.

"You're in trouble, Elise," I whisper, climbing the final stair.

When I reach my apartment, thankfully Shayna is on the phone. Still, she waggles her eyebrows at me as I hang up my coat and bypass her into my bedroom. I eye the manila envelope containing the photograph I took of Alexander and Crouch last night. There is a slight chance I could bring this to Karina tomorrow morning and earn myself a staff writer spot. But it's very slight. There is a better chance she rains down Armageddon on my head.

I sit down on the edge of my bed, settling my laptop on my thighs and opening it.

There is a folder on the desktop labeled Alexander Crouch where I compiled all of my notes on the rejected story, but I bypass it now in favor of pulling up the Google homepage.

Before I can guess my own intentions, I've typed the words "New York City journalism schools" into a search engine and hit return. The first search result is Columbia. Uh, yeah. The Ivy League won't be happening any time soon. There are several more realistic schools, however. Hunter. Hofstra. Baruch. All a subway ride away.

Could I possibly get into those?

What if I could actually commit to four years of school and become a journalist the right way? No shortcuts. No scheming. Do I have it in me?

Maybe.

My parents believed in me once upon a time. I believed in myself. And I would be lying if I said the Tram Fam wasn't inspiring this

Google search. My guys would tell me I can do it. Apply to a journalism school and work toward an actual degree. Pursue this thing I
want and succeed without trying to scheme my way to the top.

Or you might just continue your cut and run pattern.

With an impatient sound, I ex out of the webpage and pull up a
fresh document. After a moment's hesitation, I start typing, my fingers
already sluggish with guilt.

Me Plus Three
   by Elise Brandeis

*What do an egomaniacal porn star, an emotionally bullied construction
foreman and a rugby coach with crippling mommy issues have in common?*

They all slept in the same bed as me last night.

*By a simple twist of fate—and a Roosevelt Island tram malfunction—there
I was, trapped with a trio of walking red flags...*

A few hours later, I stare down at my unmoving fingers on the
keyboard. My gaze lifts to read some of the more provocative lines. In
a way, the article is way too personal. In another...it doesn't sound like
me at all. It sounds like my fears trying to convince me that these men
couldn't possibly be right for me. It's a con list with no pro side.

It's over-the-top humorous and a little mean.

And it's not how I truly feel about Tobias, Banks and Gabe
whatsoever.

Maybe in the very beginning, but not now. No way I can send it to
Karina. Right?

Just because I send it doesn't mean it's going to be published.

It could be terrible and I'll be back at square one. What I *should* do
is delete the whole thing and continue browsing schools. So I can
pursue a writing career the right way.

But it wouldn't hurt to get Karina's opinion...right?

In the end, my fear of enrolling and subsequently dropping out of school wins. Not to mention, the growing need for someone to tell me I'm not terrible at writing. The need for some positive reinforcement to reassure me I'm not chasing a pipe dream when I research journalism schools in the first place. It feels disloyal sharing this information with even one person, but it won't go any further than that. Without giving myself another second to talk myself out of it, I attach the piece to an email to Karina and hit send.

CHAPTER

Fifteen

I **PUSH** the sandwich cart through the lane of cubicles, acutely aware that everyone on staff is staring at me with fresh fascination. Fine, it's Monday morning and this is the first time I've been in the newsroom since the Tram Fam surprised me at work. And I guess it's not every day that three very attractive men show up to an office and express their interest in the sandwich girl, even if she does have great legs. Eventually, a new piece of gossip will intercept their curiosity, but not today. All eyes are on me for now.

Awesome.

It would be a lot more convenient if these working stiffs accepted their sandwich from me, as usual, without taking their rapt attention from the screens of their Mac. Because I need to speak with Karina again. I need to at least *inform* her of what I overheard at the party Saturday night, don't I? The conversation between Alexander and Crouch is way too important. I can't simply pretend I never heard it, can I? That's irresponsible as a citizen.

She told me I couldn't pursue the story—and I won't.

But if she decides to chase it down or give it to an experienced reporter, their work will be half completed once I show them the picture I'm carrying in my apron. I might not get the byline, but I can still be helpful. Although it's going to take some fancy footwork to convince Karina that I didn't actively seek out the opportunity to take this picture. It fell into my lap.

I'm sure she'll totally believe me.

Right after she tells me "Me Plus Three" is a masterpiece.

A girl can dream.

I stop at the edge of a desk of the woman who always whines about the lack of soup and wait for her to go through her spiel, but she doesn't. Instead, she is joined by the staff writer behind her in an ambush I see coming from a mile away. "So…Elise, right?" They give me that wink-wink, shoulder juggle that implies we're girls so we've just gotta dish. "Can you settle a bet?"

"I don't know. Do you want a sandwich?"

The second girl laughs at my abrupt change of topic, but girl one appears miffed. "Those guys who came here to see you last week. Some of us swear that one of them was Tobias Atwater. Was it? I'll win ten bucks if the answer is yes and it will go straight into your tip jar."

I don't have a tip jar, but I keep that to myself. "Yes, that was him. He's my…friend."

The second girl throws a handful of paperclips in the air in victory. "I knew it. I *knew* it."

That's when I realize half the office is groaning, while the other half celebrates. My face turns piping hot in a matter of seconds and all I want to do is abandon the sandwich cart and run like hell. The whole humiliating moment reminds me that I am not their equal. I haven't done the work to reach their level and I've been trying to attain it anyway. The easy way. But they'll never see me as anything but the person who delivers their lunch, unless I do the work.

Do I have it in me? I don't know. Four years of school?

I can barely keep a job for four months.

That's why, with my impulses screaming at me to run and never come back, I take a centering breath and remain right where I am, tossing a turkey on wheat to the bespectacled man on my left. Doing my best to keep my composure, I shove my cart to the end of the row and skirt past it, determined to tell Karina what I have to say. Finish up my workday—

And stick. I'm going to stick out this job. Maybe I'll find it inside of me to start attending classes, too, but I can't keep quitting and running.

The laughter and high fiving are still ongoing behind me, so I walk faster, faster, my pulse loud in my ears, until I'm pushing into Karina's icy cold office. I'm so distracted by what's happening on the floor and searching for a way to divert my own thoughts from the ruckus, that I don't see Karina waving at me. Not right away.

"Elise—"

"I know you told me not to proceed with the story—and I won't. I swear. But you need to know what I overheard on Saturday night. A conversation between the deputy mayor and—"

I'm halfway through blurting out what I need to tell her, when I notice she's frantically waving her hands at me. A split-second before my mouth snaps shut, she's ending the call, which was on speaker-phone, with a punch of a finger.

She stares at her desk for long moments, then shoots to her feet and begins to pace. "Oh fuck, Elise. What did you just do?"

"I...don't know. I'm sorry, I didn't realize you were on the phone. I just..." I shoot a helpless glance back over my shoulder. "Was it important?"

"Was it important?" she enunciates, stabbing a finger into her desk. "That was the assistant to the deputy mayor, Elise."

The blood drains straight out of my upper half, pooling inside of a stomach that has gone completely hollow. "What?"

Karina drags a hand down her features. "This is bad."

"Oh my God."

"Yeah. Oh my God." She throws her hands wide. "I wasn't just going to let the story drop, Elise. I was on it. Unlike the *Post*, apparently, no one is leaking *us* any major stories that involve the actual governor and his wife. Not without establishing a line of trust and communication, which I *was* in the process of doing. It needed to be a credentialed *Times* writer to publicly make the connection between Local 401 and the deputy mayor's office. These things don't happen overnight."

All I can do is stare as Karina paces behind her desk. I'm going to be sick.

I've just outed myself to God knows who over the phone. I might have screwed Karina's chances of effectively covering the story in the process.

"Alexander and the mayor just released a statement claiming their servers were hacked and the emails were obtained that way. But if that's a lie…if your hunch is correct and those damning emails are being leaked by the deputy mayor himself…what is his end game? Getting his competition out of the way in time for the election, so he can run without the incumbent breathing down his neck? And it suits Crouch to have this damning information continue to go public, because once the mayor is out, he'll have friends in high places and he'll win the stupid feud at the same time. It makes sense. So much for the gala over the weekend serving as a truce offering."

I can confirm a lot of Karina's speculations right here and now, based on what I overheard on Saturday night. I'm not sure why I say nothing. Probably because I already feel incredibly stupid for walking in here and blabbing sensitive information without preamble. And I think I'm savvy enough to be a reporter? "H-have I put myself in some kind of jeopardy here?"

I'm not sure why I ask this question. My gut already knows the answer. Alexander is obviously an ambitious and very skillful liar. If the deputy mayor is willing to go behind the mayor's back to further his career, he won't let a sandwich delivery girl stand in his way. Especially if he's willing to release emails pertaining to the governor. I'm not saying he'd murder me or something, but suddenly all I can think about is the scene in *House of Cards* when the girl who knows too much gets pushed in front of a train.

"What do I do?" I stammer. "How do I make this better?"

"Go home, for starters," Karina shoots back.

"Am I fired?" I ask calmly, lifting my chin, unsure if I'm ready to fight to keep the job or just take my punishment like a woman. "Please, I really need—"

"I don't know," Karina says, pinching the bridge of her nose. "Let me see what the fallout looks like."

"Am I…" I can barely voice the next part out loud. "You don't think I'm in danger, do you?" I force out on a rush of nervous laughter.

The managing editor, visibly Done With My Shit, drops down into her chair. "I would like to give you a definitive no. I really would. But if everything you've told me is true…these men are protecting a lot of self-interest." She shakes her head. "I said your name out loud when you walked in, but you're not technically an employee here, so they won't be able to find you in our system. I will protect your identity as a source, if it comes down to that. I hope it doesn't."

Numb and chilled to the bone, I turn and leave the office, leaving the sandwiches to rot in the middle of the office floor, the incriminating picture forgotten in my apron.

What have I just set into motion?

———

I spend the remaining daylight hours of Monday sitting on the edge of my bed, replaying everything that happened that morning and searching for a way to fix it, but I come up empty. Unless Alexander's assistant failed to hear my outburst of sensitive information, the fact that someone knows his boss's secret is out there.

Maybe they'll simply hire a lawyer to suppress the story.

They'll definitely deny feeding Jameson Crouch information—and I don't have much proof, besides the picture now sitting on top of my dresser, hidden away in the manila envelope. Which they have no idea is in existence. They could be totally unconcerned.

Unless they're not.

In an attempt to keep my mind from drifting into paranoia territory, I write. I open "Me Plus Three" on my laptop and make a few tweaks, delving deeper into descriptions of each of the men. Or at least I start to. Nothing about the article feels right or accurate. It's written almost like a satire. About something that feels anything but. I know when I wrote the first draft, I was trying to talk myself into believing the relationship wasn't viable.

But…I'm no longer sure I believe that.

Putting this out in a newspaper for public consumption? No, I don't think I could, but I like taking experiences that seem like dreams and turning them to cement on the page. Someday I might doubt the whole thing ever happened…and I'll have this as proof.

Shaking off the troubling thought, I continue to smooth out the rough edges of the article, despite the fact that it will never see the light of day. It's pitch black outside by the time I'm finished and I still haven't heard from Karina. I consider calling her, but after what happened today, waking her up in the middle of the night seems like self-sabotage.

I flip my phone over a few times in my hand—and then I do the unimaginable.

I start a group chat with Gabe, Tobias and Banks.

Elise: Hi. What's everyone up to?

The name of the group is immediately changed to Tram Fam. Tobias. I watch myself shake my head on the screen of my phone, but despite my exasperation, I instantly feel better.

Less alone.

Tobias: We're in a group chat with Elise. Hell hath frozen over, lads.
  Banks: What's wrong? Are you okay?
  Gabe: Watching 30 for 30. Having a beer.

My mouth twists with a smile over how different they are from each other.

Elise: I'm fine. Rough day at work. Distract me?

There's an extended pause. Then…

• • •

Tobias: To answer your original question, I'm obviously in my penthouse, standing in front of a floor-to-ceiling window in silk boxers, staring broodily out at the city lights...

Banks: A tripod set up to capture the moment, otherwise it didn't happen, right?

Tobias: The shorts are so brief, my cock looks like it could tumble out at any moment.

Gabe: Porno Bruce Wayne.

Banks: Christ.

Tobias: YES. Waiting for Elise's bat signal. Is this it? Are we fucking, Fam?

Elise: I instantly regret this group chat.

Tobias: Ah, but you're distracted now, aren't you, love?

A sound makes me jump—and I realize it's my own laughter.

Gabe: I don't like Elise having a rough day at work.

Banks: No, me either.

Tobias: Who made it rough? I'm a lover, not a fighter, but I can make an exception.

Banks: Can one even fight in silk boxers?

Tobias: Yes, as long as no one minds my tumbled out cock. Spoiler: no one ever does.

Gabe: I got challenged to a lot of fights growing up, but no one was ever my size. Didn't feel fair, punching someone smaller than me.

Elise: That's because you're a good man, Gabe.

Banks: She has a soft spot for you, Gabe. Don't screw it up.

Gabe: Maybe we could just steal something from whoever made you have a bad day.

Banks: Way to ignore my advice.

Elise: GABE! No stealing!

Tobias: Elise, do you like me yet? Have we made progress?

Tobias: Because I think of nothing but ripping your fucking panties off.

• • •

The group chat goes quiet, but it's not quiet in my room. Or inside my body. Everything is pulsing. Scrambling. The lamp glow of my room has gone from functional to seductive, the cool Manhattan breeze doing nothing to keep my skin from heating, flushing. Maybe the events of the day and my need to distract myself are making me extra brazen. Or maybe it's the safe headspace these men put me in, but for whatever reason, I find myself standing in front of the mirror hanging on my closet door and stripping off my night shirt.

I face the window, cock a hip and look back over my shoulder, snapping a picture of my reflection. Of me, long, dark hair down and messy to the middle of my back, covered only in baby blue, bikini-cut underwear. I send the picture to the chat, alone with…

Elise: These panties?
  Gabe: Fuck.
  Banks: FUCK.
  Tobias: Yes. Those ones. I can feel them in my hands right now.
  Elise: Too bad I don't like you yet.
  Tobias: Strongly considering ditching that requirement.
  Banks: Strongly considering showing up outside your door.
  Tobias: Curious about the silk boxers, mate?
  Banks: I'm talking to Elise, bonehead.
  Elise: Where did Gabe go?
  Banks: You don't know your own power, Elise.
  Elise: Meaning?
  Tobias: Meaning, old Gabe is likely having a wank to your dirty little picture.
  Gabe: I'm back.
  Tobias: Good God, man! Google the word "stamina."
  Elise: We'll work on it together, Gabe.

I type those words so easily and the chat goes quiet. Sure, I can't see their faces, but intuition tells me we're all savoring my acknowledgment that if there is work to be done between us, I'm willing to participate. That we're not only official, I might even be willing to change and grow with them. When I returned home from my work debacle, I felt like bait dangling from the end of a fishing hook. Chatting with Tobias, Gabe and Banks makes me feel protected. Supported. Surrounded by three very different forcefields.

Banks: What are you and I going to work on, Elise?

My breath accelerates and I lay down on my belly, letting the comforter rasp my sensitive nipples, my thighs flexing, toes extended. It takes me a moment to locate an answer, because honestly, there isn't much for Banks to improve on. Except maybe…

Elise: Maybe you could be gentle sometimes. Emphasis on sometimes.
    Banks: I can do that. For you.
    Tobias: And me, love?
    Elise: We're going to work on the Quiet Game. It's an American custom.
    Tobias: Sounds hot.
    Elise: Oh, you have no idea.
    Tobias: Would you like to see what you've done to me?

Dick pics are the scourge of womankind. But only if they're unsolicited, right?

Elise: Yes.

A moment later, a picture arrives in the chat from Tobias. He is actually wearing silk boxers. Dove gray. City lights glow in the background. And in the foreground?
    "Mother Mary."

A bead of sweat literally rolls down the slope of my back.

Elise: I don't think that's tumbling anywhere.
   Tobias: Fair point. Too fucking stiff to tumble, isn't it?
   Banks: Are you done?
   Tobias: Don't I bloody wish.
   Gabe: Elise, do you feel better? I need you to feel better.
   Elise: I do.
   Elise: Thanks, Fam.
   Tobias: I'm printing this out and framing it!
   Banks: Elise = traitor.
   Tobias: There you have it. The power of a dick pic. From me, obviously.
   Gabe: If you need me to walk you into work tomorrow, you call me.
   Gabe: I don't need stamina for that. 😢

I'm actually giggling into my pillow, afraid to wake up Shayna on the other side of the apartment. I don't know how to tell Gabe I'm not going into work tomorrow or if I'll even have a job going forward. This is enough. It's enough that they've reassured me just by being themselves. We all sign off with various goodnights. I tell Tobias I'll see him at the rugby game tomorrow and wish Banks good luck.

And somehow, after the upheaval of the afternoon, I manage to fall asleep smiling.

CHAPTER

WHEN I AGREED to attend this game on a Tuesday afternoon, I didn't realize it was in New Jersey, so I run late. And of course, so do the trains. Tobias texted me this morning to meet him outside of the stadium and it's not until I'm jogging down the moderately populated street of Hoboken do I start to get nervous. I'm going on a date with my go-to adult film star. A date where the plan is to watch my other love interest coach a rugby game?

Today's agenda is weird.

Stranger things have happened. Surely. Just not to me. Not romantically, anyway.

I've been naked in front of these men, but this is broad daylight and I no longer have my shield erected. I'm no longer able to reassure myself that I'll probably never see them again, so might as well enjoy it. No, now we've established rules. A relationship. Admitted feelings.

Today is different.

Frankly, I'm grateful to have an activity to occupy me. Normally I would be working. I planned to find someone to cover my shift, anyway, so I could attend the game. That became even more necessary once Karina told me to lay low. I only heard from the managing editor briefly this morning via text. She informed me she is meeting with

Alexander today to formally question him about a potential connection with Crouch. She is going to keep my name out of it. But now I'm worried about *her*.

I'm worried I've prematurely ripped the Band-Aid off the story before Karina could lay her own groundwork and made her an enemy of someone with bad intentions.

Perhaps it's this anxiousness that makes me feel like I'm being watched.

I cross an intersection and glance back the way I came, noticing there's a black SUV idling on the opposite curb. The windows are tinted, so I can't see anyone inside the vehicle. I'm probably—no, definitely being paranoid, but when the light turns green and the SUV makes no move to go through the light, goosebumps prickle my skin.

You're being ridiculous.

With one last glance over my shoulder, I turn and keep going. I take a deep breath for calm, shake off the heebie-jeebies and round the final corner of my route to the stadium—and I don't have to search the crowd very long to spot Tobias. He's a head above everyone in jeans and a fitted white cashmere sweater that very few men could pull off successfully. And bad news for my hormones, he's wearing one of those newsboy caps, his hair sort of curling around the edges. He's unshaven for once. Utterly, painfully hot.

Oh, I'm pretty sure he knows exactly what he's doing. And I'm suddenly feeling very underdressed in leggings, a sleeveless turtleneck and ankle boots. My purse is beat up and oversized, because I wanted to bring my laptop with me. While I'm waiting for Karina to let me know if I'm in the clear with Alexander, I feel compelled to keep my notes with me, which is probably ridiculous, but I decided to follow my gut.

My heart is racing as I approach Tobias, but it has nothing to do with my impromptu jog.

He's even more magnetic up close.

"Hey," I say, pulling my jacket tighter around my body. Not because it's cold—it's not. It's a refreshing sixty-five degrees. But one second in his presence has my body under a sensual attack and I can't stop remembering the way he tented those silk boxers. I went back to look at it so many times this morning that I finally gave up and saved it to my camera roll.

"Hello, Elise." He wraps a huge hand around my elbow and pulls me closer to kiss my cheek. "You're looking as fuckable as ever."

A passerby chokes on his giant street pretzel, obviously having overheard.

"Could you lower your voice?" I hiss, poking him in the ribs.

"Message received." He eases closer until our bodies meet, his lips brushing over mine. "You want me to whisper in your ear how fuckable you are—"

I shove him away, slapping the hand still holding on my elbow. "Stop."

He holds up his hands in surrender. "Sorry, love." When I can only stare up at him and attempt to replenish my lungs with oxygen, he says, "I'm a lot better at expressing myself physically than verbally, but..." For once, he looks serious. Like, he's really concentrating on it. "I'm very glad you're here. With me. I wasn't sure you would show up."

"I told Banks I would come."

"Yes." He clears his throat. "Is that the only reason?"

My knee-jerk reaction is to say yes, because he appears so cocky. I know better now, though. He's more than what meets the eye. I've seen beneath the surface to the wound he's hiding. If he can make himself vulnerable, so can I. "No," I say quietly, feeling his energy skyrocket with that single word. "No, it's not the only reason."

There's a flare of relief in his eyes, but it's cut with something innately sexual. As though he can't help it. "Thank you."

He offers me his hand.

I study it for a moment, the strength and character of it, before slipping my fingers in between each of his, letting him fold me into his grip, and we walk through the entrance together, only stopping to have our tickets scanned by a smiling senior citizen. "Wow," I murmur when the field comes into view. "I haven't been to a sporting event since I was a kid. I forgot what the grand entrance is like."

"Never gets old, does it?" Briefly, he looks down at the tickets, then at the numbers posted on the pillars, leading me in the appropriate direction. "I still remember my first Liverpool game. My parents weren't much for a day out, but I tagged along with a friend's family. I couldn't believe the players I'd been watching all my life on the telly were right there in front of me. I still try and make it to a match whenever I'm home." A line of tension rides through his back, which I am apparently watching very, very closely. "It has been quite a while."

We turn down some concrete stairs, toward the field. Most of the seats in this section are occupied, spectators holding signs and wearing jerseys. Three seats remain open at the very front and somehow, before Tobias even leads me there, I know two of them belong to us. We take our seats and I can't help but continue to study his chiseled profile. "How long has it been since you went home, exactly?"

"Five years." He hesitates, stares out at the field where the players are still warming up and stretching, but I suspect he isn't really seeing it. "Logically, I know London is a vast goddamn place and my former manager isn't going to be lurking around every corner. But just the thought of running into him..." He coughs into a fist. "I'd prefer to avoid feeling that used and helpless again. That...small."

This is not an appropriate time for a joke, but I sense he needs it. Badly. He's still holding my hand and his knuckles are pale. "Must be unusual for you to feel small."

"It is," he laughs, appreciating me with a look. "I don't like it. I'm supposed to feel big and girthy and virile—"

"Too far."

"Sorry, love." He swallows a lazy grin and we stare at each other for an extra-long moment that tugs every single string below my waist, pulling so taut that I have to tear my gaze away. Especially because his jaw is growing tighter and I know what that means.

Because I think of nothing but ripping your fucking panties off.

I release an uneven breath, ordering myself to focus on what's happening in front of me. The referees are bending and stretching, congregating in the center of the field. The players are huddled together on the sidelines. And there is Banks.

In a charcoal colored suit.

Clean cut and absorbed by whatever he's telling his team. When he sends them off to the field with a final barked command, he crosses his arms and begins to pace the sideline, intelligent eyes scanning the pitch, shouting changes and reminders as he goes. In the deep, smoky voice that has me removing my jacket due to excess heat.

Tobias watches me take off the garment, his eyes all-knowing. He's aware that I'm turned on by Banks and him at the same time. It's understood. And there really are no words in the English language to describe how freeing that is. Tobias likes me in need no matter who is responsible for it. I can also tell by the way he fists his hands in his lap that he'd love to be the one who fulfills that need.

Good God. I think I actually need her to like me first.

I watch him remind himself of this, without words, physically drawing back from me slightly, regrouping with his eyes closed. "What was your first sporting event?" he asks.

"Football." I smile. "My father is a marine and his regiment was invited to a Chargers game to present the flag during the national anthem. I got to be on the field."

"Damn." He shifts to face me slightly. "That's incredible."

"I was seven. It was kind of overwhelming," I say. "But I was proud of my dad. I saw how proud my mom was of him, too. It was…I just remember this big rush of hope that they would look at me the same way someday."

"They must, Elise. They must be proud."

I nod. Keep right on nodding, but I don't respond.

Tobias slides his arm along the back of my chair and when I get the courage to look up at him, he's studying me with a rare mar between his brows. He gives me a gentle, "What?"

My shrug is jerky. "Before I was a sandwich girl, I was an entrepreneur of businesses I didn't take the time to understand." It takes me a moment to find my voice again, but oddly, I meet Banks's eyes briefly across the pitch and that bolt of solidarity helps me continue, along with Tobias's protective and encouraging arm around my shoulder. "Like I told you guys, I'm…afraid to start anything long term because it'll go away before I reach the end, so I try and skip right to the end. Like serving turkey sandwiches in the hopes that I can charm the editor of the *Gotham Times* into letting me be a reporter. My parents used to support my go-getter attitude, but now I think they just…I think they've given up on me."

"That's not possible, Elise. I won't believe that."

"Lately, yeah." My voice cracks a little. "I think it's possible."

Tobias draws me closer, his thumb beginning to brush up and down on my arm. "Have you been happy lately?" I'm not expecting the question and I don't understand the relevance, so I turn to him with a raised eyebrow. "Parents can sense that kind of thing. When their child isn't happy. They were proud of you when you were off trying all manner of professions, because you were happy. It wasn't contingent on your succeeding. Maybe they just see you're losing hope and they don't know how to help."

"No." As much as I want to believe him, I shake my head adamantly. "I…"

"Hmm?"

"A week ago, I couldn't picture myself spilling my guts to you."

He winks at me. "Maybe it makes perfect sense. I made a living being at my most vulnerable on camera. Therefore, you probably feel safe being vulnerable with me." His throat works through a shifting pattern of muscle, his attention dropping to my mouth and flaring. "Although, fuck me. I'm not sure I've been as vulnerable with anyone as I am with you, Elise."

I gravitate closer to him, the warmth of his expensive scent making me dizzy, every nerve ending on my body sparking. "Enlisting was always in my back pocket. If I couldn't make my parents or myself proud any other way, I could do this. I could follow in my dad's footsteps. But I couldn't even do that."

It takes him a while to process that. "Did you really want to?"

"I don't know," I say honestly, only somewhat surprised by his astuteness. His ability to listen. "I'm too afraid to hope for anything."

"Love," he grates, sounding pained for me. "Maybe we start thinking differently." His fingers thread through my hair, his thumb tracing the curve of my jawline. "Maybe we stop bending to fit. Forcing things. Because something is out there hoping for you. Hoping you'll arrive exactly as you are. That's a fact."

I'm almost as surprised by the passion in his voice as I'm affected by it. How it makes me want to confide more and more. "I want to write. It's my favorite part of everything I've tried. I keep coming back to it."

He presses his forehead to mine, looking me in the eye. "Then write."

Our mouths are a millimeter away from each other and suddenly I'm thinking about Edward from *Twilight* having perfect breath to lure prey. Is Tobias a vampire? Because his warm exhale is minty with a hint of chocolate and promise of bliss. I almost lean back to check if he's sparkling. But I can't move away. Not when his lips coast over mine and he's looking so deeply into my eyes it's like he's trying to read my mind. In the back of my head, I can already hear myself moaning. Begging. What is he doing to me?

A whistle blows on the field and I flinch back, breathing hard.

Tobias hasn't moved. Hasn't stopped staring at me, his chest heaving.

It takes serious willpower to stop devouring the sight of him up close, his engine clearly revved, but I remind myself I came to the game for Banks. Sure, he sent Tobias with me, but I doubt he planned for us to make out in the front row. I release a long breath and cross my legs, earning a raspy chuckle from Tobias, and do my best to focus on the match.

And honestly, watching rugby is far from the equivalent of a cold shower. All these men piling on top of each other with their mountain warrior thighs and short shorts? Banks pressed and confident in his suit, that deep boom of a voice carrying all the way across the field? Tobias stroking my thigh with a lazy but attentive knuckle?

Yowza.

At the end of a time out, before play resumes, Banks and I lock eyes across the expanse of green and something passes between us. Warmth and gratitude and yearning. Maybe a combination of the three? I don't know, but I can barely breathe afterward.

On the heels of that, Tobias leans over and begins murmuring the rules in my ear and now I'm so hot, I feel like I'm sweating every-where. The stimuli is hitting me from all sides, continuing on for the longest forty minutes of my life. I almost dive out of my seat when halftime arrives. "I'm going to get a water," I say in a rush to Tobias. "Do you want something?"

When he doesn't answer right away, I glance up at him from my phone and find him blatantly staring at my ass with a wolfish expression. "Ehm…" Does he seem rattled? He drags his fingers through his hair twice before answering. "No. I mean, yes. And I'll get it for you."

"That's not necessary. I need some air."

An eyebrow wings up. "We're outside, love. You have to go inside to buy drinks."

I wave my hands around, nearly dropping my phone. "You know what I mean."

"No, I don't." He closes the distance between us, a smile playing around the edges of his mouth and oh, yeah, he knows exactly what he's doing. What he's been doing. And the predicament I'm in. "Explain it to me, Elise."

His mouth is so…there. "I was never this horny before," I complain, letting my head fall back on my shoulders. "Take me back."

"To your place? Thought you'd never ask."

"No, you miscreant," I fire back, smacking him in his shoulder. "To a time when I could think straight. Maybe there is a program for this kind of thing. Man detox."

"My God." He reaches out to tuck a stray lock of hair behind my ear. "You are fucking adorable when you're disgruntled."

I storm up the stairs in a horny huff and he follows, hot on my heels. "Tobias—"

"I'm supposed to protect you," he interrupts, as if anticipating my protest. "I'm under strict instructions—and I always follow the script."

I stop abruptly, which is totally my mistake—one I possibly make on purpose thanks to my traitorous hormones—and Tobias runs into the back of me. Before I can fall to my knees, he wraps a forearm around my hips to steady me, pulling me upright and we just sort of stand there, me concentrating on not having a spontaneous orgasm while he breaths against the side of my neck, his perfect machine of a body molded to the back of mine.

Feeling this way in public is new to me.

Feeling this way for *this* man is ten times as startling…because it's more than physical.

All this time, I've been able to think of Banks, Tobias and Gabe as separate people. They are a circle that isn't fully formed around me, because of my dislike of Tobias. A broken circle. But some foreign intuition tells me that once that breach is repaired, the circle will close and lock me in. Is that why I'm resisting him so hard? I'm terrified of what the full circle will mean in terms of commitment? And what happens when a fissure forms again? Which one of us will cause it? It's hard enough maintaining a friendship or romantic relationship with one person and it's always over too soon. That's why I avoid them.

But three?

The imminence of the circle forming completely scares me.

Employing every ounce of my will, I pull away from Tobias. "If you could grab me a water, that would be great. I'm just going to take a walk."

"Elise."

His voice is like gravel, but I ignore the flutter in my stomach and keep walking.

———

I walk the perimeter of the stadium, stripping off layers of clothing, periodically checking my phone to see if Karina called or emailed, but there's nothing. I use the restroom, even though I don't need it. My spiked temperature probably evaporated any potential pee in my body —and I have no idea how I'm going to live through the second half of this rugby match.

When I peek into the stadium and see there is only six minutes left until the game resumes, I groan, turn away from the pitch…

And I lock eyes with a woman who is standing right behind me. She is medium height, well dressed, her brown skin glowing youthfully, despite her age.

"Excuse me," I mutter, starting to bypass her.

I'm not sure what stops me. A familiarity about her?

I don't think we've ever met, but there is something in the staunch set of her jaw and fiercely intelligent eyes that gives me pause. She has stopped halfway up the tunnel leading to the field, seemingly hesitant about entering to watch the game.

"Do you need help finding your seat?" I venture, sort of surprised at myself. Up until recently, I was definitely the kind of person who minds her own business.

The woman looks at me like I'm daft. Maybe I am. Maybe pheromones have eroded my brain, hindering my ability to behave normally. "What gave you the impression I need help?"

"You seem...undecided," I settle on. "About going in. I thought maybe..."

She waves off my stuttering explanation. "It's fine. You're just being nice."

I nod through a hum. "Enjoy the game."

When I turn to leave, she stops me. "Wait."

"Yes?"

She's poised to speak, but it takes a moment for the words to come out. "Do you come to many games?"

"I don't. No. This is my first."

"Ah."

That seems to be that, so I start to leave again. Not because I'm worried about Tobias being worried about *me*. Certainly not. Having to check in is a big part of why I avoid serious entanglements. Still, I'd like to make sure he isn't worried...

"My son is the coach," blurts the woman, gesturing at the end of the tunnel, then crossing her arms once again. "He always leaves me a ticket at the front. This is the first time I've taken it..." She shifts. "But I can't seem to make it in there."

I'm still reeling from the revelation that this woman is Banks's mother. Then I realize, I shouldn't be shocked. The similarities in their features and mannerisms are uncanny. It's why she seemed so familiar. And thank God I convinced him to leave the ticket one more time. She might have come here today otherwise and found nothing waiting for her. "Why can't you go in?"

Her laugh only contains a speck of humor. "That's a good question." The small smile fades. "I don't think I deserve to be proud of him, I suppose. I didn't have anything to do with...all of this. His accomplishment isn't mine. I did nothing to support him and yet he keeps on leaving me that damn ticket at the front gate."

My throat feels heavy, along with my chest, and if a magic genie offered me one wish right now, it would be for Banks to overhear this conversation. Here it is. This is why I feel such a kindred attachment to this woman's son. We're both wrestling with the need for pride from our parents. It makes me wonder what a conversation would sound like between my parents and a stranger. Maybe their feelings about pride are just as complicated. Maybe I should ask.

For now, though, in this moment, if there is some way to nudge the relationship between Banks and his mother back to solid ground, I have to try.

"Well." I swallow the weight in my throat. "As someone who is in a constant battle for her parents' pride, I can tell you, I don't care how I come by it. As long as I get it."

She considers that for a few beats. "Did they support you in your chosen profession?"

"Yes. All eight of them." I laugh, but it fades. "They're starting to lose hope, though."

"Oh, I doubt that."

"No, it's true." The pressure on my chest briefly doubles, but I rub it away. "It's weird how I need their support now, as an adult, almost more than I did as a kid. The need never really goes away. It's just lurking around, hoping to be fulfilled."

When I glance back at her, she's staring out at the field. Without following her line of vision, I know Banks is back on the pitch, along with his team. The reluctant hope in her eyes says it all. "It's too late... for a second chance."

"I don't think it is." I hesitate before saying the next part, worried it's too much. But some sort of sixth sense tells me she won't budge without good reason. "I think when he stops leaving the ticket...that's when you know it's too late. But if the ticket is his way of asking for support, maybe you don't want to wait?"

The woman doesn't respond, her gaze remaining locked on the pitch.

With a murmured goodbye, I head back to the curved indoor hallway, intending to make my way back to the section where I'm sitting with Tobias. Just before I walk out of sight, I glance back and find the woman stepping into the sunlight, handing her ticket to an usher.

A flowing sense of euphoria and relief has me walking faster. The chance encounter has robbed me of my cynicism—briefly. Let's not get crazy—and I'm as light as a feather. I can't wait to…tell Tobias. Did I really just think those words? Yes. Yes, I did. But I'm too hopeful to care. Banks is going to see his mother at the game. The happiness I desperately want him to feel is kicking inside of me now, trying to burst from my throat.

That's when I see Tobias up ahead.

He's behind the counter of the portable bar on wheels.

There are two plastic cups in his hands and he's shaking them overhead, loudly rattling the ice inside. Several attendants in red shirts are standing around, watching him work with rapt attention. "The secret to a good martini is the quality of the ingredients, of course. But often overlooked is the *temperature*, lads. No one wants warm vodka. Only ice cold—" He sees me coming and his occupied hands drop to the counter. "And just where have you been?"

My smile stretches before I can stop it.

Mayday. Mayday.

Please send emergency assistance.

I officially like Tobias.

And no sooner do I watch him realize it that he's handing off the makeshift martini maker and coming toward me with enough sensual purpose to render even the smartest girl stupid.

It's me. I'm that girl.

CHAPTER

Tobias

YOU'RE BEHAVING LIKE A TWAT.

Honestly. Sweating bullets because she's not back in time for the match to resume?

She didn't leave, did she? Of course not. Ghost *me?*

I was once ordained the Jesus of Sex by The International Adult Film Corporation. I even have that title stitched on the back of my bathrobe at home. Not that I want Elise to see it. Might just toss that robe out with the rubbish next week, come to think of it. Time for a new one.

Elise is about twenty meters away from me and I'm fairly certain she wants to fuck. She has these enchanting rose spots on her cheeks and she's taken off her sweater, so I'm privy to the outline of her nipples against her tank top. Wherever she went during halftime, she's come back liking me. Against all odds. She's *smiling* at me, for fuck's sake.

Don't fuck her.

There it is again. My brain playing tricks on me. I could have sworn it just told me not to fuck the dark-haired goddess who is finally giving me the green light.

Don't fuck her yet.

Okay, slightly better. I can work with a *yet*. That might just mean… wait five minutes before banging her so hard we time travel and end up in ancient Egypt. Right?

I'm going to throw away the robe.

It's not like I can hide what I've done in the past. I'm not ashamed that I made a fortune in the adult film industry. After all, I got out before it broke me completely—and that is a feat many don't accomplish. I got out before they succeeded in addicting me to pills that kept me hard far longer than is natural. Seeing the darkest side of the job early on saved my life. Kept me from going down a path of cocaine and off-set depravity.

Perhaps I'm ashamed that I didn't cop on that I was being taken for a ride, being sold out by my manager behind my back, but I'm not ashamed of who I am or what I've done. However. Dear God, I know Elise has watched me on film and I don't want her to think about any of that when I'm inside of her. The experience between us won't be the same as a job. It won't even be in the same fucking universe. Will she believe that? Feel it?

Maybe I'll burn the robe in my fireplace.

I've reached her now and she's not putting on the brakes.

The overhead light brightens her face like a shaft of light from the heavens and it's everything I can do not to start praying to her, like she's some sort of deity.

How *does* one pray, exactly?

More importantly, how does she grow more beautiful by the day? Is it some kind of magical face cream, because I would like to borrow it. The wrinkles beneath my eyes continue to branch out. Crow's feet, people call them. Horrific. She must notice them. I'm the oldest of the three men and my past profession makes me the least ideal candidate for a boyfriend, but I can't stay away from her. I'd actually allow the crow's feet to triple if she just lets me be a part of this weird four-way relationship. And I've been in some weird four-ways, but this one takes the bloody cake.

None of us have had a successful romantic commitment.

Most of us haven't even participated in a successful orgy. Amateurs.

And none of us know what the fuck we're doing, except we are in dire need of this girl.

Elise.

Now.

I plant my lips in the center of her forehead and make a miserable sound. "My brain is telling me not to fuck you yet."

"Why?" she whispers, her head tilting back so I can see her smooth, tan neck and my cock is already starting to get extremely uncomfortable. Which is a problem, because I can't get hard in public without making a scene. It's quite obvious when I'm erect, thank you very much.

"I don't know. Maybe…" A realization hits me like a lightning bolt. "My God, I think my conscience is reminding me to follow the rules."

Her head tilts, sending her glorious hair cascading to the left. That neck.

This is pain.

If I don't get the chance to grip her hips and give her the sweetest kind of hell soon, I'm going to forget the meaning of life.

Indulgence.

Although lately, that meaning has shifted to the indulgence of *her*.

"That's right." Heaven help me, she's staring at my mouth, the color deepening in her cheeks. "We have rules."

"I think I actually give a shite what Gabe and Banks think about me. In the escape room, we mutually decided that everyone needed to be okay with…"

"Two of us having sex," she finishes. "Without the others."

Just hearing the word "sex" in her husky tone of voice has me on the edge.

"Yes," I say raggedly, pulling her close despite what I've just told her, our mouths open, panting against one another, my right hand reaching up between us to brush my fingertips over her nipple—and she moans, turning me inside out. "Fuck."

"C-can we like…" She shakes her head, as if trying to break free of a daze. "Ask them?"

"Banks is in the middle of a match." I'm already extricating the phone from my pocket and pulling up the rugby coach's contact into. With my free thumb, I punch out a one-word text to the man—*PLEASE* —hoping the desperation comes through. Meanwhile, the goddess herself starts to text Gabe.

"Tell Gabe it's a code red," I say, drawing her up onto her toes so she can feel my dick getting stiffer for her. All for her.

"Uh…" Her eyelashes flutter, remaining at half-mast. "What's a code red?"

"It means you need some action. Badly. Hopefully he'll read between the lines." I trace her jaw with my lips, adoring the way she leans into the treatment, a shiver passing through her.

She swallows. "Can't argue with that."

"Mmmm. You like me now, love?" I breathe against her mouth. "Don't you?"

"At this moment I do," she whispers, looking into my eyes. "But no accounting for tomorrow."

I slant my mouth over hers and send my tongue on a thorough tour of her delicious mouth, the way I've been dying to do since she arrived outside. "I'll take it."

Our phones ding simultaneously.

I only need a split-second to acknowledge the thumbs up on both of our screens before I have her wrist locked in mine and I'm leading her toward the stairwell.

———

Elise

There's a scene in *Willy Wonka and the Chocolate Factory* where the children and their plus ones get a tour of the mysterious plant. Everyone is oohing and ahhing. I used to rewind the scene where they enter the indoor park where every single object is edible. Flowers, mushrooms, the river—all candy or chocolate. For a long time that edible park symbolized utopia to me. Nothing would ever get better.

I never expected a stairwell to prove me wrong.

This is Shangri-La.

And all we've done so far is kiss, but it's the anticipation, knowing what comes next that has tingles sailing through my bloodstream like the Willy Wonka paddleboat, but instead of traumatizing children, they are spreading excitement wherever they go. Stirring up needs that I would normally attempt to suppress or temper, but not right now. I let them ripple and dance. I'm riding too high to do otherwise. I'm in this untouchable bubble high above the ground knowing something wonderful is happening for Banks. That I stuck to my guns long enough to feel truly, wildly drawn to Tobias, body and soul. The very thought of Gabe existing makes my chest lighter.

It's almost as though Tobias is a representative of the three men, rather than an individual. They are all here with me while Tobias's mouth feasts on my neck, suctioning an incredibly sensitive area beneath my ear until I make a frantic noise and he tears away, gripping my wrist and dragging me up another set of stairs.

"Where are we going?" I say, sounding like I just woke up from a bender.

"The roof," he says unsteadily. "I can make a case for it being romantic."

We round the metal rail and jog up one final set of stairs, a door marked No Trespassing ahead. "Do you care about this being romantic?"

"With you I do, Elise."

My heart stuffs itself in the vicinity of my windpipe. This softie has been hiding behind the legendary sex god façade all this time, hasn't he? "I'm on the same page," I manage. "Watching your butt climb these stairs is very romantic. Like, I'm ready to buy it a steak dinner and serenade it with some Luther Vandross."

His laugh isn't as guarded as it normally is. It fills the concrete enclosure, wrapping around every part of me, making me like him more. More. Although *like* doesn't feel like a strong enough word. Infatuation or attraction sound too superficial. I was waiting for him to be real, maybe because some intuitive part of me knew he could. Knew he would. I don't know exactly how to describe what I have inside me for Tobias, but now that I've let it run wild, it triples by the second.

I stop analyzing and let it take over.

Tobias pulls me out onto the roof, letting go of my hand briefly to wedge his wallet in the door opening so we don't get locked up here—and then it's a free for all. He storms over me, kissing me from above as if to set the tone that he'll be in charge, the crook of his elbow catching the back of my head and holding me steady for the assault of his mouth.

We switch directions, heads canting left, right, until I start to grow dizzy and frantic, my fingers curling into the front of his sweater. Every time we come up for air, his eyes are more and more glazed, his color higher. I thought I'd seen him aroused in the hotel room at the Conrad, but no. He must have been holding back behind that smirk.

This is Tobias ready to rumble.

The grin is gone, the walls are down.

He's hard against my stomach, hips tilting to rock against me in that slow, inviting pace that brings a hundred different videos to mind. That first obligatory five minutes of foreplay before the clothes come off. Only it's me he's kissing now. It's the seam of my leggings he's tracing with his middle finger, pressing deeper and deeper with every rake of that digit. When he travels over my clit and jostles it gently, again, again, again, I jolt with a moan and his upper lip curls, baring his teeth to me, almost like he's been wounded by my show of pleasure.

Looking me in the eye, he delves his hand down the front of my leggings, straight past the barrier of my panties, finding my damp heat with his fingers. His head falls forward and he chokes through a humorless laugh. "You deserve to have me down on my hands and knees, licking this, every time. But fuck me, love, you can't get any wetter." His middle finger presses into my opening slowly, but deeply.

Deeper and deeper until I gasp, his breath growing shorter until he's panting. And then he uses that hand between my legs to draw me up onto my toes, tilting the world on its axis. "What's say I fuck you rotten now and lick this pretty thing off later?"

"Done." Is that *my* whiny voice? "Sold."

Half of Tobias's mouth tilts up in a devilish grin, his eyes nothing short of unholy. He keeps his right fingers pressed up tight inside of me, wrapping his left arm around my shoulders and guiding me back, back, until I'm pressed up against hard metal. A waist-high box with vents every few feet. There's a hum coming from inside, some kind of engine, and the white noise gusts over me, frees me even more to groan, to whimper over his now-thrusting fingers, how they plunge with authority, then retreat almost apologetically, before he does it again. Again.

"Do us a favor and unfasten my jeans, love," he says in between erotic drags of his open mouth over mine, right to left. His saliva is smeared across my lips and cheeks and I love it. It feels appropriate. It matches my rough baseline of need for this man inside of me. "Take me out. Get used to seeing me in your hand. That's the only place it wants to be."

I'm eager, breathless, while thumbing open his button and tugging down the zipper carefully over the thick curve of his shaft. But I'd be lying to say there isn't a part of me that experiences a sudden flash of inadequacy. This man has done this professionally. With other professionals. Plus I'm younger than Tobias by seven years.

Am I going to come across like a total amateur?

That thrumming baseline of lust inside of me crashes with a flurry of cymbals when I draw him out and see him live for the first time. In the flesh, not on a screen. To say he's well-endowed would be stating the obvious. Not only that, he's groomed and smooth and...fuck it, he's succulent and ripe. My knees start to dip toward the floor, simply because it's the kind of erection a girl wants in her mouth. It's a foregone conclusion that this man gets a blow job, right? Out of appreciation for the grooming alone, he—

"Whoa, love." He uses his body to push me upright again, against the humming metal box and I see he's sweating, his throat muscles standing out more than usual. Is he even…shaking slightly? "I thought we established that I'd be slamming that tight ass up against the engine box until you can't keep your knees up anymore?"

I don't remember him talking quite like this in any of his films.

Hoarse and pleading.

I love it.

"Yes. I-I know. But that's kind of…" I'm stuttering in between gulps of cool air. "You're really going off script, aren't you? Skipping to the end—"

Something akin to panic passes through his eyes. "There is no script with you, Elise. There is no beginning, middle or end." He leans in close, rolling his forehead against mine. His hands grip the material of my leggings, shoving them down my hips, thighs, until I join the effort and kick off my ankle boots, toeing off my bottoms the rest of the way. "None of it was real. You are what's fucking real."

"I hate that I needed to hear you say that."

"I hate that I made you need to hear it."

"Okay, then," I half-sob against his mouth, because the connection between us in this moment is so great that it's causing a vicious twist in my chest. His arousal is back in my hand and I'm stroking it, exploring while his rasping breath stirs my hair. He produces a condom from the pocket of his jeans and we rip the package eagerly, rolling on the lubricated latex together.

"I have something that will make it all better," he says, savoring my mouth with a kiss.

"I'm pretty sure I'm holding it."

"Well, yes. That's a given. But…" He draws away slightly, giving himself enough room to peel off his sweater, revealing a chest and abs that look almost make-believe, they're cut so precisely, rounded and full in the most appealing of places. "Now." He stoops down and licks up my throat, his hips coming up between my thighs, which loop around him automatically, his lips raking through the hair at my temple. "Isn't that better, love?"

"Arrogant," I gasp—as he tears the panties off my body, winking as he does it.

"The arrogance is a bit warranted, though, isn't it? Don't answer now. I'll ask you again when your nails are shredding my fucking back." Without taking his eyes off mine, he reaches down and fists himself, poising himself against my entrance, shuddering, then pushing in with a slow show of force, not stopping until I feel utterly pinned. "Oh. Damn, love. *Dammit.*"

He thrusts inside me once, twice, coming to an abrupt stop. Cursing.

"Remind me to apologize to Gabe for laughing at him. For coming too soon. I get it now," he says, voice like gravel. "It's not often I'm rendered speechless but..." He punches his hips hard, my butt smacking hard against the metal, his guttural groan rousing something dark and confident inside of me. "Fuck."

"No. Fuck you. I mean, not fuck you. I'm saying fuck...about you."

He expels a deep chuckle through his teeth. "Hold on for your fucking life, Elise."

Our bodies mold together, his mouth making love to me while his lower half...it...oh my God. Does he have double-jointed hips? His chest remains pressed against mine, mouths wet, panting and semi-locked, while those hips arc up and back so dramatically that I'm being emptied and filled on every single rapid-fire punch drive.

"Tobias!" I scream into his shoulder, my claws, indeed, coming out involuntarily to bury themselves in the muscular beef of his upper back. This is going to be the fastest orgasm of my life. I'm going to be a changed woman after this. My inner thighs are strapped to his hips by some invisible force, his straining grunts in my ear causing something primal and feminine to unravel and I bury my teeth where his shoulder curves into his neck, working my hips into a gallop, even though I'm gloriously impaled and it's more of a trapped writhe, but he loves it. He loves how I circle and clench myself on him so much that his thrusts turn almost violent, his hands grappling with my knees to keep them open for the onslaught of welcome aggression.

"You should be the arrogant one," he grits out, baring his teeth against my ear. "You're going to ruin my life with this pussy. This wet little high-end pussy. Go ahead and claw and scratch at me, love, I'm not going to stop fucking it."

Everything goes technicolor as my body gives up the fight. It's the kind of climax a woman is almost afraid of because it's so intense, but I'm not scared with his mouth on mine, like he's almost talking me down from a very high height while I'm already in the midst of free falling. I seize up around his still-driving flesh until both of us make a pained sound, followed by one of relief when the clench starts to lessen in blessed degrees, leaving my head flopped over his shoulder, limp, my limbs momentarily having lost their function.

"You come like a fucking queen," he whispers into my perspiring neck, awed, bouncing me once, twice, and hello—I'm back online. "My queen. *Our* queen."

I lift my head just in time to receive his kiss, as if he's anticipating my return to the living. I expect him to press me hard against the metal box and finish. Instead the world becomes a blur of color as he carefully settles my feet on the ground, spinning me around to face the opposite direction and growling. Slamming a fist down on the box and entering me roughly from behind.

"Yes." He presses me forward with his body, moving my hands into the position he wants them. Braced, palms down. "Our queen, right?" He drives me up onto my toes and I cry out, seeing nothing in front of me. Nothing but sparks. "But you're all mine right now." He winds my hair around his fist and slowly, slowly draws my head back while his mouth drags up the center of my spine. "And I'm all yours. I've just been practicing for the day I met you, love." He pulls my hair with a hint of more authority. "Now you're going to press that ass into my stomach as high as you can and take advantage of it."

"Yes, Tobias," I whisper, shaken down to my toes.

He yanks up the back of my shirt and unsnaps my bra so quickly, it almost seems like a magic trick. Then his left hand is sliding between my body and the metal box, molding my breast in his hand, my hair still tugged back in his right. His slow pumps are divine in a way that defies description. He's defiling me and worshipping me at the very same time, sinking so deep it almost hurts—almost—then whispering praise into my hair, thanking me, as he recedes.

"Lift a bit more," he says hoarsely into the back of my neck. "I know where you need me...there. Feel that? Aw, the way you tightened up all the way to my balls says you do, love."

My eyes roll into the back of my head as the ridge at the head of his sex grazes my clit again and we both sort of grow restless at the very same moment, my libido spinning madly in the wake of his crudely beautiful speech. He works his hips harder, faster, sawing wetly over that bundle of building tension until I'm pressing my moaning mouth into the bend of my elbow to keep from screaming.

But I lose the ability to muffle my pleasure when Tobias abruptly lets go of my hair, my breast, and acquires both of my wrists, locking them at the small of my back.

"Spread your legs." He spits on my backside. Growls while slapping it sharply. "Time to put me out of my misery, you fucking temptation."

I should punch him in the face for spitting on me. Except I love it. Except I'd have to stop receiving what he's giving me, which is all-out hedonism. He's bearing down on top of me now, his hips pumping in a frenzied way that says the end is near and I'm powerless to the lust. Powerless to do anything but raise my buttocks like he told me and take the raw and wonderful conquering of my body. The spiral he loosened inside me earlier begins to coil the other direction again, faster, faster and my legs shift and dance, knowing what's coming.

"Please, please, please." I flex my wrists but he holds tight. "Keep going."

"Anything you say, love." He's breathless now. Wild. But in the eye of the storm, his voice has lost all trace of arrogance. All artifice. He's just mine. He's just ours. "Just don't stop liking me, Elise. Just keep...I don't want to lose that. This. I've never had this."

Our fingers intertwine at the small of my back. "I won't stop."

On that promise, his stomach muscles flex and strain against my backside and he moans brokenly into my back, the excessive warmth increasing even more inside of me, his movements turning jagged, his hands letting go of my wrists to scramble down to my hips, yanking them back desperately for three final drives—and that roughness at that angle blows my second fuse, forcing a closed-mouth scream from deep in the recesses of my body, both of us straining over that near-painful clench of my body around his, before he falls forward onto me, gathering me close, so close, in the circle of his arms. "Elise. My *God*."

A whistle blows somewhere in the distance and the crowd cheers.

I turn and collapse against him, our bodies swaying in a slow dance for several seconds, before we meet for a kiss. And when I see the look of completion, awe, understanding in his eyes, I somehow know they match my own.

What we've just done has snapped the circle together with a finality I can feel in my bones—and I'm pretty sure I no longer have a choice but to exist in the center of it, trusting hope to outweigh my fear. Hoping that against all odds, the circle stays intact.

CHAPTER

Eighteen

I'M STILL in an orgasmic haze when we reach my apartment.

Tobias drove to Jersey for the match this afternoon, so I have the pleasure of skipping the train and riding in his silver Audi, the interior of which smells like new leather and vanilla. We weren't able to speak much to Banks after the game, but we waved to him as he followed his team onto their idling bus, earning Tobias a very professional nod— and me, a distinctly promissory one. It was more than a nod vowing to please me later, it was a nod telling me much more. That he has something to speak to me about. Share with me.

And I'm guessing, hoping, that I know what it is.

I catch sight of myself in the glass of my building door, shocked to find that I'm smiling ear to ear. I can't remember the last time I felt free and buoyant enough to smile this broadly. Unforced. One third of the reason stands behind me while I unlock the main entrance, his hands molding shamelessly to my butt.

"You're not allowed inside, Tobias."

"Your bum?" he asks, sounding hilariously dejected.

"My apartment."

"Oh, thank God." A beat passes. "Hang on. Why not?"

"I'm renting a room from Shayna and those are her rules. No men allowed."

Tobias is pensive. Then, "I like this rule until it applies to me."

"That is the very hallmark of being a man."

He's very still for a moment. "My God, that's eye-opening."

I have the fierce urge to giggle, so I turn the key extra hard in the door to combat the sound. "You can walk me to the hallway, then it's bye-bye. You have to return to your awful penthouse overlooking the city."

"Pack a bag and come with me," he says, following me up the stairs. "We can order sashimi and play naked Twister."

"That is weirdly specific. I'm more of a trivia and nachos girl."

"We can do that, too. I've never had nachos."

I come to a halt at the top of the stairs, slowly turning around. "You've never had nachos?"

"Show me what I'm missing, Elise." He stops on the stair below me, making us almost eye level, his attention dipping to my mouth and heating. "I'll even let you bring the other two wankers, as long as they promise not to touch my Jean Louis David volumizer."

"What is that? By the way, I already regret asking."

"It's the styling mousse I have shipped from France. Banks will use it just to fuck with me and Gabe will probably mistake it for whipped cream."

My lips wobble with the need to smile, but I do my best to keep a stern expression. "Stop pretending like you don't like Gabe and Banks."

"We share a common obsession." He reaches out and frames my jaw, brushing his thumb right to left across the seam of my mouth. "Hard not to feel a sense of camaraderie when there is one girl wrapping herself around our collective throats."

A tingle swims through me, all the way to the ends of my hair follicles. "Maybe I'm just waiting for the right moment to squeeze the life out of you."

"You did exactly that back on the roof, love." He climbs the remaining stair and backs me across the landing, his hard body coming up against mine in a slow, firm press that has every nerve ending inside of me shooting sparks. "More, please," he growls into my neck.

I push him off before I get taken under, surprised by the…authority I'm feeling. And the welcome sense of obligation. "No. Next time, everyone will be there. Together." I shake my head, trying to come up with the words to explain the shift that has been taking place inside of me since meeting these three. "We were together today—alone—and… I loved it. Really loved it. But there is a balance that has to be restored now. That's up to me, I think." I study Tobias's face for a reaction. "I don't know if I'm making any sense."

"You are." Serious now, he slips his hands into the pockets of his jeans. Hesitates to speak. Then, "Even I have been feeling…anxious to get everyone back on an even surface since we made love. And I'm a classic narcissist."

"No you're not," I say on a burst of laughter. "Who told you that?"

"Everyone I've ever met."

I take the remaining steps to my apartment door and insert the key, pushing open the door, "Well, give them my number so I can—"

My heart drops like a boulder.

The apartment is in disarray.

Books are everywhere, possessions from both rooms tossed on the floor, even food from the kitchen cabinets is smeared in places, scattered in others.

Ransacked. Someone did this on purpose.

"Tobias," I whisper, reaching for him. My palm lands in the center of his chest and he gently captures my wrist, coming up behind me. As soon as he processes the scene from over the top of my head, he yanks me back out of the apartment, standing between me and the mess. "I assume it doesn't always look like that?" he asks tightly.

"No. Shayna. Oh my God, my roommate—"

"Is she home this time of day?"

"No. She works downtown, but she could have called in sick or worked virtually today." Pulse scrabbling, I wheel around him, trying to enter the apartment, but he turns quickly, wrapping his arms around my waist and preventing me from going any further. "I need to make sure she's not in there. Shayna?"

"I will check, Elise." He scans the hallway end to end. Searching for a threat? "You will wait right here." The sudden change in his demeanor, from playful to imposing, renders me momentarily speechless. All I can do is watch with my hands over my mouth as he enters the apartment, stepping over throw pillows and rolls of toilet paper, disappearing into each bedroom and the bathroom, even the closets. He emerges from the final one shaking his head. "There's no one here."

I let out the breath I've been holding and step over the threshold. My immediate—albeit ridiculous—response is to begin cleaning everything up, but Tobias stops me. He takes my face in his hands and forces me to focus on him.

"Elise. The television is still here. A laptop in the other bedroom. It doesn't appear to be a robbery." He pauses, searching my face. "Do you have any idea who would do this?"

"No. I—" Abruptly, I cut myself off, leaving the denial hanging in the air. A chill carries up my spine and washes over the back of my neck. No. No...my apartment hasn't been destroyed over the Alexander-Crouch story. Right? This kind of personal retaliation doesn't happen in real life. This isn't *The Sopranos*. Everything goes through lawyers and...

The picture.

It was sitting on my dresser when I left the apartment this morning.

My feet carry me into my room slowly. I already know the manila envelope is going to be missing when I step over the threshold, but I'm still knocked back a step. This confirms it—my apartment has been trashed by someone connected to the story. As far as I can tell, it's the only thing missing.

Tobias comes to a stop beside me at the foot of my bed. The longer I'm silent, the closer his eyebrows creep toward his hairline. "It would appear you have some idea who did this."

"I..." I'm embarrassed to tell him. To recount my flub yesterday to anyone. At some point, I will have to acknowledge what is happening here out loud. But I need to deal with the immediate problems first. Need to wrap my head around what I've caused. "I need to call Shayna and tell her what happened. Then the police—"

I pretend not to notice Tobias scrutinizing me.

But I can't ignore him when he approaches—and attempts to sweep me up in his arms like a child. I wrestle my way free, batting at his hands. "What are you doing?"

"Comforting you," he explains, attempting to cradle me again. "It's just the thing."

"No, it's not!"

Finally, he gives up, but he's extremely put out about it, the absolute nut ball. "Fine. I'm calling the lads." When I look at him in surprise, he adds, "Balance, right? If you were in danger and no one called me, I would go fucking mental."

Danger? "I'm not in danger."

"Try saying it with a little more conviction." He taps the screen and holds up the phone, the familiar chirp of a call connecting filling the vandalized room. It's not a regular old call, though, he's FaceTiming. As if a group text with four people isn't bad enough. Shoot me right now. "I can tell you're keeping something from me, Elise," he says solemnly, right before the FaceTime connects.

Keeping a problem this big from them doesn't seem right. Not at all. And I find myself murmuring, "I'll explain when we're all together, so I only have to do it once."

Two faces pop up on the screen. Banks is on top. There is a parking lot behind him, as if we've caught him walking to his car. Gabe is shirtless and holding a bottle of beer, construction grime still shadowing his jaw and forehead.

Banks is brisk. "Hello."

"Yo," Gabe says, peering into the phone, so only his eye is visible on the screen. "What's good?"

Tobias gives me a withering look. "I hereby call an emergency Tram Fam meeting. Elise's apartment has been trashed and she won't even let me hold her like a baby."

"*What?*" Banks has stopped in his tracks. "Trashed by who? Let me see her."

Tobias shifts the phone, but I can't look Banks in the eye. He's going to know I've been withholding something from him, even after he asked me about the story. I assured him I was clear of the situation, so he's going to feel that betrayal deeper than the other two. "I'm fine,"

I say, suddenly feeling a very urgent, almost shocking need to be surrounded by all three of them. The need is so crucial, a shudder winds through me.

Still connected to the FaceTime, Tobias stomps over and draws me up against his chest. "We're going to call the police and then—"

"Bring her to my place," Gabe interrupts. It's not until he growls this directive that I realize his face has been leached of color. "Meet here. I want her here."

"Queens?" Tobias wrinkles his nose. "Is there even a decent sashimi place near you?"

I elbow him in the ribs.

"Call the police from down the street. Somewhere public. In case they come back." Banks is speed walking now, getting into his car and firing up the engine. "Jesus Christ. That's burglary 101, Tobias."

"Elise is safe." He tightens his hold on me, looking very dramatic. "I'm with her."

That earns a classic Banks eyeroll. "They could have weapons. You don't. And before you ask, no, you can't swing your dick at the bad guys."

Tobias snorts. "Lucky for them."

I watch as a realization dawns on Banks's face. "Elise, please tell me this has nothing to do with the story you were chasing."

"I…" I shake my head. "I can't tell you that."

"Story." Tobias's face loses some of its color. "I thought that was over."

All I can do is focus on breathing. Staying calm.

"Are you bringing her here or do I have to come and get her?" Gabe says, looking properly intimidating, a line of muscle flexing in his jaw. "Elise, I'm sorry this happened. We've got you."

I give Tobias and Banks a pointed look. "Thank you, my sweet Gabe."

"He's the favorite," Tobias mutters. "Anyone can see it."

Gabe grins.

"Out of the apartment," Banks near-shouts, his engine gunning in the background. "Now. I'll meet you all at Gabe's." He pauses. "Elise can fill us in when we get there."

CHAPTER
Nineteen

Banks

SOMEHOW, Tobias, Elise and I arrive at Gabe's at the exact same time.

We pull into spots at the curb, parallel to each other, trading stunned glances through the passenger window of Tobias's Audi. But I shouldn't be surprised at this stage, should I? Everything that has happened from the moment I stepped onto the Roosevelt Island tram has felt...different, but oddly exact. Like I left my old skin behind on that island and stepped into a new one. If I wasn't such a pragmatic man, I could swear the hand of fate is pressing on my back, guiding me from moment to moment with Elise, Tobias, Gabe.

Of course we are arriving at the same time.

For the same woman.

I devour the sight of her through the glass, nearly ripping the hinges clean off my car in order to get out. *You're going to overwhelm her. Slow down.*

It's not easy to temper myself, however. I saw her speaking to my

mother at the stadium. I don't know how it happened. Nor do I understand how she knew to encourage me to leave the ticket one more
time. Or the circumstances of their meeting. But I am positive Elise
encouraged my mother to walk into the stands and sit down. Her very
first game of mine—ever. For that,

Elise will never fully understand the depth of my gratitude. I don't
think she has a single clue that there is magic surrounding her. She
weaves it everywhere she goes. Tobias is a different man since meeting
her. More humble, empathetic. Gabe doesn't stare at the ground
anymore. He looks us in the eye. And now, she's helped bridge a gap
between me and my mother. The meeting between the four of us is
starting to feel less like happenstance and more like fate. Some
inevitable providence that none of us saw coming.

Again, I realize I'm storming toward her with barely leashed
desperation and worry, and I forcibly slow myself down. This is what
I've been doing since the beginning. Moderating myself in every
moment that we're not intimate. Making her safe, physically and
emotionally. Trying to give her an avenue of escape, because I know
it's what she needs not to feel cornered. Pressured. Even if I have the
urge to crowd her sometimes.

Inhale her.

I'm a selfish man. But I'm learning to be unselfish with her. *For* her.

For them, too, now, I guess. I've evolved to fit.

Outside of my car now, I catch sight of Gabe in the driveway where
he's obviously been waiting, barefoot and shirtless in sweatpants that
appear to be covered in floor stain. In my life before the tram, I probably never would have known this man. Or had a reason to speak with
him, but there is no getting around this sense that we're a team now.
Our opponent is anything that makes Elise unhappy and I can't stress
how drastic that purpose feels. It's like an iron sitting on my chest at
all times—and it's not just my burden. I can almost feel Tobias and
Gabe carrying the same heaviness. It's why I have no choice but to
share her.

To be one of three, instead of her only one.

I don't know if the instinct to edge out my competition for her
attention will ever fully go away—winning is too deeply ingrained in

me—but the edges of that instinct are dulling in the face of what she clearly needs.

We converge on her in the middle of the street, our hands everywhere. Whispering comfort to her. It's insane. This behavior, this relationship. All of it. But I've never experienced anything better in my life. Not when I was named the head coach of the Flare. Not when we won our first championship. Not ever. Nothing compares to her going limp in between us, confident that we won't let her fall.

She buries her face between Gabe's pecs and he immediately begins crooning to her, petting her hair. Her fingers slide into mine and squeeze. Tobias, of course, has her rear end parked in his lap—but he doesn't appear as smug as usual. No, we lock gazes over the top of Elise's head and I can see he is clearly shaken, like me. Like Gabe.

"Who fucked with you?" Gabe demands to know. Then to us, "Who fucked with her?"

"That's what we're going to find out," I say, bringing her hand to my mouth and kissing her knuckles. "Did you meet with the police?"

"Yes." A muscle ticks in Tobias's cheek. "But nothing was missing, so they left rather quickly."

"Nothing was missing?" Gabe echoes. "I don't understand."

"Actually..." Elise takes a deep breath. "Something was missing."

Across the street, one of the neighbors is watching the three of us comfort Elise with his mouth open, garden hose forgotten in his hand, water splashing all over the sidewalk. "We should go inside."

"Tram Fam is on the move," Tobias says into a fake headset.

We remain crowded around Elise all the way to the front door, like a pack of security guards protecting a Kardashian. When we get inside, Gabe's house is exactly as I expected it to be. Cement and paint splattered work boots are discarded in the mud room. The sound of television sports emanates from the back of the house, the furniture is beat up, functional brown leather. It smells like a combination of microwave meals and aftershave, the latter of which is so fresh, he must have splashed it on right before he got here.

Fair enough. I reapplied deodorant while speeding over the Queensboro Bridge.

I'm sure Tobias checked his hair eighty times in the rearview.

We're all fucked for this girl.

"Gabe…" She bestows an incredible smile on him. "I love your house."

"Move in," he blurts, his face immediately turning the color of a stoplight.

She laughs and my reaction to her amusement is like having the wind knocked out of me. I forget how to breathe for a second. I've been hit with her being in danger and that laugh, all in the space of a couple of hours, and it's leaving me unbalanced.

In need of *her* balance.

I swallow a croak of her name.

But it's almost like she hears it anyway, her eyes tripping over to me. "I want to explain now. I just need to get it out, okay?"

Tobias sits down on the couch and pats his knee for Elise to sit, but she shakes her head.

He frowns and falls back into the cushions.

"You three remember that morning you showed up at my place of work to see me again, a totally inappropriate thing to do?"

A chorus of hums from us men. Gabe hangs his head until Tobias kicks him, gesturing for him to stop slouching. What are we *becoming*?

"Well. That morning, I told you I was following a story about Gabe's union boss, Jameson Crouch, right?" We all seem to watch with rapt attention as her throat moves in a swallow. "He's in a feud with the mayor. You've all seen it in the paper, right? On the news…" She tucks some hair behind one ear and my fingers flex in response. "Well, I started to notice that the accusations against the mayor were so specific. I wanted to prove myself to Karina, so I…I pursued my hunch that there was a mole feeding Crouch information. I started with Deputy Mayor Alexander and it turned out to be the right lead. I followed him to a meeting with Crouch that evening on Roosevelt Island." She looks at me, wetting her lips. "Banks, when you asked me if I'd dropped the story, I should have told you this part. At the Local 401 party, I overheard them making plans about leaking those emails about the governor." Heavy seconds go by. "And I took a picture of them speaking, exchanging a thumb drive. A picture that is now missing from my apartment, but still on my phone. They might have been looking for my laptop, maybe to see what I knew? But I brought it with me to the rugby game. I have it with me now."

As her explanation continues, cement is pouring into my chest.

I don't know a lot about the inner workings of local government, but everyone under the sun knows New York politics is cutthroat as hell. I hate Elise swimming in that swamp more than I hate anything. She's not even done explaining the whole story and my muscles are as stiff as an ironing board. Tobias and Gabe don't even appear to be breathing.

"Yesterday, I..." A red stain appears on her cheeks. "I walked into Karina's office to tell her about the conversation I overheard and she was on the phone with Alexander's assistant. They heard enough to be aware that I suspect them of teaming up to sabotage the mayor. They heard Karina call me by my name." She blows out a breath. "Maybe they were just searching for the correct Elise...and the picture in my apartment confirmed I was the one in Karina's office. Bottom line, I definitely think someone associated with this might have ransacked my apartment."

"You've made yourself a target, love," Tobias breathes, raking his hands down his face.

"Can't we just hand the pictures over?" Gabe wants to know. "Or delete them?"

"I don't know. Would they believe I have the only copy? They won't communicate with Karina now and they reached out to me by trashing my apartment," Elise says. "They don't exactly sound reasonable."

"You're staying here until it's safe," Gabe states, crossing his arms over his bare chest. "I mean it, Elise."

"Actually." She takes her time looking at each of us, as if memorizing our faces and I know, I just fucking know she's about to say something that none of us will like. "I owed you guys an explanation and I've given it. But for now, I think it's best if I leave. I don't want any of you getting caught up in this. Maybe getting hurt." Her nod is resolute. "Yeah, I'm going to bail, at least until this is over. Okay?"

There's a pregnant pause.

Then the shouting all starts at once.

CHAPTER

Twenty

"EXCUSE ME, MADAM?" Tobias growls.

Banks holds up his hands, palms out. "Elise, be reasonable."

"No. Nope." For once, Gabe is up to speed on proceedings and not the least bit happy. "No way. You're staying right here."

"You're safer with us than without us," Banks says, casually positioning himself between me and the front door. "There's no way we're letting you leave, Elise."

"Letting me?" I sputter.

"Does anyone have any rope?" Tobias poses the question while lunging to his feet from the couch. "Now seems like a good time to show off my shibari skills."

I back away, gasping. "You are *not* going to tie me up."

Features tight, Tobias follows me step for step while examining my face. "Turns you on a bit, though, doesn't it?"

"Not when it's used as a method to detain me," I respond through my teeth. "Guys, we talked about kidnapping in the escape room."

I realize I'm backing myself into a literal corner and duck around Tobias, only to come up against Banks's solid chest. As always, the warm strength of him makes my thighs feel like jelly, my urgent need to leave immediately waning. I'm tempted to lay my cheek on his shoulder and let him comfort me while the sky falls, but that would be too easy. I can't start relying too much on these men. I've learned to have my own back, because it's selfish to expect others to catch me when I tumble...when I know we're only in each other's lives temporarily.

This is too big. Depending on people.

It was one thing to make the independent decision to venture into this quad, but relying on them is a whole other story. I'm not there yet. I'm not there. I'm scared of pressing down on something too hard when I haven't tested the stability. I'm scared, period. And yet. I think...I might be allowing myself to freak out a little bit so they can use their potency to calm me down.

Does that even make sense?

"This relationship is moving too fast," I heave.

"No, it's not," Gabe says in my ear. Where did he come from?

Two of them are touching me now. If Tobias completes the circle, I'm screwed. I'll give in and let them play my heroes. I'll stay here and possibly put them in harm's way. Letting them share this mess with me would be the ultimate act of selfishness. With that in mind, I whirl free of Gabe and Banks, just as Tobias is about to lock me into a four-way embrace.

"It is moving fast," Banks agrees. "I think I speak for the three of us when I say, we'd be happy with it moving even faster. But we must give Elise time to catch up."

"There's no better time to think than when you're tied to a bed rail," Tobias offers.

"A better use of the rope might be strangling you," I say sweetly.

They're literally following me slowly around the room while I back around furniture and try to avoid tripping over discarded boots and remote controls. "Look, I'll keep in contact with you guys and when the situation blows over, we'll—"

Banks shakes his head. "No."

"You're pushing us away, Elise."

"Rope."

I snatch a throw pillow up off the couch and launch it at Tobias's head. He ducks, gracefully, avoiding the projectile. But he doesn't anticipate me hurling another one immediately afterward and this one hits him square in the forehead.

He's shocked and miffed, and I can't help it, I start to laugh. In my distraction, I trip backward over a remote and land on my ass near the edge of the rug. Hitting the ground without warning jars me into laughing even harder, despite the fact that all three of them are surrounding me now, worriedly asking if I'm all right and checking for injuries.

"I'm fine," I assure them, slapping numerous hands away. "You should be checking on Tobias's ego."

"It's in shambles since meeting you, thank you very much," Tobias clips, but he's looking down at me and battling a smile. "But if it makes you happy, you can grind it to dust."

I bat my eyelashes at him. "It really does."

He goes right on smiling, but there's a slight hardening of the planes of his face. "Are you done threatening to leave, Elise?"

My smile drops. "It's not a threat. It's not an irrational decision, either. These men trashed my apartment, and I don't want to involve any of you in a situation that could get worse before it gets better. Gabe, Jameson Crouch is your boss. Being involved with me might even jeopardize your job."

"Better than jeopardizing your safety, Elise," Gabe says gruffly.

Banks crouches down in front of me. "At the risk of replacing Tobias as your least favorite—"

"Hey!" Tobias complains.

"Elise." Banks sighs, shakes his head. "You're looking for any excuse to get rid of us. The urge to protect yourself from pain isn't going to go away overnight. You're searching for an escape hatch because you're afraid of going down with the whole submarine."

"Insert torpedo dick joke here," Tobias murmurs.

Banks studies my face, a pulse tapping in his temple.

The longer he looks at me, the more exposed I feel.

"Are you just the coach? Or do you double as the team psychologist?" I mutter.

His lips tilt at one end, but his eyes remain as intense as ever. "You know I'm all about giving you choices and making sure we don't overstep…" Banks reaches out and frames my jaw in his hand, tilting my face up. "But so help me God, you are not going anywhere without us until this shit is over. Is that clear?"

Oh…my God.

I don't have the words to describe what happens inside of me in that moment.

Until now, I thought I was craving the sense of control these three men give me, but that hint of dominance from Banks has riddled me with need. Maybe the circle of four is big enough, powerful enough to hold more than one kind of pleasure. More than one kind of escape. Or maybe I'm still in control after all, because Banks is eye level with me, waiting for my response, even as his hand slips down to my throat and squeezes lightly, eliciting soft groans from Tobias and Gabe. They're waiting for me to say yes to being owned. Yes, to owning them. I'm still holding the reins, but they want to take them for a while.

And it's galling for someone so independent to admit that I do want to hand over control for now. I'm in a tailspin. My job is on the line, possibly my safety, too. I don't know which direction my future is heading, and I'm scared of how much these three people are starting to mean to me. I don't want to think, I just want to feel, and leave it to Banks to sense this and gamble on it.

But so help me God, Banks said a moment ago, *you are not going anywhere without us until this shit is over. Is that clear?*

"Yes," I push past my dry throat, more than a touch shocked at myself. But eager to let go and let myself be directed for a while. Just a little while.

"That's a good girl," Gabe breathes, tone heavy. "That's our girl." A quick glance away from Banks's hypnotic stare tells me the foreman is hard in his jeans, his index finger toying with the zipper. Waiting on the edge.

"I see. It's only a problem when *I* threaten to hold her hostage." Tobias might be complaining, but his voice has gone thick. Everyone in the room has noticed the drastic change in energy. A minute ago, I was throwing pillows and now I'm on the floor in front of three men being held by my throat. "This is usually where Banks asks what you'd like from us, love. *Who* you would like. How far we're allowed to go. But the fine print seems to have been left up to me this time." Tobias removes his hat, tosses it aside and starts to remove his sweater. "What do you want the next couple of hours to look like, love?"

"Tell her we'll stop if she needs to stop," Gabe rasps, openly stroking himself now in the lowered zipper of his jeans. "She likes hearing that."

"Elise." Tobias waits to continue until I'm looking him in the eye. "We'll always stop if you say stop." He flicks open the button of his jeans. "We serve you."

Helpless power. That's the oxymoronic combination that rocks me, makes me feel exultant and weak at the same exact time. I love the hand around my throat. It's anchoring me, keeping me from floating away into the atmosphere of lust that thickens by the second. I'm supposed to say something, but my tongue is heavy in my mouth, pulse rapping in my temples, chest, every nerve ending inside of me throbs.

What do I want?

I know the answer. It feels like I've known it since the night on the tram.

"I want to feel all three of you at once."

As soon as that truth leaves my mouth, my veins seem to expand to accommodate the sudden wild rush of blood. Banks's grip around my throat tightens, an involuntary response to my words, and I whimper brokenly, my knees shifting on the floor.

"What I want is for you to share me...roughly. Overwhelm me. You..." I say, closing my eyes. "All three of you...have permission to be animals."

———

I'm not going to lie; I've watched this moment happen on the tiny screen of my phone and it did not seem appealing. The act, anyway. One woman kneeling between three men while they take turns using her mouth. No, it seemed like a lot of multitasking and motor skills. The only thing that ever prevented me from fast forwarding was the moaning men. Their reaction to watching their buddies getting pleasure, while they impatiently await their own.

In real life, with men I care about, men to whom I am painfully attracted, that enjoyment is astronomical.

I'm almost delirious with the privilege of kneeling in front of them.

I haven't done anything yet and they're already struggling to breathe, diaphragms expanding, hips flexed forward. Banks has only just let go of my throat and stood up, so he is still in the process of unzipping himself. Gabe's hand moves in desperate strokes, up and down his heavy shaft, his balls in tight knots in the V of his zipper. Tobias turns my face toward him with a glide of fingers into my hair and works my lips apart with the smooth crown of his sex and I moan while it slides back along my tongue, stretching my lips wide.

"Fuck. Me." He shudders through an exhale, exits my mouth in a slick slide, before slowly thrusting back in right to the beginning of my throat. Just far enough that my eyes only tear slightly. "If I was an animal, love, I'd fuck your little mouth the way I fucked you from behind today on the roof. Is that what you're asking for?"

Swiftly, he pulls out so I can answer.

"Yes," I gasp, never having meant that word so much in my life.

Tobias begins to pant, steps into me so my mouth is almost flush to his lap and then he's following through on his word. He's fucking my mouth with the upper half of his erection, his fist wrapped around the bottom, jerking roughly. "Maybe you're such a brat to me because you want me to fuck you like one." He fists my hair and delves an inch deeper. "Go on, then, love. Suck my dick like a little brat."

I almost forget my name and location.

I've never, ever been like this or thought I could be so enthusiastic about pleasuring a man with my mouth, but Tobias tastes like something that fell from heaven. Maybe it's the filth he's gritting out from behind his teeth or the way he strokes my cheekbone with a reverent thumb even as he's prodding my throat, holding, holding until I cough. Or maybe it's Banks and Gabe grunting in pain while they fist themselves, eager for a turn. Whatever the reason, I'm suddenly starved for their tastes in my mouth, I can't seem to do anything but give.

"Animals, huh?" Gabe exhales roughly, wrapping a free length of my hair around his fist and tugging my mouth right, pressing his broad head between my lips without preamble, my knees scrambling on the floor to change directions, my eyes at half-mast, even though I want them open. Want to see and taste and experience everything about these men. "That's what you turned me into when you sent us that picture of you in those baby blue panties. I see it every time I blink, you've fucked me up so bad."

Until right now, I haven't acknowledged how much it turns me on that I can make Gabe peak so fast. But it does. And it's happening now. He's swelling so quickly in my mouth, I know he won't last long if I keep this fast-paced drag of my lips and tongue and teeth, the smooth part of my knuckles teasing the seam of his balls. I'm crying out around his flesh, the rapid heightening of his pleasure is such an aphrodisiac.

"It's the perfect mouth, isn't it, Gabe?" Tobias asks, his voice like the deepest, darkest region of a cave, his fingers still twisting in my hair. "So beautiful and generous. So excited to be full of cock. Are you going to come in it?"

"Yes," Gabe lets out on a burst of air, his hips beginning to move roughly. Unevenly.

Yes. Please.

I wrap both fists around his inches and service him deeper, more thoroughly. I want to hear that choked sound he makes when it's too much. On an upstroke, I wiggle my tongue into the slit at the very top and he yanks himself out of my mouth with a curse. "No." He clamps down hard on his swollen flesh. "I'm going to learn to last for you."

I'm on the brink of launching a formal protest when Banks blocks my view of Gabe and then I'm being occupied nearly to the throat. He stands over me like a conqueror, stepping closer and closer until I lose balance on my knees and now I'm on my backside again, my mouth being used like a pleasure tool, male groans hitting me in surround sound.

A change has come over Banks and I like it. I like the man who always checks in with me about my boundaries, but I also love this man who knows when it's time to exploit them. I've felt him inside of me and remember how hard he gets, almost like there is no slack available in his entire body and he wants me to know that. Wants me to know he's unbendable.

He looks me in the eye while he plows slowly and deeply into my mouth, Gabe and Tobias holding me steady with hands on my shoulders, fists tangled in my hair. I meant it wholeheartedly when I asked them to be animals. To overwhelm me. And not only are they giving me exactly what I want, it's been inside of them ready to pounce all along.

"Maybe you run away because you want to be caught, Elise." He sinks thickly into my mouth until I can't take any more, drops his head back and hisses at the ceiling. Then with a visible will, he pulls himself free and draws me to my feet. "What do you think about that?"

"I don't know." I barely recognize my own voice. It sounds raw and vulnerable. "Maybe."

"Maybe?" Tobias echoes, whirling me around. "We can do better than maybe. If you want to be caught, it must be because you need the consequences. Put your hands on my shoulders." Too overcome by the potency of them to question anything, I do as he asks, my fingertips reveling in the hard ridges of muscle. "Good girl," he says, kissing my mouth in one hot slant, speaking against it. "Show off that beautiful ass to Gabe. Shake it at him a little. Tease him. We are all painfully aware that you love getting him off."

"I love doing it for all of you," I whisper urgently, because apparently, I'm allergic to lying or playing it close to the vest when every erogenous zone in my body is throbbing. But again, I tilt my hips back and writhe my butt in the air like I'm giving a lap dance and my knees almost give out over the groans that come behind me.

"Gabe, aren't you a little frustrated by how fast she makes you need to come?"

"No," he denies too quickly.

My pulse starts to pound so loud, I can barely hear what's going on. Moisture rushes between my legs and at the same time, Banks tears down my leggings and panties, baring my backside for all three of them to look at. I'm turned on beyond measure by them staring at me, yes, but this idea that Gabe might be harboring some anger toward me, my body, for getting him too horny…it's an unexpected blast of endorphins I never saw coming. Is this a kink? What is this and how the holy hell did Tobias recognize it before me?

"Gabe, be honest. Does this brat make you so hard you can't stand it?"

His swallow is audible, like an anchor sinking into water. "Yes," he admits quietly.

Hoarsely.

I whimper, the desire in my stomach doubling me over, but somehow I stabilize myself with a shoulder wedged up against Tobias's abdomen, my cheek pressed to his ribcage. He strokes my hair like a wise master of hidden kinks. "Better spank her for it, Gabe."

"Elise?" Banks questions me, urgently.

"I'm good," I say, reaching blindly for his hand, grasping it. "I want it."

"Do you want to be spanked as a consequence for trying to run away from us? Or for making Gabe need to fuck his hand all goddamn day and night?

"Both," I heave, moisture starting to leak from my eyes, my voice pulled taut like a string. Who am I? Part of me can't believe I'm giving these men so much power over me, but the other part is in control and it wants to be dragged kicking and screaming into oblivion where I don't have to think or worry. All I have to do is trust.

"Gabe, it's okay to show her your frustration." Tobias uses a foot to kick my legs farther apart, stretching the leggings around my trembling knees. "She likes it."

The foreman groans and I sense him stumbling closer. He grips my ass in both hands and kneads my cheeks roughly, then he strikes me with the flat of his palm on my right buttock, shooting off a flare inside of me that carries me up, up into the night sky and drops me toward earth. The only thing that propels me back upward is another sharp slap. And now all three of them are laboring to breathe, Banks stroking his hands up and down my back, my thighs, soothingly, muttering praise. Tobias cups my face in his hand, then begins sliding his thumb in and out of my mouth.

Every time Gabe spanks me, Tobias pushes that digit all the way in and holds it for me to moan around, to bite down on, whatever I want.

I have no idea where this leads, my body on the verge of implosion while something in my chest shifts, transforms. It's so intense. Physical buildup, sensory overload and an emotional hurricane all at once. I scream something unintelligible and all three of them seem to interpret what even I can't—and I'm suddenly being carried down a hallway, three sets of determined and purposeful footsteps echoing in my ears along with my heartbeat.

CHAPTER
Twenty-One

Banks

WHEN IT COMES to this woman, I follow my instincts.

She didn't want to leave. She didn't want to run from us, either. But she needed the decision to be taken out of her hands. Now, I know how that sounds. Like I think my male brain is superior or I think I know what's best—but that isn't it. My gut screamed at me that Elise needed something and didn't know how to ask, so I reacted.

And my God, the result is fucking glorious.

She was beautiful before, but right now? She's a masterpiece.

As we move as a single unit toward Gabe's room, she's being carried in Tobias's arms, but she appears to be floating, her eyes glazed over, mouth puffy from giving us oral. Her leggings are down around her ankles, the lower half of her body unable to keep still. Her breath shudders in and out and she whimpers, trying to wrap her thighs around Tobias's waist, but the leggings prevent it from happening, so she kicks them off along with her panties and climbs his body, attacking his mouth as if for her very first breath.

Tobias stumbles into a wall like his batteries just died, visibly overcome by the power of her mouth, her kiss, a jagged sound leaving him and filling the hallway. There is no jealousy watching this happen. Not anymore. I'm only obsessed with getting Elise what she needs. I don't give a fuck how it happens, as long as it's done among the four of us. I just want to keep that blissed out expression on her face. I would kill for it.

Elise breaks the kiss, trailing her mouth down to Tobias's neck and licking over the sinew there. I've never seen the Brit look so dizzy, so out of control as he does now. His head falls back and he moans at the ceiling of the hallway, his hands sliding down the tan globes of Elise's ass and grinding her on his erection. He does this over and over again, growing more and more aggressive each time until finally he stops with a curse.

"Fucking hell. We haven't even made it to the bedroom. I'm not even inside of her and I could finish so easily." In a lightning-fast move, he switches their positions, throwing Elise up against the wall. "What are you doing to us?" he demands against her puffy mouth.

"Nothing we're not begging for," Gabe pants to my left. He's a goner, too, like Tobias. He's blind to anything but the woman, his mind having been put on a new, different setting. Attuned only to Elise and her body. Her needs. All three of us resemble each other in this moment, our bodies stiff for her, desperate, primed.

"Tobias," she rasps, rolling her lower body sensually. "Please. Now."

"Yes, love," he responds in a gutter tone, taking his cock in his hand and positioning it between her legs. I want to beat my chest watching this happen. Witnessing Elise experience the journey where the final destination is her orgasm. I want to watch her scream and writhe and have her clit tended and her mouth fucked. I'm *obsessed* with her being fucked.

By us.

We're no longer individuals. Not right now. We're simply Elise's.

But I must maintain some vital parts of myself, because I can't help but look out for everyone's well-being. It's the coach inside of me.

"Tobias," I bark, before he can enter Elise. "Not without a condom."

His spine looks like it's going to snap, his fist connecting with the wall. "Someday," he says against her mouth, raking his lips across hers in a crude kiss that she loves, her throaty whine making me need to grip and stroke my half-sucked cock. "No rubber. Someday very fucking soon. Yeah?"

"Yes," she says on a stuttering inhale.

Gabe curses under his breath, his eyes closing as if imagining it. Being inside Elise without protection. I can't. I can't allow myself to think about it or I'll embarrass myself.

"Get her into the bedroom," I order, my voice sounding odd. Like I have something permanently stuck in my throat. "She deserves better than the hallway."

"I'm well aware of that." Tobias kisses her furiously, wetly, his hands moving roughly up and down the outsides of her naked thighs. "*You* try ending a kiss with her, mate. She tastes like the fucking sun."

God knows he's right. Her perfection is fact.

Without discussion, Gabe and I step forward and pry Tobias off Elise, making sure that her feet find the ground softly. I step between them and Elise automatically wraps her arms around my neck, her brown eyes unfocused, needy, and our tongues flicker together as if they have a mind of their own. It takes every ounce of my will to propel her toward the bedroom and get her across the threshold. Gabe's giant, unmade bed lays in the center of the room. Blue flannel sheets are hanging off one of the sides, but the room is clean, smelling of menthol and soap, the window shades drawn to make it ninety percent dark.

Elise is still trying to distract me with kisses as I set her down at the foot of the bed. Knowing we have precious little time before we lose the battle with our patience, I take a fistful of condoms out of my pocket and toss them onto the mattress and that's the last responsible thing I can manage because Gabe is kneeling behind Elise on the bed, his calloused hands rasping up the soft skin of her belly and fondling her gorgeous tits, mesmerizing me. He allows himself a few swipes of his fingers inside of her bra, before stripping off her shirt and tearing the undergarment from her body, his hands shaking all the while.

Once she's in the nude, whatever remaining manners we were capable of holding onto go straight out the window.

"Animals," she reminds us in a thready whisper.

And we fucking pounce.

Gabe

I'm not sure how Elise lands flat on her back on my bed. Maybe I pulled her, maybe Banks or Tobias pushed her down into the softness, but suddenly I'm kneeling beside her beautiful head, watching as Tobias and Banks shove open her thighs. They get down on their knees in front of her and begin taking turns licking her pussy. All I can do is stare. There will never be a time in my life when I'm not arrested by the sight of that place between her legs, so smooth and firm and glistening. It's ours to satisfy. *She* is ours to satisfy.

I watch Tobias drag his tongue through the split of her sex and tickle her clit with the tip of his tongue, staying there, keeping at it while Banks slides his crooked middle finger inside, rotating it slowly, drawing it in and out, bringing the digit to his mouth and licking off the moisture. Going back for more.

The urgency to join them in giving Elise pleasure pierces me and I take her tits in my hands, molding them, leaning down to offer my tongue to her mouth—and she loves that. She moans in her throat like my kiss was the missing piece to her pleasure, her fingers spear through my hair and we make out hungrily. Which would obviously be enough to make my cock hard, but knowing she's having her pussy eaten at the same time makes me wild. Makes the delves and strokes of my tongue more adventurous, my fingers pinching at her little pebbled nipples until she cries out.

"Gabe," she whispers enticingly between kisses. "Do you want my mouth?"

"I have it and it's perfect," I respond raggedly, my tongue creating a path down her throat to her nipples, sucking them noisily, memorizing the delicious taste of our Elise.

My God, so good.

"No…" she says, voice still soft. Just for me. All for me. "I m-mean, do you want to put yourself in my mouth? The way you did in the living room."

"Yes," I groan, without thinking. Who could think straight with this perfect woman asking if you'd like her to suck your dick? You wouldn't be human. I'm kneeling beside her face before I know it, dragging my shaft to her mouth in a shaking fist. Can't believe I'm so lucky.

"It's a trap, Gabe," Banks says to me, his speech slurred, his eyelids at half-mast. He starts to elaborate but can't seem to stop himself from pushing open Elise's knees and circling his tongue around her entrance, making her gasp and clutch at my comforter. "She wants to get you off fast."

It's beyond stupid to be outraged. This astoundingly hot woman loves making me come. What is there to be mad about? But I can't seem to help it. Horny and offended is a strange combination and it leads to a ripple of shame—and now I'm in big trouble. As a born and raised Catholic, I was taught that the sins of the flesh would send me to hell. Now I'm having a four-way in my bedroom. I'm being offered a blow job and I really want it. This is temptation and I've been taught it's wrong to give in, so I want to give in twice as much.

But I promised myself I would last for her. I promised.

"No," I say, scooting my ass toward the headboard. Just to get a breather. To wait out the clawing sensation in my balls. Don't think about her lips stretching around my inches. Her tongue wiggling around in the slit.

I squeeze my eyes closed and try to think of something gross, but I can't think of anything but her. But Elise. Our woman and her giving mouth and hands and body. I'm so overwhelmed by thoughts of her that when I open my eyes and she's crawling toward me on the bed, naked, intention in her eyes, I think I'm daydreaming.

"I want it in my mouth, Gabe," she pouts.

My back hits the pillows.

Wet, heavenly heat slides down my cock slowly. My balls coil up.

"Oh. Oh God. Oh God."

It's her mouth and it's vibrating with a savoring hum, and speaking of Catholicism, clouds part overhead in my bedroom and I glimpse the Virgin Mother while Elise goes to town on my dick. She's on her hands and knees in the center of my bed, face down in my lap, giving me the kind of blow job that men fantasize about. She's tugging me off, licking my balls and deep throating me every third suck. This is how I die.

I think I might be able to last another twenty seconds, but I'm wrong.

I didn't anticipate Banks coming up behind Elise, rolling a condom down his erection and pumping it into her roughly from behind. She screams around my dick and for a split second, my world goes black thinking she's hurt, but no. No, as Banks begins to fuck her with sharp, slapping drives, her mouth only starts to work harder.

"Jesus Christ," I growl, wrapping her long hair around my fists. I need to close my eyes. I'm already experiencing the best sensation of my life, watching her get it doggy style at the same time is sensory overload. I can't. I can't...help myself.

Banks's head is thrown back, features screwed up tight, as if the pleasure of taking Elise from the back is the ultimate pleasure/pain. Her ass cheeks shudder and shake with every slam of his hips. Tobias is standing behind Banks and to the right, watching Banks's cock sink between Elise's thighs, again, again, again, his eyes darkening each time.

"Just look at the way she lifts her hips for those pounds," Tobias grunts, touching himself. "Think about how she made us work for it. Bet you dig in a little deeper."

Banks makes a beastly sound and pumps faster, harder.

Oh my God, the scene, the shit that's being said out loud is a little twisted and a lot arousing. It's so incredibly hot the way we've forgotten to be jealous and exist for her pleasure now, no matter how she gets it—and I need to be a part of that.

I need to.

Which is why I pull out of her mouth, shouting in pain over being so thoroughly engorged and slap a hand down on my right thigh. "Get up here now." I implore Banks with my eyes and he nods after several more powerful thrusts, gritting his teeth and slipping his cock free of Elise's body. I make quick work of putting on a condom, then I guide her toward me by the hair and she loves it, her flushed body climbing over mine and straddling me. "I need to make you come, woman."

"Okay, baby," she whispers, her lips flush to mine, reaching back and guiding me to her pussy, enveloping me in snug heat. And she knows exactly what she is doing calling me *baby* while I sink into all that wetness, her hips already starting to tweak, scrambling my brain cells like eggs. "Oh, Gabe," she whimpers, licking into my mouth. "You're so big for me."

My hips bounce up and down involuntarily, the underside of her thighs smacking repeatedly on my lap. "Stop," I grit out. "Don't stop."

"Easy, love," comes a male voice. Tobias.

His face appears over her shoulder and then he's pressing Elise's tits down into my chest, aligning her upper body flat to mine, her thighs still hanging down on either side of my hips. It changes the friction between us unexpectedly and we grind into it frantically. "Gabe," Tobias rasps, dragging his thumb up and back in the valley of Elise's backside. "Can you stay hard long enough for me to groom this pretty asshole?"

He smiles like the devil and jiggles his middle finger against that back entrance. And her pussy clenches up so tight around me that I have to reach up and grip the headboard momentarily, the wooden edge biting into my palm and preventing me from spilling. For now.

"Doubt it," I pant.

Not when she continues to ride my dick up and down while looking me in the eye, breathing fast, her puckered nipples slipping and sliding in my chest hair. My view from above allows me to watch down the length of her gorgeous back as Tobias spits on her asshole and worries his middle fingers against it, Banks observing over his shoulder. And it reminds me I can do more for her, that I am dying to do more for her. Holding her mouth in a sucking kiss, I wedge my fingers between us and use the pad of my thumb to tease her clit—

"Gabe!" she screams behind her teeth, milking me faster, harder, her body in a sweaty lather now. I'm pumping my hips like a beast. This is the longest I've ever lasted with her and it's also the best fuck of my goddamn life, so I have no idea how I'm pulling it off. I'm watching two men visibly obsess over her ass while I repeatedly smack her pussy full and she's biting me now, my pecs, my shoulders, my lips. She's fucking *biting* me, her little nub swelling against the pad of my thumb. Her whimpers are getting louder. My hips drill up and up and up.

"*Come on*, you hot, slippery tease."

She gasps into our kiss, her eyes losing focus.

Even through the condom, I can feel the spread of warmth that signals her orgasm. And if that wasn't enough proof, she's cinched up around my cock like a fucking bolt cutter and I'm done. I rear up with her still impaled on my lap and bellow her name, the pleasure pouring out of me in thick, painful waves. Every muscle in my body is seized up and shaking and I'm still watching Tobias pump his fingers in and out of her tight asshole, and so help me God, it makes my orgasm last forever. For fucking ever.

"Tell me I made you come," I demand against her mouth. "Tell me over and over again."

"You made me come, baby, you made me come so good," she hiccups against my mouth, still working her pussy in hot little circles, grinding every last drop out of me. She ruined me days ago in the hotel room, but I'm renewed now. I'm her man, now.

I handle that business.

Thank God.

She's pried off of me by two sets of hands and as badly as I'd like to cuddle her up and kiss every inch of her body and talk about going on vacations and meeting each other's parents, I won't prevent our woman from finding even more pleasure.

The most pleasure.

And I never will.

Tobias

A lot of the sex I've had throughout my life was choreographed. Designed specifically to appeal to a viewer through lighting, body positioning and camera angles and acting. Yet somehow the four of us move like we've practiced this dance a thousand times. We're masters. It's seamless. And it's all because of Elise. She isn't thinking now, it's easy to see that by looking into her eyes. She's gone to some land where all that exists is gratification. That's right where we want her.

She's like a prima ballerina in the middle of a glorious lift, being passed in my hands from Gabe to Banks, her delicious body covered in a fine sheen of sweat. I haven't said a word to Banks about how we'll accomplish making love to her at the same time. Somehow, it's just understood. Somehow, we already know because the choreography is coming from our hearts, not just our heads or our junk. It's the sexual version of a shared psychosis. We're reading each other's minds and all of our minds are one hundred percent attuned to her. To each other.

I'm fucking shaken by it.

Banks receives a still-gasping Elise in his arms and turns her around to face me, holding her arms behind her back, his tongue licking up the side of her neck. I've never seen anyone in her state. Thighs spasming, breath racing, body aroused and straining. And not attempting to control or hide any of it from us. She's magnificent.

"Is her pussy still wet?" I lay down on my back in front of her, rip open one of the condom packets and apply the latex while she watches, her pupils expanding, those nipples so tight I know she's in need of another climax. One isn't enough for this woman. I'd say she's a three-man job, but she's not a job at all. She's a privilege. "Or does she need to wiggle around on my face for a while?"

Elise squeezes her spasming thighs together and moans.

Banks snakes a hand around her right hip and murmurs in her ear until she loosens the flex of her legs, then he slides two fingers into the shiny split of her sex and growls. "Still wet as fuck." He fists her hair and guides her down on top of me. She goes even more eagerly when Banks slaps her ass. Once, twice. "Still eager."

"A miracle," I groan.

"Goddamn right she is," Banks agrees, shaking his head in reverence.

And then I'm in the coveted position of kissing Elise.

I wasn't lying. She tastes like the sun. Hope and light and redemption.

The warm, wet juncture of her thighs makes contact with my lap and I make a strangled sound, reaching back to spank her tight ass, as well. It drenches her further. Makes her offer that tongue with more enthusiasm. She scoops her hips a little, reaching back and using the tips of two fingers to press me into her entrance, working her way down my shaft with whimpering kisses that really, really come close to doing my head in. In the best way. If she didn't specifically tell us what she wanted tonight, I'd lose control about now.

But her wants are our calling. They are musts.

The goddess gets what the goddess wants.

And she wants to feel us all at the same time.

"If I wasn't obsessed with granting your wishes, you'd be on your back right now, getting it filthy. Is that how you imagined us all those years while you fingered yourself in the dark? In the glow of your phone?" I grind upward with my hips and she trembles, gasps. "Poor girl needed the real thing. You're getting it now, aren't you?"

I bounce her in that elevated position, the other two men surging closer to watch her tits jiggle around—and she likes being the star of her own naughty little show. She watches us ogle her with foggy eyes, arches her back to give us a better view, God love her. I smooth my palms up her belly and ribcage, massaging those globes reverently, before delivering sharp smacks to her nipples, experiencing the ripple and flex of her pussy in response. Gritting my teeth at the perfection of it.

I'm *obsessed* with this woman.

"Come here, love," I command, no longer surprised to hear the emotion in my voice. Every single one that I possess is hers in this moment. "Banks is going to worship that gorgeous rear end of yours, isn't he?"

"God yes," he breathes.

"Lucky man, isn't he?" I'm pumping into her from below, she's rocking to meet me. Her forehead is glued to mine, our harsh exhales colliding. This is heaven. "We all want to get lucky at some point, watching our cocks disappear between those cheeks, Elise, but listen to me. You don't owe us anything." Her eyes regain a little focus at that. "If this stops feeling like it's for you at any time, we're doing it wrong. Okay? It hurts or you don't like it, we stop."

Glassy eyed, she nods. Traces my brow with her lips. "Thank you. It...doesn't feel like it's for you. I can feel the three of you considering me. Constantly."

"Good. That's what we want. That's what we're doing. Always," Banks says into her neck, his body pushing down, down, until we're sandwiching her between us. His weight presses Elise down onto my lap and blesses me with enough friction to roll my eyes into the back of my fucking head.

Banks doesn't try and enter her right away. No, he starts to move in the rhythm of our fuck, grinding into each revolution of her backside. His teeth are already clenched and sweat is popping out on his forehead and I know it's the anticipation sinking into his gut like teeth. "Beautiful woman," he chants. "Beautiful, beautiful woman."

"Gabe," she whispers, searching around blindly—and it's like he knew she'd call for him. He's already there, coming forward on his stomach, reaching out to trace her gasping lips with his fingers, pressing them one by one into her mouth, using the saliva to stroke himself back to an erection. "I'm here, Elise. We're all here."

I know the moment Banks penetrates that breach, because she jolts against me, her muscles seizing. She's no longer riding me and it's painful, but I lock down my testosterone and wait, placating myself with the fact that I get to look into her eyes while this happens. Get to witness the trepidation giving way to wonder. I hold my breath in the face of such honesty. Such beauty. All while her pussy beats around my cock, constricting a little more each time Banks gains another inch.

"Gabe," I say. "Do you have..."

"Yeah."

He leaves the bed momentarily to find something in his bedside table. A small, turquoise bottle that he hands over to Banks. Banks rips the top off with his teeth, his chest heaving like a prize fighter in the middle of a bout, and he pours the contents between the crack of Elise's ass. We watch the valley of those cheeks become coated in moisture, Elise lifts her hips up ever so slightly and Banks sinks in with a guttural grunt. We're both inside of her now. And the atmosphere changes. Dramatically.

Elise

I've left my head. I didn't think that was possible.

I can't think of a single thing around the cacophony of sensations. I'm not even sure whether or not being occupied from both sides hurts or feels good. I just know that it's like jump-starting an emotional engine that I didn't know existed inside of me. I'm shaking in a way that can't be controlled, inside and out. I'm snared inside of a three-way trap of intensity that makes my throat shrink, my eyes burn, my chest expand and expand until I swear to God I'm going to splinter into a million pieces.

I'm love. I'm the embodiment *of* love and nature and everything good.

I'm a woman. These men are desperate to praise me. And I let them, because my heart demands it. My vanity and humility and worries don't exist right now. It's just me giving the most basic, elemental part of myself what it needs. There's nothing else. I'm high.

"Animals," I whisper again.

Their awed and grateful response swells around me like radioactivity, ringing in my ears and I just give myself over to their energy. This world they've woven around me. I close my eyes and feel them fuck me, Tobias from below, Banks behind. They move hungrily, teeth snapping at my flesh, like a pack of wolves preying on me after sundown. The room is filled with the sound of groaning and slapping and me calling their names one by one. Banks. Gabe. Tobias. All of them so important. All of them here with me, lost with me, experiencing this event.

I toss a hand out seeking Gabe and murmur something unintelligible against Tobias's panting mouth. But he knows exactly what I'm trying to say, like I knew he would.

"Moving to my knees, mate," Tobias huffs, his back lifting off the mattress. Keeping me seated on his shaft, he maneuvers his legs into a kneel while Banks sits back doing the same, still inside of me, still moving in those thick drives. My thighs are wrapped around Tobias's hips and I'm writhing, working my lower body to bring him in and out of me. Banks is nearly coming undone behind me, brought to the brink by the brusque up and back tweaks of my hips. And now Gabe is standing on the bed to my left, approaching me with his erection in hand, bringing it to my mouth, where I'm aching to have it. Dying for the sense of completion that's going to rock me when I'm pleasuring all three of them. I need it. I'm living for it.

The moment Gabe slides his swollen, salty flesh into my mouth, I am pushed to the brink. Right to the precipice of something almost alarmingly beautiful.

My trembles increase and I become painstakingly aware of every pressure point in my body. My entire body weight rests on the place where I'm joined with Tobias, my clit pressing and rubbing on the base of his engorged flesh. Banks is so full, hurting me slightly with his ownership but in a way that I want. I want to feel like a corrupted virgin—I don't care if that's weird or wrong. I want to feel like a seductive vixen, too, and I'm getting that from Gabe. Tobias looks up at me with nothing short of hero worship, like I'm saving his soul. His life. I'm redeeming him.

"There you fucking go, love. All three of us. Your men. Your men for life."

And I'm all of these things. I make myself all three. They help bring me here.

I'm everything in these moments with them. I'm the universe.

We hold, just like that, nobody moving. My mouth is occupied. My sex and my buttocks are owned. We all take one deep breath together, acknowledging the importance of what we're doing together, a bond forming that goes far, far beyond just a physical one. We move in one swell of appreciation, breathing deeply of each other—and then the frenzy begins.

It's what I asked for.

It's what I need.

My men as animals.

My mouth is crammed full repeatedly, my lips struggling to take the heft of Gabe. His fingers twist in my hair and he snarls, moans, rasps my name while fucking my lips. And I revel in the treatment, scraping his ridges lightly with my teeth and using my left hand to stroke, stroke, stroke. Gabe watches the other men penetrate me from the front, the back, their bodies nothing more than desperate, sweaty machines and he plows into my mouth harder, visibly turned on. Fingertips dig into my hips, my throat, my breasts from all sides and I squeeze my eyes closed and find my path to pleasure.

"Son of a bitch," Tobias near-shouts. "I can feel how close she is."

Banks breathes raggedly into my neck. "That tight clench of hers, right? I'm getting it, too. Christ almighty."

I reach down and fondle my clit, focusing on the stiff weight of the two men pounding into me from the front, the rear. The strength of them. The daintiness of me. I feel their intense longing and it matches mine while that sensitive nub begins to tingle against my fingers.

"Yes, yes, yes," I moan, before taking Gabe into my mouth again. "Don't stop."

"Never," they respond back to me. Fucking me rougher. Without restraint.

Animals. Animals. I'm their victim and their leader.

My body ignites into a flaming orgasm and I scream, the sound coming from somewhere so deep inside of me, I've never reached it before.

It's Banks's unsteady breath on my shoulders.

It's the moisture in Tobias's eyes that seems to confuse even him.

It's the way Gabe tries to hold back, but can't, his salt greeting the back of my throat, followed by his roar of satisfaction.

It's the brotherhood I feel forming between them.

It's us. Everything.

We all go over the side of the cliff together, jerking and thrusting and straining, no one stopping until everyone has gotten through to the other side. And the other side?

Somehow, it's just as magical as getting there.

CHAPTER

I WAKE up the following morning to the sound of laughter.

It's muffled and feminine. It's not coming from inside the bedroom, that much I can tell.

I crack an eyelid and watch a shadow pass along the outside of Gabe's bedroom window. There's more laughter, followed by the bump and screech of car wheels. The slam of a door. The crinkle of a paper bag. Then a deep male voice joins the first one.

Someone stirs in the bed beside me and I realize it's Gabe. He lifts his head, glances between me and the window and gives me a resigned shrug.

It's Candace and his brother, I realize.

Everything that has taken place since walking through the front door of this house has been...distracting to say the absolute least. I don't feel like the same person who arrived here embarrassed and shaken and scared.

I could fight a war one-handed.

That's how I feel right now.

However, I am afraid of moving my body and finding out how sore I am. Our first round together bled into round two. And then three.

I've been face up, face down, backwards and bent in half by three men whose sexual appetites for me have no limits. I'm starving.

Gingerly, I lift my head and observe the fallout around me.

Gabe is at my feet, cradling one of them liked a stuffed teddy bear. Banks is to my right, sprawled out face down, for once looking as though he has relinquished control to the universe. Tobias is to my left and unlike the rest of us, he did not bother putting on underwear last night. He's face up and...fully...awake. *Extremely* awake. And his hand is cupping my wrist, as if he was afraid I might take off in the middle of the night.

As I lie there absorbing their presence, there is a wild expansion inside in my breast. It happens so quickly that I grasp at my chest, struggling through a breath.

I think I might be in love.

I think I might be in love...with us.

Maybe that's why the feeling is so huge. It's for four people, not one. I'm in love with who I am when I'm with these men. I'm in love with who they've become for me. How they imbue me with confidence and protectiveness and power.

Oh mama. I need a deep breath.

Also, I need to get out of this bed before Tobias tries to use that morning wood on me. Not before I get some corn flakes or a bagel. Or a shower. I've been licked up one side and down the other. Been sweaty and sweated on. I wouldn't erase a single moment of last night, but it's time for some coffee and soap. Not necessarily in that order.

I gently extricate myself from everyone's clutches and tiptoe out of the bedroom. After retrieving my overnight bag from the living room, I lock myself in the bathroom—and halleluiah, it's clean. I stand under the hot spray while scenes from the previous evening flash like a strobe light behind my eyelids. Tobias's head thrown back in bliss, his chest flexed and covered in scratch marks. Gabe's breath puffing in and out against my neck while he took me from behind, Tobias coaching him on how to last longer. Banks making love to me slowly with his hand over my mouth to trap my moans while the other two were sleeping.

Yeah. The sex is…I don't think a word exists to describe the sex, but I'll try.

Fulfilling.

Empowering.

Satisfying.

Elevating.

Cardio.

But it's the quiet moments in between, too. It's Banks laughing at Tobias's jokes when I never thought I would witness such a moment in a million years. It's Gabe explaining his recipe for tortellini soup, leading to a conversation about the best meals we've ever had. It's me pulling up a stupid video on my phone, four heads gathering close to watch the screen in the dark and all of us dissolving into hysterics over it.

I think we might be good for each other.

Amazing, actually.

I think all of us sensed something powerful here all along and I'm the only one who has been in denial. I'm finding it harder and harder to remain there after last night.

My soul is lighter. Maybe they're each carrying a little piece of it.

After getting dressed and putting on some light makeup, I leave the bathroom for the kitchen. When I set down my bag and hear the *thunk* of my laptop, the problem that sent me to Gabe's house in the first place comes back in a massive rush. Right. It's possible I've made myself the enemy of a corrupt politician and an equally corrupt union boss.

I shoot a quick text to Shayna to make sure she's still somewhere secure and she replies with a thumbs up. Safe to say she's not thrilled with me at the moment, but who could blame her? Next I open my laptop on the kitchen table and do a quick scan of my email.

My spine snaps straight when I see there is one from Karina.

Elise,

.   .   .

My contact at Alexander's office is no longer returning my calls, even after being asked outright about your apartment break-in. I don't have a great feeling about this. Please continue to remain vigilant. Where are you staying? Somewhere safe, I hope. Please remain there, even if you're in the arms of an adult film star, etcetera. I am working on this. Please trust me.

Karina

I'm barely given time to process the managing editor's email when a set of footsteps comes down the hallway. That heavy tread belongs to Gabe, I decide, before he turns the corner into the kitchen and proves me right. I close my laptop and smile at the shirtless foreman, curious about the bashful expression on his face. The way he rubs his palm against the nape of his neck, redness high on his cheekbones.

"Morning, Elise."

"Morning."

He kind of paces around the kitchen, apparently without having a destination in mind. "You're not self-conscious, are you?" I murmur, coming to my feet and wrapping my arms around his neck, a move that requires me to stand on my tiptoes. I kiss his jaw, his mouth, purring involuntarily when he groans and tilts his hips against mine. "I didn't think that was possible after last night."

"Maybe *you* have no reason to be self-conscious…"

"Is this about the whole endurance thing again?"

"No." He chuckles against my mouth. "You've done a great job of letting me know how much you enjoy my…early arrival."

I'm giggling. We're swaying together in the middle of the kitchen floor. The lightness I felt walking out of the shower is only increasing by the second. Is this what happiness feels like?

"Then why are you blushing?"

He tilts my face up and examines it. "I was raised to respect women. My mother always told me girls should be treated like gold." He shakes his head. "There were times last night where it felt like three big dudes ganging up on one woman. We were really aggressive with you, Elise. I...spanked you for doing nothing wrong. I spanked you hard—"

"Careful, Gabe. You're turning me on." My smile fades when I see he's actually concerned about this. "Hey." I wrap my arms more securely around his neck and the pressure of his hold on me increases. "I knew I could say stop and all of you would stop. Or I wouldn't have been here in the first place. I loved every single second of last night. Even the spanking." I nudge his nose with mine. "Maybe even especially the spanking."

"Really?"

I hum into a long, winding kiss, loving the way I can predict the hardening of his body, the length and slant of it inside of his sweatpants. His big hands clutch my bottom, I lick the tattoo on his neck and I'm being lifted onto the kitchen table, my thighs pushed apart eagerly...when my stomach growls loud enough to shake the cabinetry.

Gabe pulls back from our kiss looking stricken. "Oh my God. You're starving."

Now it's my turn to pinken. "I could try to deny it but apparently my stomach is doing the talking."

He lunges for the fridge. With an erection tenting his sweatpants.

I don't even try to stop him. I might be in the first, flushed stages of arousal, but it's too much of a pleasure watching this man crack eggs into a bowl, rip bagels in half in his bear-sized hands, pour orange juice into a Mets memorabilia day glass. Besides that, I really want to ask him about what I heard this morning while lying in bed. "Gabe..." He glances back at me over his shoulder, nods for me to continue. "I knew your brother and your ex-wife lived next door, but...you can hear them in your *bedroom*."

"Yeah, they have kind of a ritual." He takes a fork out of a drawer to whisk the eggs. "My brother goes out to get bacon, egg and cheeses most mornings. When you heard them this morning, he was coming back from his breakfast run."

It's hard for me to imagine how painful this must be. How hard it must have been, especially right after the divorce. Gabe might not have been deeply in love with Candace, but for his brother to walk all over his feelings, to invade his space, must be so hurtful.

I have a really, really big problem with anyone hurting Gabe's feelings.

My skin is starting to feel a little extra hot when I saunter to the side window and peek out through the blinds, looking across the driveway to Gabe's brother's house. There is a light on inside, but I can't see anyone. However, I do notice that the car belonging to Gabe's brother is parked on Gabe's lawn. There is more than enough room to get all four wheels of the vehicle in the driveway, so it must be a choice.

I remember Gabe telling me how much it bothers him.

I remember the fact that Gabe only got called outside to hang with his brother and the rest of the neighborhood kids if the football got stuck in the tree and they needed him to get it down. These were just stories until now. Until I'm looking at the stupid tires on the lawn.

I release the blinds with a little too much force and circle the kitchen, considering sliding a knife out of the butcher block, taking it outside and stabbing it into the wheels of Gabe's brother's car. As satisfying as that would be, it wouldn't solve Gabe's issue, though. The issue of his brother not only disregarding his feelings but almost taunting him.

"I smelled sustenance," Tobias says, walking into the kitchen. In a wide open robe that I'm pretty sure belongs to Gabe, nothing but a pair of white briefs underneath. "I'll have a double espresso and eggs Florentine, please."

Gabe snorts. "I've got eggs and bagels."

"Fine. God. I'm so hungry, I'm willing to eat gluten." Tobias drops into the chair in front of my laptop and crooks his finger at me. "After breakfast, I'll go back to eating Elise."

I roll my eyes at him, but I definitely saunter close enough—on purpose—that he can catch me around the waist and yank me down into his lap. He growls into the crook of my neck and strokes my hair, seeming to count each strand as they sift through his fingers. And I can't even lie, it's exactly where I want to be. Where I'm *supposed* to be.

I can feel it in the depths of my chest. "What does everyone have planned today?"

Banks enters the room fully dressed. "I have a post-game meeting with the staff this morning." He pulls out a chair, his gaze heating as it roams over me. "Will you please stay here while I'm gone? I won't be able to concentrate otherwise."

"I was going to say the same." Gabe adds more plates to the counter, then briefly turns from the stove. "I have to clock in this morning and delegate projects for the day, but I can be back by this afternoon."

"No worries, men. I'm free to play bodyguard all day." Tobias drags his open mouth back and forth across my shoulder. "Don't worry. I'm going to guard the shit out of her."

"Something tells me your focus isn't going to be on protecting her," Banks says dryly.

"You're right. I need to make a condom run."

At the stove, Gabe's shoulders shake with laughter.

I can't help but sit and marvel over how much the dynamic between us four has changed in a week. For one, I'm no longer running. I spent the night and didn't bail at the crack of dawn. And two, Gabe, Banks and Tobias seem to be forming a friendship. They're no longer jealous over each other and I can't help but hope my equal attention toward them has spurred the positive change. Because my feelings for these men are genuinely balanced. We're a circle. A weird one, but a circle nonetheless.

"I can take care of myself. I don't need a bodyguard." Banks and Gabe open their mouths to protest. Tobias bites my neck like an actual vampire. "But." I bop Tobias on the head and he un-sinks his teeth, licking the marks gently. "I'll stay here for the day so you guys don't have to worry."

"You don't like us being worried," Banks remarks, nodding a thank you to Gabe when he sets down a glass of orange juice in front of him. "That's new."

There's a lit sparkler in my chest, but I give a casual shrug. "I guess I don't."

Tobias drops his chin to my shoulder. "Say more."

They've all suspended their movements to stare at me. "I mean...I just..." More casual shrugging that isn't really casual at all. "If the shoe was on the other foot and one of you was in possible danger, I would want you to take precautions."

"Because you care about us," Gabe says gruffly.

"Yes," I murmur, forcing myself to look each of them in the eye, even if saying these words out loud feels risky and scary to some deeply ingrained part of me. "I care about the three of you. A lot."

I might even be in love with this. With you. With us.

Banks drops a fist softly to the table. "How am I supposed to leave now?"

"I was thinking the same thing," Gabe sighs.

Tobias plants noisy kisses all over my hair and face. "I've never been happier to be rich and unemployed."

We eat breakfast like a family, asking more specific questions about Banks's team meeting. How they'll watch game film and make adjustments for the next match. Gabe tells us the condos he's building will sell for eight million dollars apiece and our jaws drop into our scrambled eggs. Tobias tells us he had a therapy breakthrough recently and we all raise our glasses of orange juice to celebrate. And there's bickering, of course, because it's us. About which one of them will take me on the best dates and sleeping arrangements. Balled up napkins are thrown at heads. It's so comfortable and yet breathtakingly new. Unique.

I move to Banks's lap mid-conversation and he tucks my head under his chin, his magic fingers stroking down my back without missing a beat, still arguing with Gabe about rugby being superior to football. Gabe plucks me up a few minutes later and I rest back against his chest while they all pepper me with questions about work. I tell them about each staff writer at the *Times* and how they all have weird food quirks. Soup girl makes them laugh the hardest.

Talking to them is so easy that I'm telling them my secret before I can stop myself.

"I tried to become one of them. I thought I could take a shortcut. Impress Karina and make it into the club without putting in the work, but..." I don't realize I'm fidgeting until Gabe lays a hand on mine and brings it to his mouth. "I think I'm going to enroll in the journalism program at Baruch. I'm going to try and walk before I run. For once."

Everyone sets down their utensils, like this is the news of the century.

"That's brilliant, love," Tobias says, beaming at me.

"Good for you, Elise." There's pride in Banks's eyes that makes me feel weirdly choked up. "What made you decide to do that?"

I purse my lips and shrug a shoulder. "I don't know." Gabe wraps his arms around me and squeezes until I squeal. "Fine. A lot of it was me hitting professional rock bottom. But…maybe it was kind of sort of the Tram Fam that knocked the realization loose. You guys and your staying power make me…think permanency is possible again."

After a decade of guarding my feelings like the crown jewels, spilling my guts like this is a lot at once. As soon as I make the admission, I start gathering plates from the table and bringing them to the sink, distracting myself from this new vulnerable feeling. In seconds, however, they're behind me at the sink, tugging dishes out of my hands and wrapping me in their now-famous three-way hug where my feet barely touch the floor and I feel like I'm floating.

"That's right," Gabe says into my neck, his voice husky. "Permanent is possible."

Banks tips up my chin. "It's not only possible, it's happening."

"You're going to be a smash at university, Elise." Tobias kisses my forehead. "And we'll be smashing you non-stop along the journey."

"Jesus Christ," Banks groans. "Way to ruin the moment."

"Excuse me, I added to the moment." My body is shaking with laughter and Tobias takes a moment to watch me, pleasure softening his handsome features. "Are you sure the two of you can't call in sick? She needs all three of us this morning."

As if on cue, Banks's phone starts to ring. "Believe me, I want to stay more than anything. God." He leans in and brushes our lips together. "But you'll have to keep her satisfied until tonight. My staff is already waiting for me at the team offices."

"I'm going to break traffic laws getting back here," Gabe growls, raking a hand down my bottom and kneading roughly. "Keep her happy."

Tobias takes a deep inhale of my neck. "It's my new life mission." He nods at the other two. "*Our* new life mission."

Something serious, like a vow, passes between them and my stomach gives a slow, happy, perhaps slightly nervous flip. I'm not completely cured of my fears surrounding people passing in and out of my life, but I'm getting there. And I'm willing to stick until those fears are gone.

Voices fill the kitchen.

A lot like this morning in the bedroom. It's the same feminine lilt and masculine boom that woke me up from the other side of the window. Gabe's brother and his ex-wife. We can actually hear them talking about their plan to meet at the pub for a drink after work. Not for the first time today, I marvel over Gabe's ability to live like this. So up close and personal with the two people who played fast and loose with his feelings. His life.

Tobias, Banks and I all look at Gabe.

He starts to glance away, embarrassed, but something changes in him. Maybe it's the fact that we're locked together, a literal united front. Or maybe we're just witnessing a personal change in him, but he suddenly appears determined.

"Take up your space, Gabe," I whisper in his ear, echoing what I told him the night of the gala. "Don't apologize for it."

Tobias and Banks clap him on the shoulder.

I hold my breath as he leaves our embrace and moves across the kitchen. An imposing figure with his chiseled back and tattoos, while on the inside, such a sensitive man. He hesitates with his hand on the doorknob, before pulling it open. "Hey," he calls in a steady, no-nonsense tone. The conversation that had been taking place in the driveway cuts out abruptly.

Banks, Tobias and I exchange a look of shocked anticipation, then we run to the blinds to peek through the slats. Gabe's brother is leaning against the hood of his car and he is visibly stunned by the sudden appearance of Gabe. "Yeah?" he says slowly.

Gabe steps out of the house, barefoot in the morning light and...oh my God.

For the first time this morning, I notice that he is covered in scratches from my nails and there are hickeys all over his neck. And nipples. And stomach.

Gabe's brother rears back with wide eyes.

"Holy…" I breathe.

"Yeah," Tobias drawls. "You're a fucking wildcat. You should see my back."

Banks clears his throat. "My ass looks like someone played tic-tac-toe on it."

My face heats. "Wow. I guess I'll trim my nails."

"No," they both say at the same time. "Leave them," Banks says, kissing my hand.

"I'd get mine tattooed on if I could bear to mar this incredible skin of mine—"

"Looks like you had quite a night," Gabe's brother remarks.

"Yeah. I did. And it's none of your business. Just like your romantic life is none of mine. But it seems like something you're determined to share with me."

"Hey, man. We're just living our lives."

"Right." Gabe's arms are crossed now. I've never seen him look more confident. "Is there some reason you're parked on my lawn?"

His brother doesn't bother to glance at the tires, which leads me to believe he's well-aware of what he's been doing. "It's a small driveway. I like to leave room on both sides of the car, so we can get in easily."

"That sounds like your problem, not mine," Gabe says without hesitation. His brother snorts, but his amusement disappears quickly when Gabe remains stone-faced. "This is the last time. You park on my lawn again, you'll wake up to flat tires."

The other man gapes. "Are you threatening me?"

Gabe winks at his brother, turns on a heel and strides back toward the house. "You bet your ass I am."

Candace has been silent up to this point, but she finally speaks. "Jesus, Gabe." There's a mystified smile on her face. "What has gotten into you?"

He points at the blinds where all three of us are watching the proceedings—and we've definitely been spotted. "They have."

We hit the floor like children caught eavesdropping.

Gabe's shadow darkens the door, but his brother calls to him, stopping him just short of entering the house. "Hold up, man. Wait."

"What?" Gabe asks.

"Listen, uh…" A loud gust of breath. "It's not about leaving room on both sides of the car. I was just trying to get a reaction out of you. This whole thing with the marriage and divorce…you have no idea how much I regret how it all went down. I hurt my brother. I hurt Candace, too, by letting her go in the first place, but she forgave me in due time. You…you didn't even get fucking mad at me. You just accepted us getting back together without a fight. I *wanted* a fight. I wanted you to tell me I'm a prick and punch me in the face. I deserve it."

Gabe is silent for a full ten seconds. "*That's* why you've been parking on my lawn?"

"Yeah. What else am I supposed to do?" A chagrined laugh from Gabe's brother. "Communicate with you like an adult?"

"That would have been nice."

"You're one to talk. Hiding in your house. Signing the divorce papers without so much as a middle finger for us. You wouldn't believe the guilt I've been living with."

Gabe walks into the house calmly and takes a knife out of the wooden block. After shaking his head at the three of us huddled under the window, he goes back outside. And then there is the very distinct sound of a tire being punctured. "Happy?" Gabe asks.

The ex-wife is laughing.

"Not really," mutters his brother.

"Well, I am," Gabe says, letting the words hang in the air. "I'm happy. I don't need you to feel guilty for me. Matter of fact, I don't want it. There's no reason for it when I'm this happy. You take up your space and I'm going to take up mine."

"Is there any chance of us being…friends?"

"I don't know." Gabe doesn't elaborate right away. "I'll let you know when I'm ready."

"Well done, mate," Tobias murmurs.

A moment later, Gabe steps over the threshold and marches into the kitchen. His attention zeroes in on me and he keeps coming, intention etched into his features. My pulse speeds into a haywire sprint as Gabe hauls me to my feet. My breaths already sound like hiccupping half-sobs and I don't even know what's happening yet. I'm not in the dark for long, though. Gabe leads me into the kitchen by my wrist, kneels long enough to tear my panties down my ankles, and then I'm being lifted, my ass slapping down on the kitchen table, rattling the remaining breakfast plates and orange juice glasses.

"I want some pussy."

Slowly, I trace the growing ridge in his sweatpants with a single fingertip. "Then you better take it."

I've enjoyed every second of having Gabe inside of my body. But when Banks hands him a condom and Tobias spits on my already dampening sex, allowing Gabe to buck home inside of me with a vile, gritted curse, there is a new, distinct difference in his energy. His confidence is tenfold. He's not just making love to me with an air of gratitude like before, though that sentiment is still there in spades. No, he's owning me. He's looking me right in the eye and conquering me, because he was finally able to conquer some loose end in himself.

"Don't stop," I gasp.

He captures my throat and bears down harder, faster. "Don't worry."

The table rocks underneath us, silverware falling off the table. His hips are machines.

"Now, mate. That's how you fuck our woman."

Pressure is building inside of me and it's no wonder. I've got this man huge and thick inside of me, the intensity and purpose in his gaze stealing the air from my lungs. And my other two lovers stand behind him, watching with unconcealed lust as I'm brought to the brink of screaming. No, I *am* screaming. A plate falls off the table and smashes on the ground. My toes curl up and that quickening sensation I became very, very acquainted with last night is starting to make itself known. It's the kind of orgasm that only comes from the inside. No outside stimulation. Just the incessant rubbing of that deep, secret place and the knowledge that I'm the key to my man's pleasure and the only way he can achieve his release is through this. This wild, animalistic rutting. This unabashed enjoyment of my body.

"Come on it," he growls against my mouth. And before I can take a single breath, he's pushing me down to the table, pinning me there with his hand on my throat and looming over me, entering me so swiftly now that there is barely a breath of time between one aggressive drive and the last. "I could never give enough back to you, Elise. Never. You've given me so much already. But I can protect you and feed you and make you moan, can't I? I can fuck you the way you need it. Dirty and mean, baby. Come on it."

The rush of pleasure is so sharp, it's almost painful. My back wrenches off the table into an arch and I wrap my thighs around Gabe like a vise, holding him in a deep thrust and he grits his teeth, grinding it into me deeper, all three of them roaring in triumph while I shake, my muscles popping and straining. I'm trapped between this world and the next, my core flexed dramatically, my flesh converging on Gabe's and rippling, squeezing. I don't know how to come down. I'm lost up here and I can't see the ground.

But finally I regain some sense of reality, thanks to Banks and Tobias kissing me in turn, their mouths moving on my neck and shoulders.

And Gabe is still hard.

I must have made that discovery out loud, because everyone's heads move on a swivel. We look at him, then down at his still extremely erect penis. With a cocky smile, he pulls up his sweatpants and swaggers down the hallway. "I think I'll save it for tonight," he calls back over his shoulder.

We all stare at his retreating back like he's an alien lifeform.

Tobias exhales. "I feel like a proud father—"

Gabe comes running back down the hallway coated in sweat. "I lied. I can't wait that long. Please, Elise. Even a hand job..."

"Bloody hell," Tobias mutters.

Laughing freely, my heart swelling inside of me, I slide off the table onto my knees.

CHAPTER
Twenty-Three

IT MIGHT BE November and slightly chilly outside, but I haven't had a backyard in a long time, so I feel I must take advantage of Gabe's. I go through his closet until I find the biggest, thickest fleece he owns and pull it on. Tobias watches from his lean in the bedroom doorway, visibly amused as the garment drops to well below my knees. He continues to watch me as I slide past him down the hallway, his amusement giving way to thoughtful silence.

We've been quiet since Banks and Gabe left for work, but there's nothing uncomfortable about the quiet. It's like we're caught in a welling of anticipation. We're enjoying being together, the lack of pressure, the fact that we have feelings for one another. It's companionship with a wild undercurrent of attraction that keeps my senses alive at all times.

I sit down on a plastic chair in the backyard and bundle my knees up to my chest, tucking them into the fleece with the rest of me. It's quiet here. Nothing but the sound of wind and the occasional car driving by on the other side of the house. I let my breath out and watch the outline of it dance in the air, allowing my neck to loosen and tip back, resting it on the chair. After a few minutes, the back door opens again and Tobias emerges holding two cups of something hot, steam twisting around his knuckles.

He hands me one and sits down in the chair beside mine. Cautiously. Like he's not sure if the plastic chair is a viable piece of furniture.

A drowsy giggle finds its way up my throat. "You look like so out of place. Like someone accidentally put their Rolex in an old toolbox."

His grin comes easily. "I'm not a complete snob, you know," he says, nudging the leg of my chair with his toe. "My upbringing was entirely modest. Typical. It's just been a while since I've spent any real amount of time outside of my flat. Suddenly I'm in Queens eating bagels."

He says bagels in an American accent and I come very close to spitting out my first sip of hot chocolate. Thank God I manage to keep it in my mouth, though, because it's glorious. "Wow. Gabe had this in his cabinet?"

"No, I found some chocolate bars and melted them down on the stove. Added milk." He watches my mouth drop open. "You think I'm useless for anything but fucking, don't you?"

It appears I'm not going to be able to drink this hot chocolate without choking. "That's not true at all. I'm just in awe of your initiative." I squint out at the slightly overgrown yard. "Although, I guess I shouldn't be. The three of you have shown so much of it."

"You're a powerful motivator, Elise."

The even thrum in my veins is no longer quite so steady. Not when his blue gaze travels over the tumble of my hair with open adoration. I have the urge to go sit in his lap, but we would end up kissing. We'd be in the bedroom before I knew what was happening—and I really want to use this time alone to find out more about him. So I stay put.

"You said your upbringing was modest. What was it like?"

Tobias's gaze zeroes in on mine and narrows. Almost like he's surprised that I'm asking about his life before he started acting in adult films. As I'm sitting patiently, waiting for him to answer, it occurs to me that maybe no one ever asks about his background without bringing up his profession. It must take up so much air. "Well..." he says slowly. "My father drove a school bus. My mother ran a nursery school out of the house."

"Like...daycare?"

"I suppose that's what you'd call it. She minded children." He takes a long sip from his mug and takes his time swallowing, as if he hasn't thought of the distant past in a while. "Sometimes I helped out."

I concentrate on keeping my features schooled, but it is a challenge and a half. "You helped out watching children?"

"Yes." Even Tobias looks somewhat incredulous over this revelation. "I mean, I didn't change nappies or anything, but I brought them to the park if my mother needed a smoke. They walked behind me, two by two, holding hands." The fondness in his expression fades gradually. He taps a finger against the side of his hot chocolate. "It must be a great story now. For them to tell at parties. Tobias Atwater used to walk me to the park. I'm sure it gets a laugh."

There's a prolonged pang in my ribcage. "Maybe they do tell the story. I hope so. You deserve to be thought of as more than who you were for twenty-minute intervals on camera. Because you are. A lot more."

He sniffs. Throws his ankle up onto the opposite knee. "Forty-minute intervals."

"My apologies," I say, lips twitching. "So, did you push them on the swings?"

"Of course," he responds, offended. "Looked out for playground bullies, too. There's always one."

"Do you like children?"

"I like them for other people." It's an off-handed comment, but as soon as he says it out loud, his face becomes stone cold serious. "Do *you* want kids, love?"

I take a deep inhale and let it out, seriously considering the question. "I've never thought about it before. I've been too busy figuring myself out. But...I'm leaning toward no. When I think about having kids, it's only my parents that come to mind. I'd be doing it mainly for them."

Tobias continues to study me. "I'd say Banks feels the same as me.

But I'm not sure about Gabe. He strikes me as a traditionalist." He hums. "We can get him a dog."

That does it.

I spit hot chocolate all over Gabe's fleece.

Tobias's laughter fills the backyard, the sound lacking in all artifice. It's pure and real and I realize I've never heard it like that before. Well worth the cost of replacing the coziest article of clothing in Gabe's closet. "Look what you made me do!"

He's swiping at his eyes. "I was serious about the dog. He's the bulldog type. I know it."

"Stop making fun of your brother."

"He's the favorite. It's only fair that I get to take the piss once in a while."

"I don't have a favorite," I say, looking him in the eye. "I just…"

"What?"

"I don't know. I just have this weird…sense. When it comes to…"

"What each of us needs?"

Having it put into words out loud causes my blood to pump faster. "Yes."

A moment passes while we look at each other, the wind picking up around us.

Tobias slowly sets his mug down on the stone patio and stands. He takes two steps until he's towering over me, then pulls me to my feet. The only part of him that's touching me is his hand, which encircles my wrist, but I'm close enough to feel his body heat and that alone turns me into a winded mess. In seconds, I'm trembling.

"Can you sense what I need right now?" he asks, his words feathering my mouth.

I can only manage a nod. "You need to know I'm sleeping with you for more than what your body can give me."

That statement makes him start, his breath going choppy. "I…Elise…"

I wasn't expecting to say that either. Maybe that's when truth is in its rawest form. When you don't think about letting it out, it just flies free on its own. "I'm in this for your heart, too." I wind our fingers together and tow him behind me to the back door. "Come inside and I'll make sure you feel it."

———

Time is ceasing to have any meaning within these four walls.

I make love with Tobias in the cool dark, looking deeper than I have before and finding so much untapped strength and vulnerability inside of him. So much that he's willing to explore with me over time. I look him in the eye as he moves on top of me, showing him how much I like who he is. Who he'll become. Who we are together, within the circle of four. It's a shattering experience that leaves us both shaking and gasping, holding on to one another's hands. The hours together deplete us and we drop into a deep sleep.

I could never have expected to wake up and find that everything has turned to shit.

It's late that afternoon after yet another shower and I'm staring down at my email inbox in disbelief, rereading the message from Karina for the third time, positive I made a mistake or looking for some winking emoji to tell me she's joking. There's nothing to reassure me, though, just those same damning lines in the body of the email.

Elise,

The timing of this isn't ideal, but I'm hoping you'll see this as a bright spot of sun in the middle of a storm. You're going to be published! I passed your piece on to the human-interest editor, Lisette, and she ate it up like chocolate gelato. Now for the amazing part—it's going to run in tomorrow morning's paper. The tram power outage is still fresh in everyone's memory and she thinks that might lead to more shares of the online version. We're going to make it anony- mous, considering the private nature of the material, not to mention we're trying to keep you less visible until we figure everything out with Alexander. Congratulations, nonetheless! You're a writer. I'm not hiring you, so don't get too excited. But you're a writer. A good one.

. . .

Karina

I leave my laptop open on the bed beside a napping Tobias and pad to the kitchen, pouring myself a glass of water from the tap. I set it down without drinking, because my arm is too weak to lift the glass to my mouth. My article is going to be published.

My *article* is going to be *published.*

There might be a part of me that's extremely proud of the accomplishment, but there is a far bigger part of me that's reeling from shock and denial. I didn't submit it to Karina to be published. I sent it to her for notes. A critique. A professional eye. I didn't expect it to be good enough for publication—and I haven't even told Tobias, Gabe and Banks about what I wrote.

Everything has changed since I sent that story to Karina.

When I think of the tone I used, so flippant, I full body cringe. These men are layered and complicated and I reduced them to surface level descriptions that I would never use now that I've...bonded with them. In a way that feels almost spiritual. I'm in love with them.

And there is no way I can let the article publish. *No way.*

Not until it has been repaired and rewritten. Not until I've had a chance to speak to the men about it. Anonymous or not, I can't publicly cheapen this relationship or let people think it's a temporary fling. A joke. I treasure it too much. I treasure *them* too much.

I take my phone out of my pocket and text Karina.

Thank you for the encouragement, but I don't want the piece published. Repeat: I do not want it published. Please confirm when it has been pulled.

Then I pace the kitchen for ten minutes. No text back. I try calling her office line and a message greets me explaining that Karina is working in the field today and won't be back at her desk until tomorrow morning. She's still seeing her texts, though, right? She'll still be able to pull the piece.

My stomach starts to churn. Maybe I'll email her, too, in case she's monitoring that. This is important. I need to try every available avenue to reach her.

I walk into the bedroom and stop short. Tobias is sitting up in bed, his bare back in the pillows, his hair still in disarray from my fingers. My laptop is open on his stretched-out thighs.

Every hair on my body stands up straight.

He doesn't look up immediately when I walk into the room, but when his guarded blue eyes finally tick to mine, my stomach plummets to the ground. "I was going to change your background to a picture of me, but the email caught my eye." His voice is flat, not jovial as usual and heat instantly presses up behind my eyes. "I was curious which piece she was referring to, so I looked back at the attachment on the previous email and...wow. Egomaniacal adult film star, hmm?"

"Tobias, I wrote that before." I sound like I'm choking. "I wrote it before everything changed. And I didn't think it would actually get published—"

"Ah, but it is. Congratulations. Guess taking your shortcuts worked out this time." He sets aside the laptop and swings his legs over the side of the bed, standing. "Were you just hanging around until you had enough material for the sequel?"

"What? No. No—"

"You think I'd be used to this by now. Someone taking advantage of what I am so they can further their own interests. But I feel like dying right now, so I guess not."

His words hit me like a brick to the throat. "You can't be comparing me to your manager—"

I stop short when the front door of the house opens and closes. Two sets of footsteps move through the living room, approaching the hallway. When the voices reach me, I know it's Banks and Gabe. They're talking about the fact that Gabe's brother is parked properly in the driveway and I want to turn and run into their arms, but all I can do is stand stiffly as they walk into the room. They absorb the tension immediately and grow openly confused.

"What's going on?" Gabe asks, setting down a brown paper bag that smells like it has cookies or some other baked good inside.

"You okay?" Banks mouths at me, frowning.

Tobias speaks before I can. "Where do you keep the bubbly, Gabe? We're celebrating."

"Bubbly what?"

"It's champ—never mind," Tobias sighs at the ceiling. "Elise is getting published. Thought you might like to celebrate, but apparently, we'll have to do it with Budweiser."

Banks's chest rises and falls. "Elise, tell me you didn't submit the mole story. The whole situation is way too volatile—"

"The article is about us, actually," Tobias interjects. "It's about *us*."

Gabe shifts right to left, hesitantly amused. "You wrote an article about us?"

"Why didn't you say anything?" Banks asks, his expression unreadable.

"Perhaps she wanted it to be a surprise for her—and I quote— rugby coach with debilitating mommy issues and an emotionally bullied construction foreman."

The twin devastation on their faces is almost too painful to witness, but I force myself to stand there and take it in. The ground is moving underneath my feet, my breakfast on the verge of coming up. I can explain this to them and repair the hurt. I can. They will read the article and they will forgive me. Tobias is angry, lashing out. They're sure to follow. But I can mend this.

That's what my heart is telling me.

My gut is another story. It's telling me this is the beginning of the end that I predicted since getting involved with these men. Everything was shiny and new and wonderful, but this is going to burn away the top layer of what we have. Then we'll argue again in the future and another layer of this relationship will get skinned off. Another and another until we're down to the bone. And then someone is going to leave. The thought of that happening, the idea of any of them walking away is causing a horrible, serrated punch of pain in my midsection. I've avoided any situation that might cause me to feel a sense of loss, the kind I felt so many times growing up, but here I am. I'm in the thick of it. I opened myself up for this.

I need to face the consequences like a grownup.

My throat is dry, eyes are burning. "I'm really sorry," is all I can manage. "I wrote it in the beginning of us. When I was in denial that this was something important and special. I would write it very differently now." I move to the bed under Tobias's watchful eyes, open the laptop and hand it to Banks. "Read it. Whatever you need to do, I'll understand."

I leave the room, closing the door behind me.

The house looks very different now. Dimmer. More ominous. There's no laughter or movement. The low murmur of voices behind me causes the hair on the back of my neck to stand up, my skin prickling with dread. There is a severe urge to bolt tickling the soles of my feet that I'm trying to ignore. Tobias hates me right now. Gabe and Banks could very likely follow in his footsteps. Avoidance would be so easy. Leaving now and pretending the whole thing never happened. My insides will be a shipwreck without them, but I know from experience that if I pretend to be aloof about something long enough, eventually I will convince myself that it's true.

Do I want to do that, though?

Do I want to be aloof over these men? Or do I want to leave my floodgates open and take whatever comes because they deserve to be treasured? Because the way they make me feel deserves to be celebrated?

Yes.

Yes.

I decided to stick and that's what I'm going to do.

My heart won't allow me to run this time. I'm in deep, times three.

No running this time, Elise.

My phone buzzes in my hand and I quickly tilt the device so I can see the screen. Finally, Karina is texting me back. Thank God. I need to get the article pulled immediately…

. . .

Karina: Got your text and email. I understand you've had a change of heart about the article. Pity. It's utterly absorbing. Unfortunately, like I said, I'm not in the office today and I can't get a hold of Lisette. I've managed to have the online version delayed, but the physical paper gets sent to the printers at six. I'll do my best to track her down between meetings.

That's not good enough.

I need it stopped.

It's three forty right now. If I leave this very second, I can make it to the *Times* by four thirty. That would give them an hour and a half to remove the article and replace it with something else. I physically cannot bear the idea of that article going out into the world. I don't care if Karina thinks it's good. Those words on the page were lies I told myself. They aren't good enough for Gabe and Banks and Tobias. I can't let them get printed.

I pocket my phone and glance toward Gabe's bedroom door.

Will they even care if I leave right now?

My heart tells me yes—and I desperately want to believe that.

But I can't run the chance of them preventing me from leaving. They might tell me it's not worth the risk right now when the situation with Alexander and Crouch is still unresolved. They might not understand this is something I have to do.

Might as well admit what terrifies me the most, though.

They won't care if I leave.

I take a step toward the bedroom door and my stomach shrinks in on itself, preventing me from going any closer. I don't deserve to go in there and crawl into Gabe's lap and cry until they forgive me. That's not the kind of woman I am, either. I'm going to make myself *earn* their forgiveness. I'm going to make this right and show them how much my heart has changed since I wrote that article.

Resolved, I order an Uber, relieved when one pops up two minutes away. Gathering my things as quietly as possible, I leave them to come to terms with what I've done.

I leave the house to do damage control.

CHAPTER

Twenty~Four

Tobias

I FEEL as though I've been doused in ice water.

My skin is cold and clammy. I can't seem to sit still.

I'm pacing while Banks and Gabe read the article, refusing to acknowledge the prongs of dread that dig themselves deeper into my chest with every passing second. I do not like how sad Elise looked when she walked out of this room. I am growing increasingly seasick over it. But I remind myself of those words, how they ridiculed me in stark black and white. Egomaniacal porn star. Shallow. When I confronted my manager about him buying the rights to my catalogue out from under me, profiting off my name and years of work, he said something along the same lines as Elise. That I was a human dick joke.

Seeing them from Elise's point of view hurt infinitely worse—and I didn't think that was possible. But of course it is.

I'm in *love* with Elise.

Blindingly in love with her.

The way she reduced me to a pile of adjectives…she might as well have carved between my ribs with the tip of a blade. She sees me no differently than anyone else, as much as I tried to convince myself otherwise. I allowed her behind my walls this afternoon more than ever and she ranks me as nothing more than a selfish prima donna. Maybe that's all that I am. If I can expose everything to someone and they still find me nothing more than an ego on legs, perhaps it's true.

"Wow," Gabe says, handing the laptop back to Banks.

Banks closes the lid, sets aside the computer and sits in silence.

"Well." I circle the bed to stand in front of them. "Isn't it nice to know that we've been torn up for this woman and she's been laughing behind our backs?"

Gabe's brows draw together. He looks down at his hands. "No, I wouldn't call it nice…"

"You heard what she said, right?" Banks doesn't sound as sure of himself as usual. "She would write it differently now."

"Yes, I heard." I rub at the empty feeling in my sternum. Five-year-old memories are racing back, leapfrogging what's happening currently. Smoke and mirrors. Betrayal. The ache I'm experiencing is telling me it's happening all over again. Once again, I've wrongly believed someone gave a shit about me. "Can you trust that so easily?"

Banks stares hard at the ground beneath his feet for several moments. Then, slowly, he begins to nod. "Yeah. I can."

Gabe's expression goes from desolate to hopeful. "How?"

"What the fuck do you mean how?" Banks asks, pushing to his feet. "You know Elise. You think everything she's given us has been for an article? Are we done here, Tobias? Or do you need to overreact some more?"

That dread I've been ignoring gets louder in the wake of that question.

"Kindly bring us up to speed on your thought process, mate," I sputter.

"Gabe." Banks backhands the big man in his shoulder. "Don't you dare join this pity party."

"Too late."

"Jesus Christ." Banks splits a disgusted look between the two of us. "Do you know who called me this morning on my way to the

meeting? My mother. She hasn't called me in years. She told me...
fuck." His emotions seem to get the better of him momentarily. "She
told me she's proud of me and she wants us to be more involved in
each other's lives. If it wasn't for Elise, I never would have left that
last ticket at the front of the stadium. And my mother admits she
never would have gone in without running into a stranger. A
stranger who, she says, spoke about me with so much affection, it
took her breath away. It reminded my mother how much she
loves me."

My legs are beginning to lose strength.

I can't stop thinking of Elise's stricken face when she walked out of
here.

The venomous way I spoke to her.

"Gabe." Banks isn't finished. In fact, he seems to be getting angrier
by the second. "Tell the truth. Would you have finally stood up to your
brother this morning if it wasn't for her?"

"No," Gabe responds automatically. "I'd have kept hiding. It
started when she came to the gala with me. I...I don't know. It's like
my confidence has been snowballing since then. She makes me feel like
I count. I'm around for a reason."

"Exactly."

Banks turns his disgust on me and I sit down on the windowsill. Or
maybe I stumble backward and fall, because my knees have finally
given way. My heart is beating in an unnatural rhythm now. It feels so
heavy and uncomfortable that I want very badly to rip it out of my
chest.

"And you, Tobias." Banks paces toward me in full coach mode.
"You aren't the same person now that we met on the tram. You were a
caricature. A sad walking innuendo. You were everything she said in
that article and more, weren't you? Until she forced you to take off
your mask before she would give you the time of day. Why would she
bother if all she wanted from you was an entertaining story? If that
was the case, she would have been better off leaving you unchanged."

My throat drops into my socks.

I'm going to be ill.

Banks drops the final hammer. "She was lying to herself. She was pretending this was all one big joke, that we were one big joke, because she was afraid."

She was lying to herself.

She was afraid.

I should have expected Banks to see through Elise quicker than myself or Gabe. It's always been that way. His loyal defense of her now boils me in shame. "You're right," I say in a threadbare voice. "I over-reacted. I let the past get the better of me. I fucked up."

"I doubted her, too." Gabe lets out a frustrated exhale, his gaze staring a hole through the bedroom door. "How could I do that?"

"You—we—are all going to make this right with her. Because Elise...she's not an accident, all right? She was put in our paths—"

"To make all of us better," I finish raggedly. "And she was put in ours..."

"So we could worship her for it." Gabe lunges to his feet and yanks open the bedroom door. "Elise."

I'm right behind him, stumbling through the door, prepared to throw myself down at her feet and beg for mercy. How could I assume the worst in someone who searched for the best in me? I'm a dog. A slug. I'm the lowest form of organism.

My tongue and I have a lot of apologizing to do.

If she lets me.

Lord, what if she doesn't forgive me?

I'm made so dizzy by the horrible possibility that it takes me a moment to realize Banks and Gabe are starting to look nervous. They enter room after room shouting Elise's name and all I can do is stand there, my feet encased in cement. No. No. No. She can't be gone.

"Elise!" I roar, my fist striking out involuntarily and punching a cabinet.

Banks re-enters the kitchen with a yellow, square sticky note in his hands, Gabe following behind him with a pale complexion. "She left this on the door." He slaps it down in the center of the dining room table. "She went to stop the article from being published."

Those words don't penetrate right away. When they do, my skull caves in on itself.

I sent her out into danger. I doubted her, I took out my insecurities on this incredibly giving woman and now she could be hurt. Because of me.

I take a lunging step and lose the entire contents of my stomach in the sink.

Elise

My Uber pulls up in front of the *Times* and I leap out, my badge already in hand. Traffic wasn't as horrific as usual, so I've managed to make it here earlier than expected, a New York miracle to say the least. On my way over the bridge, my phone started to ring, so I silenced it. All three men are taking their turn calling me, but I am fully focused on my goal. I'm not looking right or left until it is achieved. When I'm face to face with them again, I want to do it knowing I made every effort to correct my mistake. I want them to know it, too.

I pull open the heavy glass and brass door, jogging through the lobby toward security and scanning my badge. Throwing my purse into a plastic tub and walking through the metal detector. I'm trying not to think about what Tobias, Banks and Gabe would say if I answered the phone—and it's not too difficult to distract myself at this very moment, because I'm scanning the lobby, looking right, left and over my shoulder for any kind of threat.

There's nothing out of the ordinary, but I can't totally ignore the voice whispering in the back of my head that I'm missing something. It started on the ride over from Queens and now, as I enter the elevator, it's getting louder.

A few moments later, I'm stepping onto the floor where human interest is located.

"Excuse me," I say breathlessly to the receptionist. "I'm here to see Lisette."

"She's downstairs in production."

"Production? Do you know if they've sent tomorrow's edition yet?"

"They're doing a test run on our in-house printer, actually." She frowns slightly. "You didn't mention your name…"

I'm already speed walking back to the elevator, throwing myself inside and hitting the button for the basement level. I've only been down there once, and it was by accident. I'd gotten onto an elevator that already had the button pushed. At a glance, it's a vast, underground network of servers, sectioned off in the back by a mailroom. I didn't realize they ran test prints downstairs, but why *would* I know that? I'm the sandwich girl.

The metal doors open to reveal the basement. It's a lot quieter than I expected.

No employees that I can see.

Like I remember, there are servers running and they create a static hum. In the distance, there is a trundling sound that makes me think the printer lies in that direction. Shouldering my bag, I step off the elevator and weave through the six-foot-high servers, desperately trying to reduce the warning voice in my head that has gone from a whisper to a shout. I just need to find Lisette, do everything I can to stop the article from running and then I can concentrate on whatever my sixth sense is trying to tell me.

I've almost located the source of the rolling sound when voices reach my ears.

A man and a woman are talking. I can't make out any of the words. I'm too close to the noise now and it's mostly drowning the conversation out. But when there is a break in the mechanical whir of the printer, I hear the woman's voice and recognize it immediately.

Karina?

I thought she was working in the field today.

Did she come in personally to prevent my piece from running?

If so, I will worship her forever.

I start to take a step around the server blocking me from view, but before my foot touches the floor, the man's voice responds to Karina—and my blood becomes ice.

Deputy Mayor Alexander.

My heart starts pounding like a jackrabbit. That shout in the back of my head is more urgent now. It's telling me to get out of there. Now.

There is no reason Alexander and Karina should be talking in hushed tones in the basement of the *Times*, is there?

"You said printing her little bullshit article would be a distraction from the real story," Alexander says. "You guaranteed me this would cause her to back off. That all she wanted was something of hers to be published. So why is it being yanked?"

"I don't know. I can't ask too many questions without her getting suspicious. She didn't respond when I asked her where she was staying. I'm a journalist. I know when to push and when my subject is getting jumpy."

Heavy footsteps tell me Alexander is starting to pace. "When you came to me with her suspicions, I told you to suppress the article. In exchange, I was going to give you inside information, as soon as I took over as mayor. That deal is very close to being off the table. I'm quite happy with our arrangement with the *Post*."

"Listen to me, Elise isn't even a reporter. She isn't *employed* by the *Times*—"

"That makes her more of a liability. Not less. She could take it to another paper."

Karina sighs. "I said, I've got her under control."

I'm already backing up as slowly as possible, but it's hard to focus on my steps when my mind has turned into a wind funnel. "Me Plus Three" wasn't good enough to be printed. It was all about placating me. So I would drop the mole story. And worst of all, I've been played by Karina. That's what I've been missing.

I can't believe I didn't see it.

Karina tried to find out where I was staying. Why? So Alexander could...come get me?

Thank goodness he didn't recognize me from the gala. If he'd known who I was, he could have connected me to Gabe. I would have been putting my men in danger simply by hiding out at Gabe's house. My God. My pulse is going so fast, it's making me dizzy. I'm in danger of tripping over my own feet. I need to get out of here now—

My back runs into something soft. Soft on top of hard.

I turn around and find a suited man smirking down at me.

It's Jameson Crouch.

"Excuse me," I whisper, trying to go around him.

He grabs my arm. Holds on tight when I try to pull it free. "Not so fast, girly."

My temples pound. Mouth goes dry. "Let me go. Please, let me go."

"Hey, Alexander," Crouch shouts. "I found what we're looking for."

Karina and the deputy mayor step into view on the other side of the server. Alexander looks nonplussed, but it slowly gives way to amusement. Karina is stunned, but she can only look me in the eye for a moment, before horror takes over and she looks away.

The suited man starts to drag me toward the back of the basement. Where are they taking me? Is there a rear exit?

"Karina, please," I say in a strangled scream, my vocal cords pinched shut from fear.

"I couldn't let the *Post* continue to scoop us. My job was at stake." Eyes closed, she shakes her head. "I told you to stick to delivering sandwiches, Elise."

———

Banks

To put it mildly, I'm losing my shit.

Elise is not answering her phone. We know she is enroute to the *Times*. We are most likely going to find her there safe and probably a little closed off—and frankly, I can't blame her. The four of us are mere days into this relationship and her faith is already being shaken. Believe me, I would love nothing more than to blame Tobias. It is very difficult to be angry with him, however, when he is continuously banging his head off the passenger side window.

"I've never understood those macho Americans who ask people to punch them in the stomach as hard as they can, but I completely get it now. They are emotional shite piles like me and they just want to relocate the suffering."

"You need to take a deep breath," I mutter, weaving in and out of traffic as fast as possible without running the risk of being pulled over. Every car we pass with an Uber decal in the window, I glance into the backseat in case Elise is the passenger. "I can't deal with your hysterics right now."

"Please know that I'm holding back!"

Another purposeful bang of his head against the window.

"I can't believe we let her walk out and close the door," Gabe is saying, though it's hard to discern whether he's talking to us or himself. "We should never let her walk out when things are up in the air. She has to stay. She has to hear everything we're saying. Didn't we decide that in the escape room? Everyone on the same page."

Tobias clutches at his chest like he's been stabbed and howls at the ceiling.

"I take responsibility for that, too, Gabe," I say, finding it necessary to clear my throat. It is very difficult to remain calm right now, but I can't lose it when I am the designated stable one of the group. Today, at least. That being said, it's taking every drop of my willpower not to floor the gas pedal and bellow like a wounded beast at the top of my lungs.

I saw on her face that something was wrong. I saw that she was crumbling and I didn't properly take control of the situation. Now I'm paying. I'm paying in fear and regret. This woman has completely transformed my world since we met. I'm in love with her. I want her to be a part of every moment of my life. God help me, I want these two shitheads there, too.

Anyone who threatens what we've made here is going to regret it. I don't care if that someone is one of the most influential men in the city —what we have is more powerful.

Finally, I'm off the bridge. Unfortunately, crosstown traffic this close to rush hour is abominably slow and lights seem to be taking forever.

"Okay," I say, trying unsuccessfully to calm my own nerves. "Unless Elise told someone where she was going, no one knew she was leaving the house besides us. We have no evidence that someone is actively looking for her. I could be having a panic attack for nothing."

"You're having a panic attack?" Tobias temporarily stops abusing his cranium against the glass to shift around and face me. "You're supposed to be the calm one."

"I'm not calm at all. I'll be calm when we find her at the *Times*."

"When is that going to be, approximately?" Tobias asks. "I have no idea where we are. I barely leave my apartment unless it's for therapy. This could be Miami for all I know."

"We're in Midtown," Gabe says, still sounding dazed. "Do you guys miss her?"

"Yes," I say very precisely.

"Yes," Tobias echoes, his voice a scrape of sound. "Very much."

It remains dead quiet in the car through the next block.

"All three of us love her, don't we?" Gabe asks, though he obviously doesn't expect an answer.

He doesn't need to. The truth is palpable. My stomach winds up into a knot when I think about her smile, how she listens so intently, how her eyes water when she feels cornered. Her bravery. I have known her for such a short amount of time and yet I can't picture a future where she isn't making her mark on every day, every hour, every moment.

"I'm a traditional man. I've always imagined myself getting married. Again." Gabe coughs into his fist. "But I won't be able to marry Elise. None of us will."

"God, man. I'm just hoping she talks to me again." Tobias exhales roughly. "But since we're on the subject, I've done some internetting and...there *are* commitment ceremonies."

I watch Gabe sit up straighter in the rearview. "There are?"

"Yes," I say, trying to keep my voice even. "I checked into it, as well."

Gabe curses. "I really need to figure out the internet."

"When that day comes, you're going to learn a lot more about me," Tobias says. With a laugh that sounds pained, he asks, "How hard do you think it would be to convince Elise to exchange vows on the beach in a white dress while a violinist plays softly in the background?"

"Next to impossible," I answer, strings tightening in my chest.

"We'd have to trick her," Gabe laughs.

We join him. For about five seconds.

Then the car goes silent again. The air around us weighs a thousand pounds.

"Please. We really need to find her." Tobias says, sounding winded. "Fast."

It takes us another five minutes to get in the vicinity of the *Times*. By unspoken agreement, I find a metered parking spot and we don't bother putting a ticket on the dashboard before we start to run.

"Elise took back her pass," Gabe calls behind me. "I have no idea how we're going to get in this time."

"We'll figure it out when we get there," I say, picking up my pace.

I'm running through a host of options to get to Elise's floor. But when we enter the lobby a moment later, I see a woman that looks familiar. She's on her phone in the corner of the lobby. Elise was speaking to her the day we ambushed her in the office. The managing editor, Karina, right? The one who has been keeping her apprised of the situation with Alexander and Crouch? She looks...agitated.

"I don't like that she looks agitated," Gabe says, startling me by echoing my thoughts.

"Me either," Tobias says, already storming in that direction.

It's not until this moment that I realize Tobias never bothered to put on a shirt.

At least he managed pants.

"Excuse me," Tobias says, putting all of his effort forth into a broad grin, though he doesn't really have to bother, because the editor stops speaking mid-sentence to gape at his bare chest. "Have you seen Elise?"

Karina's expression doesn't change, but I watch very closely as the color leaches slightly from her face. She opens her mouth to speak and closes it, her eyelashes fluttering a hundred miles an hour. "I'm..." She begins to fan her face, regret clouding her features. "I'm sorry. Oh God, I never thought it would come to this. I'm trying to make it right—"

Panic is trying to shut my organs down one by one, but I manage to take her by the shoulders and look her hard in the eye. "Where is Elise?"

"They have her," Karina whispers. "Alexander and Crouch."

There's a screeching sound inside of my skull. Blood rushes so quickly to the backs of my eyes, my head becomes one giant throb. Never in my life have I lost the ability to speak, but that's what happens. I physically can't force out a single syllable. We were only being cautious by keeping her at Gabe's. I never really believed someone would try and physically hurt her. Another mistake. I've made two mistakes today and one of them could set my world on fire.

She could be in pain. Right now.

Worse.

Oh my God.

I turn to look at Tobias and Gabe. They're in the same condition as me—being driven into the ground by denial. Gabe rakes shaking fingers through his hair. Tobias looks like he's staring into the mouth of hell.

"Where did they take her?" Tobias asks through his teeth.

Karina is already shaking her head. "I don't know." Moisture spills down onto her cheeks. "You have to believe me, I didn't realize I was making a deal with the devil. This is standard shit in journalism. Moral gray areas when it comes to collecting information. Having the mayor in my pocket would have been a windfall. I told Alexander and Crouch that I would keep a lid on Elise, dissuade her from pursuing the mole story about them teaming up to take down the current mayor. It shouldn't have been hard—she's not even employed by the *Times*. When they overheard her on our phone call, it was out of my hands. They thought I'd been playing them. I don't...I don't know what they're going to do. What they're capable of."

"If something happens to her..." I manage, right before my voice deserts me again.

"We need to call the police," Tobias rasps. "Now."

"That's who I was speaking with when you arrived," Karina says. "They're on the way."

I don't feel an ounce of relief over that news. Zero.

"Jesus. By the time we explain to them what's happening..." For once in my life, I can't think of a logical solution and I'm reeling. I'm losing my shit. "By the time we find a way to track them down, what if it's...they might have already..."

"Enough of that," Tobias growls. "We'll find her. We have to."

Gabe steps in front of us, ushering me and Tobias away from Karina. In a low, uneven tone he says, "Is this a good time to admit I stole Elise's phone last night and turned on the location tracking?"

———

Elise

I'm shoved forcefully into a chair.

The man who drove me, Crouch, and Alexander to this construction site in Morningside Heights stoops down behind me and ties my wrists together with his own shoelace. He looks nervous the whole time he completes the task, too, sweat pouring down the sides of his face.

"First kidnapping?" I ask, as casually as possible when I really want to cry. It's taking everything inside of me not to let out the sobs building inside of my chest. But some untapped source of self-preservation tells me I need to keep a level head. If I can just make these men see reason, I can get out of this, right? I'm not going to die today. Right? "I'm just a sandwich girl."

"Shut the fuck up," says the driver, standing again and pointing his gun at me.

A firearm has been aimed at me for the last twenty minutes, although it was in the hands of Jameson Crouch. I should be used to it by now, but I'm not. My skin crawls and acid climbs the sides of my throat. I can't control the trembling of my body. Alexander and Crouch are arguing in the corner of the half-built room where they've taken me. Just like they argued in hushed tones on the drive to this place. They were in the middle seat of the SUV. I was in the back, lying down on my side as instructed, a gun leveled at me from its place in Crouch's hand.

The fact that they're arguing now is good, right? They're unraveling. My gut tells me they were in over their heads the second they kidnapped me from the *Times*. They didn't plan this. It was a spur-of-the-moment decision and now they don't know what to do.

The bad part? They can't just let me go now.

I know too much. I've now been kidnapped by the deputy mayor and a powerful union boss and they have an explosive secret to hide. Power and money are at stake. I know they leaked emails about the governor. I know they planned to have the *Times* in their back pocket.

On the ride over, I promised them if they just pulled over and set me free, I would never tell anyone about this. They would never hear my name or see me ever again. I swore on my life. But those vows fell on deaf ears. I was only told to shut up. I'm not a human being to them. I'm nothing but a problem to be solved.

This is bad. This is *bad*.

I can't help but try again, though. Now that the use of my hands has been taken away, I feel tragically powerless and it spurs me into begging, even though I hate the pitiful tone to my voice. "Please. It's not too late to let me go," I shout across the empty concrete room to Crouch and Alexander. "You've scared me. That was the goal, right? To scare me into keeping my mouth shut about what I know? Fine. I was already planning on it. Just let me go. *Please.*"

Behind my back, I start to twist my wrists, hoping to subtly loosen the shoelace. The driver used one of those thin, starchy dress shoelaces, I realize, looking down at his matching shoe. They're not great for knot tying. If I can get loose and run, there is a chance this man won't pull the trigger. He didn't sign up for this—it's there in his nervous movements. The conflicted way he continues to look at me.

"What's the plan?" whisper-shouts the driver, shifting in his wingtips. "The longer we're here, the greater the chance of being found. I don't want to be found with some tied-up girl, man. I've got a family."

"Relax," Crouch says sharply. "We're waiting for approval on permits for this site. No one is scheduled to be here until they're granted. No one is coming."

Has Gabe worked on this project?

As soon as I allow that musing to slip to the forefront of my mind, the floodgates open. I can no longer stop the tears from tracking down my cheeks. I miss Gabe and Tobias and Banks so badly, it winds me. Bereaves me. I shouldn't have ignored their calls. I should have stayed at Gabe's and accepted their anger over the article like a big girl, instead of running off half-cocked to get it omitted from tomorrow's paper. Just one more time in my life that I behaved impulsively, but now it could get me...killed.

Might as well admit it. This could be the end.

I don't see how they can let me off with a warning now.

Not with the mayoral seat hanging in the balance. Or the potential wrath of a governor.

My parents are never going to find out what happened to me. I'll never have the chance to enroll in classes at Baruch and set myself up for real success at something I love, instead of trying to skip to the end. Of course, I'm not afraid to commit now, when it could be too late.

I continue to twist my hands within the confines of the tightly tied laces. I can't tell if I'm making any progress, though. I don't think I am. My circulation is beginning to cut off.

God. I would give anything to be in Tobias's lap right now.

He'd make some dumb joke about bondage and Banks would shake his head.

Tears fill my eyes to the brim and pressure pushes outward from inside of my ribcage. Pressure so strong that I know it's coming from love. My love for three men.

And I feel a slight loosening in the ties.

Alexander and Crouch go silent. Abruptly.

Hands on hips, Alexander hangs his head. Crouch can't look directly at me.

My gut pitches violently.

Not good. Not good.

They approach slowly, Crouch giving the driver a grave look.

Blood drains from his face, his arm briefly losing enough power to keep the gun aloft.

"Killing me isn't going to solve your problems," I rush to say, my voice unnaturally thick. "What about Karina? She knows you took me."

"If we go down, Karina goes down, too. She's culpable here," Alexander says smoothly. "She'll look the other way."

He's right. I don't know Karina at all, do I? I thought she was my friend, but she sold me out. Even if she wants to help now, she won't be able to tell the police where they brought me. They threw my phone out the window of the SUV and into a trash can several blocks before we reached this construction site. There's no way anyone will ever find me. My dead body is going to end up encased in cement with a building on top of me. And my murderers are going to run this town. Probably go on to kill more people who stand in their way. I'm just the first of many.

"Do it," Crouch says to the driver.

"Are you serious?" He hesitates, blinking as if he's dizzy. But he keeps the gun raised. "I don't think I can do it," he wheezes. "She says she's just the sandwich girl."

There's an extended silence and I realize Crouch is staring at me. With recognition this time. "Hold on a second. I know you were at the gala because you took that picture, but I didn't remember seeing you until now. Pink dress. You were with one of my foreman. Gabe." He adjusts his stance, the lines around his mouth increasing with tension. "What does he know?"

Cold purpose blankets me in a split-second. The noise in my ears recedes.

Apparently, this is a level of fear I've never reached before, because it involves someone I love being hurt. Throw in my protectiveness when it comes to Gabe and I'm nothing but a swarming hive of denial. They've made the connection between me and Gabe. He's in danger now. And it's only a matter of time before Banks and Tobias are, too. The very thought of them being hurt surges my fear to the highest point where it transforms into anger so sharp I can feel it cutting straight through me. In a burst of fury, I twist my wrists with all of my might and feel a snap, though I don't dare show it on my face. My adrenaline has surged so fast, my vision grays at the edges.

Crouch gets in my face. "*Answer me.* What does he know?"

"Go to hell."

The union boss backhands me across the face so hard my ears ring.

I can't breathe around the sting. A metallic taste fills my mouth.

Crouch wrestles the gun out of the driver's hand—and I know it's now or never. The union boss is red-faced and irrational and I'm the target. I'm going to get shot. And then they're going to go after Gabe. Tobias. Banks. I can't allow this. Without giving myself another second to hesitate, I lunge out of the chair and knock the gun out of Crouch's hands. The weapon goes flying across the half-constructed room and it's a race, three against one. My odds of making it to the gun first are pitifully low, but I dive toward it anyway.

Falling a couple of inches short.

I'm dragged backwards by the ankles, taking the weapon farther and farther out of my reach. Alexander retrieves the gun with a resigned expression on his face that terrifies me. I twist around onto my back just in time for him to point it straight down at my head.

"Sorry about this, kid."

There is something behind Alexander, though. Something that wasn't there before. It's the muzzle of a gun peeking around the entrance to the room. It's followed by a police officer.

No...his bulletproof vest says SWAT.

Oh my God. It's a whole team. They crowd into the entrance, seething like one single entity, then scatter, coming in and spreading in all directions, automatic rifles with scopes raised. Aimed at my three captors.

"Put your hands up!" roars the first law enforcement officer entering the room.

None of it seems real. The sea of black uniforms just keeps on pouring in until finally they've filled the room nearly to capacity. My three captors are wrestled into face down positions, their bodies being searched for more weapons. Handcuffs are snapped shut around their wrists. All of it seems to happen simultaneously while I struggle to breathe through the inundation of relief and sky-high adrenaline from my position on the ground.

My relief doesn't fully connect, tough. Not completely. Not until Banks strides into the room, flanked by Gabe and Tobias.

Karina, too. The managing editor is there, visibly deflating with relief to see me alive, but she can kick rocks for all I care. Seeing her only floods me with betrayal. Shock.

I'm going to survive, though, because Gabe, Banks and Tobias all reach me at once. I'm scooped up off the ground into a three-way bear hug. My legs wrap around Gabe's waist and I'm crushed between a trio of chests, their hands everywhere, raking over my back, thighs and hair.

"She's bleeding!" Gabe roars, loud enough to drown out the room full of shouting men. "She's fucking *bleeding*."

"Her lip is cut." Banks relays this information like the gravest sin imaginable has occurred. "And her eye."

"Which one of them did it, love?" Tobias asks through his teeth, every syllable packed with malice. "Who is going to die today?"

"It doesn't matter. I'm fine." A sob wracks me. "I just need you guys, okay?"

They look at each other hard, visibly putting a leash on their tempers.

Or maybe agreeing to put them on hold. Temporarily.

"Goddammit, Elise," Banks grinds out, his chest to my back. "Don't ever put yourself in danger like this again. You were almost killed. We would have died along with you."

"I'm sorry. I know, I'm sorry."

"No, I'm sorry," Tobias says against my ear. "I'm so sorry, love. Please forgive me."

"There's nothing to forgive. You were right to be mad—"

"No, I wasn't. You let me know you. I know your heart and I still let my trust slip."

"It's okay." I turn my head and kiss Tobias, feel him shudder. "It's okay now."

Banks sinks his fingers into my hair and tugs my head back at an angle, sealing his mouth over mine hungrily. Gabe's mouth rakes up my exposed throat and my legs tighten around him in anticipation, before I remember we're far from alone.

In fact, we're the main focus of a thirty-man SWAT team.

"Um…" I struggle to catch my breath. "H-how did you find me?"

"Gabe strikes again," Banks responds wryly, brushing my hair back. "Our resident thief stole your phone last night and turned on the tracking feature."

"The blue dot stopped moving a quarter mile from here, but I could see the direction you were heading. I know this site. I supervised the laying of the foundation."

I shake my head, sniffle. "I'm password protecting my next phone, but you get away with your thievery just this once, since your criminal behavior saved my life."

"He gets away with it every time," Tobias mutters, but he's smiling. "Always the favorite."

"You're all my favorite. We are my favorite," I say, dropping my feet to the ground so I can face all three men at once. Look up into their incredible faces and marvel over the swelling inside of me. "I love all three of you equally." My voice catches, the emotion of the last hour clobbering me over the head. "I love all three of you so much."

Gabe's chest hollows and inflates dramatically. "Maybe it won't be so hard to get her on a beach in a white dress with a violinist after all."

My throat burns. "You mean a commitment ceremony?"

"Yes," Tobias says.

Banks nods, seemingly unable to speak.

"I looked it up," I admit, wiping at my damp eyes.

For some reason, the three of them find this admission quite remarkable—and they all converge on me at once, enclosing me in an unbreakable circle.

"I love you, Elise," Tobias growls into my neck.

"I love you," Gabe whispers into my hair.

"I love you," Banks says, his voice unsteady, followed by a hard kiss.

"I don't suppose I can convince you to let me publish the piece about your relationship?" Karina says hesitantly to my right. All three of the men bristle, but a kiss to each of their cheeks eases their muscles of tension. "I wasn't lying when I said it was good."

"Maybe someday." I raise an eyebrow. "For now, I think my mole in the mayor's office story is going to look great on the front page with my byline. Don't you? Having that kind of clout on my application for journalism school isn't going to hurt, either."

Karina inclines her head. There's a sparkle of appreciation in her eye, along with a request for forgiveness. I'm not quite ready to give it to her yet, but something tells me I will. Soon. There's so much room in my heart to fill now. So much grace to offer. Love to the power of three can do that to a person.

I take my time looking each of my guys in the eye. "As far as the relationship piece?" I shake my head. "Not until we spend some time writing more of the story. It could be a while."

"Because this story doesn't have an end," says Banks, every word laden with affection.

And as usual, he's right.

Epilogue

Gabe

Four Years Later

I STILL STEAL THINGS.

Right now, I have my eye on one of the white daisies in Elise's flower crown. She's wearing it on the dance floor, her arms wrapped around her father's neck as they dance. I can already see how that flower will look in the scrapbook I'm keeping. Technically, I guess, I'm not really stealing, since everything I take is kept inside of the leather-bound pages where all four of us can easily find it.

There are ticket stubs from our first concert together. Ed Sheeran in Forest Hills. I don't remember a lot about the show because I was too busy watching our girl sing along with her best friend, Shayna. Me and the guys basically took turns bringing them drinks and standing in the endless line for merchandise. That was well over three years ago—and one of the best nights of my life. Our life.

That's the night she got drunk and told us living apart wasn't working anymore.

When we started this relationship, the plan was to keep separate residences. Elise could see us separately during the week, followed with a group date on the weekends. It's so laughable now to think we could control this. Tidy the four of us up into a schedule.

We're not containable.

Don't get me wrong, it was amazing having Elise to myself on those solo dates. I even got her to a few Mets games. But returning her home the next morning was awful. Accepting it would be several days before seeing her again. Knowing she was spending the night in Banks's or Tobias's bed without me never seemed right. The evening of the Ed Sheeran concert, we all finally admitted to feeling to same way. Solo dates were still an option, but the majority of the time, it needed to be all of us. These men I consider my brothers now. And our Elise.

We bought a house together, not too far from my old place in Queens. Elise spent two years at Baruch earning her associate's degree in journalism, before being accepted to Columbia where she got her bachelor's. She's taking her time deciding which news outlet she wants to work for. After her legendary expose in the *Times* four years ago, she can have her pick.

But trust me, we'll be keeping a close eye on whoever ends up as her managing editor.

Along with anyone else who comes within ten feet of the center of our universe. Speaking of whom, she's no longer dancing with her father, because the song is over. Tobias claims her with a kiss on the forehead, swaying her into the next dance.

It's amazing how much the Brit has changed over the years. He's relaxed in his own skin. Quicker to laughter. Our boarding passes to London are another item in my scrapbook. He overcame his fear of returning home last year. Having us along for the ride helped. Now, he is the top investor in a series of high-end sashimi restaurants throughout Queens. *I can't be the only one who wants decent sashimi in this borough,* he once said. Apparently, he was right.

I have a whole separate scrapbook dedicated to ticket stubs for the Flare. Tobias, Elise and I have attended so many matches, I've lost count. We sit in the family box alongside Banks's mother, who hasn't missed a game in four years. They added another championship banner to the rafters of the stadium recently—and the night of the ceremony, somehow, we just knew. It was time to propose to Elise.

She wanted to wait until she got her degree to plan the commitment ceremony. Not going to lie, there were some days I thought I would die without having some kind of vow exchange between us. Not because I feared I would lose them without it. More from a need to express out loud how much they mean to me.

Speaking of Banks's mother, she's dancing with her son right now. She must feel me observing them from my spot at the bar, because she raises a hand and waves. I give an exaggerated tug of my bow tie, pretending that it's cutting off my oxygen and she laughs, before going back to her conversation with Banks.

I look around the room at everyone in attendance. My parents are here. My brother and Candace—also known as our former neighbors. Elise's parents. Shayna. Tobias's therapist and his parents. An entire rugby team. Some of Elise's classmates. People that have accepted our unorthodox relationship, despite some skepticism in the beginning.

Especially from Elise's parents. The weekend we met them for the first time takes up an entire five pages in my scrapbook.

The napkin her mother wept into when we broke the news.

A transcript of her father's phone call to the police.

The label off the bottle of whiskey he drank when the police informed him no laws were being broken.

A picture of their faces when Tobias told Elise's parents how he made his fortune.

A shard of the plate that Elise's father threw at Tobias's head.

That was an interesting weekend, to say the least, but it ended in Elise's parents being overjoyed for their daughter. Finally believing her claim that she'd never been happier. The final picture in that weekend's section of the scrapbook is the six of us posing in front of our new house, a SOLD sign swinging in the breeze to our left. Since then,

I've added a guest room onto the back of the house, so they feel welcome to come visit as much as they want from California.

Yeah, it's hard to believe how far we've come with Elise's parents in the last four years—and no one can say it isn't still awkward when we all retire to the same room at the end of the night—but we've grown to love and respect each other.

Enough for Elise's parents to attend our commitment ceremony today on the shores of Rockaway Beach.

The song ends. Elise kisses Tobias, their mouths lingering together for a moment in a way that makes my heart flip over. And then, like I knew she would, she searches me out for my turn to dance with her. Memories come flooding back from that first night we danced, at the gala. It seems like a hundred years ago, but somehow it also feels like it happened yesterday. *Take up your space,* she told me that night.

I like to think I've done her proud since then. When Crouch went to prison on kidnapping and conspiracy to commit murder charges, among many others, I filled his vacant position as Local 401 union boss. I'm a lot busier these days, but nothing can or will stop me from making time for Elise. Or my brothers who love her as much as I do. We're a family. And we don't merely work, we thrive.

Now, I push off the bar and meet her halfway on the dancefloor, my pulse surging when she steps into my arms, somehow devilish and angelic at the same time in her long, white dress. She places her hand on my shoulder and I glance down at her ring, a wide gold band stamped with the outline of the Roosevelt Island tram. We each wear an identical one.

Tobias threatened to have his inscribed the Tram Fam.

We surprised him by having it done to all four.

"My Gabe," she sighs, laying her cheek on my shoulder. "Do you ever wonder what would have happened if we hadn't all been on Roosevelt Island that night?"

"I wonder all the time." I wrap her more securely in my arms. We're barely dancing, more just hugging and swaying slightly, but it doesn't matter. All that matters is holding her. Absorbing as much of her as I can. "And I think we all would have met some other way.

Maybe in a park. Or on a ferry. But it would have happened. Our paths would have crossed."

"Yeah?"

She lifts her head, eyes sparkling. Radiating love, as always.

God, she never stops taking my breath away.

I can see both men in the distance watching her, and I know it's the same for them.

She overwhelms us with her strength and beauty every single day.

Today she promised she always will.

"What makes you think we would have met no matter what?"

"Something this perfect can't be happenstance," I say confidently.

"I have to agree," Tobias drawls, coming up behind Elise, planting a kiss on her bare shoulder. "Banks?"

"You'll get no argument here," Banks concurs.

"I'm glad we met exactly how we did," Elise says, turning her head to receive a kiss from Banks. Then one from Tobias. And me. She gives me a little extra, since our dance has been interrupted. Not that I mind, she simply has a way of balancing everything out and she never, ever compromises. "I wouldn't change a thing."

Tobias shudders. "I could have done without the kidnapping."

"Don't remind us," Banks and I say at the same time.

"I wouldn't even change that. I would do everything exactly the same. Each little thing that led us right to this spot." Her expression turns solemn. "Even your socks on my floor."

I throw back my head and laugh.

We tried. We really did. Socks just kind of end up on the floor when three men are constantly disrobing in a hurry.

And we do. Frequently. In fact, we're probably only going to last another fifteen minutes before we're dragging Elise out the door to the limousine waiting to bring us to the airport for our honeymoon in St. Lucia. That's if we don't get her alone in a broom closet or a deserted hallway first. I didn't think the need for her could get any more urgent than it was that first week together, but hell if it doesn't deepen and grow more meaningful with every passing day.

We never fail to fuck her in a frenzy. The kind she screams for.

As if she has read our minds, her voice is breathy when she says, "I guess we should do the whole garter belt ceremony. Which one of you is going to take it off?"

She's teasing. We know she'd insist on it being all three of us.

At least, she would if I hadn't already stolen it.

I take the garter belt out of my pocket with an apologetic wince, dangling it between the four of us. Three mouths drop open simultaneously.

"Gabe!"

THE END

About the Author

#1 New York Times Bestselling author Tessa Bailey can solve all problems except for her own, so she focuses those efforts on stubborn, fictional blue collar men and loyal, lovable heroines. She lives on Long Island avoiding the sun and social interactions, then wonders why no one has called. Dubbed the "Michelangelo of dirty talk," by Entertainment Weekly, Tessa writes with spice, spirit, swoon and a guaranteed happily ever after. Catch her on TikTok at @authortessabailey or check out tessabailey.com for a complete list of books.

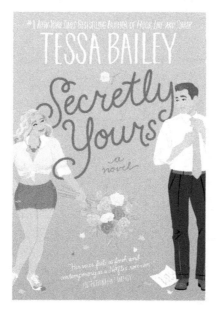

From #1 *New York Times* bestselling author and TikTok favorite Tessa Bailey comes a steamy new rom-com about a starchy professor and the bubbly neighbor he clashes with at every turn...

Hallie Welch fell hard for Julian Vos at fourteen, after they *almost* kissed in the dark vineyards of his family's winery. Now the prodigal hottie has returned to their small Napa town. When Hallie is hired to revamp the gardens on the Vos estate, she wonders if she'll finally get that smooch. But the grumpy professor isn't the teenager she remembers and their polar opposite personalities clash spectacularly. One wine-fueled girls' night later, Hallie can't shake the sense that she did something reckless—and then she remembers the drunken secret admirer letter she left for Julian. *Oh shit.*

On sabbatical from his ivy league job, Julian plans write a novel. But having Hallie gardening right outside his window is the ultimate distraction. She's eccentric, chronically late, often *literally* covered in dirt—and so unbelievably beautiful, he can't focus on anything else. Until he finds an anonymous letter sent by a woman from his past. Even as Julian wonders about this admirer, he's sucked further into Hallie's orbit. Like the flowers she plants all over town, Hallie is a burst of color in Julian's grey-scale life. For a man who irons his socks and runs on tight schedules, her sunny chaotic energy makes zero sense. But there's something so familiar about her... and her very presence is turning his world upside down.

Coming February 7, 2023!

Preorder here: https://bit.ly/3g6slFO

CPSIA information can be obtained
at www.ICGtesting.com
Printed in the USA
LVHW011247291122
734186LV00003B/189

9 781087 893600